TEARS FOR THE BRIDE

THE WIDOW AND THE WEB

Robert Martin

Introduction by
Brian Greene

Stark House Press • Eureka California

TEARS FOR THE BRIDE / THE WIDOW AND THE WEB

Published by Stark House Press
1315 H Street
Eureka, CA 95501, USA
griffinskye3@sbcglobal.net
www.starkhousepress.com

TEARS FOR THE BRIDE
Originally published by Dodd, Mead & Company, Inc., New York,
and copyright © 1954 by Robert Martin. Reprinted in paperback by
Bantam Books, Inc., New York, 1955.

THE WIDOW AND THE WEB
Originally published by Dodd, Mead & Company, Inc., New York,
and copyright © 1954 by Robert Martin. Reprinted in paperback by
Bantam Books, Inc., New York, 1955.

"Meet Robert Martin and Jim Bennett" by Brian Greene
copyright © 2025.

ISBN: 979-8-88601-142-5

Text design by Mark Shepard, shepgraphics.com
Cover design by Jeff Vorzimmer, ¡caliente!design, Austin, Texas
Proofreading by Bill Kelly

First Stark House Press Edition: April 2025

TEARS FOR THE BRIDE

When Jim Bennett agrees to join his secretary Sandy
for a weekend of hunting with her family, the last thing
he expects is to find himself thrust in the middle of an
accidental shooting. Then someone takes a shot at him
as well, and the "accident" suddenly becomes very
personal. Sandy's brother Ralph now lies in the
hospital, his previous girlfriend wracked with guilt at
having fired the shot that put him there. But Bennett is
not convinced that she's as guilty as she seems. After
all, someone fired at him as well. Could Earl Seltzman,
in love with Ralph's fiancée, have tried to remove the
competition? All Bennett knows is that he won't be
satisfied until he finds the person who tried to kill him.

THE WIDOW AND THE WEB

Jim Bennett is working for the Industrial Welfare
Commission's Department of Investigations on a
routine case. George Shannon has fallen from a ladder
and died from a head injury. It looks like an industrial
accident, and Bennett is ready to give his okay for
payment to the widow. But someone sends him a note,
suggesting that Shannon's death is no accident. When
Bennett follows up with a few questions at the plant, a
shadowy figure clubs him in an alley, threatening worse
if he doesn't lay off. Now Bennett is determined to find
out what happened to Shannon. If only his widow
weren't so distracting…

Robert Martin Bibliography
(1908-1976)

NOVELS

Jim Bennett series:
Dark Dream (Dodd Mead, 1951; Pocket, 1952).
Sleep, My Love (Dodd Mead, 1953; Dell, 1953)
Tears for the Bride (Dodd Mead, 1954; Bantam, 1955)
The Widow and the Web (Dodd Mead, 1954; Bantam, 1955)
Just a Corpse at Twilight (Dodd Mead, 1955)
Catch a Killer (Dodd Mead, 1956; abridged in
  Mercury Mystery Book Magazine)
Hand-Picked for Murder (Dodd Mead, 1957)
Killer Among Us (Dodd Mead, 1958; Detective Book Club, 1959)
A Key to the Morgue (Dodd Mead, 1959; Detective Book Club, 1959;
  Ace, 1960)
To Have and To Kill (Dodd Mead, 1960; Ace, 1961, abridged)
She, Me and Murder (Hale UK, 1962; Curtis, 1971)
A Coffin for Two (Hale UK, 1962; Curtis, 1972)
Bargain for Death (Hale UK, 1964, Curtis, 1972)

Standalone Mystery:
The Echoing Shore (Dodd Mead, 1955; Bantam, 1957,
  as *The Tough Die Hard*)

As by Lee Roberts

Little Sister (Gold Medal, 1952)
The Pale Door (Dodd Mead, 1955; Detective Book Club, 1955;
  Bantam, 1956)
Judas Journey (Dodd Mead, 1956; Popular Library, 1957)
The Case of the Missing Lovers (Dodd Mead, 1957)

Dr. Clinton Shannon series:
Once a Widow (Dodd Mead, 1957; Detective Book Club, 1957; Dell, 1959)
If the Shoe Fits (Dodd Mead, 1959; Crest, 1960)
Death of a Ladies' Man (Gold Medal, 1960)
Suspicion (Hale UK, 1964; Curtis, 1971)

7

Meet Robert Martin
and Jim Bennett
by Brian Greene

11

Tears for the Bride
By Robert Martin

143

The Widow and the Web
By Robert Martin

Meet Robert Martin and Jim Bennett

by Brian Greene

I've lived in or near Virginia since I was twelve years old, yet before doing research on crime novelist Robert Martin (1908-76), I'd never heard of the author's birthplace area of Chula, VA. But then neither Chula nor the commonwealth of Virginia are significant to Martin's life story or his literary work. His family moved to Ohio when he was a kid and that's where he stayed. He spent much of his adult life in or near Cleveland, as a family man who moved up the ladder in an industrial goods firm while writing detective fiction as a moonlighting gig. He died in the town of Tiffin, OH, the same small burg in which he attended high school.

Martin's serial fictional character Jim Bennett lives and works out of Cleveland. Bennett, narrator and lead figure of thirteen Martin novels published between 1951-64, is the lead investigator in the Cleveland branch of the New York-based National Detective Agency. While Bennett's office is located in the city, most of the cases he works on take him into smaller towns in and around Ohio. Reading the books, you get the sense that Martin felt an affinity for the relatively humble locales, that his heart was more attached to Tiffin than to Cleveland.

Martin—who had a healthy stream of short stories (many of them Jim Bennett tales) appears in prominent detective fiction magazines in the 1930s and '40s before market considerations had him turn to full-length literary efforts starting in the early '50s—was a well-read guy. He appreciated novels by like-minded scribes such as Hammett, Chandler, and Cain. But he was also a versatile reader who could enjoy straight literary writing by authors like Steinbeck, Fitzgerald, and Hemingway. One pictures him putting in a day of work in the personnel office at the Sterling Grinding Wheel Company, then coming home and, after the kids were off to bed, sitting in his favorite chair and savoring the pages of *Farewell, My Lovely* or *East of Eden*.

Jim Bennett is an intriguing character when considered alongside other notable lead men of classic detective fiction. As an unmarried, childless fellow, he shares the societal outsider's detachment with Chandler's Philip Marlowe and Ross Macdonald's Lew Archer. But he's not a chronic wisecracker like Marlowe and he doesn't deeply psychoanalyze the people he encounters in his investigations, à la Archer. He's more like Hammett's operatives in being a no-nonsense detective who keeps things straight and to the point as he investigates the murderous entanglements he gets called on to unravel. In one way, he's reminiscent of Carter Brown's Al Wheeler character when it comes to women. While Bennett isn't the full-on hedonistic horndog that Wheeler is like Brown's protagonist, he always has a hungry eye on the female persons he meets in his work, and Martin always has him giving detailed descriptions of the physical attributes of the many attractive women who populate the stories. But unlike Wheeler, Bennett is a cautious guy who is usually able to keep it in his pants.

The two Robert Martin novels you're about to read are the third and fourth in the Jim Bennett series. Both were originally published in hardcover by Dodd Mead in 1954 and brought out in Bantam mass market paperbacks in '55 (the back cover of my copy of the Bantam edition of *The Widow and the Web* mistakenly refers to the lead character as "Pete" Bennett—sheesh).

Sandy Hollis is Bennett's secretary at the Cleveland office of the National Detective Agency. Sandy's a pretty, amiable single lady who shares an ongoing flirtation with her boss. It seems that if any woman could ever make an honest man out of Bennett (who often expresses mixed emotions about being unattached), it'd be her. *Tears for the Bride* opens with Jim agreeing to accompany Sandy on a weekend visit to her family's farm 100 miles Southwest of Cleveland, the focal point of their stay being a pheasant hunting expedition (the author enjoyed hunting, so worked one of his hobbies into the story). But this is a Robert Martin crime novel, so of course more than just outdoor gaming recreation occurs when Jim and Sandy venture out to the sticks.

As is the norm with Jim Bennett yarns, a complicated web of romantic relationships among small town inhabitants with interconnected lives drives the story here. There's a classic good girl versus bad girl setup, both the humble sweetheart and the provocative vixen having involvement with Sandy's brother. Heartsickness, jealousy, and amorous rivalries propel the people in and around

Sandy's family's orbit to desperate, sometimes fatality-inducing actions. It's up to Jim Bennett to untangle the web and get to the bottom of who's perpetrating all the violence.

The Widow and the Web, the second Martin novel collected here, represents a departure in the Bennett series in that it finds the investigator pulled into work that's outside his usual line of duties. The money-hungry owner of National (Bennett's always grumbling about the man's callous greed) has yanked Bennett out of Cleveland and placed him on a temporary assignment as an insurance investigator who works for a mid-Southern state on claims related to accidents or deaths suffered by employees on the job in industrial workplaces. So, here we see Martin utilizing knowledge gained in his own work experiences in his fiction.

In the story, Bennett is asked by the commission he represents to look into the death of a man who perished when he fell twenty feet from a ladder while performing warehouse work for the Ferris Abrasives Company. The deceased left behind a widow who is entitled to a $10,000 insurance payout and Bennett has to go around and talk to involved parties and make certain there was no foul play involved in the workman's fatal accident. Initially everything seems to be on the up and up and Bennett's all but ready to sign off on a recommendation that the widow—a hottie who's also the stepmother of a young daughter the man had—receives her benefit in full. But then the operative receives an anonymous note from one of the deceased's former co-workers, stating that the death was no accident. And now the case becomes more like the work Bennett usually performs: a potential murder investigation.

Both of these books, like all of the Jim Bennett novels, contain a wide swath of characters—both well-meaning and sinister people— whose lives are intertwined. The reader goes inside the various relationships and other personal motivations that drive the actions of each town's inhabitants. Sex and violence are ever present but never described gratuitously. Bennett investigates multiple murders in both stories, and in so doing finds that hurt feelings and cheating ploys in the characters' love lives are generally at the core of all the mayhem, with financial greed an additional factor at times. They're crime stories that double as society novels. They're suspenseful and fast-moving, and the word-for-word writing is sound, as you might expect from a guy as well read as Martin.

Bill Pronzini enjoyed a written correspondence with Martin during the handful of years leading up to Martin's passing. Pronzini describes their pen pal relationship, and his impressions of Martin's personal character, in his introduction to Stark House's Black Gat edition of Martin's 1952 novel *Little Sister* (a non-Bennett title written under Martin's pseudonym Lee Roberts). Pronzini got to know Martin at a time when the latter's life was not going well. He was a widower living alone after his longtime wife's illness-related death; changes at his workplace had forced him into retirement before he wanted that, and he wasn't able to get his current writing published by anyone.

Pronzini's depiction of Martin shows him to be a generally good guy: thoughtful, modest, kind-hearted. Reading that, it makes you think that Martin might have been a lot like Jim Bennett. Although the author was never a detective who investigated murders, his literary creation Bennett is likewise a basically nice guy who's ever reliable and who's an empathetic soul always ready to sympathize with the people he gets involved with while he explores the causes of violent crimes. The Jim Bennett books are too edgy to be called cozy mysteries, yet there's something comforting about the presence and voice of the good-natured character of the detective. These two excellent books provide readers with a great opportunity to get acquainted with the likable Jim Bennett and his creator, the equally affable Robert Martin.

—December 2024

Brian Greene writes short fiction, as well as journalism features on various arts. His short stories have been published online by Jerry Jazz Musician, Retreats from Oblivion, Punk Noir magazine, and others, and in print by *Bachelor Pad* magazine. His articles, essays, and reviews concerning crime fiction and film have appeared on the web via Crime Reads, Criminal Element, The Strand, Crimeculture, Crime Time, etc., and in hard copy publications by PM Press, *Paperback Parade*, and *Mystery Scene*. Brian lives in Durham, North Carolina.

TEARS FOR THE BRIDE

Robert Martin

For Lee

CHAPTER ONE

One gray Thursday afternoon in November Sandy Hollis said to me, "Jim, do you like to hunt?" I lowered the sport page of *The Cleveland Plain Dealer* and gazed across the office at her. Sandy was not only a good secretary, but easy to look at. She had brown hair which almost exactly matched her eyes, a faint scattering of freckles over her short nose, and long handsome legs. "Man or beast?" I asked.

"Birds," she said. "Ring-necked pheasants."

"Sure," I said. "I'll use my .38."

"Quit bragging," she laughed. "Even James Tobias Bennett, the famous private investigator, can't hit a pheasant with a revolver—unless it was sitting. And one doesn't shoot sitting birds."

"Tell me more," I said, folding the paper. Sandy and I had cleaned up some routine desk work, and the week's reports, with the required carbons, had been mailed to New York. It had been a dull day, and we were waiting for quitting time.

Sandy pushed her chair back from her typewriter and crossed her slim legs. "I had a letter from Dad today. He says there are a lot of birds on the place this fall. He wants me to come down for some shooting. He's got plenty of guns, and Mom's fried chicken is super, and Ralph will be there, and some other people. It'll be kind of a party."

"Who's Ralph?" I asked. "The boyfriend?" I realized instantly that I shouldn't have said it. I knew that Sandy didn't have a boyfriend—not yet. She had been engaged to a jet pilot, and three or four months previously he had been reported missing on a test flight over the Pacific.

Her eyes clouded for just an instant, and then she smiled. "Ralph's my brother," she said gently. "He's just been discharged from the army. We haven't seen him for over a year."

"Sounds like a family affair," I said. "Why should I butt in?"

"You won't be—and I want them to see what a nice boss I've got." She smiled.

"Aw, shucks," I said.

"You'll come, then?"

Suddenly the idea seemed attractive to me. "If you really want me."

"Good. I'll call home tonight."

I got up, put on my hat and overcoat.

"Where're you going?"

"Out to buy a hunting license."

She looked pleased. "We'll leave tomorrow afternoon, and come back on Sunday."

"Tally-ho," I said, and went out.

The Hollis farm was about a hundred miles southwest of Cleveland near a village called Ridge Center. It was pleasant driving in the crisp sunshine with Sandy beside me and the radio tuned to a program of soft dance music. Although Sandy had been with the agency for over two years, she had never told me much about her family. Now, as we drove along, I learned that her brother, Ralph, was a year younger than she and was engaged to marry a girl named Eileen Fortune. "She's a nice girl," Sandy said, "but I think I liked Judy better."

"Who's Judy?"

"Judy Kirkland. We all thought she and Ralph would get married, but just before Ralph went into the service they had some kind of a quarrel—and the next we knew Ralph was engaged to Eileen. Judy's—well, a little wild, maybe—but I like her. She has, oh, more personality than Eileen...." She paused and sighed. "I guess it'll work out all right, but I just hope that Ralph's engagement to Eileen wasn't one of those rebound things."

"Second choice is best choice—sometimes," I said.

She turned and smiled at me. "Why didn't you ever get married, Jim?"

"I guess I'm not the parent-teachers association type. Maybe, if I ever get a regular nine to five job, I might scout around and see if I can find a woman who'll have me."

"Have you ever been in love?"

"Madly," I said, "but she married a wholesale grocer from Columbus."

"I'm sorry."

"Don't be. She's fat now, and president of a garden club."

"How horrible," she said, laughing. "I'm glad she didn't marry you."

"So am I," I said sincerely.

She didn't mention the missing jet pilot, and neither did I, and after a while we passed through the four traffic lights on the main street of Ridge Center. It was five-thirty when we drove into the barnyard of the Hollis farm and stopped beneath a towering windmill. A tall lean man with a tanned leathery face came from around a corner of a fine big white barn and waved at us. He was wearing blue overalls over a heavy gray sweater and a sheepskin cap with the ear flaps turned up. Sandy got out of the car and ran to him. They embraced, and she led him over to me. He had a shy smile and clear friendly blue eyes.

"Glad to meet you, Mr. Bennett," he said, as we shook hands. "Sandy has written us a lot about you."

"Call me Jim," I said, smiling at him.

"All right, Jim. My name's Homer." He smiled his shy smile. "You don't look much like a detective—not, leastways, the way I figured a detective should look."

Sandy said, "Dad was a little dubious about my starting work in a detective agency. He thought I should get a respectable job in an insurance office, or a bank, I guess."

Homer Hollis smiled ruefully, "Well, after hearing some of those radio programs . . ."

"You should see the television stories," Sandy said. She pointed a finger and cocked a thumb. "Bang! Bang!" She looked up at the roof of the house. "I don't see an aerial yet, Dad."

"Not yet," Homer sighed. "But the pressure is on—especially since Ralph came home."

"How is Ralph?" Sandy asked.

Homer shook his head slowly. "He's not the same boy, Sandy. Kind of moody, and he's thin. I'm a little worried about him—but don't say anything to your mother."

Sandy's brown eyes clouded. "Maybe, after he's home a while . . ."

"Maybe," Homer said, and took my arm. "Come on in, Jim. That wind's raw."

The three of us walked across a neat lawn to a screened back porch. A row of milk cans sat beside the steps. A short plump woman with gray hair tied severely back from her head came out of the back door wiping her hands on an apron.

Homer said, "Mom, this is Jim Bennett."

Her pleasant face lit up and I took her warm moist hand. "Land's sake," she said, "Homer's been looking for you since noon." She kissed Sandy. "You look thin, honey. You don't get enough to eat in those city restaurants."

Sandy laughed, and then we all were in the kitchen. There was the warm smell of roast chicken and baking biscuits. They led me through the big house into a long living room where the flames from a fireplace crackled pleasantly and filled the twilight glow with flickering shadows. There were comfortable chairs, several divans, bright rag rugs over the polished hardwood floor. Through a long window I could see across a sweep of lawn. The highway at the end of the lane showed faintly in the dusk. As I watched, the lights of a car came up the highway and turned into the lane.

Mrs. Hollis peered out of the window. "Here comes Ralph and Eileen now."

"When are they going to get married?" Sandy asked.

Mrs. Hollis lifted her plump shoulders. "You ask him, honey. He don't seem to want to talk about it." She sighed heavily. "Something's worrying that boy. He's restless, and he don't eat right...."

"He'll be all right," Sandy said. "Come on, Mom. I'll help get up the chicken and stuff." She and her mother left the room.

Homer Hollis said, "Excuse me, Jim. I've got to go out and give Rex a hand with the milking."

"Who's Rex?"

"Rex Bishop, my hired hand. Been with me for years. He can run this farm better than I can, even if he is Lord knows how old—past eighty, I guess. But you'd never know it. His father was scalped by the Senecas over in Big Tree township. Rex is what you'd call a pioneer, I guess. You'll meet him at supper."

He went out and I sat down by the fireplace and stretched out my legs. Voices and laughter came from the kitchen, and then Sandy came into the living room with a tall, lean, dark young man and a small blond girl.

And so I met Ralph Hollis, late of the U.S. Army, and his pretty bride-to-be, Eileen Fortune. He was pleasant and quiet, with the same clear blue eyes of his father and same half-shy manner. Eileen Fortune clung to his arm and stood close beside him. Her small rather thin-lipped mouth and her large wide-spaced gray eyes prevented her from being beautiful, but she was attractive and very neat. Her simple wool dress held the same deep grey of her eyes, and I caught the tiny sparkle of the engagement diamond on her left hand. She took her melting gaze from Ralph long enough to acknowledge Sandy's introduction to me, and then she led Ralph to a divan, where she cuddled close beside him.

Sandy left the room and returned with a tray bearing gin, vermouth, ice and a bowl of olives. "Surprise, Jim," she said. "I'll bet you didn't think we served cocktails out here in the sticks, did you?"

Ralph Hollis looked across the room, grinning. "Gosh, this *must* be a special occasion. I never saw a martini in this house before I went away."

Sandy laughed. "Two special occasions, Ralph; you're home and I pried Jim away from the wicked city."

Homer Hollis entered the room. He had changed his overalls for a dark suit, and his thick iron-gray hair was neatly combed. With him was a ramrod-straight old man with the face of a mummy, like the pictures of Rameses II I used to see in my history books. He was tanned almost black, his cheeks were hollow and his nose was curved and knife-thin. His small black eyes beneath a sharp ledge of brow moved quick and bright. He was wearing a clean blue shirt and faded dungarees, which fitted his long thin legs tightly, like a cowpuncher's Levis.

Homer said, "Rex, this is Jim Bennett."

"Howdy, Jim." His voice was high and quavering, and his hand felt like dried leather, but his grasp was firm.

Sandy said, "Jim, you do the mixing."

I stirred a batch of martinis. When they were ready, everybody accepted one except Homer Hollis, Rex Bishop and Eileen Fortune, who said demurely, "I don't drink, thank you."

Homer left the room and came back with a bottle of bourbon and poured two small glasses for himself and Rex. The rest of us sipped our martinis, with Mrs. Hollis making a wry face at her first taste. She handed her glass to Ralph. "That's worse than Doc Mazzini's cough medicine," she said, and added hastily, "No offense, Mr. Bennett. I didn't mean . . ." She paused in confusion.

Everyone laughed, and Sandy said, "Mom, I'll have you know that Jim's the best martini-mixer in the state of Ohio. If you don't believe it, just ask him."

"We all have our small talents," I said modestly.

"I guess sweet cider is my speed," Mrs. Hollis said. "Come on, you girls. Help me dish things up."

She and Sandy and Eileen Fortune left the room. We four men sat quietly, listening to the crackle of the fire. It was full dark outside and I could hear the November wind moaning around a corner of the house. Ralph Hollis sat moodily by the fire, the flames making moving shadows on his lean young face.

Old Rex Bishop tossed off his whisky in one quick swallow, brushed the back of a hand over his puckered mouth and said in his shrill quavering voice, "Jim, Homer tells me you're one of them dee-tective fellers. You carry a gun?"

"Sometimes," I said, smiling.

"What kind?"

"A Smith and Wesson .38, mostly."

"Got her with you?"

"It's in my bag."

"You a pretty good shot, hey?"

"Fair," I said, remembering for the first time in years that I'd held the off-hand shooting record for hand guns at the agency school in New Jersey. It seemed like a long time ago, those days when I was just out of law school with visions of becoming a great trial lawyer, the champion of the people, the defender of justice. And then I'd met the sly, shrewd, cigar-chewing old man who ran the agency and all its branches, all over the world. He'd been old then, nobody knew how old, but his scratchy scrawl still signed the communiques, the directives, and all the paychecks.

He had been a lawyer, too, before he founded the agency, and he'd gotten my name from the college and he'd come to see me, chewing on a soggy cigar, which I came to learn was as much a part of him as his clipped white mustache, his heavy cane, his black Homburg.

"Jim," he had said, "they showed me your record, your psychological tests, and all that crap, and you're too damned honest. You'll starve to death, by God. Come with the agency, my boy. Be a part of the organization, and to hell with the law. You'll get plenty of law, anyhow, and you'll be living. Why, son, the FBI comes to me when they get stuck. My top men were lawyers once, and you've got the build and the brawn and not too much brain, just the right amount of brain—oh, hell, son, give it a try. The pay . . ."

He had stared at me fiercely, chewing on his cigar, and I had laughed and felt a kinship with him, and I suddenly knew that all along I hadn't really wanted to be a lawyer, and I was young and naive enough to think that there was glamour in the work of a private investigator. Besides, I had thought, I could always open a law office, whenever I wanted to. And so I had gone to the agency school, and the work had seeped into my blood and bones and I knew at last, after seventeen years, that I would never do anything else.

Rex Bishop's cracked old voice said, "I got me a Colt .44. My pappy brought it from Texas. Maybe tomorrow you and me can do some target shooting down by the creek."

Homer Hollis said, "Jim's going after pheasant with us in the morning."

"Shotguns!" the old man snorted. "Murder! Why, back in the old days I could hit a quail on the wing with a muzzle-loading musket. Jim, I got me a flintlock, too. My pappy said Daniel Boone carried it in Kentucky. She's a sweet gun, walnut stock as smooth as grease, notch sights. She can take out a squirrel's eye at a hundred yards, by God. Got me a bullet mold, too, and I make my own wadding. Them fancy new guns . . ."

Mrs. Hollis appeared in the doorway. "Everything's ready. Come on, now, before the mashed potatoes get cold."

We entered the dining room, where the table was loaded with heaping platters of golden-brown chicken, snowy mounds of mashed potatoes, deep bowls of giblet gravy, fluffy hot biscuits, pickles, preserves, relishes, delicacies without end. And for the first time in many years I bowed my head in thanks as Homer Hollis' deep humble voice began, "Dear Lord, we thank Thee for this food, and for all Thy blessings . . ."

CHAPTER TWO

After dinner, Homer Hollis and Rex Bishop went outside to finish up the evening chores and Ralph and I helped to carry the dishes into the kitchen. We offered to help dry them, too, but Mrs. Hollis shooed us out, saying that we would only be in the way. Ralph winked at me and we returned to the living room. He said, "Jim, if you want to get your bag, I'll show you your room."

"Fine," I said, and went out to my car. I got my bag, and Sandy's, and on the way back to the house I paused a moment to look at the night. It was clear and cold, with a bright moon and many stars. Over the hill on my left I could see the faint glow in the sky from the village of Ridge Center. A few cars were humming along the highway, and as I entered the house by the front door I saw a pair of headlights turn into the lane and come up toward the Hollis farm. Inside, I said to Ralph, "Looks like company's coming."

"Yes," he said, as I followed him up a wide-open stairway off the entrance hall. "It's probably Jake Fortune—Eileen's father. Mom asked him for supper, too, but he said he couldn't make it, but might stop in afterward." We reached the top of the stairs and he opened a door off a long hallway. "Here's your room. The bath is right down the hall. If you need anything, just holler." He moved away, carrying Sandy's bag.

My room was big and high-ceilinged, with white-painted woodwork and flowered wall paper. An old-fashioned porcelain pitcher and bowl stood on a marble-topped dresser beneath an oval mirror. The bed was a high four-poster covered with a patchwork quilt. The mattress sank luxuriously beneath my testing hand, and I realized that I was tired. I hoped that the Hollis family retired at the traditionally early country hour.

After unpacking my bag I hung in a cedar-smelling closet the few clothes I'd brought along; a stiff new gabardine hunting coat with a fleece lining, corduroy slacks, a blue flannel shirt. On the floor I placed the heavy shoes I wore on the rare occasions when I found time to fish for bass in the Michigan woods. I hadn't bought a hunting cap, having decided that the gray felt I was wearing would be adequate.

In the bathroom I washed my face and combed my hair, realizing, as usual, that I needed a haircut. Back in my room I decided my soft white shirt was clean enough, re-tied a blue knit tie, brushed my gray flannel suit, and went back downstairs to the living room.

Someone had put more wood on the fire and several bronze floor lamps added a soft glow to the light dancing on the walls. A man was standing by the fireplace talking to Ralph Hollis, a big man with a tough weathered face, rather small gray wide-spaced eyes, thin blond hair graying over his ears. Even if Ralph hadn't told me, I think I would have known that he was Eileen Fortune's father. He was wearing gray tweed slacks and a heavy gray flannel shirt, the pockets of which bulged with notebooks and yellow lead pencils. In one hand he held a small glass of whisky, the stub of a cigar in the other.

Another man sat nearby, idly leafing the pages of a magazine. He was young, about Ralph Hollis' age, I guessed, and was dressed in sharp contrast to the man by the fireplace; dark blue suit, sober tie, polished black shoes. He was thin, with a pale delicate face and dark hair clipped in a crew cut. The firelight gleamed on his rimless glasses.

Ralph Hollis turned away from the fireplace and made the introductions. The big man was Jake Fortune, the father of Eileen, as I had guessed. The young thin man was named Earl Seltzman. Fortune's grasp was firm and hearty; Seltzman's was limp. His voice was nasal, and immediately he sat down again and resumed his listless leafing of the magazine. The big man grinned, showing strong yellow teeth. "Pleased to meet you, Bennett. Homer told me that Sandy worked for a private dick—is that what you are, honest to God?"

"Yes," I said, a trifle wearily. Over the years I'd become a little surfeited with people who regarded my profession as outlandish, something away from the norm, a fantastic, slightly sordid occupation, not real, except in fiction, on the radio, or the television and movie screens. I suppose that every one of the hundreds of private investigators, either on their own or with one of the big agencies, as I was, from Miami to Seattle, had the same naive reaction from the rest of the world.

"Well," Jake Fortune said heartily, "it takes all kinds, I guess." He grinned at me, showing that he held no hard feelings.

Mrs. Hollis came into the room, followed by Sandy and Eileen Fortune. Mrs. Hollis smiled at Jake Fortune, and said to the thin young man, "Why, hello, Earl. How have you been?"

He gave her a wan smile without getting up. "I haven't seen Ralph since he got home," he said, "and Jake asked me to come along." He looked at Eileen, and added bitterly. "I hope it's all right."

Eileen flushed. "I—I'm glad to see you, Earl," she stammered.

"I knew you would be," he said with a kind of sly, cold sneer, and I decided in that instant that I did not like Earl Seltzman.

Sandy said in a too-gay voice, "Well! It looks like we need some ice and glasses." She went into the kitchen, and I followed her. While she got glasses from a cupboard, I broke ice cubes from a refrigerator tray. "Having fun, Jim?" she asked over her shoulder. I noticed that she'd changed to a soft cashmere sweater and a rust-colored skirt. Her shining brown hair curled crisply just above her shoulders, and I decided that she was one of the prettiest girls I knew.

"Sure," I said. "Tell me about the people; the big bluff character with the pocketful of pencils is the father of Eileen, the father-in-law-to-be of your brother, Ralph?"

She nodded, polishing glasses. "Jake Fortune. He's a widower, and

Eileen is an only child. They say he gambles a lot, and he likes the women, and he drinks, and makes frequent trips to Cleveland and Toledo. He's done a little of everything—farmed, dabbled in oil, raised horses, sold farm implements. At present I hear he's dealing in cattle."

"And the sullen young man with the poetic face? Seltzman, is that it?"

Sandy frowned a little and paused in her glass polishing. "To tell you the truth, Jim, I'm surprised that he's here. It's liable to create a—a situation. You see, Earl was in love with Eileen Fortune for a long time—still is, I suppose. He and Ralph went to Ohio State together to major in agriculture. Then, after Ralph and Judy Kirkland quarreled, Ralph began to see Eileen, and, well, I guess she liked my brother better than Earl, and she and Ralph became engaged just before Ralph enlisted. I told you about it."

"I remember," I said. "And then Earl Seltzman and Judy Kirkland got together?"

She shook her head. "No, it didn't work out that way. I'm afraid that Earl isn't Judy's type. I think it worried Ralph a little—after all, he was Earl's friend—but he never talks about it."

"All's fair," I said.

"I know," she said soberly, "but I wonder if—well, if Ralph really loves Eileen."

"She sure loves him," I said. "It sticks out all over her."

Sandy sighed. "I know."

"I'm just a nosey old bastard," I said, "but what's the connection between Jake Fortune and Earl Seltzman? Outside the fact that Earl is sweet on Jake's daughter? They came here together."

"They've probably been out on a cattle-buying trip," Sandy said. "Earl is quite wealthy. His parents are dead and they left him half a dozen farms around here. Dad wrote me that Earl has the idea that he wants to compete with the Texas beef market, and is building up a herd. I suppose Jake Fortune is doing the buying for him."

"All right," I said, "now tell me more about Judy Kirkland. She sounds—uh—interesting."

Sandy gave me a mocking look. "Banish that glint from your eye. You won't see Judy—not if I can help it. I didn't bring you down here to make passes at the local gals."

"Please don't be crude, Miss Hollis. I'm merely curious."

Sandy said, "Judy is frigid and unresponsive and she does as she pleases, no matter who gets hurt. She hates men. Every unattached male in these parts with enough courage has courted her without success, including my brother, Ralph."

"She must have money—or something," I murmured.

"Money *and* something," Sandy said. "Some girls have all the luck. Judy is pretty, of course—in a kind of pixie way, and although a trifle thin, her figure is marvelous. Her folks died a long time ago, and she lives with two old aunts on the family estate near here, or at her own place in town—that is, when she isn't in New York, or Los Angeles, or Bermuda, or someplace. I went to high school with her, and she likes dogs and horses and guns. She's a crack shot, an expert horsewoman, and it's rumored she's had affairs with a movie star, a young congressman, a rodeo cowboy, the author of a sexy bestselling novel, and Dr. Mazzini, who has an office in town. She drinks old-fashioneds for breakfast, champagne for lunch, martinis for dinner and Scotch in between times. She has wonderful clothes and she's a super gold-plated witch—and I like her."

"Hmmm," I said.

"Pooh," Sandy said. "Help me carry this stuff in."

In the living room Ralph Hollis and Jake Fortune were in conversation by the fireplace. Eileen had left Ralph and was now sitting beside Earl Seltzman. He was talking to her in low tones, his head bent forward, his eyes bright and intense behind his glasses. She was listening, but I saw her gaze dart to Ralph, who very carefully avoided looking at her. Mrs. Hollis was sitting comfortably in a rocking chair on the far side of the fireplace with a darning needle and a basket of heavy wool socks.

Sandy called for drink orders, and motioned for me to help her. Jake Fortune said he believed he'd have another straight whisky. Ralph wanted a highball, with soda; Earl Seltzman the same, with ginger ale. Eileen Fortune said sweetly that she really did not care for anything, thank you. Mrs. Hollis also declined, saying that she'd make herself a cup of tea after a while. Homer Hollis came in, bringing with him the cold smell of the November night, and accepted a straight whisky. When they all were served I made a whisky and water for Sandy and myself and carried my glass over to where Homer had sat down by a table on which was a stack of farm journals mixed in with the latest women's slicks and copies of *Time*.

I pulled up a chair beside him, said, "Where's Rex?"

"In bed. He gets up at five o'clock in the morning, winter and summer. He wouldn't need to, but he still lives in the old days, before we had electric milking machines and tractors and automatic feeders." He smiled his shy smile. "Of course, we still have to see that the right buttons are pushed."

"Oh, sure," I said, laughing. "You farmers certainly have it easy."

He smiled, more with his eyes than his mouth, and sipped at his whisky.

"I like Rex," I said.

"He's one of the family," Homer said. "He won't work for anyone else. This place belonged to him at one time—until the Depression. He lost it in '32, and the bank eventually sold it to me. I guess he thinks he still owns it, the way he acts sometimes." He laughed softly. "Rex is more of a partner than a hired hand. He has a share of the wheat and corn, and all the truck stuff, and the pigs are his."

"Can he really shoot—like he said?"

"He's a fine shot, as old as he is. Got quite a little gun shop out in the barn. He's all excited about you—thinks you'll give him some competition. If you get time tomorrow, maybe you wouldn't mind doing some shooting with him."

"I'd like to," I said, and I meant it. "How much land do you farm?"

"A hundred and forty acres now. I've been selling land, and going in more for blooded stock." He told me with quiet pride about his Hereford bull which had won a ribbon at the county fair that fall, and then our talk turned to hunting. He said there seemed to be quite a few pheasants, and that he had left some corn shocks and brush standing to provide cover for them. He also told me that the morning hunting party would consist of himself, Sandy, Ralph, Eileen Fortune and her father, and myself.

"Aren't you going to invite young Seltzman?" I asked.

He lit his pipe and said shortly, "That's up to Ralph."

I gazed around the room. Sandy had joined Ralph and Jake Fortune at the fireplace. Mrs. Hollis was contentedly darning socks, but I saw her glance over her glasses at Eileen and Earl Seltzman on the divan. Seltzman was still talking in low tones; she was listening with a grave expression. I had the feeling that everyone in the room was ignoring them with an elaborate indifference, a sort of everything-is-normal air. But looking at Earl Seltzman's pale intense face, at the glitter of his glasses, at the movement of his lips as he muttered into Eileen's ear, I thought that he was acting very badly, here in the home of Ralph Hollis, who was going to marry the girl beside him. I wondered why he had come, and I thought, *Forget her, son, and buck up. The best man won and all that and stop trying to talk her out of it. She's made up her mind and you'd better find a new girl.*

Sandy moved away from the fireplace to a phonograph console at the far end of the room. In a moment the soft piano magic of Frankie Carle filled the room. I settled back in my chair with a sigh of contentment. Sandy came and stood beside me. "Another drink, Jim?"

I handed her my glass, and we smiled at each other. She looked at her father. "Dad?"

Homer Hollis shook his head. "Not now. Don't expect me to keep up with you wild city people." He smiled up at her, half shyly. "I wish you'd come home more often, honey."

She leaned down and kissed him. "I would, Dad, but Jim works me too hard."

"Really cracks the whip, does he?" Homer's eyes glinted with amusement. "Maybe you need it. I remember when you were a little girl your mother could never get you to make your bed."

"I have a terrible time with her," I said. "I'm thinking about getting a new girl—a blonde, this time."

"Now, listen—," Sandy began, and then she gazed out of the window. "Oh, fun. More company."

The lights of a car were streaking up the lane. They disappeared and we heard the rattle of stone as the car braked to what must have been a skidding stop.

"That's Judy," Sandy said. "Nobody else in the world drives like that."

The room was suddenly quiet, and the piano melody from the console was soft and bell-clear. Even Earl Seltzman stopped his low monologue, and both he and Eileen Fortune looked toward the archway leading to the front hall. Ralph Hollis and Jake Fortune turned expectantly from the fireplace, and Mrs. Hollis stopped her gentle rocking. Homer puffed silently on his pipe.

Sandy moved out into the hall. The front door opened and closed, there were voices of greeting and a woman's quick laughter. Sandy returned to the living room with an arm around a slender black-haired girl, who was murmuring in protest, "But you have guests...."

"Nonsense, Judy," Sandy said. "I'm glad you came." The two of them stopped and faced the room.

I got to my feet, as did Homer Hollis, who said it quietly, "Good evening, Judy."

She smiled at him, swept her cool gaze over me, and looked beyond me. She was dressed in a soft leather jacket, dark green skirt, buckskin moccasins and a snugly fitting pale green turtle neck sweater which blended nicely with the odd gray-green of her eyes. My first impression of her was of gauntness, but as I gazed at her I became aware of the high firm breasts beneath the sweater, the slender waist above rounded hips, the straight sturdiness of her legs. Her mouth was very red and almost too large for her rather thin face. She wore her hair long with straight bangs across her forehead and there was an elfin look about her as she flung her hair back from her face and gazed expectantly across the room. She seemed to be waiting for something, her lips slightly parted.

And then from behind me I heard Ralph Hollis' grave voice. "Hello, Judy."

"I—I heard you were home, Ralph," she said breathlessly. "I just wanted to say hello."

"Thank you, Judy," he said in the same grave voice, and then everyone in the room seemed to speak at once, greeting Judy Kirkland. It was as if it all had depended upon Ralph, upon how he would react to her unexpected visit.

When the flurry had died down, Sandy said to Judy, "You'll *freeze* driving in that open convertible."

"I like the cold," she said, looking at me, her eyes cool and appraising.

"This is Jim Bennett," Sandy said. "He's my boss. We're going after pheasant in the morning."

Judy Kirkland held out her hand. Her fingers were as cold as death. She said easily, "I've heard of you, of course. You really *are* a detective?"

"Really."

"How amusing," she said. "That is something different." A glint, a something, showed in her eyes. "Do you carry a gun in a shoulder holster, and keep a bottle of rye in your desk? And do gorgeous blondes make passes at you, day and night?" Her red lips curved in faint mockery.

"You've been reading too many mystery books," I told her. "Besides, I prefer brunettes."

Sandy gave me a reproachful look, but Judy Kirkland's eyes widened a little and she said in a cool crisp voice, "How very interesting."

Ralph Hollis sauntered up and said, "Don't get any ideas, Jim. Judy hates men and devotes her life to her dogs and horses."

I thought I saw a shadow of pain cross Judy's eyes, but I could have been wrong, and immediately Sandy said nervously, "Judy, will you have a drink? We have martinis, and whisky...."

Judy's red mouth twisted in distaste. "Martinis? At this hour of the night? Whisky, please, honey. Straight."

Sandy said defensively, "We had the martinis before dinner."

"Of course, darling," Judy said brightly. "I was just being bitchy." She gazed across the room at Earl Seltzman, Eileen and Jake Fortune, and Mrs. Hollis. "Relax, all you people. I'm only staying a minute." She took my arm and led me to a divan on the opposite side of the room. "Come on, Mr. Bennett. Tell me more about those blondes you don't prefer."

Sandy said, "Don't forget, Judy—I'm the gal what brung him."

Mrs. Hollis resumed her rocking and knitting. Ralph poured himself a double whisky and carried it to the fireplace and stood staring into the flames. Earl Seltzman left Eileen's side at last and moved to the window and stood staring out at the night. Eileen, alone on the divan, gazed intently at her clasped hands, a small forlorn figure. Jake Fortune walked over to Homer Hollis and began talking in loud tones about the price of beef at the Chicago stockyards. Judy Kirkland sat close beside me, her hand still exerting a gentle pressure on my arm. Sandy brought us each a drink, and Judy said in a brittle voice, "So sweet of you, Sandy, honey."

I saw Eileen look up at Ralph with a worried, pleading expression, but he seemed not to notice. She continued to gaze at him anxiously.

Judy, her eyes on Eileen, said to Ralph, "Come on over, Ralph, and tell us about the army." She patted the divan beside her.

As Ralph turned toward us, I saw Eileen's small chin tremble, and a swift expression of dismay crossed her face. Ralph stood before us, holding his glass. "There isn't much to tell," he said carelessly. "I'm glad I'm out of it."

Judy said sweetly, "You haven't even kissed me yet. Aren't we still friends?"

Ralph stammered something, and looked uncomfortable. Judy laughed softly, stood up and moved to him. "For old time's sake," she said, and gently pulled his head down and placed her lips against his. It was a lingering kiss, and Ralph didn't pull away.

Eileen sprang to her feet. She stood trembling, her small fists clenched. There were tears in her eyes and she opened her mouth as if to speak, but she didn't say anything.

Judy released Ralph and laughed a little breathlessly. Eileen turned away and walked swiftly out of the room. I expected Ralph to follow her, but I was wrong.

It was Earl Seltzman.

CHAPTER THREE

For a brief space of time there was silence in the room and I realized that the Frankie Carle album had ended some time ago. Now Sandy moved to the console, turned over the stack of records, and started the player. The clean silver notes of the piano filled the room like a gentle shower of stars, and almost immediately everyone began to talk. All except Ralph Hollis. He moved to a chair, sat down and gazed intently at the glass in his hand. Mrs. Hollis rocked and knitted grimly.

Judy Kirkland resumed her seat beside me and gave me a bright wicked glance. "Did I do something?" she asked with elaborate innocence.

"You know damn well you did."

"Oh, hell," she said carelessly. "Eileen shouldn't be so touchy." Her gaze strayed to Ralph, but he didn't look at her. I had a clear view of her profile and the pouting curve of her lower lip.

Homer Hollis stood up, yawned, took out a gold watch and began to wind it. "Well, guess I'll turn in. If I'm going hunting in the morning, I'll have to get up early and help Rex with the work."

"I'll help, Dad," Ralph said suddenly.

"No, son," Homer said gently. "You take it easy for a while. We got to get some meat back on your bones."

"Don't baby me, Dad." Ralph grinned at his father. "I'm a big boy now."

"So I notice," Homer said dryly. He nodded at the room in general. Mrs. Hollis arose, too, said, "Goodnight, everyone," and followed Homer from the room.

Jake Fortune glanced at a wristwatch and said to no one in particular, "Eileen and me should be going." He moved over to the table and poured himself more whisky.

Sandy knelt on the floor and peered intently at the titles on the row of record albums in the phonograph cabinet. Ralph Hollis sat very still, staring at the glass in his hand. Judy Kirkland began to talk quietly and pleasantly to me about a pair of Irish setters she owned and I decided that she could be very attractive and likeable, when she wanted to be.

Suddenly we heard the sound of a car starting and through the window I saw the lights of a car going down the drive. At the highway it turned right, toward Ridge Center. Judy saw it, too, and she said to Ralph Hollis, "Ralph, it looks like Earl is taking your gal home."

He stood up and said carelessly, "Yes, it looks like it," and moved to the stairway in the hall. "Good-night, everyone."

We all said good-night, and I looked at Sandy. She was watching Ralph go slowly up the stairs and there was sadness in her eyes. She made a move as if to follow him, and then stood still.

Judy said softly, "That's right, Sandy. Let him go. He has nothing to worry about." She paused, and then said hesitantly, "I—I'm sorry for what I did, but you can't blame me for being just a little jealous, and Eileen is so—so possessive."

Sandy looked at her, and she didn't say anything.

Jake Fortune cleared his throat. "Well, my daughter seems to have gotten a ride home—I may as well get going." For some odd reason it seemed to me that he had a smug, satisfied look. He nodded at me, "See you in the morning, Bennett. Get your shooting eye in shape." His laugh boomed out as he left the room.

I said to Sandy, "Does he have a way home? I'll take him if—"

She shook her head. "He came in Earl's car, but he lives just up the hill. He can walk." She looked at Judy. "The party seems to be breaking up, but there's no reason why the three of us can't have a drink."

Judy stood up. "Thanks, honey, but no. I seem to have messed things up nicely. I should never have come. It was a crazy thing to do...."

"Your intentions were good, I'm sure," Sandy said with a hint of malice.

Judy patted her cheek. "My intentions were nothing of the kind, darling, as you well know. But I seem to have lost my perspective. If I had an eye for the long pull, I'd be married to Ralph now."

"Yes," Sandy said.

"Eileen will make him a good wife," Judy said. "They'll have a cute little love nest, and lots of babies, and it'll be very cozy, and very dull."

"But if they're happy . . ." Sandy said helplessly.

"That's what counts every time," Judy said briskly. "We must be happy, if it kills us." She looked at me. "It's been nice meeting you, Mr. Bennett. Will you be here long?"

"Until Sunday."

She gave me a level look, and the glint, the something, showed again in her gray-green eyes. "I have a place on the other side of town," she said, "on River Road. There's a white picket fence, and a brass coach lamp on a green pole. I call it Sanctuary. Do you like Faulkner, Mr. Bennett?"

"Some of him," I said. "The earlier things."

"I go to my little house when I get bored with my aunts," she said. "I'm going there now, for the weekend. Do you ever get bored, Mr. Bennett?"

"Frequently."

"If you like, stop at my house and we'll be bored together." She smiled at Sandy. "That is, if Sandy doesn't mind. Do you mind, Sandy?"

"Not at all," Sandy said sweetly. "Would you like to join us in the morning? For pheasant, I mean? We plan on leaving around nine."

Judy picked up her leather jacket and moved across the room. At the archway she turned and said gravely, "Thank you, Sandy. You always were a nice gal. But I'd better not. It might make things— complicated." She turned away, and we heard the front door slam. Her car started and roared down the lane. Through the window I saw it turn toward Ridge Center, in the same direction Eileen Fortune and Earl Seltzman had gone.

Sandy sighed and said, "Well, you've met Judy. What do you think of her?"

"I don't know. Is she mad at the world, or something?"

"She's just spoiled, and she's always had too much money. I told you that she and Ralph were engaged, and they broke up, and now she can't bear to see any other girl get him. That's why she came here tonight—to embarrass poor little Eileen."

"I'm no authority," I said, "but I think Judy Kirkland needs a man who will beat her three times a day and keep her pregnant and barefooted."

Sandy laughed. "Maybe you're right. I was surprised that Eileen had the spunk to leave with Earl tonight—but maybe it's not surprising, either. She knows that Earl is still in love with her, and maybe it helped her ego—although it wasn't fair to Ralph; he couldn't help what happened."

"What did he and Judy quarrel about?"

"Ralph never told me, and I sometimes think he's still in love with her." She sighed again. "Well, I can't do anything about it. I'm going to bed. We'll have breakfast about eight. Can I make you a nightcap before I go up?"

"I'll get it—if I want one."

She moved toward the stairway, and then hesitated, her gaze avoiding mine. "Are—are you going to see her? Judy, I mean?"

I went up to her and placed my hands on her shoulders. "Of course not."

"Maybe—you'd like her."

I grinned at her. "I'm sticking with the gal what brung me."

She looked up at me then, and she smiled, but there was a suggestion of tears in her brown eyes. "Sometimes you're—nice, Jim," she said softly.

On a sudden impulse I leaned down and kissed her. I felt her stiffen, and then her arms slid around my neck. Her lips were cool and soft, and it was a nice kiss, brief, and as light as a summer breeze. Then she stepped out of my arms, murmured, "Good-night, Jim," and went up the stairs.

I poured myself a small drink of bourbon, turned off the lights and sat before the dying fire. It was the first time I'd ever kissed Sandy. She'd worked for the agency for over two years, and I'd never even thought of kissing her, until tonight. Maybe it was because I knew she was very deeply in love with the boy in the Air Force, and because I'd grown accustomed to her quiet, friendly presence. I sighed, and thought that I'd be smart if I picked a girl like Sandy Hollis and married her. The kiss had surprised us both; I hadn't intended to kiss her, but I was glad that I had. It was something nice to remember, a little island in my memories of other women and other kisses, other times and other places, and all the things that make a man's life.

I thought of Judy Kirkland, arrogant and selfish, who had been engaged to Ralph Hollis, and had lost him, and of the pale sullen Earl Seltzman, eating out his heart for Eileen, who was now engaged to Ralph. I thought of Homer Hollis, a quiet, friendly man, and of his pleasant motherly wife; of old Rex Bishop, looking backward to the past down the long years; of Jake Fortune, loud and hearty, the father of Eileen, the father-in-law-to-be of Ralph Hollis. I thought of all the people I'd met since coming to this farm, of their loves and worries and feelings, each living his own life, and I thought that nothing in this life was ever exactly right, not ever the precise way we wanted it to be. I sat by the fire, feeling sad and nostalgic and faintly sorry for myself, and my thoughts returned to Sandy....

In the morning everything seemed fine, at least on the surface. At breakfast Sandy and Ralph joked with each other, and once Sandy gave me a special sort of smile. Homer Hollis was quietly humorous, and Mrs. Hollis bustled about urging us to eat more pancakes, scrambled eggs and fried ham. I asked about Rex Bishop, and Homer said he'd had his breakfast hours ago.

"He cooks it himself about dawn," Homer said, "and he won't let Mom do it for him."

"And thank heaven," Mrs. Hollis said, laughing. "I've lived on a farm all my life, but five o'clock in the morning is a little too early for me."

Jake Fortune and Eileen arrived. They said they'd had breakfast, but accepted coffee and sat at the big table with us. Eileen glanced anxiously at Ralph, but he smiled at her and presently I noticed that they were holding hands beneath the table. A melting look came into her eyes, and I guessed that she could hardly wait to get Ralph alone to tell him that she was sorry for her impulsive action, born of jealousy, in leaving with Earl Seltzman the night before. She looked pretty in a red hunting cap and a heavy bright plaid shirt. Jake Fortune talked loudly and laughed a lot. The notebooks and yellow pencils still bulged the pocket of his flannel shirt.

At last we pushed back our chairs. I put on my new hunting coat and we went outside. There was an array of guns on the back porch, and Homer Hollis handed me a 12-gauge double-barreled shotgun and a handful of shells. "That's a good gun, Jim," he said. "I think you'll like her."

I hefted it, raised it to my shoulder and sighted at a lightning rod on the barn. "It's a sweet gun," I said. "If I don't get a bird, it won't be the gun's fault."

Homer laughed, and the six of us started out across the barnyard toward the open country beyond. It was a fine day, cold and clear, with a bright sun shining over the brown fields. In the woods the remnants of autumn leaves clung to the bare branches and the earth was spongy with their matted mouldy dampness. We left the woods and walked across a big field filled with corn stalk stubbles. I breathed the sharp cold air and the gun was a pleasant weight in the crook of my arm. We spread out, with about ten yards between us. Homer Hollis was on my left, Jake Fortune on my right. Sandy and Ralph were on the wings, with Eileen between her father and Ralph.

Off to our right a pheasant left the shelter of a corn shock and shot into the air, the sun glinting on the bright red, green and gold of its feathers. Homer shouted, "Sandy! Take it!"

Sandy brought her trim little 16-gauge to her shoulder, the gleaming blue barrel following the swift flight of the bird. The clean crack of the shot echoed over the fields and the bird dropped. Sandy ran to pick it up and held it proudly aloft.

Jake Fortune's laugh boomed out. "First blood," he said. "Homer, we'll have to do something about that. Can't let the women get the best of us. How about you and me going over to my place—to a berry thicket I've been watching?"

Homer smiled, his proud gaze on Sandy, and he said absently, "All right, Jake," and he followed the big man across the field. "See you at dinner," he called over his shoulder at the rest of us.

I was glad the party had split up. I figured that six in a bunch was too many for safety, even if we had been spread out. Suddenly Jake Fortune stopped and called to Eileen, "Want to come with us, honey? That'll make it even—three and three."

Eileen looked questioningly at Ralph. He grinned and said, "Go ahead. I'll see you at noon."

She said something to him that I couldn't hear, and then moved slowly to join her father and Homer. They walked across the field and disappeared over a pine-crested hill.

Sandy, Ralph and I moved across the field, our guns ready, but we didn't see any birds. We reached a fence and I saw the tall thin figure of Rex Bishop walking toward us. A gleaming coil of wire was lopped over one shoulder, and he carried a long-barreled rifle. He waved at us, and I went over to the fence. We grinned at each other in the sunshine. The gun he held was an old-time flint lock. "Going to fix a fence at the far end of the ravine," he said, "down in the bottom. Thought I might get a shot at a bird."

I nodded at the musket. "With that?"

"It's a dang sight better weapon than that fancy scattergun you're toting." He peered out over the fields. "Where's Homer, and the rest?"

"We split up."

"Try the ravine," he said. "It goes clean across Homer's land, east to west. It runs across the Kirkland boundary, and them two old women don't allow no hunting at all—except Judy, she hunts once in a while. Should be plenty of birds in there."

"Thanks, Rex."

He peered at me in the sunlight. "Do you suppose you and me could do a little target shooting this afternoon?" he asked hopefully. "Before chore time?"

"Sure."

He grinned like a kid who had been promised a new bicycle, and as he moved away he said, "Tell Homer I might not get up to the house for dinner, but I got me a couple of side meat sandwiches in my pocket."

"I'll tell him," I said.

He waved at Sandy and Ralph and moved on along the fence, balancing the heavy coil of wire easily on his lean shoulder. I went over to Ralph and Sandy and told them what Rex had said about the ravine near the boundary of the Kirkland place. Ralph nodded. "He's probably right. We'll give it a try."

We climbed two fences, went through a patch of stunted pine and emerged in a rolling meadow. Ahead I could see a winding row of trees and bushes which marked the crest of a ravine which stretched across the land as far as I could see. "It runs for miles," Ralph said. "There was water in it at one time, but it's dried up now."

Beyond the ravine was a long sloping hill and a distant house outlined against the sky. Ralph pointed at the house, said, "That's where Eileen and her father live."

I grinned at him. "Your girl lives right next door, huh?"

He laughed and said, "Sandy and I grew up with Eileen."

As we approached the ravine, we heard the sound of gunfire. I looked questioningly at Ralph, and he furrowed his dark brows in a frown. Another shot rang out in the cold November air. It seemed to come from the far side of the ravine.

"Is that your father and the Fortunes?" I asked Ralph.

He shook his head. "I don't think so—they headed the other way, toward the house. It's probably some city hunters on the place without permission. Every Fall, out-of-town hunters flood this whole section. Folks here post 'No Hunting' signs, but it doesn't do much good. But Dad never minded if they hunted on his place—if they asked permission. Come on."

We reached the edge of the ravine, and Ralph went down the steep side, running stiff-legged to keep his balance, and started up the other side. Sandy and I followed him, holding our guns clear of the underbrush. A gun cracked nearby, and the dry branches of the trees around rattled faintly. Something struck my hat brim, like a pebble falling.

"The fools," Sandy said angrily. "They're shooting too close to us."

Ahead of us and above, Ralph gained the top of the opposite side of the ravine, and for an instant his tall form was silhouetted against the bright blue sky. In that instant the unseen gun spoke again, two quick shots, and I saw a pheasant rise over the crest and wheel away to my right. I raised my gun to my shoulder, began to lead the bird with the sights, and put slow pressure on the trigger.

Sandy's stricken voice stopped me. "Jim! Ralph's hurt!"

I turned and looked upward, and I saw Ralph swaying on his feet. He dropped his gun, leaned briefly against the trunk of a big beech tree, and then slid slowly to the ground.

I reached him first. There was no blood yet, but I could see where the bird shot had entered. Thin black furrows slanted in horizontal lines across his right shoulder and chest, leaving ragged tears in his leather jacket. He laid his cheek against the brown leaves and he began to cough, and the leaves were suddenly stained a bright red.

CHAPTER FOUR

I kneeled over him and snapped at Sandy, "Run to the house and call a doctor. I'll bring him in."

For an instant she stood frozen, looking down at her brother, her face drained white. Then she turned and ran like a young deer down the ravine, her brown hair glinting in the sunlight.

Gently I turned Ralph on his back and unzipped his leather jacket. The shotgun pellets had penetrated deeply and blood was already soaking his flannel shirt.

"Ralph," I said sharply.

He tried to grin at me, but caught his lower lip between his teeth in sudden pain, and started to cough again. I gathered his long body in my arms as gently as I could, and I stood up and gazed out over the countryside. Not a moving thing was in sight. I looked down at Ralph, saw that blood from his mouth was staining the sleeve of my hunting coat. Carefully I started down the side of the ravine.

There was a sound behind me, and I turned. Judy Kirkland was coming up the hill on the far side, from a small valley below. She was wearing the same soft leather jacket, but had changed her skirt for trim-fitting jodhpurs. Her generous mouth looked redder than ever in the bright sun, and she wore big dark sun glasses. Over her black hair she wore a red cap with a long bill, like a baseball player's. She reached the crest, panting, and looked at me dumbly, and at the form of Ralph in my arms. He was limp now, and his eyes were closed. Bright blood stained his mouth and chin.

At the sight of the blood, Judy's face went gray and pinched-looking. She opened her mouth, but no sound came out.

"Were you doing that shooting?" I snapped.

"Yes, I—I guess so. I was standing down there in the thicket, and I saw a bird fly out of the ravine. Did I . . .?"

"Yes," I said grimly, turning away. "You hit Ralph." I started down the side of the ravine, holding Ralph as gently as I could.

She scrambled after me. "Wait," she panted. "I—"

"Wait, hell. This boy has got to get to a doctor. Bring the guns, if you want to help."

She gathered up the two shotguns, and I could hear her following me, slipping and sliding on the hill.

I guessed Ralph Hollis to weigh about a hundred and sixty. I tip the scales at one-ninety, but before I reached the farmhouse my arms felt paralyzed. It was a long walk across the fields and through the woods, and getting Ralph over the fences was the worst, but I made it. Judy Kirkland trudged silently beside me carrying the guns, and she tried to help me when she could. When we reached the barnyard at last I could feel the sweat drenching my body, and I was panting like a relay runner after the last hurdle.

Sandy and her mother were waiting on the back porch. They stared at Ralph dumbly, and Sandy opened the door. A sheet and a pillow had been placed on one of the divans in the living room, and as I laid Ralph down Mrs. Hollis moaned, "Ralph, my baby...."

Sandy said in a strained voice, "Dr. Mazzini is on the way. He should be here by now...."

I unbuttoned Ralph's shirt. There was a lot of blood now, but I couldn't tell how badly he was hit. Three little black pellets clung to his undershirt, and I thought that it was a good sign; the shotgun charge had apparently been nearly spent when it struck him. And then I remembered the blood on the leaves, and I knew that at least one of the pellets had gone deep.

Ralph opened his eyes. They were slightly glazed, but they searched and found his mother, and he tried to smile. "Hi, Mom...."

"Quiet, son," she whispered, and laid a hand on his forehead.

I had forgotten about Judy Kirkland until she spoke. "Those damned sun glasses. I—I didn't see Ralph. All I saw was the bird rising...." Her voice choked off.

We heard the crunch of wheels in the drive, and the sound of a car door slamming. Sandy ran to the front door and came back into the room with a tall man, a dark hatless man who wore a blue woolen muffler and a gray tweed overcoat. He had short, curly black hair and a lean dark Indian-like face, alert black eyes. He ignored all of us and we stood aside while he knelt beside the divan. From a black leather bag he took a pair of scissors and skillfully cut away Ralph's blood-soaked undershirt. He took one intense look, and stood up.

"Hospital," he said shortly. "Two of those shots are pretty deep—might be in the lung. I'll take him in my car."

I said, "He coughed some blood, right after he was hit."

The doctor gave me a quick look, bent over, and grasped Ralph beneath his shoulders. "Get his feet," he said to me.

The two of us carried Ralph out to the doctor's car, a new blue Ford sedan, and laid him gently on the rear seat. Sandy handed me a blanket. I folded it around Ralph and sat beside him on the edge of the seat. The doctor got behind the wheel. "All set?" he snapped.

Sandy said, "Can—I go along?"

"Sure," the doctor said. "Hop in."

Swiftly Sandy got in beside him, and he started the motor. Judy Kirkland appeared beside the car and fumbled at the door latch.

"No," the doctor snapped, "you stay here."

Judy backed away with a faintly dazed expression. The Ford's rear wheels skidded on the stone as we swung in a circle and took off. I looked out of the rear window and saw Judy and Mrs. Hollis standing in the drive gazing after us. As we turned into the highway, the doctor said, "Who shot him?"

"Judy," I said.

His lean jaw tightened, but he made no comment.

Sandy stared straight ahead, and said nothing. Ralph muttered something, and I tried to make him more comfortable. It took us maybe ten minutes to reach the hospital in Ridge Center, a long low-roofed building on the edge of the village with a cement parking area around it. The doctor stopped at a rear entrance labeled *Emergency*, blew a blast on the horn, and got out. Almost immediately two white-uniformed nurses appeared with a wheeled white-sheeted stretcher and rolled it up to the car. The doctor barked quick orders as we lifted Ralph out. Then we were inside the hospital and moving down a long corridor. Sandy was beside me, but the doctor had disappeared. They pushed Ralph through swinging doors into a room that gleamed dazzling white for an instant before the doors swished softly shut. A sign above said, *Surgery.*

Sandy and I stood helplessly in the corridor. An old man in a faded bathrobe limped slowly past us, paying no attention to the rest of the world. A telephone rang, nurses hurried by on silent rubber soles. There was the smell of antiseptic and soap. Dr. Mazzini, in hospital whites, appeared from somewhere and went past us without speaking. His black eyes looked angry and remote as he pushed through the swinging doors. The doors whispered shut.

I looked at Sandy. She was watching the doors, her face pale and drawn. I lit a cigarette, touched her arm. She looked at me. I gave her the cigarette. She smiled her thanks and inhaled deeply. I lit a cigarette for myself. We waited. After a little while I left her and walked to the end of the corridor to a little sun-filled alcove, where I sat on a bench and leafed copies of old magazines. I could see Sandy standing by the surgery doors. I went back and stood beside her. The doors swung open and I got a whiff of ether. They wheeled Ralph out. He lay very still, swathed in white, his lean young face calm and reposed. The doctor followed. He wiped sweat from his face and said to Sandy, "He's got a chance. Two of the slugs penetrated the lung wall. How did it happen?"

Sandy glanced helplessly at me, and I told the doctor all I knew about the accident. When I finished, he looked thoughtful and said quietly, "I see. Who are you, by the way?"

"My name's Bennett—Jim Bennett."

Sandy said, "Doctor, he's my boss, in Cleveland. We came down together yesterday."

The doctor snapped his fingers. "Of course. The fact that Sandy works for you makes her a kind of celebrity around here." He smiled and held out a hand. "Glad to meet you, Jim."

We shook hands, and he said, "I've got to run. Three women ready to pop babies any minute, and my office will be full." He glanced up at a big clock on the wall. "But first I've got to run out past your folk's place, Sandy. Can I give you a lift?"

"No, thanks," Sandy said. "I'll stay here for a while. Will Ralph be—all right?"

He hedged, as all doctors must. "I'll check him in a couple of hours."

As he moved away, I saw Mr. and Mrs. Hollis and Eileen Fortune coming up the corridor. Sandy went to meet them and I heard her say, "Now, don't worry. He'll be all right."

Homer Hollis said, "Judy came over to Jake's place and told us. I got Mom and drove right in."

"You can't see him for a while," Sandy said, and the four of them sat on a bench along the wall. Mrs. Hollis looked as if she'd been crying, and Homer's lean face was grim. Eileen Fortune was sobbing openly. I moved down to them, and Homer said, "Jim, I'm sorry this had to happen—to spoil your visit."

"Don't worry about me."

Mrs. Hollis said brokenly, "To think what that boy went through in the army, and then he comes home . . ."

Homer patted her plump shoulder. Eileen Fortune's sobs grew louder, and she bunched a wadded handkerchief to her nose. It seemed to me that she looked quite unattractive, but I sternly told myself that I should he more charitable. After all, Ralph was her betrothed.

I saw Dr. Mazzini, dressed in street clothes again, standing at the far end of the corridor. Sandy saw him, too, and she said to me, "Go with him, Jim. There is no need for you to wait around here. I'll see you at the house."

"All right." I moved down to the doctor, asked him if I could ride with him as far as the Hollis place. He nodded, and we went out to his Ford. As we drove away, he said, "I've got to see a patient on the next road past the Hollis place."

We rode in silence for a while, but after we left the village limits the doctor said suddenly, "Judy's too damn careless—about everything. All she was thinking about was killing that bird, and she didn't pay attention to anything else. She should have seen Ralph, standing like you said on the top of the ravine."

"Yes," I said, noting that we were in the country and approaching the lane leading up to the Hollis farm. "Let me out at the top of the hill."

He looked at me quickly. "Is that near where it happened?"

"Fairly near. It was back off the highway, beyond the woods."

He compressed his lips and he didn't speak again until he'd stopped the Ford on the edge of the highway at the top of the hill overlooking the Hollis farm and the adjoining land where Jake Fortune and Eileen lived. And through the distant trees I saw the gables of a tall old house and decided that it was the Kirkland place, where Judy's aunts spent their days in what I imagined was decadent loneliness. And from the hilltop the tree-fringed ravine wound across the land of all three farms.

Dr. Mazzini said carefully, "It was an accident?"

I looked at him in surprise. "Of course."

He sat with his hands on the wheel and his eyes were bleak as they surveyed the countryside. "You wanted out here," he said, "and not at the Hollis lane. To me, that means you're going to look over the scene, where it happened. You're a detective, with a big agency. You're almost the same as the law, and I know how your mind works. When I was just out of Western Reserve and interning I had a part-time job with the medical examiner's office. We had some homicides, of course. I helped on some of them, and I got to know some of the city detectives." He paused, his eyes on the horizon.

"Go on," I said gently.

He turned toward me. "I assume that you are aware that Judy Kirkland is a hellion, that Ralph Hollis jilted her for Eileen Fortune?"

"I had the impression that it was the other way around," I said. "Didn't Judy give Ralph the gate?"

He shrugged. "What's the difference? I suppose you're wondering why I'm so interested?"

"I can guess," I said. "Good luck."

He laughed shortly. "I know what you mean. She's spoiled and bored and selfish, like a high bred horse or a blue-ribbon dog—she needs somebody to crack the whip." He gave me a sidelong look. "And why in hell am I telling you all this?"

"I don't know," I said, "unless you figure you're the guy to crack the whip. That's why I wished you good luck."

His gaze shifted away from mine, and he gunned the Ford's motor.

I opened the door. "Thanks for the lift, Doc."

"What do you expect to find over there?" He jerked his head toward the fields.

"Probably nothing."

"But you've got to look?"

"Habit," I said. "Maybe just plain nosiness. I was with Ralph when he was hit. Maybe I can figure out how it happened. Anyhow, I've got the afternoon to kill."

He opened his mouth as if to speak, and then apparently changed his mind. I got out and closed the door, and he drove away, down the hill and around a curve. I saw his car again, a blue dot on the highway as it came up the far side, and then it disappeared. I crossed the ditch, climbed the fence, and struck out across the fields. It was almost twelve o'clock noon. I guessed that Ralph Hollis had been shot between ten and ten-thirty in the morning.

I climbed a second fence, crossed another stubbly field, and entered the woods. It was still and quiet, and as I moved through the trees I felt a vague uneasiness. It wasn't like the city, and yet it was the same. A man can be terribly alone in the city with people all around him, and I had a feeling of loneliness now, a vague sensation of danger. I was oddly relieved when I left the woods and began to cross the open meadow. The ravine was directly ahead, and I saw the big beech tree where Ralph had fallen.

I went down into the ravine, imagining that I was Ralph, and I climbed up to the ridge and stood by the beech tree and gazed down into the valley below and the stretch of meadow I had just crossed and the fields beyond. Directly below me I saw the thicket where Judy Kirkland had said she had stood when she had fired at the pheasant rising from the ravine behind Ralph Hollis. I shifted my position until I thought I was standing in the same spot I'd seen Ralph just before the shotgun charge struck him. I stood beside the tree, still imagining that I was Ralph, and that Judy Kirkland was standing in the thicket directly below me with her gun poised for a quick shot at a bird rising behind me.

Two hours ago, if I had been Ralph, I would have been facing the sun, and the sun would have been at Judy's back—she could have seen me clearly, if she had been looking. And then I put myself in Judy's place, standing in thick underbrush, and wearing dark sun glasses, and sighting swiftly on a bird winging fast into the sky. Would I have noticed a man standing above me, between me and the bird?

I lit a cigarette and leaned against the beech tree. At my feet Ralph Hollis' blood was now a part of the earth, only a faint darkness on the brown leaves, and I thought, *Bennett, you're just a suspicious old son of a bitch. This shooting was an accident, pure and simple, and—*

A gun cracked, not too far away. The sound rumbled up the ravine in an obscene echo, and splinters of bark sprayed out from the beech tree close beside my head, I jerked away and dropped to the ground, my hand reaching automatically for my inside coat pocket. But my gun wasn't there, of course, not in the bulky new hunting coat. It was in my bag in an upstairs room back at the Hollis farmhouse. I hugged the damp leaves and waited.

The woods were silent. The only sound was the excited chirping of sparrows in the branches above me. I waited some more, lying very still, and at last I cautiously lifted my head. I heard another shot, but it was farther away, and there was no bullet whine near me. I pushed myself to my hands and knees. Below me in the thicket a cockbird called to its mate and I saw a drab brown hen rise from the field beyond and fly toward the thicket. And then there was more silence, oceans of it.

I waited maybe five minutes before I began to crawl backward down the side of the ravine. My coat got bunched up beneath my arms and I was covered with burrs and dirt before I reached the bottom. I stood up and gazed upward at the exposed ridge I'd just left. The shot which had struck the beech tree had come from my left, from the general direction of the highway. I walked that way along the bottom of the ravine, but when I emerged on the open fields I saw nothing but the rolling country and the white ribbon of highway beyond. A few cars were moving along the highway, tiny little bright bugs, and on the horizon there was a trail of smoke from a distant train.

As I moved across the fields toward the Hollis farm house, I wondered if some people in this part of the country hunted pheasants with rifles, because it had surely been a rifle bullet smacking the beech tree beside my head. I decided that most pheasant hunters would use a shotgun—except Rex Bishop who, I remembered suddenly, had carried a musket on his fence-fixing job "down in the bottom." I stopped and looked around, but I didn't know where "the bottom" was located, or even what it was; a flat low place, I had always thought, usually near water, but I could have been wrong.

I walked on up to the farm and as I turned the corner of the barn I saw Homer Hollis standing on the back porch filling his pipe. I moved up to him, said, "Hi, Homer."

He regarded me over a lighted match. "Hello, Jim." I sat down on the porch step. Homer came and sat beside me, puffing thoughtfully on his pipe.

"Sandy still at the hospital?" I asked.

"Yes. She and Mom stayed there. I came on back home. Nothing I can do."

"Any change?"

He shook his head, and we sat in silence for maybe a minute. Then he said, "Jim, I want to thank you for carrying our boy all that way."

"It was nothing."

"I won't forget it. I kind of blame myself for leaving you and Sandy and Ralph. Maybe, if I'd stayed with you . . ."

"No," I said. "We saw Rex, and he suggested we try the ravine. By the way, he said to tell you that he might not get up to the house at noon. He's got some sandwiches with him."

Homer nodded. "He was determined to fix that fence today. It's just as well, I guess; there won't be any womenfolk around to cook."

"I can fry eggs and bacon," I said.

"We'll find something, I reckon. Would you like a drink?"

"No, thanks. Maybe I'd better go back and tell Rex about Ralph?"

He shook his head. "There's no need. He should be up to the house before long."

"We've got a date to shoot target," I said. "Where's Jake Fortune? I saw Eileen at the hospital."

"Oh, after we left you and got near his place he remembered he had to make a phone call. We waited for him, and when he came back out he said he had to stick around and wait for a cattleman from Cleveland to call him back. Eileen and I hunted a while, and were working our way back here when we saw Judy running to tell us about Ralph. We got Mom and went right to the hospital. I don't know where Judy went. She was pretty cut up about it."

"Yes," I said.

"Damn it," he said suddenly, and I looked at him in surprise. It was a harsh word for him. "That Judy has always been harum-scarum and irresponsible. It seems to me she could have seen Ralph before she shot . . ."

"Accidents happen," I said.

He sighed and nodded gloomily. "I suppose so, but I'm glad that Ralph broke off with her. She would have led him a merry chase. Eileen will make him a better wife, but Judy was sure sweet on him—maybe she still is, for all I know. She shouldn't have come here last night and stirred things up, but she's like all the Kirklands. Troublemakers, I always said, and downright mean, sometimes.

Especially when they're crossed. Her dad had the wildest temper in this county. I saw Orville Kirkland kill a mare once, with a singletree. It was a good mare, too—just balky because a stallion was in the next stall. Of course, Orville was sorry afterward...."

"Like Judy is now?" I asked softly.

He looked at me quickly, but I avoided his eyes and gazed out over the fields. "Jim," he said quietly, "what were you doing back in the woods?"

I shrugged. "Trying to scare up a bird." Immediately I knew I had slipped.

"You didn't have a gun with you," he said gently.

I looked at him then, and I tried to smile, but it was a poor attempt. The wicked thunk of the bullet into the tree beside my head was still a vivid and terrifying memory. I shivered a little in the cold sunshine.

Homer said, "You went back to where it happened?"

I nodded.

"I figured you did. Learn anything?"

"No." I didn't tell him about the bullet hitting the tree. I hadn't fully made up my mind about that yet. "What about this Earl Seltzman, the fellow who left with Eileen last night? Sandy told me that he was in love with Eileen, before she got engaged to Ralph— after Ralph split up with Judy."

"That's right." Homer knocked out his pipe on the edge of the step. "Earl went around with Eileen a long time. He was turned down for the service—sinus trouble, I heard—and after Ralph went away he tried to make hay with Eileen again."

"Did he get anywhere?"

Homer shrugged his spare shoulders. "How can you tell? Maybe Eileen did see Earl while Ralph was gone, but she and Ralph seem to hit it off fine, now that he's home. I know that Jake Fortune was in favor of Eileen marrying Earl. I guess he wanted his girl to marry the Seltzman money, and our Ralph is just a poor farmer boy." He smiled wryly, and added, "I mean, in comparison. This place is paid for, and it'll be Ralph's someday, but Earl Seltzman is really wealthy. His folks owned half of this county, and Earl got it all. I figure that Jake Fortune could use a son-in-law like Earl. Jake's in a bad way— this summer I heard he came out on the short end of a stock gamble, and before that he borrowed money to drill some oil wells north of here. All dry holes. Now Jake is buying cattle on commission, and the bank took over his farm. They're letting him and Eileen live there until it's sold."

"And then what?" I asked.

"Well, Mom says that Ralph and Eileen, after they're married, figure on staying with us for a while. That's all right—we've got plenty of room—but we'll probably have Jake, too."

"Maybe not," I said. "Not if Earl wins Eileen back."

He nodded slowly. "I've thought of that, and it might be a good thing. Ralph's a good boy, but something's bothering him—he's mixed up. After the trouble he had with Judy—whatever it was—he started seeing Eileen right away. It was too fast. And then he was away all that time, and now he's home, and I don't think the boy knows himself what he really feels, or what he wants. You saw what happened last night. I never particularly liked Earl Seltzman— always thought there was something sneaking about him—but I give him credit; he's made his land pay. He has what he calls a 'foreman' on each farm, like a factory, and this year he had some of the finest wheat and corn raised in these parts, and now he's going in for beef."

I said, "Do you suppose Eileen would marry Earl Seltzman, if it weren't for her engagement to Ralph?"

"Maybe," Homer said shortly. "I don't know."

"She might marry Earl," I said, "but not while Ralph is alive?"

He gazed bleakly out over his land and said in his gentle voice, "I wasn't going to say that, Jim."

I flicked my cigarette out over the grass and I knew what I had to do. It wasn't so much what Homer had told me; it was the memory of the bullet hitting the tree. Death had leered at me then, no matter if the bullet had been aimed at me or not. When you're dead you're dead as you'll ever be, no matter what the cause, and I wanted to live a while. I could lie low and return to Cleveland the following day, but that would be running away, even if I did not know from what I was running, or if I was running from anything. But I had to find out, and I decided dismally that I'd better go whole hog.

CHAPTER FIVE

From inside the house we heard the telephone ringing; Homer Hollis stood up, said, "That'll be Mom." He went inside and returned in a few minutes. "Ralph's just coming out of the ether. Mom and

Sandy are going to eat in town and wait at the hospital for Dr. Mazzini to come back."

"How is Ralph?"

He shook his head slowly. "Mom didn't know. She said the nurse told her he was doing as well as could be expected. She said Eileen was carrying on pretty bad, and won't leave the hospital to eat." He paused and sighed deeply. "Jim, I don't feel much like eating, either, but you fix anything you want. There's ham, and eggs and bacon, and cold chicken...."

"Never mind," I told him. "I think I'll go into town for a while."

He gazed at me gravely, and then said, "What's on your mind?"

"Nothing." I grinned at him.

"You know," he said slowly, "when Sandy wrote that she was working for a private detective—well, Mom and me were a little doubtful. I guess I figured you for a loud-mouth, a kind of shady character." He smiled shyly. "But now, since I've met you, I'm glad Sandy is working for you."

"Thanks. She's a fine girl."

"Always was, from a baby up, and Ralph, too. We were lucky with our children. So many of them, well—they don't turn out like you hope and expect. Right now Ralph's mixed up, like I said, and I guess Sandy is too, a little. She feels bad about Russell, but she never lets on . . ."

I remembered that Russell was the jet pilot, the boy Sandy had been engaged to. "I know," I said. "Sandy told me." I stood up, crossed the porch, and entered the house. Up in my room I got the .38 from my bag, put it in a side pocket of the hunting coat, and went back down again. Homer was still sitting on the back porch steps. I said, "See you later," crossed the barnyard to my car. As I drove down the lane, Homer waved to me.

The village of Ridge Center was jammed with a Saturday afternoon crowd. Every parking space around the square and along the main street, each with its meter, held a car, and the sidewalks were swarming with people. All of the business establishments, the supermarket, the drug, department and hardware stores, the bars and the beer joints were booming with trade. I finally found a parking space in front of the courthouse on the far side of the square and walked in the sunshine until I came to a place called Jerry's Diner. I entered, saw one empty stool at the counter, and ordered two ham sandwiches and a glass of milk. When I had finished, I stood on the sidewalk and smoked a cigarette. Nobody paid any attention to me.

I had known for some time what I intended to do, but still I loitered. At last I walked slowly back around the square to my car. A pretty girl with two kids clinging to her skirts came out of a drugstore. I asked her if she could direct me to River Road, and she told me, with gestures, that it was the first road beyond the village limits, going south. I thanked her, and as I walked away, I heard one of the kids asking insistently, "Who's that man, Mommy? Do we know him . . .?"

The village limits was maybe a hundred yards past the last traffic light, and a big sign read, YOU ARE NOW LEAVING RIDGE CENTER. DRIVE SAFELY AND COME AGAIN. I turned at the next road and drove through softly rolling country spotted with new bungalows and small frame houses under construction. In time, I supposed, this section would no doubt be called South Ridge Center and would compete with Ridge Center in the basketball tournaments and the county football championships. I didn't see the river from which I assumed the road got its name, until I saw the gleam of water through trees behind a fair-sized frame house with high windows and peaked gables. There was a white picket fence in front and a brass coach lamp on a green-painted pole beside a stone drive. I turned into the drive and stopped behind a red Buick convertible with the top down. I sat for a moment gazing at the house. The only sign of life was a thin spiral of smoke drifting from a red brick chimney. I got out and walked along the drive to the Buick. There was a rifle in front leaning against the dash. I stopped and peered at it, saw that it was a lever-action Winchester carbine. I glanced up at the house. The windows were blank and no curtains moved furtively. I picked up the rifle, opened the breech. It was empty, as all guns should be, except when ready for use. I leaned it back against the dash and walked on up to the house.

There was a small front stoop flanked by wrought iron railings. The front door was painted green to match the lamp post. In place of a bell button there was a huge old-fashioned knocker. I rattled the knocker and waited. On the road behind me a car went past. I turned and looked. It was a beat-up muddy sedan dragging a makeshift trailer filled with empty chicken crates. The back seat was packed with dirty-faced kids. A man with a pipe in his mouth was driving, and a woman with a fat face and straggly hair sat beside him. She peered at me curiously as they went past. I lifted the knocker again, banged it down three times. No response. I tried the knob. It turned, and the door swung inward.

"Hey!" I called, and stepped inside.

I was in a small reception hall with a bare polished floor. Through an archway I saw part of a stair railing leading upward. There was the smell of cigarette smoke and burning pine. I stepped through the archway into a long room that had probably once been two rooms, but had been made into one by removing the partition. At the far end burning pine logs in a sandstone fireplace cast a pleasant warmth into the room. There were a number of chairs, most of them rustic with cane seats, a huge worn leather divan, a round wooden card table with a built-in ledge for glasses and ashtrays. The top of the table was scarred and the edge crimped by countless and neglected burning cigarettes. The floor was bare pine, polished and worn to a warm saddle color. Wide windows, draped with monk's cloth, overlooked the drive, the front lawn and the road beyond. At the far end was another archway leading to the back of the house. The place looked rather shabby, and yet comfortable, like a resort cottage filled with cast-off furniture.

I stood still and sniffed the air, like a beagle on a rabbit scent. The cigarette smoke was fresh. I moved slowly across the room. One of the logs in the fireplace dropped, sending up a small shower of sparks. I reached the archway, and stood still.

Judy Kirkland sat facing me.

"Go away, you," she said. "I'm poison."

She was sprawled in a low canvas deck chair, and was still wearing the jodhpurs. Her feet were bare. They were small and white, the nails neatly clipped, no polish on them. Her bright red flannel shirt was unbuttoned, revealing the narrow band of a brassiere, white against her slim tanned torso. Her black hair was smoothly combed, and there was a smoldering look in her gray-green eyes. She held a glass on the arm of the chair. On the floor beside her was a squat brown bottle. I squinted at the label. Vat 69. Behind her was a miniature bar made of knotty pine, complete with four bar stools and a shelf of assorted bottles and glasses. Through a window at the side of the bar I saw the bare branches of trees and the bright glint of the river. On a card table beside the window was a portable typewriter.

I said, "Didn't you hear me knock?"

"Yes. I hoped you would go away."

I nodded at her glass. "Now that I'm here, you might offer me a drink."

She shrugged. "Help yourself."

I moved past her and stepped behind the bar and peered at the bottles. One of them was bonded bourbon, half full. I carried it to another canvas chair opposite Judy and sat down. I took off my hat, laid it on the floor, and uncorked the bottle.

She said sullenly, "Don't you want a glass? And ice?"

I shook my head, tilted the bottle. It was good bourbon, hot, and silky as milk.

She said, "Is he dead?"

I looked at her over the neck of the bottle. "Not yet."

Her eyes brightened. "Then there's a—a chance for him?"

"Maybe." I took another sip.

Tears ran down her cheeks. "I still don't see how I hit him. All I saw was the bird rising in the sun...."

"Sure," I said.

She brushed away the tears with the sleeve of her shirt. "Did—did you come to tell me about Ralph?"

"I thought you might be interested." I cradled the bottle between my knees. The bottle was my pal, my friend; maybe it would help me forget the rifle bullet zinging at me from across the fields.

Judy said, "I ran and told Eileen and Ralph's father what—what I had done, and I couldn't stand to face them anymore, and I came here...."

"To your sanctuary?"

"I know it's trite," she said, "but that's what it is, this place. I come here a lot. My aunts don't mind. All they care about is clipping coupons, listening to the radio soap operas, and having tea and lettuce sandwiches at four o'clock." She paused and added in a pleading voice, "Do Sandy and the others blame me? Are they bitter?"

"I don't think so. It was an accident . . ."

She drank from her glass, fumbled briefly with a button of her shirt, and let it hang open. "I'm poison," she said. "Just call me Poison Kirkland."

I had another small drink myself and then asked, "Why didn't you marry Ralph when you had him? And why did you have to stir things up last night?"

"I'm just bitchy," she said, "and jealous, I suppose. I was very fond of Ralph, but at times he was tiresome. You know?" She smiled brightly. "Even so, I would probably have married him—if something hadn't happened. I could have still had him if I'd made the effort, but I let him go. I was amused when I heard that he was engaged to that little Sunday School girl, Eileen Fortune, the All-American girl, so wholesome. They made a good pair. And, besides, Ralph was going into service, and so I dropped it. But when he came back last week, I knew I wanted to see him again just to—to—"

"To see what would happen, and maybe convince yourself that you could still have him—if you wanted him?" I asked.

She nodded gloomily. "Something like that, I suppose. Afterward I was sorry. I'm always sorry—afterward. I knew you all were going hunting this morning, and I decided to go out, too, hoping that I would see Ralph and Eileen, and tell them I was sorry."

"You saw Ralph, all right," I said.

"Damn you," she said evenly. "Get out."

"This is a sanctuary. Remember?"

"Not for you."

"Button your shirt," I said. "It distracts me."

"I'm flattered," she said coldly, making no move to button the shirt. "Simply charmed."

"What happened between you and Ralph? Or is it too personal a question?"

The anger seemed to have left her as suddenly as it had come. "It's a very personal question, my friend. very, very." She leaned over for the Scotch bottle and filled her glass. "Do you mind if I get drunk?"

"Not at all."

"Ralph caught me in bed with a man," she said. "It was all very innocent, really."

"Of course," I said. "Ralph must be frightfully narrow-minded."

"It didn't mean anything," she said sullenly. "Not to me or the man, just one of those things, like the birds and the bees. I was deathly bored that day, and this man stopped to see me, a friend, a writer, from New York on his way to the coast—if I told you his name, you wouldn't believe meand we got to drinking and talking and I forgot that I had a dinner date with Ralph, and—well, Ralph walked in on us here."

"Then what?" I was very interested.

She shrugged. "Nothing. Ralph just looked at us and then turned around and walked out of the bedroom. I let him go. After all, I couldn't run after him naked." She drank from her glass.

"He didn't follow the script," I said. "He should have thrown the man out and beaten the hell out of you."

"Not Ralph," she said. "I wish he had."

"And so Eileen Fortune got him?"

She nodded. "Sweet little Eileen, the high school cheerleader."

"And Earl Seltzman was left out in the cold. To make things fit, you and Earl should have gotten together."

She shivered a little. "That creep. He used to ask me for dates, but I just laughed at him. I've hated Earl Seltzman ever since he put a snake in my desk in the sixth grade." She finished the Scotch in her glass, sighed and stretched and wiggled her bare toes. "I seem to be weary," she said, yawning.

I said, "I saw a rifle in your car."

She looked at me quickly. "What of it?"

"You don't hunt pheasant with a rifle."

"Of course not. I thought I'd go over to the big place after a while and shoot rats. It amuses me, and the noise makes my aunts nervous."

"Would your aunts rather have the rats than the noise?"

"They insist that I should poison them, but I'm afraid to use poison because of my dogs. Most of the rats are in an old barn at the back of the place. This morning when I opened the door the floor was moving with them, big brown ones. So I'll shoot them for a while, for fun, and then I'll get rid of all of them."

"How?" I asked curiously.

"Well," she said seriously, "first you catch one alive in a trap. Then you tar and feather him, and let him go. He'll run straight back to the other rats and then you'll hear a tremendous squealing and hundreds of rats will dash out of their holes and run off, and the tarred rat will try to keep up with them. They are his friends, and he wants to join them, but the faster he runs, the faster the others try to get away from him. So they all run away to some other place and they won't come back for a long time. My father used to say that the other rats thought the tarred and feathered one was a ferret, a deadly enemy of rats. Anyhow, it works—just an old Ohio trick. Would you like to come and watch?"

"Yes, but not today."

She said with a faint sneer, "I suppose you have some more snooping to do?"

"That wasn't a nice thing to say."

"I'm not a very nice person."

"That could be a matter of opinion," I said.

Her eyes softened. "You *could* be nice," she murmured, "if you wanted to. Are you married?"

"Nope."

"Why not?"

"Why aren't you?"

"I'm poison."

I placed the bottle on the floor, stood up, moved over to her and leaned over her with my hands on the arms of her chair. She didn't move, and I saw the gray-green flecks in her eyes, and the mocking light. "You just need someone to show you who's boss," I said.

Her face was up-tilted, her lips parted. "You, maybe?"

"Maybe," I said, placing a hand beneath the small of her back. She arched up out of the chair and her arms slid around my neck, and as she pressed her body against me I watched her glass roll over the floor with a musical tinkling sound. I held her tightly for a moment, keenly aware of her soft slimness, and she moved her mouth over my cheek and we kissed, not passionately, but softly, even tenderly, and it was very nice.

And then she pushed gently away from me, her face averted, and I saw the tears on her cheeks. "I haven't been kissed like that for a long while," she whispered. "Not for a long, long while...."

"It's about time, then," I said, and I kissed her again. Presently we stood apart. Her face was flushed, and she avoided my gaze. "I've got to go," I said.

"Must you?" There was faint surprise in her voice.

I nodded.

"Will—will you come back?"

"Maybe."

"Tonight?"

"Maybe."

"Please come. I'll want to know about Ralph, and I can't face them...."

"I'll let you know."

"Will he—live?"

"I don't know."

"He's got to! If he doesn't, I—I'll kill myself."

"Don't talk like that."

Her eyes were wild. I grasped her shoulders and shook her a little. "Relax," I said.

"Kiss me again—like you did."

"Not now," I said. "Let's just be chums—for now."

"To hell with you."

"Yes," I said, and I left her.

Outside, as I passed the Buick, I lifted out the Winchester without slowing my stride or glancing back to see if she was watching me, and I laid it on the rear seat of my car. As I backed out of the drive, I thought dismally, *Bennett, you're sure hell with the women today....*

CHAPTER SIX

The hands of the courthouse clock on the square in Ridge Center stood at two-thirty in the afternoon. I drove on through town and out the highway leading to the Hollis farm. At the top of the hill, where Dr. Mazzini had dropped me at noon, I pulled well off the road and stopped. From the tool kit in my car I took a screwdriver and a hammer, put them in one of the voluminous pockets of my hunting coat, and locked the car. I stood on the hill for a while, gazing out over the countryside below me. It looked very peaceful in the afternoon sunshine, and except for some cows grazing in the meadow beside the woods on the Hollis farm, I didn't see a moving thing. At last I climbed the fence and headed across the fields toward the place on the ravine where Ralph Hollis had been shot, and where I had stood by the big beech tree.

When I reached the ravine, I walked along the bottom until I came to the spot below the beech tree. I stood still a moment, listening and watching, and then slowly I climbed the steep slope to the crest of the ravine. As I reached the top I lowered myself to my stomach, like an advance wagon train scout looking for Indians, and surveyed the terrain. An occasional car droned along the distant highway, but that was all.

I stood up and went to work on the tree with the screwdriver and hammer. The bullet was buried deep, but I finally dug it out and held it in my hand. It was flattened and out of shape, and it looked to be about .30 caliber, but I wasn't too sure. I put it in a pocket of my shirt and buttoned the flap. As I turned and started back down the steep side of the ravine, I heard a sound behind me, maybe the rustling of leaves, and I swung around.

I don't know where he had come from, but Earl Seltzman was standing above the crest of the ravine, six feet away, watching me. He was clad in the fanciest hunting outfit this side of Fifth Avenue;

bright red wool knee-length coat, silky whipcord breeches, polished cordovan boots, a long-visored corduroy cap. Green-tinted sunglasses fitted over his rimless ones. He was holding a beautiful hand-made 12-gauge shotgun with a glossy blued double barrel, ventilated sights, and graceful silver scroll work on the satiny walnut stock. His thin face was pale behind the dark glasses, and his mouth was slack.

"Mr. Bennett, I do believe," he said in his nasal, adenoidal voice, and he bowed mockingly, swaying on his feet.

"Hello, Earl. I didn't hear you come up."

"That is not surprising, considering the noise you were making with your little hammer."

I admitted ruefully to myself that he was correct.

"A horrible racket," he said, wagging a finger reproachfully. "You'll scare all the birds away."

"Sorry," I said, realizing that he was as drunk as a man could get and still be on his feet.

He swayed, leaned forward and peered at the jagged hole I'd dug in the beech tree. "Carving your initials?"

"Yes," I said wearily. "Clumsy, aren't I?"

He turned slowly, steadied his stance, carefully switched the shotgun to his left hand, fumbled inside his coat and extracted an over-sized silver flask. He unscrewed the cap, let it dangle by a silver chain, and held it out to me with a wavering hand. "Have a drink?"

I took the flask, tilted it to my mouth. It was brandy, and it blended very well with Judy Kirkland's bonded bourbon. "Thanks." I handed it back to him.

He took a long swallow, carefully replaced the cap, and bent over to lay it carefully on the ground. He almost lost his balance, but steadied himself, straightened and teetered backward on his heels. Then he stood still, except for a slight weaving, and peered at me. "What're you doing out here, anyhow?"

"I might ask you the same question."

"I'm brooding," he sighed. "Communing with nature." He stooped down, reached a wavering hand for the flask, finally grasped it and held it up triumphantly. "Damn thing tried to get away. Have a drink?"

"No, thanks."

He peered down into the ravine. "Are they down there? Eileen, and the rest?"

"No."

"All alone, Mr. Bennett?" he raised his eyebrows.

"Listen, Earl; Judy shot Ralph this morning."

He gazed at me dumbly. "Shot?" he mumbled. "Ralph? Judy shot Ralph dead?"

"He isn't dead, not yet. Don't get your hopes up. It was an accident, and it happened right here, while they were hunting. Judy was down there in the thicket and she shot upwards at a bird, and she hit Ralph."

"Maybe she had a right to shoot him," he said. "Maybe it serves Ralph right."

"It was an accident. Were you out hunting this morning—around ten-thirty?"

"I wasn't invited," he said stiffly. "Ralph didn't invite me, because of Eileen, you know. He's jealous of me."

"Maybe he has reason. You took Eileen home last night."

"It didn't mean a thing," he said sadly. "She told me that she went with me to make Ralph jealous—because he kissed Judy. Did you ever kiss Judy?"

"No," I lied.

"I did once. She bit me."

"Good for her."

"What?" he asked thickly.

"Never mind. Good-bye, Earl." I turned away from him and started down the ravine.

"Hey, you. Wait."

I turned and looked up at him.

His loose lips closed over his prominent teeth and he leveled the shotgun over the crook of his arm, a finger on the trigger. He stood swaying, his feet apart, and I stared at the twin blue barrels. A black cloud seemed to drift over the ravine, and I had the same fear I'd had when the bullet had struck the tree beside my head. Earl Seltzman was drunk, and love-sick, and frustrated, and I didn't know what he had in mind, and I tried not to think of what a blast of bird shot would do to my stomach at point-blank range.

"Earl," I said, trying to keep my voice steady, "point that gun the other way."

He backed up a little and tilted the gun a trifle. The barrels now bore on my chest. I looked into the twin eyes of death, and I had a sudden wild impulse to turn and run like hell. My revolver was in an inside pocket of my hunting coat, but I still held the hammer in one hand, the screwdriver in the other. Earl stood above me. If he shot, the blast would knock me halfway down the side of the ravine, and I'd roll, very limply, the rest of the way. I managed a smile. "Put that damn gun down, and let's have a drink."

"I resent your manner," he muttered. "Demand apology."

I took a step toward him. "Sure, Earl, I apologize," I said, and I swung the hammer against the barrel of the gun. It made a sharp clanging sound and the gun swiveled away. Seltzman stumbled backward, and he must have pulled both triggers, because I heard the double blast and the thudding and the rattling of the shot in the trees behind me. I dropped the hammer and screwdriver, got my hands on the now harmless gun, wrenched it from him, dropped it, and bored right on in. My fingers closed over the front of his thick red coat, and I pulled him close and slapped him, palm and backhand, across the mouth until my fingers stung. His knees gave way, and I let him fall. He sprawled on his back, his legs moving a little, his fingers scratching the leaves. His open mouth was bloody, and there was blood on his teeth. I looked at the palm of my hand. It was bloody, too. I wiped the blood on a sleeve, thinking wryly that with Ralph's blood on the other sleeve, my new hunting coat was really getting broken in. It seemed a shame that so far it was all human blood, and not a drop of fowl or animal blood.

I picked up Seltzman's expensive gun, and noted with sadness the dent in the barrel made by the hammer. I broke it, ejected the two empty shells. He'd fired them both, all right, either intentionally or by accident. I leaned over him, took six extra shells from his coat pocket. I couldn't see his eyes behind the dark glasses, but from the position of his head I knew he was watching me.

"For God's sake, get up," I said. "You're not killed."

He got slowly to his feet and brushed off his clothes. Then he wiped his mouth with a handkerchief. As he did this, he stared absently out over the fields, and once he hiccoughed slightly. He looked at the blood on the handkerchief, and then tossed it away with a gesture of distaste.

I handed him the shotgun. "I'm sorry about the barrel," I said. "You'd better have a smith look at it before you fire it again."

He took the gun, and stared once more out over the fields, toward the distant highway. His swollen lips worked a little, and a tear slid down one cheek from beneath the dark glasses.

"There are other girls," I said gently. "The woods are full of them."

"Not Eileen," he said in a choked voice. "I'll never find another Eileen." He was quite a boy. First he'd been drunk and arrogant; now he was drunk and maudlin.

"Go home, Earl," I said. "Forget it, for now. When you're sober, we'll have a little talk. I'm sorry I had to hit you; I'm just a city boy, but I know enough not to carry both a loaded gun and a bottle into the woods."

He turned silently away and walked unsteadily along the ridge. I saw the silver flask still lying in the leaves, and I called after him, "Hey, Earl, you forgot your flask."

He kept on walking.

I watched him until he disappeared into the woods at the far end of the ravine. Presently he reappeared, a small red-coated figure, moving slowly across the green meadow. He climbed a fence, correctly pushing the gun through before him, muzzle first, even though it wasn't loaded, and I knew that someone had trained him properly. He went over a hill, and I didn't see him anymore.

I picked up the flask, moved down the side of the ravine to a spot where I couldn't be seen, sat down and had a drink. Two swallows emptied the flask. I lit a cigarette. My anger was gone, but the memory of fear was still with me. Thinking back, I could bring myself to feel a little sorry for Earl Seltzman, and for Judy Kirkland, and Dr. Mazzini, who was obviously in love with Judy. I was sorry for Eileen Fortune, and for Sandy and her parents, and for Ralph Hollis, fighting for his life in the Ridge Center hospital. And then it came to me again, the ugly sound of the bullet thudding into the tree two inches from my nose, and the sight of the twin barrels of Earl Seltzman's shotgun pointing at my stomach, and I began to feel sorry for myself.

I wished there was more brandy in the flask, and I smoked and watched the red sun sink lower in the afternoon sky.

CHAPTER SEVEN

It was after four o'clock when I reached the Hollis farm. The place was deserted. No cars were around, and the cows were bunched up at the pasture gate waiting to be milked. Their plaintive bawling was somehow sad and lonely. Chickens were swarming in the fenced-off area of an apple orchard, and from the henhouse there came a raucous squawking. From somewhere nearby pigs were grunting and squealing. Two gray cats were bunched up on the back steps making pink-mouthed meows. As I approached, a stranger, they scampered away, stiff-tailed. Obviously, it was feeding time for a variety of creatures, and no one around to feed them. I looked about for the hired man, Rex Bishop, but I didn't see him, and I thought of our target shooting date. The back door was unlocked. I went through the quiet kitchen and the deserted house and up the wide stairway to my room.

I undressed to my shorts, went down the hall to the bathroom, shaved and took a bath. Back in the room I lay on the soft bed for a while, half dozing, and decided that I wasn't adjusted to the fresh country air and the exercise. I could still hear the faint bawling of the cattle, and I thought uneasily that it wouldn't be like Homer Hollis to let his stock go unattended. Presently I heard a car come up the lane, and decided I'd better get dressed.

To me, the hour before dinner is the best time of day; a bath, clean clothes, a drink or two, the pleasant feeling of relaxation. But now my mind would not let me relax. As I dressed, I thought of the day's events and I knew whatever I did about them, if I was going to do anything, would have to be done tonight. Tomorrow was Sunday, and I was returning to Cleveland, with a full Monday's work facing me. I was scheduled to be in Toledo before noon, at the boss's orders, to help the agent there on a blackmail deal involving a famous industrial executive with connections in Washington. My one full-time assistant was on a job he couldn't leave, and if Ralph Hollis' condition grew worse, or if he died, Sandy would want to stay here, at least for a few days. That would mean calling in the part-time office girl to hold the fort in Cleveland.

I put on a clean white shirt, blue knit tie, the gray flannel suit I'd worn from Cleveland, pocketed keys, cigarettes, wallet, handkerchief and silver, and was thinking seriously of having a drink from the bottle in my bag, to bolster Earl Seltzman's brandy, when somebody knocked on my door. I opened it and gazed at Sandy's white face.

"Jim, Ralph's worse. We stayed at the hospital all afternoon. Dr. Mazzini is with him now, and Mom insisted upon coming home and getting supper for all of us. Eileen's here, too, and, well—I guess there's nothing to do but wait."

"What does the doctor say?"

"Not much, except that Ralph has a high fever...."

"How high?"

"A hundred and four, when we left. Dr. Mazzini didn't tell us, but one of the nurses did. They put Ralph in an oxygen tent, and we can't see him." She began to cry quietly, her hands over her face.

I closed the door to my room, put my arm around her, and we walked along the hall to the stairway. She stopped, wiped her eyes. "Jim, I—I'm sorry. I thought it would be fun having you down here, with my family, and the hunting, but—"

"Never mind." I patted her cheek. "It couldn't be helped."

Something like anger shone in her eyes. "You'd think that she'd have the courtesy to at least ask how Ralph is. *She* shot him, and she hasn't called, or been to the hospital to ask about him."

"Never mind," I said again, thinking that now was not the time to tell of my visit with Judy Kirkland.

She said, "Dad told me you went into town for lunch. What did you do all afternoon?"

"Oh, gawked at the people, had a couple of drinks, took a walk in the woods."

"It's been boring, hasn't it?"

"Not at all," I said, and I meant it.

She took my hand. "Come on. It'll be a little while until supper. You make us a drink."

Down in the big living room I saw that she'd put out gin, ice and vermouth, and a fresh fire was burning in the fireplace. Eileen Fortune sat on a divan near the fire, and from the kitchen I heard Mrs. Hollis bustling about. Homer, I thought, was out in the barn helping Rex Bishop with the evening chores. At least, the bawling of the cattle had stopped. Eileen Fortune turned and gave me a wan smile. She was pale, and she needed some lipstick on her small thin lips. I smiled at her, said, "Hi," and moved to the table bearing the martini ingredients.

Sandy said, "Make me one, Jim. I'll be right back." She went out to the kitchen, where I heard her talking to her mother.

I measured gin and vermouth, poured, stirred gently, filled three cocktail glasses and carried one over to Eileen before I remembered that she didn't drink. She looked up at me with sad eyes and shook her head. "No, thank you," she said softly.

"I forgot," I said. "Sorry."

"That's quite all right," she said seriously. "I don't smoke, either."

"Good for you," I said, trying to make my voice sincere, and I thought of a corny old gag. The rest of it went: *Do you eat hay? No. Then you ain't fit company for man or beast.* I sat down beside her and sipped from the glass intended for her. She gazed solemnly at the fire, and I had an opportunity to size her up at close range.

Her pale hair fell to her shoulders in soft curls. Her small face was delicate, but not quite in balance. As I'd noticed the evening before, her gray eyes were too far apart. Her chin was too sharp, her small nose almost too cutely tilted. She had left her vigil at the hospital long enough to change from her hunting clothes to a bluish tweed suit and a frilly white blouse. Stubby, high-heeled blue suede pumps were on her small feet, and she smelled faintly of one of the more obvious brands of drugstore perfume.

But taken as a whole, Eileen Fortune was a girl any man could be proud of, and I guessed that she'd make a good wife for Ralph Hollis and they'd probably be very happy. And I gave her grudging credit for competing for Ralph, and apparently winning, against a girl like Judy Kirkland. But I liked Ralph, and I was a little dubious about his second choice of women. Eileen seemed pale beside Judy, and it seemed to me that she would have been quite happy with Earl Seltzman, and he, most certainly, would have cherished her dearly. I sighed, and wondered once more why nothing ever worked out right; Earl loved Eileen. Eileen loved Ralph—anyhow, she was going to marry him, if he lived. Judy loved Ralph, too, or did love him. Dr. Mazzini was no doubt crazy about Judy. But what about Ralph? Did he still love Judy and was contenting himself with Eileen, because he couldn't forget or forgive what he saw in Judy's house that afternoon? Ralph was the vortex, the key figure. If he died, Earl Seltzman would be free to woo Eileen again. Judy could forget her jealousy and the haunted feeling of guilt and betrayal. Dr. Mazzini, with Ralph gone, could have Judy to himself—if that was what he wanted.

I said to Eileen, "I'm very sorry about Ralph."

"Thank you." Her small thin lips quivered.

I hesitated, and then I said, "Judy feels very badly about it."

"I hate her." Her voice was low and intense.

"Because of the accident?"

"No." She shook her head slowly. "Things like that happen, I guess. But she had him once, and she lost him. Then we—we got engaged, and he enlisted, and everything was fine. I wrote to him, and waited. When he came home last week, he didn't seem the same. Maybe it was the army—I don't know. I trust Ralph, but I don't trust Judy. I know she wants him back, but she doesn't really care about him. It's just to spite me. Once, while Ralph was away, when she had been drinking, she told me that if she couldn't have Ralph, I would never have him, either. She's smart, and clever, and I'm not. I know I shouldn't have let Earl talk me into leaving with him last night, but when Judy kissed Ralph last night, I—I couldn't stand it anymore, and—"

"I know," I said, feeling a hundred and ten years old. I had merely met Eileen Fortune briefly, but here she was, telling me about her love life. Maybe I looked fatherly, and so I added in a fatherly tone, "Ralph will be well soon, and then you can get married, and everything will be fine."

"I wish I could believe that," she said, with a catch in her voice.

I said casually, "This Earl Seltzman seems like a nice young fellow."

"He *is* nice," she said seriously. "Earl is a wonderful fellow. I—I feel sorry for him, and sometimes I think I should have just stayed engaged to him. Papa likes him, and he is very wealthy." She gave me a look of coy boastfulness. "I can still marry him—he wants me to."

"That's nice."

"But I can't now, of course," she said demurely, "because I'm promised to Ralph. He has always been my hero, ever since the fourth grade, but he would never look at little old me." She looked into the fire, reminiscing. "All the girls were crazy about him. He was captain of the basketball team, and president of the senior class. Judy thought she had him." She paused, and went on with a satisfaction I could almost taste, "But in the end she lost him, and he picked me, the little girl with the pigtails who had always adored him from afar."

"What happened between Judy and Ralph?" I asked innocently.

"Ralph never told me," she said primly, "but I suspect—the worst."

I cleared my throat. "Uh—the *worst?*"

"I do not wish to discuss it," she said in the same prim voice, and she compressed her thin little mouth in a disapproving expression that would become very unattractive as she grew older.

Behind me Sandy said, "Jim."

I turned in my chair. She was standing in the hallway. A frilly apron was tied over her print dress. I said, "Excuse me," to Eileen and went to Sandy. She said in a low voice, "Dad wants to see you. He's on the back porch."

I nodded, patted her shoulder for no reason at all, and walked back along the hall. As I passed through the kitchen, Mrs. Hollis, busy at the stove, said, "Supper in ten minutes."

"Good." I smiled at her, and went out to the back porch. Homer Hollis was standing by the steps in the cold November dusk. A wind was blowing from the northwest, rustling the dry corn shocks in a field nearby and swaying the branches of the pines above us. "I want you to go with me, Jim," Homer said. "Rex hasn't come home yet. You'd better get a coat."

I shivered in the cold wind. "Something wrong?"

"I hope not," Homer said bleakly. "Rex is always here for the milking, and he made a date to shoot target with you, and—well, he's pretty old, and we better go get him."

"All right." I left him and walked around the house to the front door, quietly climbed the stairs to my room,

I got my overcoat and hat, and the gun from my hunting coat, and rejoined Homer. I felt a vague uneasiness, and wondered suddenly why I'd taken my gun. Homer held a lighted gasoline lantern. "He was fixing the fence down in the bottom," he said. "You follow me."

The dusk quickly faded into night as I walked behind Homer across the fields, the lantern making a wavering circle of light around us. We climbed three fences, walked through a dark woods with bare whispering branches above us, and entered a grassy meadow glowing faintly with the first light of the moon. At last we reached another fence, and Homer walked more slowly. Presently he stopped. "Jim," he said.

I moved up beside him. Beside the fence lay a coil of wire, gleaming bright in the lantern light. The ancient flint lock musket stood against a post. We could see the new wire woven into a break in the fence where Rex Bishop had been working, and we stared silently. Then Homer began to move slowly along the fence, holding the lantern ahead of him.

We found the old man lying on his back in the fence corner, maybe fifty yards from where he'd been working, his bright eyes staring up at the dark sky. There was a wide black stain on the bib of his overalls. Homer stood still and said something in a voice so low I couldn't hear. I gazed past him and I saw the dark outline of the trees marking the ravine which crossed this land, the ravine where Ralph had been shot, where the bullet had struck the tree beside me, and where I'd encountered Earl Seltzman. I moved past Homer and knelt beside the body of the old man. The yellow lantern beams and the faint moonlight told it all. I didn't need to touch him, but I did. Rex Bishop was dead, already cold and stiff.

CHAPTER EIGHT

An hour later I stood on the back porch of the farm house. Light from the kitchen window fell across Homer Hollis' face and I saw the deep lines in his leathery face and the dull look of fatigue and shock in his eyes. The county sheriff and a deputy had come out and supervised the removal of Rex Bishop's body to a mortuary in Ridge Center. The sheriff, whose name was John Morrissy, had impressed me very favorably, a sharp contrast to a number of rural peace officers I'd encountered during my years with the agency. He was an elderly soft-spoken man who asked the correct questions, performed the necessary with a strict attention to detail, all in exact accordance with the chapter on the finding of dead bodies from the *Police Officer's Manual*. He expressed the preliminary opinion that Rex Bishop had been accidentally killed by a stray rifle bullet fired by a careless hunter in the area, but added cautiously that he would not issue an official statement until after the coroner had examined the body and the wound.

The coroner, it developed, was an aged and semi-retired doctor who had held his office for over thirty years. The sheriff gravely entered my name, address and occupation in a little ten-cent-store notebook, along with a few details Homer Hollis gave him about the time of morning Rex Bishop had gone to his fence-fixing job, and the time we had found him. I told the sheriff about seeing Rex, and what he said about not returning to the house for the noonday meal.

"That's why I didn't miss him until evening," Homer said. "Rex often stayed out all day."

Sheriff Morrissy nodded and said, "This has been a kind of miserable day for you, Homer—what with Ralph getting hurt, and all."

"Yes," Homer said. "It has."

The sheriff politely expressed the hope that Ralph would soon recover, made a rather vague comment about "irresponsible parties," referring, I assumed, to Judy Kirkland, and the unknown person who had fired the shot killing Rex Bishop.

Homer said, "Tell Dick Brandis that I'll take care of Rex's funeral."

Dick Brandis, I learned later, was the mortician who embalmed and buried most of the people who died in Ridge Center and the vicinity.

The sheriff nodded gravely, said he would be in touch with Homer, shook hands with both of us, and left with his young deputy in a battered Chevrolet, into which, I had noticed earlier, they had placed the coil of wire and Rex's old musket.

Homer and I watched them go down the lane. After we had found Rex's body, no one had eaten much of the huge meal prepared by Mrs. Hollis, and shortly before the sheriff had left, Sandy had driven her mother and Eileen Fortune back to the hospital to continue their anxious vigil outside Ralph's door. Homer felt that he should stay until the sheriff was finished, and Sandy had promised to call him if there was any change in Ralph's condition. The death of Rex Bishop, on top of Ralph's injury, had upset the family considerably, and I hadn't had a chance to talk to Sandy at all.

Now Homer said, "How do you figure all this, Jim?"

"I don't know. I've been thinking about it."

"So have I. Nobody around here hunts birds, or rabbits, either, with a rifle. It must have been some stranger hunting without permission. Of course, Rex used a rifle, that old flintlock of his, but he was an old-timer."

I thought of the rifle bullet striking the beech tree beside me, and of the sound of the second shot afterward, and of the lump of lead I'd dug from the tree. I thought, too, of Judy Kirkland's rifle in the back seat of my car, and I knew that Rex Bishop would never have fired a careless shot. And back in my brain a cold little voice told me that the bullet which had so narrowly missed me had not been accidental. I was suddenly tempted to tell Homer Hollis about my experiences during the afternoon, but decided against it; with his son in the hospital, and the death of Rex Bishop, he had enough on his mind.

I said, "Homer, I guess I'll go into town for a while."

He gazed at me thoughtfully, and then said in his quiet voice, "Any special reason?"

I shrugged, avoiding his eyes. "I may stop at the hospital, and maybe buy a drink or two." I didn't want to ask him where Earl Seltzman lived, and I hadn't forgotten my promise to see Judy Kirkland.

"Go ahead," he said heavily. "I've got to finish the chores around here. I—I'll sure miss Rex, in more ways than one. Sandy will call me from the hospital—if there is need."

"Can I help with the work?"

He gave me his shy smile. "It's nice of you to ask, Jim, and I appreciate it, but you'd better go to town. Maybe, when you get back, we can have a nightcap and talk a little."

"Sure," I said bleakly, thinking that I wasn't fooling him too much, maybe not at all. I left him standing there and went to my car, a year-old Mercury, and drove into Ridge Center.

When I entered the hospital corridor I knew that things were not good. The three of them were standing outside Ralph's door—Sandy, Mrs. Hollis and Eileen Fortune. Mrs. Hollis's plump face was pale and she twisted a handkerchief as she watched the closed door. Sandy's face was as grave as I'd ever seen it, and Eileen Fortune was sobbing openly. Sandy stood a little apart from her mother and Eileen, and I went up to her. She turned to me, and I touched her arm. "How is he?" I asked, realizing that I spoke in the hushed tones of a visitor in a funeral parlor.

"He's worse, Jim," she said quietly. "Much worse. The doctor is with him now...."

I looked at the closed door. The light above it suddenly glowed red. A nurse hurried up, entered the room, and for an instant I had a view of Ralph's long white-sheeted form beneath a transparent oxygen tent. Dr. Mazzini was bending over him, peering intently. He looked around as the nurse entered and said something in a quick sharp voice. The door closed.

Mrs. Hollis saw me then and smiled tremulously. Eileen Fortune stopped sobbing long enough to wipe her nose and dab at her red eyes, but she paid no attention to me, and she made no effort to conceal her distress to the people passing in the corridor who gazed at her curiously. It was my sudden opinion, probably an unkind one, that she was enjoying the spectacle of her grief.

"What does the doctor say now?" I asked Sandy.

"He hasn't told us much, except that Ralph's condition is critical. He says we'll just have to wait and see...."

The door to Ralph's room opened, and Dr. Mazzini stepped out. He closed the door and gazed at me gravely. His dark Indian face looked drawn, and his black eyes were hot and bright. "Hello, Bennett," he said.

I moved toward the door, but he shook his head. "I'm afraid you can't go in. He needs absolute quiet. We'll know by morning."

"Know what?"

He glanced at the persons standing in the corridor behind me, and said in a low voice, "If he'll live."

Before I could answer, Mrs. Hollis came up. "Doctor...."

He smiled at her, but it was a weary smile, I thought, without warmth. "Everything is being done," he said. "His right lung is punctured and in spite of precautions a severe infection has set in and his respiration is affected. We'll keep him under oxygen, and do everything possible, including drainage. You are free to call in another doctor, if you wish, but—"

"No, no," Mrs. Hollis said. "We—we know that you are doing the best that can be done. Is—is there a good chance . . .?"

"Fair," Dr. Mazzini said shortly. "We'll know by morning." He looked at me, at Sandy and Eileen. "I suggest you all go home and get some rest. The desk has instructions to call me if there is the slightest change." He touched Mrs. Hollis' shoulder briefly, and walked away down the corridor.

Sandy looked at her mother and said helplessly, "Well...."

"I'm staying right here," Mrs. Hollis said firmly. "You can go home and keep Dad company, but not me. Ralph's my boy and I'm going to see him through this."

"I'll stay, too," Sandy said, "but I'd better call Dad." She moved toward a telephone booth at the far end of the corridor.

Eileen Fortune uttered a little broken cry and began to walk in an aimless forlorn circle, holding a handkerchief to her nose. The high heels of her suede pumps made a small clicking sound on the tile floor.

A big man came striding up the corridor. He was wearing a cream-colored felt hat and a bulky camel's hair overcoat and I didn't recognize him immediately. Then I saw that it was Jake Fortune. He moved to Mrs. Hollis and took her hands. "Maude," he said in his booming voice, "I just got back from Cleveland a few minutes ago and heard about Ralph down at the gas station. It's a damn shame. How is he?"

Mrs. Hollis said something I didn't catch, and Jake Fortune nodded sympathetically. "Now don't you worry," I heard him say. "That boy's made of good stuff, and he'll pull through."

Eileen Fortune ran to her father. "Papa," she sobbed and clung to him. He patted her awkwardly. "There, there, honey. Everything will be all right." He looked at me over her head and nodded soberly.

I returned his nod, and said to Sandy, "I'll see you later."

"All right, Jim."

As I went out the hospital's front door I could still hear the sound of Eileen's sobbing.

It was almost nine o'clock and I was all alone in the November night. I stood on the hospital drive and looked up at the high white stars and the three-quarter moon hanging over the town. A few brown leaves rustled across the drive and the bare trees along the street waved gently against the blue-black sky. I thought of Ralph Hollis, and of all that happened since the evening before, and there was a loneliness on the cold wind. It seemed that there was evil abroad in the night, wailing and snuffling in the shadows; I had felt its obscene breath, and yet I could not point and say, "There it is. Stamp it out." The evil was a bullet thunking a tree in the bright noon sunshine, and an old man lying stiff and cold in a fence corner. And maybe there was evil in the fact that Ralph Hollis had been shot down. It was all around me in the night, and the gun in my overcoat pocket was suddenly a welcome and friendly weight.

And beneath the loneliness and the vague awareness of danger I felt a slow smoldering anger. It was a personal anger, almost a rage, against an unseen something, a nebulous leering something in the darkness. And no one could share my anger; I could not tell anyone, because I did not know if I truly had a reason for the anger. But the feeling persisted that the pawns were being slyly moved in a chess game with very special rules. Homer Hollis, I thought, felt a little as I did, but he had kept his silence, as I had, and I suddenly regretted that I had not confided in him.

I drove to the business section of Ridge Center. Saturday night cars were parked in a solid line all around the square and the stores were brightly lighted. I drove four blocks past the square before I found a parking space before a new brick church. I walked back along the sidewalk beneath the trees to the lighted area of stores and asked the first person I met, an old stooped man in a baggy overcoat, where I would find Dr. Mazzini's office.

He pointed a cane across the square. "South side of the courthouse, between the jail and the library. Sign in front. Can't miss it."

I thanked him and started to move on, but his thin voice stopped me. "Stranger in town, huh?"

"Yes," I said, smiling.

"Thought so," he said with satisfaction. "I know everybody in the county. Lived here for fifty years. Anyhow, if you wasn't a stranger, you'd know that Doc don't keep office hours on Saturday nights."

"Maybe you can tell me where he lives, then?"

"Sure I can. He rooms at Daisy Brown's." He swung around and pointed his cane again, in the direction I'd come. "You go down past the Methodist Church—that's about four blocks—and Daisy's is two houses past the church, a white shingle, built in 1920. Claude Brown died in '42—had a stroke. He was fourteen years older than Daisy. Claude always made good money at the post office, but he never saved anything. Daisy works in the bank, and she takes in roomers, and tourists, too. Daisy's a hard worker. I hear she's got the place pretty well paid off by now. Never got married again, but she's had plenty of chances. She's a looker, all right. By golly, if I was twenty years younger—"

"Thank you," I said, edging away.

"Hunter from the city, huh?"

"Yes."

"Thought so," he said, obviously as proud of his powers of deduction as he was of his knowledge of Ridge Center residents. "You ain't dressed like one now, but I figured you was one. I suppose you heard what happened today? It was sure too dang bad about Homer Hollis' boy getting shot by that Kirkland girl, and I just heard in the hardware store about poor old Rex Bishop. Knowed Rex all my life. Kind of quiet, Rex was, but a good hand with stock. He was older than me. He was born in '72. Dang shame about Rex, but he always said he'd die with his boots on." He made a cackling sound that might have been laughter. "Too many city hunters coming here for pheasant. They get liquored up and go out in the woods and don't pay no attention where they shoot. Last fall there was two horses and four cows killed in this county by city hunters. Ain't no wonder the farmers hereabouts are posting their land. Don't blame 'em. The city hunters are killing off all the game, and causing a lot of damage. Take Rex, now. Hard telling who fired the shot that killed him. From a rifle, I hear." He shook his head. "Can't understand it, shooting a rifle in the woods. It ain't safe. Carries too far. But maybe Sheriff Morrissy will find him, the one that shot Rex, I mean. He's out asking questions tonight, but it's like looking for a needle in a haystack. Homer posts his farm, not that a 'No Hunting' sign keeps 'em out, but his place is right up against the old Kirkland property and the farm that Jake Fortune had. The Kirkland sisters don't allow no hunting, but Jake, he don't care. Why should he, I ask you? The bank owns his place, and he and his girl are just living there until the bank finds a buyer."

He peered at me in the light from a drugstore, his bright old eyes shrewd and prying in his thin sly face. "You got kinfolk here?"

"No. I'm just a danged city hunter."

He cackled again. "No offense. You probably got permission. You look like the kind of a man who'd ask permission to hunt a man's land."

"Thanks," I said.

He said slyly, "Staying at the Ridge Hotel, I suppose?"

"Yes," I said, deciding it would be simpler.

"If you ain't feeling so good," he said, "and you can't locate Doc Mazzini, old Doc Sweet is probably home. He won't be sober, seeing as it's Saturday night, but he'll fix you up. Now, if you want to see Doc Sweet—" He turned and pointed his cane.

"Thanks," I said, and walked rapidly away. When I reached the shadows of the trees along the sidewalk, I looked back. He was leaning on his cane peering after me.

Daisy Brown's place was indeed two houses past the church, where I'd left my car. A lighted sign on the front lawn said: *Brown's Tourist Home—Rooms by Day or Week*. It was a fairly large house, well kept, with a cement walk leading to a wide front porch. A lamp with a rose-tinted shade glowed behind a window. I went up to the door and turned the handle of an old-fashioned bell. It made a startling jangling sound.

Almost immediately a woman opened the door and said in a low pleasant voice, "Good evening."

"Good evening. I'm looking for Dr. Mazzini."

"I believe he's gone out, but I'll see." She opened the door wider. "Will you come in?" She was a medium-sized woman, a little plump, but not unpleasingly so, and probably past forty, although she didn't look it. Her gray-tinged hair held a crisp permanent, her skin was remarkably white and soft-looking, her mouth full and carefully lipsticked. She wore a partially fastened quilted house coat over a pink slip, and held a honey-colored cocker spaniel puppy in her arms. The puppy squirmed and bit at her fingers with tiny white teeth.

I stepped inside, took off my hat, and she closed the door. It was a conventional room, with conventional furniture; dark blue rug, maroon divan and matching chairs, lacey doilies on end tables beneath flowered china lamps, a small television in a corner, a glass-doored book case against one wall which actually held books. On a glass-topped coffee table before the divan was a china ashtray in the shape of a sea shell, a metal box containing cigarettes, an empty Coco-Cola bottle, a half-eaten sandwich on a saucer, a miniature ivory radio.

"Please sit down," the woman said, placing the puppy on the blue rug. "The dog is a present for my grandson. Tomorrow's his birthday—he'll be five."

"I see," I said. "It's a nice dog."

She laughed, a rich pleasant sound. "No dog is nice until it's housebroken. This little rascal isn't."

I sat down on the edge of one of the chairs and held out a hand to the puppy. It stood on wobbly legs, its head cocked, regarding me with bright questioning eyes. "Come, boy," I said.

"It's a female," the woman said. "Her name is Taffy."

"Come, Taffy," I said, snapping my fingers.

"Excuse me," the woman said. "I'll see if the doctor is in." She left the room, her robe rustling.

The puppy pounced at my fingers, her little teeth gnawing viciously. "Nice Taffy," I said. "Good dog."

The small radio beside me was humming. The dial was lighted and I heard faintly the opening announcement of a news broadcast. Evidently, Daisy Brown had been listening and had turned it down when I rang the bell. I leaned over and turned up the volume.

A man's practiced homespun voice was saying . . . *Mr. Bishop was killed instantly, according to county coroner, Dr. Gerald Sweet, who said that the bullet, apparently fired by a hunter in the area, had entered his heart. The sheriff's office is making an investigation, but with so many hunters in the county considerable doubt is expressed that the person who fired the shot, and unknowingly killed Mr. Bishop, will be difficult to locate, although Sheriff John Morrissy expressed the opinion that the fact that it was a rifle bullet will narrow it down. However, many hunters here today have returned to their homes in Cleveland and other cities and there is therefore considerable doubt that the person who fired the fatal shot can be located immediately. It was the second hunting accident in the area today, both of them occurring on the Homer Hollis farm north of town on the state highway. This morning, Ralph Hollis, twenty-three, who was discharged from the United States Army last week, was accidentally struck in the chest by a shotgun charge fired by Miss Judy Kirkland, River Road. Hollis is in Ridge Center Hospital and tonight his condition remains very critical. Closing grain prices at the elevator today were . . .*

I turned the radio down and looked up to see the woman standing in the doorway. "That was too bad about old Mr. Bishop," she said. "I knew him quite well. I know Ralph Hollis, too, and his family. They are fine people." She shook her head. "It's about time the farmers here just closed their land to anyone hunting but local people. It's getting worse every year."

"Yes," I said, and stood up. "I understand that the Kirkland girl lives here."

She pulled her finely plucked brows together in a faint frown. "You can't really call Judy Kirkland local, though. She's away much of the time, and when she is here, she just causes trouble. She was always wild, and if I were her aunts—" She stopped and smiled. "But I'm sure you're not interested in local gossip. I'm sorry, but the doctor is not in. If you would care to leave a message . . ."

"No thanks. It was a business matter. I can see him later. Thank you for your trouble."

"It was no trouble," she said. "Living alone, the evenings get, well, boring. Of course, on Sundays, I visit my daughter. Her husband teaches history and coaches basketball at the high school. They'll drive in and get me in the morning. The dog is for—but I guess I told you that."

"Yes," I said. The puppy was tugging at my pants cuff and I tried gently to kick her away.

"Taffy!" the woman scolded. As she stooped down to pick up the dog I got a whiff of freshly applied perfume. The robe fell open and I saw that she had changed the pink slip for what looked like a lacey white nightgown. She straightened up with the dog, which tried to lick her flushed face. "Behave," she said, "you naughty girl."

I backed toward the door. "Thanks, again, Mrs. Brown."

She smiled archly in surprise. "You know my name?"

"A man told me down town—when I asked him where Dr. Mazzini lived."

She sighed. "Everyone knows everyone else here. It is really quite boring. I—I'm sorry the doctor isn't in. If you'll give me your name,

I'll tell him you were here."

"My name's Bennett," I told her. "But don't bother. It isn't important."

"I know you're not local," she said. "I'm not, either, really. I was born in Toledo, and moved here after I was married. There is so much more excitement in the city, so much doing. Really, I get very, well, bored here, especially in the evenings. Since my husband died, I've worked in the bank, but that's boring, too—just seeing the same people every day, the same old faces. I'll bet you're from Cleveland, Mr. Bennett." The dog was still trying to lick her face, and she held it away from her.

"Yes," I said, and opened the door.

"Maybe if you would come back later," she said hastily, "the doctor might be here. I never go to bed early on Saturday nights, since the next day is Sunday, and I'm all alone here, except for the few tourists that stop, and the doctor, but I hardly ever see him. After Claude died, I started renting out rooms, and the doctor has two rooms at the back of the house upstairs. I kept the downstairs for myself, and it's really more room than I need, being alone and all, but it's home to me."

"I suppose it is. Good-night, Mrs. Brown."

"If you're coming back, I'll tell the doctor when he comes. I'll be up anyhow. On Saturday nights I just stay up until *all* hours.... Will you be back, Mr. Bennett?"

"Perhaps," I said, thinking that it might be the truth, if I couldn't locate Dr. Mazzini in the meantime.

"Taffy! Behave!" She bent over to put the dog down, and this time there was no doubt about the lacey nightgown. She straightened, her face still flushed. "I'll wait for you," she said in a low voice, and her eyes shifted away from mine.

I went out quickly and closed the door. A drive ran along the side of the house. I moved on the grass to a garage in the rear. Daisy Brown did not have a car, I thought, since she had told me that her daughter and son-in-law were picking her up in the morning. It was a one-car garage, and it was empty. Out on the street I didn't see Dr. Mazzini's blue Ford parked anywhere along the curb.

I left the Mercury parked in front of the Methodist Church and walked back to the business section of Ridge Center. Most of the stores had closed, and the Saturday night crowd had thinned out considerably. There were now plenty of parking places around the square and the moon was high over the courthouse dome. A red neon sign over the sidewalk told me that I was approaching Dan's Place. I went in and was immediately immersed in the smell of beer, frying hamburger and tobacco smoke. Muted music came from a jukebox in a far corner. There was a long bar, booths and tables. A television, competing with the jukebox, was apparently emitting a fuzzy mystery drama featuring a handsome private eye in a slouch hat and a neatly belted trench coat. There were people in the place, but it wasn't crowded, with only a lone man at the bar.

I sat on a stool and ordered a bourbon and soda. When the bartender brought it, I asked him, "Can you tell me where Earl Seltzman lives?"

"He lives on the north corner of Crawford and Tymocktee, south of the high school—when he ain't staying at one of his farms." He leaned on the bar and grinned at me. "But if you want to see Earl, he's in the back room playing poker."

"That's service," I said. "Thanks."

"You're welcome." He moved down the bar to fill the other customer's beer glass.

I finished my drink, slid off the stool and walked to an alcove in the rear. Beyond a door labeled *Gents* was another door. I opened this second door and peered inside.

The room was small and filled with smoke. Eight men sat at a big round green-covered table with a green-shaded lamp hanging over it. They were playing with chips, but there was also a mound of bills in the center of the table. Earl Seltzman sat facing the door, still dressed in his hunting clothes. The thick red coat hung over the back of his chair. His lips were puffy from the slapping I'd given him and his thin sullen face looked chalky in the white light. There was a glass in front of him, but he looked sober. When he saw me, he rose half out of his chair and the light glinted on his rimless glasses.

"Finish the hand," I told him. "I'll be at the bar."

He stared dumbly. The other seven men in the stud game looked at me with irritated expressions. "Sorry to interrupt," I said, and went back to the bar.

I had another bourbon and soda and waited exactly five minutes by the clock back of the bar, keeping an eye on the alcove. Then I went back to the cardroom. Earl Seltzman's chair was empty, and his coat was gone. The seven men kept on playing, elaborately ignoring me. "Where'd he go?" I asked the room at large.

A man facing me chewed a cigar and spoke without taking his gaze from his cards. "To the john."

Another man said, "I'll raise it five." The chips rattled.

I backed out, slammed the door. I was certain that I hadn't seen Earl leave the cardroom, but I entered the door marked *Gents*. Inside, two men were arguing in loud beery voices. Neither was Earl Seltzman. The argument, I gathered, was about artificial cattle breeding. I opened the doors of the two stalls. Both empty.

One of the men said, "By God, it ain't natural, them test tube calves. Now, I ask you—is it natural?"

"Maybe it ain't exactly natural," the other said, "but it works. Now, take that heifer of mine. A guy from the bull farm came right out to the house and it was over in no time, and no fuss. Last spring that heifer dropped the prettiest little calf you ever saw, and *it* was a test-tuber. Course, it's kind of expensive, but you get blooded stock, and—"

"It still ain't natural," the first man broke in. He turned to me as I was going out. "Now, I ask *you*. Is a thing like that natural?"

"Maybe not from the bull's viewpoint," I said. They were both guffawing as I left.

Once more I entered the cardroom, and again the players ignored me. Across the room I spotted a door I hadn't noticed before. I said, "Thanks, boys. You meant the lady's john, no doubt." I crossed to the door, opened it, and stepped out into a dark alley.

I stood still for a moment, a little surprised. I had assumed that the door led to another room, or to a part of the bar. A cold wind blew up the alley, and I turned up my coat collar. This was the way Seltzman had left the cardroom, but which way had he gone? At one end of the alley was the lighted street, casting a faint glow back to where I stood. The other end was dark and apparently led to back lots, or the open countryside. Once more I felt the chill loneliness and my hand closed over the gun in my pocket. I turned my back on the street end of the alley and began to walk slowly. Behind me I heard the faint sounds of cars passing on the main street, and the occasional toot of a horn. The sounds seemed curiously far away.

Ahead of me, on the opposite side of the alley, I saw a bulky object which looked like a huge trash can. In the instant that I saw it I heard a tiny sound, a sound like metal moving on bricks. Somebody, or something, was crouching behind the can and had moved it slightly. I stopped, placed my back against the wall, lifted the gun from my pocket and waited.

The can didn't move again, and there was no sound, except the faraway noises in the street. I had been sniffing along an almost trackless trail, and here I stood at last in a cold and black alley with the wind raw on my face and my unknown quarry crouching twenty feet away. Or maybe it was only a cat, or a dog. And then I saw a movement, a shadow, and I knew that it wasn't any animal, that a human was huddled behind the can. I stood very still and waited, and the minutes ticked by.

Then I took a deep breath and said loudly, "All right, Earl, I see you. Come on out."

My voice must have indicated my position, because instantly the narrow alley roared and seemed to shake with gunfire, and bright bursts of flame stabbed out from behind the can. I dropped to the bricks and I fired back, and I heard the returning splatter of lead against the wall above me. A bullet hit the bricks directly in front of my face. Dust stung my eyes, and for a moment I couldn't see, but I fired blindly. I heard footsteps running rapidly up the alley and I stood up in time to see a shadowy dark figure disappear into blackness.

CHAPTER NINE

I wiped the dust from my eyes and walked slowly up the alley toward the street. Behind me I heard the door to the cardroom burst open and I saw the reflection of light, but I kept on going. Ahead of me a small crowd had gathered at the mouth of the alley. An officious voice said, "Stand back, folks, stand back."

That would be the local law, not the sheriff, but a policeman or the village marshal, and I didn't want that, not yet. On my left was a small court, and I saw the spidery shadow of a fire escape. I ducked into the court, felt for the fire escape, found it, and started climbing. Below me, a voice called loudly, "Hey! What's going on back here?"

I kept climbing. The voice called again, farther away. I reached a landing, saw a door. The door was locked. I looked upward. The roof was low and slanting. I swung to the roof, crawled over stiff tar paper to the peak, started down. My fingers encountered a metal eave trough, clogged with dried leaves. Below me, in the light from the street, was another roof, maybe a shed or a garage. I lowered myself to it, reached another eave, peered over. The ground was maybe ten feet below. I swung over and dropped into dried weeds. Faint light showed the outlines of two buildings. I moved between them to the sidewalk and stood once more on the main street of Ridge Center.

I walked to the far side and kept moving. A crowd was gathered at the alley beside Dan's Place. A man said, "Aw, hell, it musta been a car backfiring." The crowd began to drift away.

I drifted, too, back to the Methodist Church. My car was all alone at the curb now. The rose-tinted lamp still glowed in Daisy Brown's window. I thought of Daisy Brown with a faint sadness, wondering how many lonely and bored Daisy Browns there were in this world. Too many, I thought, and it wasn't right. Every woman should have a man, and every man should have a woman. And yet, I was almost as old as Daisy Brown, and I didn't have a woman; it was men like me who were responsible for the Daisy Browns.

I moved along the drive beside her house. The garage was still empty, but that didn't matter. I could still ring Daisy's bell and ask if the doctor had returned. I peeked over the porch railing into the front window. She was sitting in one of the maroon chairs, apparently watching the television. I heard muted music and gay voices. I left her sitting there in her boredom and went back to my car.

By the dash light I checked my gun. I guessed I'd fired three shots, but four cartridges were pin-dented. Four, then. Four bullets apparently wasted. I tossed the empties into the street, refilled the chambers from a box in the dash compartment, and put the gun back in my overcoat pocket. The rose-tinted light in Daisy's house glowed alluringly. Two cars went past. Along the quiet street the lights in the houses began to go out. The dash clock said ten-thirty. Time to roll up the sidewalks in Ridge Center, time to go to bed. Gotta be up bright and early for church and Sunday school, to get the chicken on for the Sunday dinners. Time to check the furnace, put out the cat, and go to bed. Tomorrow was another day.

But there was no tomorrow for me. I had two memories now; the bullet in the tree and the bullets in the alley. Somebody wanted me dead, and I felt the anger, and the fear. It was a personal thing, between me—and somebody. I wasn't getting paid for playing out this lone hand. I wasn't getting anything out of it except the hot whisper of death. I trembled a little, and I knew I had to keep going.

I started the Mercury, turned around, and drove slowly through the village to the hospital. Only a few cars were parked around it, and most of the lights in the rooms were turned off. Inside, the corridor was dimly lit. A couple of nurses swished silently by. A young nurse behind the desk was reading a copy of *Life*. From somewhere a baby cried fretfully. There was the medicine smell of all hospitals, and the night hush. Sandy and her mother were sitting on a bench near Ralph's door. Homer Hollis, dressed in his sober dark suit, stood a little way down the corridor gazing at a weight chart on the wall. I didn't see Eileen Fortune. Sandy got up and came to meet me.

I knew by her face that Ralph was no better, but she answered the silent question in my eyes. "No change, I guess," she said in a low voice.

"You guess? Hasn't the doctor been here?"

"He came about a half hour ago and went into Ralph's room. When he came out, he—he looked rather grim, and he didn't tell us anything. He went away."

"I see," I said, and looked over her shoulder at her mother and father. They nodded at me gravely.

Sandy said, "What have you been doing, Jim?"

"Just moseying around." I hesitated, and then added, "Look, Sandy, have you thought about calling in another doctor?"

"Yes. Dr. Mazzini said we could, if we wished. But old Dr. Sweet is the only other one in town, and he'll probably be drunk." She smiled a trifle bitterly. "If we called anyone else, it would have to be from Wheatville—that's the nearest town of any size. There are several doctors there."

I remembered Wheatville very well. I'd spent a week there several years previously on a job that had involved a doctor, a surgeon, but he was serving a life sentence in the Ohio Penitentiary. I had put him there. There had been other people in Wheatville, good people and wicked people, including a woman with a horribly scarred face and the figure of a goddess. I remembered Wheatville very well indeed, and I said to Sandy, "I'll go there and bring a doctor back, if you want me to."

"Don't you feel that Dr. Mazzini is doing all he can?"

"I hope so."

"Jim, is there something you should tell me?"

"Yes," I said, thinking that it was time for me to tell someone— maybe past time. It had been on my mind too long, and it seemed that somebody should know what I knew before I began once more to stalk something I couldn't see, a something that maybe I would not recognize if I did see it. I moved my head, indicating to Sandy that I wanted her to follow me outside.

We stood in the shelter of the hospital entrance. I lit cigarettes for both of us and the sparks flew away on the cold wind. I told her quickly all about it, about everything; about the bullet striking the tree beside me, my visit with Judy Kirkland, my encounter with Earl Seltzman in the woods, the bullets in the alley. She listened quietly, drawing on her cigarette and staring out at the night, and when I had finished she didn't speak for a while.

At last she threw the cigarette across the drive and turned to me. "Jim, I—I don't know what to think."

"Maybe your father suspects a little," I said, "but don't say anything to him, or to anyone. I wanted you to know—before anything else happens."

"I'm glad you told me."

"Where's Eileen?" I asked.

"Her father persuaded her to go home with him." She touched my arm. "Jim, what are you going to do now?"

"Mosey around some more."

"You can't get away from it, can you?" she said sadly. "This was supposed to be a vacation for you, and now . . ."

"Don't worry about it," I said, more harshly than I'd intended.

"Maybe you should tell the sheriff?"

"Not yet. It isn't time for that."

"But who . . . ?"

"Somebody," I said. "I'll find him, or her, if I'm lucky. I've got to try. You can understand that, can't you?"

"Yes," she said. "Can I go with you?"

"No."

"Why not? I can't do anything for Ralph, just sitting here."

"You stay with Ralph."

"Why don't you just drop it, Jim? You don't have to keep on. Wait and see—what happens. Forget it, for now."

"I can't."

She began to cry silently. It was the first time I'd ever seen Sandy cry. I put an arm around her and said, "Don't."

She came against me and whispered brokenly, "What are we going to do?"

"Maybe I'm all wrong," I said. "Maybe it was just some drunken trigger-happy bum in the alley, and I'm building it up too much in my mind, all of it. Maybe—"

"Stop it," she said. "You don't have to talk that way to me." She began to shiver.

"You're cold," I said. "Go inside."

"Jim, I'm afraid. Please be careful."

"Sure."

She lifted her face and I saw the glint of tears on her cheeks. Her arms went around my neck and she pulled my head down. It was the second time I'd kissed Sandy, and I liked it even better than the first. Presently she pushed gently away from me. I reached for her again, but she shook her head. "Not now. I—I'm fine now. I'd better go back with Mom and Dad."

"Chin up," I said, and moved away from her and across the drive to my car. She watched me, and half lifted a hand as I drove away.

CHAPTER TEN

The house on the north corner of Crawford and Tymocktee Streets, across from the high school, was a stucco bungalow built maybe a hundred feet back from the curb. The lawn was well-kept, as were the midget pines clustered around a cement stoop. There was a blacktop drive leading back to a one-car garage. The light from the corner street lamp was strong enough to show me that the garage was empty, and that a rolled magazine was sticking in the metal clip beneath the mail box beside the front door. The bungalow was dark, and it appeared that Earl Seltzman was not at home, that he probably had not been home for some hours.

I made a U-turn, drove to the main street, and headed for River Road. As I passed Daisy Brown's house, I saw that the rose-tinted lamp was still glowing in the front window. I had a half notion to stop and see if Dr. Mazzini's car was in the garage, but the upper floor of the house was dark, and I kept going. I passed the city limits sign, turned into River Road, and came at length to the house with the high windows and the brass coach lamp on a green post.

There was a light shining across the lawn from a side window, and I guessed that it came from the knotty pine bar. As I drove slowly past I saw that Judy Kirkland's red Buick convertible was still parked in the drive. Behind it was Dr. Mazzini's blue Ford sedan. I braked my car, swung over to a grassy shoulder, turned around, and headed back. Just beyond the house was a clump of tall bare-branched maples. I pulled off the road, stopped there, turned off the lights and walked back to Judy Kirkland's front lawn. I passed the Ford, stopped at the rear of the Buick and felt its tail pipe. It was cold. The Buick hadn't been driven lately, at least not within the last hour.

I moved silently along the house to the side window and cautiously peered in. The room looked the same as it had in the afternoon—the knotty pine bar, the stools, the canvas chairs, the typewriter on the card table. But there was no one there. That surprised me. I turned and gazed toward the rear of the house, saw a faint glow of light. I walked back. The light was coming from what appeared to be a kitchen window, but it was a high window, beside a small back porch. The window was open about two inches, and a blind was pulled half way down. I looked around for something to stand on and found a case of empty beer bottles beside a gas meter at the side of the house. Carefully I laid the bottles on the grass, one by one, turned the case on end beneath the window and stood on it. Slowly I raised up until I could see inside.

Judy Kirkland and Dr. Mazzini were seated at a table directly opposite the window. I could hear them talking, very plainly. They faced each other, the doctor on the edge of his chair, leaning forward, his dark lean face intense. Judy sat slouched, her chin in her hands, her eyes focused on some distant spot beyond. Her shirt was still unbuttoned, and a strand of dark hair dangled over her forehead. Her mouth held a sullen, pouting look. Between them was a round glass coffee pot and two cups. The doctor's cup was empty, and as I watched he poured more. Judy's cup was full, and growing cold, no doubt.

The doctor said sharply, "Judy."

"What?" Her voice was slurred and thick, and I guessed that she'd spent the afternoon with the Scotch bottle.

"Drink your coffee, and listen to me."

"Don't want coffee. Hell with coffee."

"Damn it, this is serious."

"Serious," she said.

He spoke in a voice a parent uses with a balky child. "Please drink your coffee."

"Hell with it. Want Scotch."

"No," he said firmly. "You've had too much now. Listen, Judy; Ralph may die. Do you understand?"

"Love Ralph," she said. "I killed him."

"It was an accident, Judy. It *has* to be an accident. Just remember that, no matter what happens. Listen, Judy, I want to marry you. Tomorrow."

"Tomorrow's Sunday."

"Monday, then. I love you, Judy."

"Gonna marry Ralph. Be a dead man's bride."

"Talk sense," he snapped. "You don't love Ralph."

"Owe it to him. I done him wrong. He's a nice boy. Pure boy. He loves me, want to make it up to him. Wanna marry him before he dies. Least I can do, if he'll have me. I'm poison, but maybe he'll have me."

"You don't owe Ralph anything," the doctor said in a low desperate voice. "It was an accident. You want to marry me. You know you do."

"Yes," she said, "but not while Ralph is alive."

"But if he dies? Will you marry me then?" The doctor's voice cracked a little.

Slowly she moved her head and gazed directly at him. "Is he going to die?"

"He—he's very bad, Judy. I'm going back to the hospital pretty soon. I shouldn't have left him, but I wanted to see you."

"I killed him," she said.

Dr. Mazzini banged his fist on the table. "Stop it! I want an answer now, whether Ralph Hollis lives or not. I've waited for you a long time, and you can't keep me on the string any longer. I can't take it anymore. You've got to forget this silly obsession about Ralph. You don't love him—you just feel that you've wronged him, and subconsciously you want to make it right. Forget Ralph. He doesn't want you anymore."

"I'll make him want me," she said slyly. "I know how."

Dr. Mazzini reached across the table and slapped her. The blow knocked her head sideways, and her elbows slid off the table. She sat back in her chair and gazed at him with wide eyes.

He said grimly, "Are you going to marry me?"

She began a slow smile.

"Answer me," he shouted, and he lifted his hand again.

She said something in a voice so low I didn't catch it. He leaned forward, his eyes blazing. "Damn you."

She began to laugh. Neither the sight of the laugh, nor the sound of it, was pleasant. "No use, Tony," she said. "I'm no good. Cheated on Ralph, and today I shot him. Gonna make it up to him, crawl to him—if he lives...."

It was the first time I'd hear Dr. Mazzini's first name. Anthony Mazzini, M.D. He gazed down at her a moment, and then he said something in a low bitter voice, swung around and left the kitchen. Judy lowered her head on her arms, her hair falling like ink over the white table top. From the front of the house I heard a door slam, and the angry roar of a car starting. I jumped off the beer case, ran around to the front. Up the road the doctor's car was a diminishing pair of red tail lights.

I ran down to where my car was parked beneath the maples, got it going, and pushed it hard up River Road. I caught him at the city limits sign, and then a half block behind. As we passed Daisy Brown's house, I saw that the rose-tinted lamp was turned off at last, and that the whole house was dark. Ahead of me, the Ford kept steadily on, through the business section, across the square. It was almost midnight, and Dan's Place was one of the few establishments still showing lights. I followed the Ford along a dark street to a point where the houses scattered out, and the country began. Then it turned left, and I saw the lights of the Ridge Center Hospital. I pulled over to the curb and stopped. The Ford circled the hospital drive and parked beside the ambulance ramp in the rear. Dr. Mazzini got out and hurried through a door beside the ramp.

I drove to the front entrance, quickly, went inside, and ran up the short flight of tile steps to the corridor and peeked around the corner. I didn't see Sandy, or her mother and father. Dr. Mazzini was hurrying toward me, carrying a small black bag. He paused at the desk, said something to the nurse, and she leafed some papers on a clipboard and pointed a finger. He leaned over the desk, peered, nodded, and hurried on. At Ralph Hollis' door he stopped, carefully turned the knob and stepped Inside. The door closed.

I stepped to the corridor and stood against the wall, sweating with indecision. A cute little red-headed nurse breezed by, paying no attention to me. I waited a little longer, and then made up my mind. I crossed to Ralph Hollis' room, opened the door and stepped inside.

Dr. Mazzini was bending over the bed, a hypo needle in his hand, peering intently at the still form on the bed beneath the transparent oxygen tent. The sound of Ralph's breathing was harsh and labored. The doctor lifted the side of the tent, but dropped it and swung toward me, his eyes wide with surprise.

We stared at each other for an instant, and then he smiled. "Oh, hello."

I closed the door behind me. "Hello."

"You—you rather startled me," he said.

"How is he?"

He turned his head and gazed down at Ralph. "Not good," he said in a low voice. "I can't—"

"What're you giving him now?"

He looked at the needle in his hand, and then at me. The dim light made shadowy planes on his lean dark face. "Penicillin," he said, and then added with a trace of mockery. "Do you approve?"

"How much?"

"Three hundred thousand units, but—"

"Give me the needle." I held out a hand.

"Certainly not," he snapped. "It's sterile." A light flamed in his eyes. "Please step outside."

Ralph's breathing seemed to grow harsher, filling the room with an ugly thick rasping sound. "I want that hypo," I said.

"Get out," he snapped. "I think you're drunk, Bennett. Is that your name?"

"The hypo," I said.

He took a menacing step toward me. "If you don't get out of here . . ."

"I don't want any trouble, Doc," I told him, and I lifted the .38 from my overcoat pocket, pointed it at him, and held out my hand.

He looked at the gun in shocked surprise, and then at me. "You really mean it, don't you?"

"You bet."

"I suppose you have a reason?"

"Yes."

A queer, bewildered expression crossed his face. Silently he handed me the hypo needle, plunger first. As I took it, he said quietly, "Ralph needs that."

"He'll get it. Get a nurse. Tell her to bring some more."

"This is crazy—"

"The nurse," I said.

He reached under the tent and pressed a button on a cord beside Ralph's pillow. Then he turned to face me, his dark face flushed. "Damn it—"

"Shut up."

We glared at each other like a couple of strange dogs.

The door opened, and the little red-headed nurse stepped inside. I put the gun back in my pocket. "Yes, Doctor?" the nurse said.

He said in a tight voice, "Please bring me a hypo and three hundred thousand units of penicillin."

She nodded, glanced at me curiously, and left. Dr. Mazzini said, "What the hell is this all about?"

"Never mind."

He shrugged helplessly and turned back to the bed. Ralph stirred a little and muttered something incoherently. The doctor watched Ralph, and I watched the doctor. We didn't talk. Presently the nurse returned, handed him a needle. He said to her, "Will you give it to him, please?"

"Of course." As she bent over the bed, the doctor looked at me with dark brooding eyes. As the nurse turned and moved for the door, he said to her, "I'm going home now. I'll be back in the morning. If his condition changes during the night, call me. It's all on the chart. You'd better tell Miss Donovan, too."

"Yes, Doctor." The door clicked shut behind her.

He said sardonically. "Satisfied?"

"For now." I backed to the door.

"Why, in God's name—?" he began.

"Doctor," I broke in. "If I'm wrong, I'll apologize. Do you mind if I keep your hypo?"

"Would it make any difference to you if I did?" he asked bitterly.

"No."

"It's loaded with cobra venom," he said mockingly. "Or maybe arsenic. If you hadn't stopped me in the nick of time, Ralph would be dead by now. I suppose, being a famous detective, you know my motive?"

"Yes," I said.

He gazed at me silently. Then he smiled a little and moved to the door. "You're wrong," he said quietly.

I sighed. "Maybe I am. I hope I am. If Ralph lives, let's just forget the whole damn thing."

"And if he dies?"

I shrugged.

"Bennett," he said in a level voice, "I should beat the hell out of you."

He was big enough to do it, and much younger besides, but I said, "You're welcome to try. We'd better go outside, though."

For a moment I thought he was going to take me up on it. But he didn't. "That wouldn't prove anything," he said. "But I can call you a son of a bitch."

"You don't even have to smile," I told him.

He smiled anyhow, a bitter twist of his lips, and went out, leaving the door ajar. When I stepped to the corridor, I saw him talking to the nurse on the desk. Then he left, without looking at me. The little red-headed nurse swished past me. I touched her arm. "Miss."

She stopped and turned. Her eyes were sky-blue and she had freckles over her short nose. I took a twenty-dollar bill from my wallet and handed it to her. "Take good care of him tonight, will you?"

She glanced at the twenty, and then at me. "Of course, but you don't need to pay me."

"Just stay with him." I tucked the twenty into a pocket of her white uniform beside the clip of a thermometer.

"Thank you," she said. "Are you a relative of Ralph's?"

"Just a friend. What's your name?"

"Mary Lou Doyle."

"I'm counting on you, Doyle," I said, thinking that there should be someone I could count on. I left her standing there and went out into the windy night.

Dr. Mazzini was turning into the drive at Daisy Brown's house before I caught up with him. I cut my lights and coasted to a stop in front of the church and watched as he put the Ford in the garage and entered the house by a rear entrance. Light showed at an upstairs window, and a blind came down. Dr. Mazzini was home at last, but too late for Daisy Brown to give him my message.

I turned on the Mercury's lights, swung around in the street, and drove back to the square. I had a growing feeling of futility, maybe despair. I'd done a lot of spying and slinking about this night, and had probably made a fool of myself, and all I had to show for it was a shapeless lump of lead, a Winchester carbine, and a filled hypo needle. And the memory of death as it reached for me....

CHAPTER ELEVEN

The lights in Dan's Place were still bright. I parked at the curb and went inside, thinking that a little bourbon might boost my sagging spirits. There were several men at the bar, a few couples in the booths. The jukebox was turned low on the old Bunny Berigan recording of *I Can't Get Started*, a long-time favorite of mine. The soft smooth melody carried me back to a night in September and a girl in a taffeta dress moving lightly in my arms as we danced on a moonlit terrace to Bunny's music the year before he died. I had been just out of law school, and the girl was a Shaker Heights debutante, a small dark girl with a velvet pouting mouth. She had married a banker's son from Rocky River, a fat boy who wore the Ivy League uniform of cordovan and gray flannel, and who no doubt slept in Oxford button-down collar shirts. For the first time in years I remembered the girl and her cool silken kisses and the hot restlessness of her slim little body, and I hoped the fat boy had been good to her.

As I climbed to a bar stool, Bunny's long-dead voice was filling the room like a dream with the sweet, sadly dated words of the song:

> *. . . I've been consulted by Franklin D.,*
> *Greta Garbo has had me to tea . . .*

"Well, sir?" the bartender said.

"Bourbon and soda."

He nodded, and then squinted at me. "Ain't you the guy that asked for Earl Seltzman tonight?"

"Yep."

"Find him?"

"Nope."

"He musta left the card game."

"Yes," I said.

"Had some excitement tonight. Shooting. A trash can out in the alley is full of bullet holes. Happened right after you was in here. Some damn city hunter, drunk, I suppose, and—"

"Bourbon," I said gently. "And soda."

"Yes, sir." He turned away.

A big man three stools down swung to face me. He had been talking to two other men in overalls. "Hello, there," he said heartily, and stuck out a big red hand. "Remember me?"

"Sure," I said, taking Jake Fortune's hand.

He grinned at me, showing his big yellow teeth, and snapped his fingers. "Bennett, that's it. I never forget a name. Homer Hollis' girl works for you."

"That's right." The bartender brought my drink, and I sipped at it.

Jake Fortune frowned. "Too damn bad about Ralph. Have you heard how he is?"

"No change. I was at the hospital around midnight."

He shook his head. "A hell of a thing. Ralph's a fine boy. He's engaged to marry my daughter, you know."

"I know. Tough on her, too."

He nodded in agreement. "She wanted to stay at the hospital, but I took her home. Nothing she can do, and she needs her rest, if—" He paused and sighed.

"If Ralph dies?"

He nodded again, gloomily. "I made her go to bed, and I came back to town for a nightcap. Can I buy you a drink?"

I held up my glass. "This will do me, but thanks."

He turned on the stool and said to the two men, "Boys, I want you to meet Mr. Bennett, from Cleveland. He's visiting Homer Hollis."

The two men, both red-faced and middle-aged, were drinking beer, and one of them was chewing tobacco. I wondered how you could chew tobacco and drink beer at the same time, but he was doing it. Jake Fortune mentioned their names, and we shook hands and mumbled to each other, and they went back to their beer.

Jake Fortune said in a low voice, "My daughter told me that Judy Kirkland hasn't even bothered to ask about how Ralph is getting along."

"I know," I said. "Sandy told me."

"Sandy's a good girl," he said. "A mighty fine girl. A lot like Homer, a square shooter."

"Yes," I said, finishing the bourbon.

The bartender looked at me expectantly, and Jake Fortune said, "Fill it up, Edgar. On me."

"Thanks," I murmured, as Edgar took my glass. The jukebox began again with *I Can't Get Started*, and I silently approved of someone's taste.

The bartender brought a fresh drink, and I lifted it to Jake Fortune.

He held up his own glass. "Mud in your eye, and all that."

One of the red-faced men said, "Jake, I saw you over Seltzman's place around supper time. Is he figuring on buying more beef?"

"Yes," Fortune said over his shoulder. "He's building up a big herd."

The other laughed shortly. "Maybe he knows what he's doing, but I can't see raising Texas steers in Ohio."

"Why not?" Fortune asked. "They get better feed here, and plenty of water, and Earl's got acres of grazing land."

"The climate ain't right," the man said. "Them longhorns won't thrive up here."

Fortune made a scoffing sound, turned to me and winked. "Try anything new around here," he said, "and everybody thinks you're crazy. Just a few years back they thought it was outlandish if a man rotated his crops. If you raised corn in a field, you kept on raising corn in that field until the land burned out. Now they all rotate.... Did you get any birds this morning?"

I shook my head. "Sandy got one, and right after that Ralph was hurt."

"That Judy," he said, shaking his head. "She's always been wild, but she's handled guns since she was twelve years old. It seems to me that she could have seen Ralph—unless she was drunk."

"She wasn't drunk," I said, more sharply than I'd intended, "and Ralph came up over the top of the ravine just as she fired."

"It could happen," he agreed. Then he mentioned the death of old Rex Bishop, blaming it on a strange hunter in the area. "Maybe a city hunter hit Ralph, too," he added.

"No—Judy was the only one around that I could see, and a shotgun doesn't carry far. She must have fired at the bird twice, because I heard two shots, and the second one hit Ralph. I saw Judy this afternoon. She blames herself, and feels pretty badly about it. She's hitting the bottle, too, and hates to face Ralph's folks."

"I suppose she does," he said heavily, "even if it was an accident. My girl's taking it hard, too."

"Yes," I said, remembering Eileen's obvious grief at the hospital. I finished my drink and slid off the bar stool.

"How about another?" he asked.

"No, thanks. I'd better get back out to Homer's place. They'll be wondering what happened to me."

"Going to be in town long?"

"Just until tomorrow."

"Come down again before the season's over," he invited. "Maybe we'll have better luck then." He held out his big hand. "Glad to have met you, Bennett. I get into Cleveland pretty often. Maybe I'll look you up, and we can have a drink."

"Do that," I said, shaking his hand. I nodded at the two red-faced men, and they nodded back over their beer glasses. I went out.

The night had turned colder and I closed the car windows and turned on the heater. When I was a mile out of town I glanced in the rearview mirror and saw the car following me. It was fairly moonlight, but I couldn't tell what kind of a car it was, except that it was light-colored. Its lights were off and it stayed maybe fifty yards behind me, a silent shape on the road, with the moonlight occasionally glinting on chrome and glass. I reached the Hollis farm, drove up the lane. The car went past the lane slowly and disappeared up the road.

One dim light burned in the living room of the farmhouse. I stopped my car in a conspicuous place in the drive by the front porch, turned off the lights, and waited. In a minute I saw the shadowy outline of the car drift back again. It stopped by the lane a moment, and then moved back along the highway toward Ridge Center. I was tempted to follow, but decided against it. Whoever was driving the car would be watching for that, and they wouldn't let me get close.

I entered the house quietly and moved along the dark hall to the archway leading to the living room. Sandy was sitting alone by the cold fireplace. She wore a blue flannel robe over blue pajamas. Her soft brown hair was brushed severely back from her pale face and tied with a blue ribbon. In the soft light, and without lipstick or makeup, she looked about sixteen years old.

She gazed at me silently as I moved across the room and stood beside her. Then she looked up and said gravely, "Hello, Jim. Have—have you learned anything?"

I pulled a hand down over my face and sighed, "I don't know what's going on…. I stopped at the hospital. Ralph is the same." I didn't tell her about my little scene with Dr. Mazzini. There was plenty of time for that.

"Mom wanted to stay there all night—so they gave her a room next to Ralph. Dad and I are going back early in the morning."

"You should be in bed, then."

"I was waiting for you—worrying about you."

I touched her cheek. It was cold. "Don't worry about me. Anyhow, I've got to go out again."

She grasped my hand. "No, Jim. Let it go. Just tell the sheriff…."

"Not yet. Can I borrow your dad's car?"

She looked puzzled. "Of course, but—"

"Somebody followed me out from town. I parked my car by the front porch, where they can see it. I want to leave it there in case they check later."

"So they'll think you're still here?"

"Something like that."

Her fingers tightened on my hand. "Jim, I—I'm scared."

"Keep the doors locked. You've got guns here. I'll be back as soon as I can."

"I want to go with you."

"No. Go to bed. And I want all the lights off." I looked away from her clear steady gaze. "Where are the car keys?"

"On a nail by the kitchen door. Jim...."

I left her and went to the kitchen. I groped in the dark until I found the keys, and walked back along the big dark hall. Sandy was standing in the archway. She looked surprisingly small and slight.

"Be careful, Jim, please."

"Sure." I went past her and out the door. Homer's five-year-old Dodge sedan was in a shed beside the barn. I backed it out and headed down the lane with the lights off. As I swung into the highway, I looked back. The house was already dark, but I had the feeling that Sandy was standing by the window watching me.

I drove in the opposite direction from Ridge Center, up a hill and around a long curve. When the road leveled off I turned on the lights and looked for a mailbox. I found it sooner than I'd expected, slammed on the brakes and backed up until the headlights hit it. Black letters on the white metal box fastened to a white pole at the edge of the road said, *J. E. Fortune*. I pulled the Dodge off the road, cut the lights, and walked on the grass beside a rutted stone drive to a small white house on a hill. A dim light burned inside. When I reached the front porch I gazed out over the valley and the woods and the fields on the Hollis farm. Homer had told me that this place adjoined both the Fortune and Kirkland acres, and I guessed that the Kirkland land lay somewhere to the rear of the Fortune place, with the boundaries of both farms close to the ravine where Ralph Hollis had been shot. I moved quietly around the house and peered about in the moonlight. I didn't see any cars parked in the drive, or in an open area before a barn. I went back to the porch and banged loudly on the front door.

Through the partially curtained window I could see a small rather shabbily furnished room, with a steep narrow stairway leading upward. A lamp burned yellowly on a low table beside a worn divan. I banged again. Then I saw Eileen Fortune coming down the stairs.

She moved to the door, peered through the glass at me, and a porch light came on. I blinked in the sudden glare, and had the uneasy feeling that I'd make a perfect target for anyone caring to try their luck again. I felt the fear again, and I motioned impatiently to Eileen. A key turned, and the door opened. I stepped inside quickly, found the switch beside the door and turned off the porch light.

Eileen Fortune gazed at me with big eyes, her small mouth trembling. Her face looked puffy and her gray, wide-spaced eyes were swollen and red. A strand of blond hair fell over one cheek. She wore a faded high-necked nightgown of a soft cotton material which, I recalled, used to be called muslin, and her feet were bare.

I started to speak, but she cut me off. "It's Ralph," she moaned. "He's gone." She began to sob loudly, her face contorted in an ugly mask of grief.

"No, listen—"

"He's dead!" she cried. "You've come to tell me he's dead. Don't try to spare me." Her sobs grew louder. "Judy killed him!"

I grasped her shoulders. "No, he's not dead."

She stopped sobbing and gazed at me wildly. "He's dying. Ralph's dying, and you have come to prepare me—"

I shook her, rather roughly. She pounded my chest with small fists. "Tell me the truth!"

I shook her some more, and she began to scream, a hideous sound in the small room, and her eyes rolled. Her mouth was open so wide I could see her tonsils. I slapped her then, not hard, and the screaming stopped abruptly. She put a hand to her cheek. "You hurt me," she whimpered.

"Get hold of yourself. Ralph's just the same. Is your father home?"

"W-what?"

"Is your father home?"

"No."

The faint red marks my fingers had made on her cheek did not improve her general look of dishevelment. With the right make-up and hairdo, she would be a fairly pretty girl, but she certainly wasn't pretty now. And yet, as I stood beside her, I was aware of the slenderness of her body beneath the nightgown. I stepped away from her a little and said, "I'm sorry to have alarmed you. Where is your father?"

"In town, I guess," she said in a dead voice. "He brought me home from the hospital, and then left. He's probably at Dan's Place. I've tried to make him change his ways, but he persists in drinking, and . . ." Her voice trailed off and she began to dry her eyes with a sleeve of the nightgown.

I handed her a handkerchief, and said, "I saw him at Dan's Place earlier this evening, and I thought he'd be home by now."

She took the handkerchief and dabbed at her red eyes. "I—I couldn't sleep," she said brokenly, "thinking about poor, dear Ralph."

I patted her shoulder in what I hoped was a fatherly manner. The shoulder was round and firm and warm beneath the thin nightgown. "Do you think your father will be home pretty soon?"

"I—I don't know." She used my handkerchief to blow her nose. "Sometimes he stays out all night. I just don't care about anything anymore. All I can think about is Ralph, lying there in the hospital." She took a deep shuddering breath and her breasts moved beneath the nightgown. "Papa could have stayed with me tonight, of all nights. I've been so lonely, and afraid." She lowered her eyes. "It's just little old me," she sniffed, "out here all alone . . ."

I backed away and put a hand on the door knob.

She took a tiny step toward me. "Papa will probably be gone all night. On Saturday nights he often plays cards, or something, until daylight." She sighed forlornly and fumbled at the high neck of the nightgown.

I opened the door. The cold air felt good on my face, but Eileen Fortune shivered and folded her arms over her breasts. "It's cold," she said plaintively. "Please close the door." She inched toward me, shivering.

I put an arm around her. There wasn't much else I could do. She huddled against me. "C-close the door," she said with chattering teeth.

I kicked the door shut, and once more I thought bleakly that this was certainly my time with the women. First, a wild, restless and driven girl, who was now very probably sodden with Scotch whisky; then a plump bored widow, and now a lonely and grieving farmer's daughter. The detective and the farmer's daughter. Even Sandy had kissed me, and that was the nicest memory. Ridge Center was quite a place. People got shot at and women made passes and the liquor flowed and nothing added up.

I had the whole story, and I had nothing. I was out in the wild darkness, and events drifted around me, and there was a sly whispering that I could not quite hear. Somewhere in the blackness there was a voice trying desperately to tell me something, but the words shifted and slurred and receded leeringly into the caverns of my brain. I got the garbled echoes, and that was all, and once more I felt the rage at the memory of the personal impact of the bullets aimed at me, and at last I admitted it to myself; Ralph Hollis could die, Rex Bishop was dead, and I was truly sorry, but they meant nothing. What did mean everything was that someone wanted to kill me. It was a selfish and personal thing, with roots probably in the jungle, but that's the way I felt, and I knew that I would not go back to Cleveland until I'd found and faced and smashed the thing, the it, whoever or whatever it was, that wanted me dead.

In the morning I would take the lump of lead, the rifle, and the filled hypodermic needle to Cleveland. I would see a ballistics man, and a chemist, and then I would come back to Ridge Center. Somewhere there was a rifle that matched the bullet in my pocket, maybe the Winchester I already had. Who else owned rifles? Earl Seltzman, Jake Fortune, Dr. Mazzini? Maybe Eileen?

She said, "Are—are you going back to Cleveland tomorrow?"

"I don't know."

"You might stay—because of Ralph?"

"Maybe—Sandy will want to stay."

"And you, too?" She looked up at me shyly.

"Why?"

"I—I just wondered."

I pushed her gently away. "Go back to bed, Eileen. I'll see your father later."

Her eyes were bewildered. "Are you—angry with little old me?"

"No. Good-night, Eileen." I opened the door and went out.

The porch was drenched with moonlight. I crossed it quickly and kept in the shadow of trees and bushes until I reached the Dodge. I hadn't learned anything, except that Eileen Fortune had apparently been at home since her father had taken her from the hospital, and that she was a girl with romantic dreams, in love with the thought of love, filled with petty vanity and self-pity, but still eager for the spotlight. As I drove away I saw that she hadn't turned off the light, and I thought of all the lights in the windows tonight—Daisy Brown's, Judy Kirkland's, Sandy's, Eileen's. Candles lighting the way for those abroad in the night, for all the wayward ones....

CHAPTER TWELVE

It was a quarter after one o'clock in the morning when I stopped once more at the curb in front of Dan's Place. The lights were still on, but through the cracks in the Venetian blinds I could see chairs stacked on tables and the tired figure of a man moving a mop around. I went up to the door and peeked in. Except for one lone man draped over the bar with his head in his arms, the place was empty of customers. The bartender shook the shoulder of the sleeper at the bar, who aroused sufficiently to stumble blindly to the door. I got back into the Dodge. The drunk came out and weaved up the street. Through the glass I saw the bartender locking the door.

I drove down the street, past Daisy Brown's dark house, and on to River Road, and I turned in the moonlight and kept on until I came to Judy Kirkland's sanctuary. The drapes were pulled, but there was a light downstairs, probably in the little knotty pine bar. The red Buick convertible was still in the drive. I stopped behind it, making no effort to be quiet. I was tired of skulking about, and besides I had a half-date with Judy Kirkland. I slammed the Dodge's door, went up to the front door and rattled the brass knocker. No response. I tried the door. It was unlocked, and I walked in.

"Judy," I called, and I kept moving until I reached the bar. This was where the light was, but she wasn't there. I looked into the kitchen. Light from behind me showed the table, the two coffee cups, a saucer filled with cigarette stubs. The whole house was very quiet. Uneasily I turned around. The bar looked the same. A bottle that had once contained Scotch whisky was on its side on the floor by the card table. The typewriter was still on the table. There was something different about it. Suddenly I knew what it was; there was a sheet of paper in it. I moved over and looked at the paper, and the typed words on it:

I tried to kill Ralph Hollis because I was jealous and I did not want him to marry Eileen. It was not an accident. I was afraid Mr. Bennett was suspicious and I got my rifle and watched the ravine. When he came back to look around I shot at him. I thought I hit him and ran away. Rex Bishop saw me and asked questions and I shot him, too. When Mr. B. came to see me I was surprised and scared. When he left

I followed him all day and I saw him go into Dan's Place tonight and go in the back room. I ran around and waited in the alley and when he came out I tried to shoot him. I am no good and I am sorry. Goodbye. Judith Kirkland.

I read the confession twice and left it in the typewriter. I straightened up and listened. The house was so quiet that my own breathing seemed loud in my ears. Then a car went past on the road, a distant lonely sound. From somewhere a clock ticked. I looked at my wristwatch. Ten minutes until two o'clock in the morning. The silence rolled over me. And there was something else. A faint acrid smell drifted past my nose, the smell of raw natural gas. I entered the kitchen, saw a gas range with six burners, and felt the control levers. They were all turned off tightly.

I moved back through the bar and into the front room. The gas smell was stronger. The stairway slanted up into darkness. I went up the steps quickly and stood in a dark hall. Reflected moonlight from a window at the far end showed me three doors. I opened the nearest one. An empty bedroom, bright with moonlight from two windows, a neatly made bed with a flowered counterpane. The next room was dark, but I smelled soap and perfume and knew that it was the bathroom. The third door was locked. I rattled the knob, pounded, and then knelt down and put my nose to the bottom of the door. The gas smell was strong.

I stood up, backed away, and lunged a shoulder against the door. It held. I lunged again. Something cracked, and there was a splintering sound. My right shoulder was numb, and I used the left one. More splintering, and the lock let loose. I stumbled into the room.

The gas was all around me, thick and deadly. I coughed and ran to a moonlit window, fumbled for the catch, pushed it upward. Cold November air blew in. I turned, aware of a steady hissing sound. The moonlight fell across a bed and I saw Judy Kirkland lying there, reposed, serene. Like a corpse.

The hissing sound came from across the room. I ran to the door, found the wall switch, turned on the lights. At one end of the room was an old-fashioned fireplace which had been converted to gas. Fake clay logs rested on brass andirons. The control valve was turned on full. I shut it off, sprang to the bed and gathered Judy Kirkland in my arms, carried her down the stairs and laid her on the leather divan. Light from the bar fell across her and I saw that she was dressed as I had last seen her, and her shirt was still unbuttoned. Her eyes were closed and she was smiling faintly and she was beautiful, like a child. I knelt beside her and laid an ear to her chest. It seemed to me that her heart was beating, very slowly, but I wasn't sure. It could have been my own heart.

I opened all the windows wide and then I left her and hunted for a telephone. I found it in the kitchen, on a shelf beneath a jutting breakfast counter. I lifted the receiver and asked for Dr. Mazzini.

He answered right away. "Dr. Mazzini," his calm voice said.

"This is Bennett—"

"To hell with you."

"It's Judy," I said, ignoring his bitter tone. "Suicide. Gas. She's—"

"Where is she?" he cut in sharply.

"At her place, on River Road. I found her—"

"My God," he said. "Stay with her." The receiver slammed in my ear.

I ran back into the front room, lifted Judy from the divan and laid her face down on the floor, trying to remember what I knew about artificial respiration. I knelt over her with my hands on the small of her back and began to swing slowly backward and forward, regulating the pressure of my hands. Her body was limp beneath me, but I kept it up until the sweat ran down my face, and I kept thinking that it was no use, that she was dead. But I kept on, I don't know how long, and at last I heard the screech of brakes and the sound of flying stone. Light swept past the front windows, a car door slammed, and feet pounded on the porch. Dr. Anthony Mazzini burst into the room, carrying his bag, his eyes wild in his dark face. He had thrown his tweed overcoat over red-striped pajamas, and his shoe laces were untied.

He saw what I was trying to do, and he said, "Good, good," and pushed me away.

I stood up. He knelt beside the still form of the girl, and his hands went over her swiftly. He muttered something, and began the respiration motions I'd been making. "Blankets," he snapped at me. "And coffee—hot and black."

I ran upstairs, tore blankets from the bed in the first room I'd entered, carried them down and laid them on the floor beside the doctor. He paid no attention to me. I entered the kitchen, filled a copper kettle with water and put it on a burner. Then I emptied into the sink the soggy grounds from the glass coffee maker on the table, filled it with fresh coffee from a can in a cupboard, and waited for the water to boil. Cold air blew through the kitchen from the open windows in the front room and struck my wet face. I shivered, and lit a cigarette. On a shelf beneath the cupboard I spied a bottle. I picked it up, saw that it was about a quarter full. I pulled the cork, sniffed, and took a long swallow. Scotch. It made a hard hot knot in my stomach, and I decided I didn't feel like drinking. I entered the bar, took the confession note from the typewriter, folded it carefully, and placed it in the breast pocket of my suit. When I returned to the kitchen, the kettle was beginning to hum a little. I went to the phone and asked the operator for the Homer Hollis residence.

Sandy answered quickly, and I knew that she hadn't gone to bed, but had been sitting downstairs in the darkness. Quickly I told her what had happened, and asked her to take my car and come to Judy Kirkland's.

She asked no questions, but said simply, "All right, Jim."

The kettle began to whistle. I poured the boiling water into the coffee pot and listened to the slow drip, drip, drip. When there was enough in the lower half of the pot I filled a cup and carried it in to Dr. Mazzini. The cold wind was still blowing in the windows, but sweat was dripping from his face, as it had from mine.

"I think she's coming around," he panted, and he turned her gently over on her back.

She still looked dead to me, but I wasn't a doctor.

"Close," he breathed. "Damned close." He lifted her into his arms and pulled one of the blankets over her. It was then that I saw her eyelids quiver. He saw it, too, and suddenly he laughed, a wild crazy sound. He held her close, folding the blanket around her, and he said softly, "You crazy little fool, you sweet little bitch." He kissed her cheeks and her eyes and I was embarrassed.

He reached out a hand for the coffee. I handed the cup to him. He tasted it first, testing it, and he blew on it briefly. Then he held the cup to Judy's lips and made soft coaxing sounds, like a mother with a stubborn baby. She took some of it, and she choked and almost strangled, and he patted her and said soothingly, "There, there, my darling." The coffee trickled over her chin and throat, but he kept feeding it to her, little by little, making soft love sounds, and I had the uncomfortable feeling that I was a Peeping Tom viewing an intimate and personal scene not meant for a stranger's eyes.

I turned away, thinking that I would get some coffee for myself, but his soft voice stopped me. "Bennett."

I turned and looked at him.

"Thanks," he said.

"You don't have to thank me. Sandy Hollis is coming over. I called her."

"Good. She can stay with Judy tonight."

"Somebody better stay with her," I said. "She might try it again."

He frowned. "How did you happen to find her?"

I looked at him steadily. "I wanted to see her about a personal matter. She didn't answer my knock, and I came inside. I found a note in her typewriter, and I smelled gas. She was upstairs in a bedroom, the door and windows locked. I smashed the door and found her on the bed with the gas turned on."

"Note?" he said, with a puzzled frown. "What did it say?"

"Nothing about you."

"I wasn't thinking of that," he said quietly. He looked down at Judy Kirkland. She had a little color now and appeared to be sleeping peacefully. "She'll be pretty groggy for a while," the doctor said, as if talking to himself. He looked up at me. "Let me see the note."

I moved around the room closing windows. From the basement I heard the sound of a mechanical furnace running, probably gas or oil, as it tried to get the house warm again. The doctor laid Judy Kirkland on the divan and covered her with one of the blankets. She stirred restlessly and sighed. He turned to face me and held out a hand. "Let me see it."

I shook my head. "I'm sorry. I'm turning it over to the sheriff." I paused, and then added, "It's a confession the of murder. She killed Rex Bishop, and she tried to kill Ralph Hollis."

"You're crazy," he said. "Why would she—"

"People kill for a lot of reasons. Jealousy is one of them."

"But I know she never really loved Ralph Hollis," he said. "She—"

"Maybe not," I said, "but he spurned her, if you'll pardon the expression, and she couldn't stand that. If she couldn't have him, she didn't want anyone else to have him, either. Dog in the manger stuff. The psychologists have a name for it."

He looked bewildered. "But why did she try suicide?"

"Remorse," I said. "Self-blame. Reaction to what she'd done, maybe fear of discovery. And she'd been drinking since noon. That probably helped."

Once more I heard a car in the drive, and saw the lights flash across the windows. "That'll be Sandy," I said.

He said desperately, "Let me talk to Judy before—before you call the sheriff. Will you promise to wait until I can talk to her?"

"All right," I said.

Sandy came in and looked quickly at the figure of Judy Kirkland. "She'll be all right," I told her.

"Thanks to your friend, Bennett," the doctor said with a trace of irony.

Sandy untied a red woolen scarf from her head and took off a loose gabardine topcoat. Except for stockings, she was completely dressed in a red skirt, black sweater and saddle oxfords. She looked like a high-school freshman.

The doctor said, "Sandy, would you bring some more coffee, please." He bent over the divan.

Sandy gave me a puzzled look, and I shrugged. She entered the kitchen, and I went up the stairs. At the landing I glanced back. Dr. Mazzini had turned and was watching me. He looked away quickly, and I went on up to the hall and down to the room where I'd found Judy.

I closed the window I'd unlocked and opened. There were two windows, and the other was locked with the same type of catch on the inside. The quilted cover on the bed showed the long slim depression of Judy's body. She had lain quietly, waiting for death. Her fingerprints would be on the gas valve, if I hadn't smeared them, and on the inside door knob, and the key. I moved to the door. The bolt had splintered the casing, but the key was still in the lock. I got down on my knees, dropped a handkerchief over the key, and turned it. The bolt slid back, and I removed the key. It was an ordinary house key with an open ring at one end, a slender old-fashioned key, unlike the short flat modern ones.

I stood up, moved over beneath the ceiling light, held the key in the handkerchief and inspected it carefully. Just a steel key, rather dull and a little rusty. On the inside of the ring a tiny something glinted in the light. I squinted, and held the key closer, thinking that I needed glasses. The object was a yellow speck, a tiny flake of something. It disappeared when I touched it, and I cursed softly. The laboratory boys would scream and tear their hair at my clumsiness. But there weren't any lab boys within a hundred miles, and it probably didn't mean anything, anyhow; just a minute fleck of yellow something on the inside ring of the end of an old-fashioned key in the lock of a room where a driven and remorseful girl had turned on the gas and waited in quiet drunken despair for the long sleep.

I put the key back in the lock for the sheriff to examine, if he wanted to examine it, turned off the light and stepped out into the hall. I took two steps toward the stairs before heard the whisper of sound behind me. I turned, but far too slowly. A dazzling light exploded behind my eyes, and then there was nothing, not even blackness.

CHAPTER THIRTEEN

The bare wooden floor was cold beneath my cheek. I moved my legs and my arms, and then my head, and felt a deadly drowsiness. I pressed my cheek against the floor and slept. There were dreams, and shadows swirled. I opened my eyes, but the lids were too heavy. I sighed, yawned, and maybe I slept some more. Time did not matter. There was no world, no people, and none of the things tagged love, hate, money or death. There was just a vast lovely silence and peace and rest. It was wonderful. I wallowed in it.

But slowly and cruelly the world crept back, leering at me obscenely, chuckling gleefully. And the people. I muttered in protest, wanting to return to the wonderful silent world, but something wouldn't let me. I opened my eyes slowly, cautiously pushed myself to my knees and squatted on my haunches, like a cave man before his puny flickering fire. My head pounded, and I explored with my fingers, found a lump behind my right ear. I swayed and lost my balance and fell sideways. I closed my eyes again, hoping for the beautiful silent world. But it didn't come. I whimpered for it, longing for it, like an embryo longing for its womb. I whimpered piteously, but I stayed in the other world, the harsh, cold and wicked one, and I cringed from it. And from the people. The world would be fine if it weren't for the goddamned people. And money and love and hate and death. Not death, maybe. Death was a consummation devoutly to be wished. The end of pain and of all life's burdens, the beautiful, silent and lovely end to everything. And the beginning. Tomorrow and tomorrow and tomorrow creeps in this petty pace from day to day.

With a great effort I pushed myself to my feet and stood rolling against the wall. Below me the light from the front room of Judy Kirkland's house cast a glow up the stair well. Judy Kirkland, Dr. Anthony Mazzini, Sandy Hollis—they were all down there, I thought, gathered at the foot of the stairs like parents on Christmas morning, and as I went down the steps they would sweetly sing a jolly carol. I lurched for the steps, but I stopped, swaying. I wasn't ready to face them yet. Not yet. I turned slowly around, peered into the darkness. The bathroom was the middle door, I remembered that. I groped along the wall, found the door. It stood half open, and again I smelled the soap and the delicate perfume. I found a wall switch, flicked it. The bathroom came at me like a train out of a tunnel. I flinched and blinked in the bright light. An old-fashioned bathroom. Metal wash bowl, enameled tub on legs, a chain hanging from a tank over the toilet. Medieval. But the water in the tap was cold. It felt very good splashing over my head. I soaked a towel, rubbed my face, and looked in a mirror over the bowl. I winced. Straight black hair, too long as usual, because I was a week past due at the barber's, black whisker stubble tinged with gray, foggy blue eyes, dark pouches beneath them, deep lines around the mouth, wrinkles in the forehead. A hell of a looking face. Dissipated, degenerate. Gently I pressed the wet towel to the lump behind my ear. No blood, a neat job. I dropped the towel and lurched out to the hall. The stairway gaped like a hippopotamus' mouth. I shrank from it, fearfully, leaned against the wall, fumbled for a cigarette. I found a mashed pack, dug one out, hit my mouth. More fumbling for a match. Strike, connect flame, inhale. Nausea. Cigarette on the bare wooden floor. Stamp it out. Help prevent fires. National Fire Prevention Week.

Get control of yourself, Bennett. Take a deep breath and throw out your chest. Walk firmly to that goddamned stairway. Go down and see what the hell is going on. Assert yourself. You're the law. Almost. And this is pretty shady business, dark stuff going on here. Sinister. Yellow speck on a key. A clue, Bennett. Hah! How about a double-double martini? Or a triple Scotch? Or six aspirin tablets?

I went down the stairs very slowly, my hand on the rail. I felt remote, superior, above the sordid sins of the world. Pure, like Lancelot. Step by step I went down, down....

Sandy stood at the foot of the stairs, her face a white blur. "Jim, what's wrong?" she asked sharply.

I pushed her gently aside and stood up straight and focused my eyes on Dr. Mazzini, who sat on the divan beside Judy Kirkland. I staggered a little, supported myself against the stair railing, and I said distinctly, "What did you hit me with, Doctor?"

"Does it matter?" he asked quietly.

I pushed myself away from the railing and stood erect. It made me happy to realize that I swayed only a little and that the room was circling quite slowly. The doctor swung into focus again, and I said, "No, it doesn't matter, I guess. But *why* did you hit me?"

"You should know," he said. "I'm sorry I had to do it."

I concentrated upon standing erect, and then I concentrated upon what he had said. Presently his meaning filtered through my fuzzy brain and slowly I began to feel in my pockets, one by one. Wallet, gun, silver, pencil, pen, comb, spare handkerchief, cigarettes, matches, tobacco crumbs, two old letters, a couple of broken toothpicks, the filled hypo, which pricked my finger. It took me a little while to realize that the missing item was Judy Kirkland's confession. I had known all along that it would be gone, and I wondered wearily why I'd gone through the motions of looking.

"Give it back," I said.

"I can't," the doctor said, and nodded at a big glass ashtray on a low table near the divan.

I peered at the ashtray. It contained three cigarette stubs, and a little pile of black debris, the burned and crinkled remnants of what had been a sheet of paper. I pointed a wavering, accusing finger at Dr. Mazzini. "Burning evidence," I said. "Obstructing justice."

"Prove it," he said softly.

Behind me I heard Sandy say in a strange voice, "Jim …"

Ponderously I turned toward her, and I heard my voice saying, "And where were you, Miss Hollis, when the good doctor sneaked up the stairs and knocked me cold and took a paper from my pocket?"

"I was in the kitchen, making more coffee. I didn't hear—"

"Don't blame Sandy," Dr. Mazzini broke in. "She didn't know that I went upstairs. And you'd better sit down. I injected sodium pentothal into the vein of your right arm. It knocked you out completely for about ten minutes, and it'll take a little while to wear off. We use it quite extensively for quick and minor surgery." He smiled. "It's harmless, and I had to be certain that you would remain unconscious long enough for me to do what I had to do." He nodded at his bag on the floor beside the divan. "I used a sap first, but I disliked hitting you hard enough to make certain you'd be out long enough."

"Thanks," I said.

"I've carried the sap since my intern days—when I was on accident duty along the lake front in Cleveland," he said.

"Handy gadgets," I said. The room seemed to have stopped its interminable circling, and now just the floor was moving, up and down slowly, like the deck of a schooner in a lazy off-shore swell. "It won't do you any good, though—burning her confession. If she wrote it, she'll tell it."

"I don't think so," he said quietly. "Writing a confession with the intention of suicide is not the same as confessing when you're alive, and sober, and no prospects of dying."

"Let's ask her," I suggested, trying to peer around him at the form of Judy Kirkland on the divan.

"She can't talk for a while," he said. "I've given her a sedative."

"You're a tricky bastard," I said, "but she's got to talk some time."

"Not until I talk to her first," he said calmly. "And it's all right about the bastard—my father's name was O'Brian, I believe."

"I'm sorry as all hell," I said. "When I tell the law—"

"About Judy's silly confession? She was drinking, and emotionally upset, and she blames herself for what happened to Ralph Hollis. In a crazy way she was trying to atone—"

"And so she killed Rex Bishop. Was that atonement, too?" I reached for a cigarette, but remembered my experience with the last one, and changed my mind.

"She lied," he said. "The whole damn thing was a lie. I know her, Bennett."

"And you love her."

"Yes," he said.

"And you'll protect her at any cost?"

"You can't prove that she wrote a confession. You can't prove any of it."

He was right, and I knew it. I had the bullet I'd dug out of the tree, but if I couldn't match it with a certain rifle, I had nothing. And I had a hypo needle filled—with something. I looked at Dr. Mazzini, and I suddenly realized that if the needle contained anything but penicillin, he would have taken it from me, along with Judy's confession. I didn't have anything now, but some ugly memories, and I couldn't go to the law. But they came back to me, the sounds of the bullets. They had been aimed at me with ugly and serious intent, and once again I felt the lonely climate of my personal little world, and with it came the slow surge of rage.

I wouldn't stop, not yet.

Fingers plucked at my sleeve and I turned slowly to see Sandy at my side. She held a cup in her hand, and she said quietly, "Jim, you'd better have some coffee. And then you'd better go out to the farm and go to bed. I'll stay with Judy tonight." She avoided my gaze, and her face was very pale.

"What's the matter?"

"I just called the hospital. He's no better."

Dr. Mazzini stood up. "I'd better have a look at him."

I took the hypo needle from my pocket and held it up. It glittered in the light, and the fluid in the glass looked like milk. I said, quoting what I remembered of the Oath of Hippocrates, "I swear by Apollo, the physician . . . and all the gods and goddesses . . . I will give no deadly medicine . . . With purity and holiness I will pass my life...."

"To hell with you," Dr. Mazzini said, and he turned to Sandy. "She'll sleep for maybe six hours. I'll be back before she wakes up."

"All right," she said.

He moved past me, ignoring me, and went out, carrying his bag. Through the window I saw his car lights back out of the drive and go down the road. Sandy went and stood by the divan and gazed at Judy Kirkland. I sipped my coffee. Sandy said softly, "She *looks* like— like an angel."

"Yes," I said, thinking of Dr. Mazzini, on his way to the hospital. Maybe I should follow, but I couldn't be everywhere at once. I had to trust him. I had to trust somebody. I was tired and still dizzy. My head hurt, and although the floor was quite steady now, there was a dullness in my brain. I pulled up my right sleeve, noticing that the shirt cuff was unbuttoned. On the inside of my forearm was a small patch of adhesive tape. I pulled it off, saw the tiny red puncture in the vein.

I looked at Sandy, standing over the sleeping form of Judy. I thought of all that had happened, and I knew that I still had unfinished business. And it couldn't wait. In Ohio in November it would be dawn before seven o'clock. I looked at my wristwatch. Ten minutes until three. Four hours, give or take a little, and it would be another day, and I would either have to pack up and return to Cleveland, or stay and finish my business, whatever it was.

Sandy turned to face me, and her lips quivered. "Did she really do—do that to Ralph, on purpose? I heard what you said to Dr. Mazzini, part of it, and . . ."

I gazed at the pale, peaceful face of Judy Kirkland, and she really did look like an angel, and I said, "Of course not. It was an accident."

She gave me a level brown-eyed stare. "Do you believe that?"

"Yes," I said.

After all, I was going to leave her alone with Judy for what was left of the night.

Beyond the headlights of my car the road was black. The night was black, too, and so was the sky. The stars were gone and the moon was a misty crescent over the tops of bare swaying trees. Rain spattered on the windshield, and was gone, and the wind moaned across the half-open window beside me. I wanted the cold air, and I sucked it into my lungs. It helped. My brain cleared slowly, and after a while I began to shiver. I rolled up the window and the sound of the wind died to a low rustling. The rain came again, and the trees caught in the lights began to thrash wildly.

I reached the end of River Road and turned, cruised slowly along the main street of Ridge Center beneath the double line of trees. Daisy Brown's house was still dark. Further on the square was dark, too, with only an occasional dim night light inside a few stores and a meager string of street lamps. There was not a moving thing in sight. Dan's Place was dark, too, like the rest. I drove past it, and saw the courthouse, looming high and dark, and the squat building that was the county jail. I remembered the old man's directions and I stopped at the curb, the headlights shining across a lawn. Gilt letters on a black sign glinted. *Anthony D. Mazzini, M.D.* I wondered what the *D.* stood for. Probably Daniel, a gesture to O'Brian. The small building was dark, but next to it, in the county jail, there were lights. Not at the row of barred windows in the rear, behind which the prisoners languished, but in front, where the sheriff's office would be. The battered Chevrolet was at the curb. I got out of my Mercury and went up some cement steps to a glassed door with the blind pulled down. I knocked and waited. The door opened, and Sheriff John Morrissy peered out at me.

"Do you remember me, Sheriff?"

He smiled. "Of course. Bennett. You and Homer Hollis found Rex Bishop's body."

"How're you making out?"

He sighed. "Not so good, but we're trying." He paused, and then said, "You know, I didn't realize who you were until after I'd left Homer's. Your agency is famous, and of course I've heard of you. Come in." He opened the door wider, and I stepped inside.

It was a small bare office containing a battered desk and several straight chairs. A number of *Wanted* circulars were pinned to the walls, and in one corner was a modern little finger printing outfit. In one of the chairs sat a chubby executive-type man with a clipped gray mustache and a sun lamp tan. He wore elegant corduroy hunting clothes and was smoking a fat cigar. He stared at me with cold eyes, a banker's eyes, I decided, and I was glad I wasn't asking him for a loan. He was quite drunk, in a dignified way, and cuddled a bottle of Canadian Club against his fat, round little stomach. If he wasn't drunk, he would have never, never carried a whisky bottle to the sheriff's office.

Through a half-open door I saw a cement floor and the glint of bars and smelled the strong disinfectant smell of all jails, from Bangor to Pasadena. From a cell near the door I could hear a man mumbling drunkenly in a hoarse, sinister monotone: "Now, listen, babe, I don't take that stuff, see? I been buying your groceries and keeping you in cigarettes and gin and you been telling me you was going out Mondays, Wednesdays and Fridays to choir practice and all the time you been laying with that sonofabitch Rudolph and I don't take that stuff, see? I might be dumb but I ain't that dumb and I don't take that stuff, see, and by god you gotta—"

The sheriff closed the door and winked at me. Then he nodded at the executive type and said politely, "This is Mr. Bennett, Mr. Forbes."

Mr. Forbes fixed me with his cold eyes and said, "Blah."

The sheriff said, "Mr. Forbes is one of the few hunters still remaining in town this weekend—and the only hunter that we have found who brought a rifle with him. Mr. Forbes, it seems, was under the impression that there were deer in the vicinity of Ridge Center, and he wishes some antlers to grace his fireplace. I have explained to him that deer are found across the Pennsylvania line, but not in this section, as a rule, and that this is strictly pheasant and rabbit country, requiring a shotgun only. Mr. Forbes—"

"C. Delbert Forbes," the executive type snapped. The sheriff smiled and nodded. "Pardon me." He turned to me again. "Mr. C. Delbert Forbes has in his possession a rifle which he admits he fired today, at some sparrows, in the vicinity of the Hollis farm. Dr. Sweet, the coroner, has extracted from the body of Rex Bishop a bullet which appears to be about .30 caliber, or perhaps a trifle larger. However, I am sorry to say that we do not have the facilities here to accurately check it against the rifling in Mr. F—in Mr. C. Delbert Forbes' gun. I plan to go to Cleveland in the morning to have the bullet and the rifle checked by ballistics experts."

"I see," I said.

The sheriff turned to the executive type, and said gravely, "I should know by noon tomorrow whether or not you accidentally, while shooting at sparrows, sent a bullet across the fields which hit and killed Rex Bishop. If the bullet we have matches your gun, then it will be my sad duty to file manslaughter charges against you."

The executive type took a drink of Canadian Club, said, "Blah," flicked cigar ashes on the floor, and belched.

Sheriff Morrissy said to me, "To you, our feeble bucolic methods may seem amateurish, but we mean well."

"You're doing fine," I said. "Is Mr. C. Delbert Forbes alone on his hunting trip? I mean, are there others in his party who may also have brought rifles?"

The sheriff said politely, "Mr. C. Delbert Forbes is accompanied by a young lady with auburn hair. Apparently she has no weapons. We left her at the hotel."

The executive type said stiffly, "My wife, sir, does not hunt."

The sheriff raised his gray eyebrows. "There must be some mistake. Her driver's license states that she is single, and that her name is Edith De Cicco."

The executive type blinked, but recovered quickly. "Of course. We're—uh—traveling incognito." He took a long pull of Canadian Club.

The sheriff looked at me blankly. I grinned, and asked, "What kind of a rifle?"

"An old army Springfield, .30 caliber, bolt action. I've got it locked up."

"Get rid of C. Delbert," I said. "I want to talk to you."

The sheriff said to the executive type, "You may go now. Please stay in town until you hear from me."

"This is an outrage."

"I'm sorry," the sheriff said in his grave voice, "but you should never shoot a rifle in the woods, unless you are certain where the bullet will strike. A rifle bullet carries far, often to areas you cannot see. A shotgun has a short range, and is more effective for small game, because the pellets fan out, thus increasing the target area." He lifted a finger, like a teacher explaining patiently to a dull pupil. "Always remember that."

"Blah," the executive type said, and tilted the bottle.

"Listen," the sheriff said in a deadly cold voice, "maybe you killed a harmless old man this morning. If you did, I will personally see that you are charged with all the law will allow. Now, get out of my office and don't leave town until I say so."

Mr. C. Delbert Forbes was on the point of saying, "Blah," again, but he saw the look of subdued fury in the sheriff's eyes and he changed his mind. He corked the bottle, stood up stiffly, as if he were about to address a board meeting. "You will hear from my attorney." His cold little eyes seemed to swirl in his head.

"Fine," the sheriff said wearily. "Now get the hell out."

He strode past us in a stately manner, carrying the bottle under his arm as if it were a brief case containing the papers for a billion-dollar loan at six per cent. The sheriff slammed the door behind him.

"He'll skip," I said.

"My deputy will watch him."

I grinned. "Tail job, huh?"

"Yes." He sighed. "I'm tired."

"Don't they have a police force here?"

"Just a marshal, part time. I handle everything in the county, and I need more help. The village council is supposed to vote another deputy for me, but they won't meet until next month." He smiled. "But I asked for it, when I ran for sheriff. Had a hardware store here for twenty years and sold out, after my wife died. Kids are all married and moved away, and this job gives me something to do. I've read up on criminology and police procedure and all that, and even attended the FBI school. The pay isn't much, but I kind of like the work—anyhow, somebody has to do it."

"No law enforcement officer is ever paid enough," I said. "I think I'll start a crusade, like the one for the teachers."

"It's an important field," he said seriously. "The pay should be better, to attract capable men."

"Who takes care of the jail?"

"I do. I live in a couple of rooms in the back. The prisoner's meals are sent in from a restaurant, and a woman comes in to clean. And my deputy helps."

I had always had respect for all the sheriffs like John Morrissy, in all the villages and counties all over America, doing a vital work, necessary for the public welfare, and being paid a pittance, much, much less than any adolescent boy who operated a drill press, or a punch-button lathe, for eight hours and then went home and to hell with it. Here was John Morrissy at three o'clock in the morning, with no overtime pay, trying to learn who had fired the stray bullet which had killed an obscure old man.

He said, "I've got some coffee. Would you like some?"

"Sure," I said.

He opened the door to the cell block and disappeared. I sat in the chair vacated by C. Delbert Forbes and lit a cigarette. The sheriff came back carrying two thick cups and a blackened pot. "I hope you don't want cream," he said. "I have sugar."

"Neither."

He poured the coffee. It was black and thick, but it tasted good. He sat behind his desk and began to fill a pipe. I guessed him to be about sixty, but he looked much younger. His skin was clear and firm, and his eyes were bright. He leaned back in his chair, sipped the coffee, and puffed at his pipe.

I said, "Sheriff—"

"Call me John," he said. "That way I can call you Jim, and tell people that I know you well. I first heard of you when you were in on that mess over in Wheatville a couple of years ago. Folks around here still talk about it—what was that woman's name? With the scarred face?"

"Donati," I said. "Marianne Donati." I stirred restlessly. Memories are never any good. Most memories, anyhow. Except the memory of Sandy's kisses. I thought suddenly of Sandy, alone with Judy Kirkland.

The sheriff said, "And the doctor who cut the throat of Mrs. Donati's husband—his name was Griffith, I remember. He got life, but he should have been sent to the chair."

"Yes," I said, not wanting to remember. "Listen, John, I'll start with the shooting of Ralph Hollis this morning—yesterday morning."

He gave me a quick alert look, and said quietly. "All right."

CHAPTER FOURTEEN

I told it to him, all of it, from the beginning to Judy Kirkland's attempted suicide. I didn't skip anything, and I told it as it happened, all I could remember, and how I felt about it. I felt much better after I'd told it, and I ended by saying, "And now Dr. Mazzini is at the hospital with Ralph, and Sandy is staying with Judy Kirkland. And

I've still got people to see."

"Earl Seltzman, for one?" the sheriff asked softly.

"For one."

"Everyone knows that he's been eating out his heart for Eileen Fortune," he said, "and that there's bad blood between him and Ralph Hollis—because of Eileen."

"I know. What about Jake Fortune?"

He shrugged. "Jake's all right. He's a woman chaser, since his wife died, and he's broke and in debt, but trying to keep up a front. He and Earl Seltzman seem to be pretty thick—Jake's been negotiating some beef deals for him. Jake is generally well-liked, but Earl isn't so popular. Something, I don't know what—something unpleasant about him. I suppose it's his upbringing. His folks were very strict, and Earl didn't cut loose much until after they died, and he came into all the Seltzman money. Judy Kirkland is what we call a character. She does what she pleases, and to hell with what anybody thinks. This summer she'd go into the supermarket wearing the skimpiest pair of shorts and halter you ever saw. Created quite a stir, and some of the good church ladies started some kind of a decency movement, but nothing ever came of it. She drives too fast, and drinks whisky in Dan's Place, and everybody knows about her affair with Doc Mazzini, and Ralph Hollis. In the summer time she lays naked in her backyard on River Road. Saw her there taking the sun myself one day." He laughed softly. "Right attractive sight, too. Personally, I think that all Judy needs is a regular tanning with a limber hickory stick."

"Dr. Mazzini slapped her tonight," I said.

"Doc's got a temper, when he's riled. He's part Italian, and hot-blooded, the kind of a man Judy needs." He gazed at me over his pipe. "We think a lot of Doc in this county. You don't have to worry—he'll take good care of Ralph Hollis, regardless."

"What about Judy's aunts?" I asked. "Can't they do anything with her?"

He shook his head slowly. "They're both old and they live in the past. Nobody hardly ever sees them. I hear that Judy spends part of her time at their place, and kind of keeps an eye on them. And Doc Mazzini calls there once a week—one of them is pretty well crippled with arthritis."

"Do you think I should see them? Tell them about Judy?"

"Not tonight. From what you've told me, she's all right now. But suit yourself." He knocked out his pipe in a heavy ashtray. "It's an odd series of circumstances, and I think I know how you feel. But there's nothing you can put your finger on—Judy's typed confession, for example. When she wrote it—*if* she wrote it—she was liquored up and feeling low, but you can't prove anything. What's your next move?"

"I want to see Earl Seltzman."

"I'll go with you," he said. "And maybe we'd better go out to Judy's place too, although there's nothing definite I can officially act on—unless you file charges, but it's all suspicion. If you want to slap a shooting with intent to kill charge on Earl, I'll do it."

"No," I said. "Not yet. It's my fight. It's a kind of personal thing, and maybe I've built it up too much in my mind, but I've got to find out."

"I understand," he said. "I'll be on call, if you want me. I plan on leaving for Cleveland around seven."

I took the hypodermic needle from my pocket and laid it on his desk. "Have that checked, too, but I'm sure it's just penicillin. The bullet I dug out of the tree is in my room at the Hollis place. If I have time, I'll get it and bring it here before you leave. Judy's rifle is out in the car. I want you to take that, too."

He nodded. "Maybe by tomorrow noon we'll have something to go on."

"Maybe," I said, and I finished my coffee.

He followed me out to my car and I gave him Judy's rifle. "I'll be here if you want me," he said. "Good luck."

"Thanks." As I drove away, I thought that I couldn't do any more, as far as official action was concerned. That part was over, done. The law would now take its course, if there proved to be a course for it to take. I was glad I had talked to John Morrissy. It had lifted some of the load.

But I was still all alone.

I drove slowly around the square and through the dark village and past the high school, to the corner of Crawford and Tymocktee Streets. Except for a dim and distant street lamp, the neighborhood was dark. I stopped at the curb and gazed at the windows of Earl Seltzman's house, at the vacant drive, the yawning emptiness of the garage. A car without lights drifted like a ghost up beside me. I caught the movement out of the corner of my eye and turned my head. Instinct made me duck in the instant the shot exploded loudly beside me. I saw the reflection of fire, heard the crunch and tinkle of breaking glass, and it seemed that a hot wicked whisper filled the car. I huddled low, waiting for the second shot, but none came, just the snarl of gears as a car sped away. I raised my head. The ghost car was turning a corner a block away, a swift glinting bulk in the darkness.

My nerves were like taut and twanging rubber bands, and my hands were too numb to get the car in motion, to give chase. I let the ghost car go. Whoever was driving it knew the alleys and the cross streets and the out-lying byroads. Play dead, Bennett. This is the third time—let 'em think they got you at last. For now. A cold jet of air brushed my face, and I turned my head. The bullet had made a splintered hole directly beside the spot where my head was now, and another hole, but bigger, in the opposite window. If a line had been drawn between the two, it would pass through my ears. I sighed deeply and lit a cigarette, and after a while my nerves settled down and feeling returned to my hands.

I turned the Mercury around and drove back to the square. On the far side a small dog snuffed along the curb beneath a yellow street lamp, and there was no other sign of life. Everyone's dead, I thought, dead in their beds. This is a ghost town, and I'm the only one alive. The person in the ghost car is a ghost, too, and I'm stalking someone, something, in a silent world, and this night will go on forever.

Dan's Place was still dark. I parked down the street a short distance, walked back, and tried the door. Locked tight. Far in the rear was a tiny glow of light. I left the door and moved to the mouth of the alley beside the place, and it seemed that I was again hearing the shots, feeling the sting of brick dust on my face. I didn't want to go back there into that darkness. But I did, and held the gun in my pocket like a baby clinging to its mother's hand. I walked slowly back, my shadow tall before me. Then even the shadow was gone, and I stopped by the back door to Dan's Place. A thin ribbon of light leaked from beneath it and across the rough bricks. I stood in the wind and the blackness and gazed down the alley, saw the bulk of the ashcan on the far side. I shivered, remembering, and tried the knob on the door. Locked, of course. I swore, and pounded with my fist. I waited.

The door opened a little and I saw an eye and half of a man's face. I said, "Is Earl Seltzman there?"

From behind the half-face a voice called, "Who the hell is that, Fred?"

The eye in the half-face moved and I saw an ear. "It's that guy looking for Earl again." The ear disappeared and I saw the eye again. "Earl ain't here."

"Mind if I come in?"

"This is a private game."

I lifted a foot and kicked the door violently. It flew wide open. Somebody shouted as I stepped inside and the eight men at the poker table jumped to their feet, all except one, who appeared to be asleep with his head on his arms. A voice muttered, "A hold up, by God."

Not counting the sleeper, I recognized four of the men as being in the game earlier in the evening. They all watched me silently as I stepped to the table, grasped the sleeping man's hair, and tilted his face. It wasn't Earl Seltzman. He mumbled, and tried to brush my hand away. I let his head fall back to the table, and stepped away. It could have been a holdup, all right; there was enough money on the table to make it worthwhile. Here, then, was Ridge Center's night life, vice in the corn belt. Maybe Dan's Place even had girls upstairs.

A burly man in a heavy plaid shirt said blusteringly, "Now, looky here—"

"Shut up. Where's Earl?"

"That ain't none of your goddamned business." The burly man moved toward me threateningly. The rest closed up a little, like a pack of wolves. The half-face who had opened the door began to edge along the wall toward the door leading into the bar. I showed them the gun then, and it froze them all. Maybe it wasn't necessary, but a gun is a great ego-salver, and my ego was suffering an inferiority complex. A gun puts you in the driver's seat, most times, and it was time for me to drive a little.

I said, "Where is Earl?"

The burly man said sullenly, "He ain't been in the game since you come looking for him the first time."

"Why did he duck out, and why did you cover up for him?"

"He said you was an insurance salesman hounding him, and he didn't want to talk to you." He looked at the rest. "Ain't that right, boys?"

Three of them nodded silently, the three who had been in the game before, and they eyed the gun.

"Anybody know where Earl would be right now?" I asked. "Or Jake Fortune?"

They realized that their money was safe, and they felt better about the whole thing. The man by the wall volunteered, "Earl's probably making hay with Eileen Fortune—now that Ralph Hollis is laid up." He giggled nervously.

The burly man said, "Jake was in here early a couple of times, but I ain't seen him since midnight."

I backed to the door, put the gun in my pocket. "Thanks, boys." Seven pairs of eyes watched me as I closed the door.

I stood in the alley a moment listening to the excited voices inside. Then the lock clicked. Apparently, none of them had pursuit in mind. They were happy that it hadn't been a holdup, and they could continue their illegal gambling, a form of amusement outlawed in a public place in Ohio. I walked up the alley and down the street to my car. I tried not to notice the holes in the windows. Viciously I started the motor, gunned the car around the square, and was hitting sixty when I left the village limits.

I guess I was frustrated.

Eighty miles an hour, ninety, and the road was a straight flat ribbon in the moonlight. Ninety-five. The telephone poles whipped past and the fields were a gray blur. The wind screamed through the little holes in the windows and made an icicle streak across my face. I didn't look in the rearview mirror to see if I was being followed. I didn't give a damn. Let them try and catch me, and to hell with them or him or her or it. The headlights couldn't keep up with the car. A curve sign slammed at me. I pushed hard on the brakes and fought the wheel. The rear end skidded sickeningly on gravel and the tires made a horrible screaming. I fed gas again, let up on the brakes, and made the curve. Ahead the road was straight again. Seventy, seventy-five, eighty and the motor wound up. Far behind I heard a faint banshee wail that sounded like a siren, but it could have been the blood singing in my ears. I laughed aloud. Maybe I was going crazy.

Far ahead I saw a cluster of lights and I slowed down. A white-and-black route sign said, *Junction—20*. Good old Route 20, I thought, a coast-to-coast highway. I could turn left on it and it would lead me straight into Cleveland and home. Did I have a home? It seemed to me that I'd been in Ridge Center since the dawn of history. The lights were a truck stop at the intersection. Big outfits were lined up in a vast parking area beyond the gas pumps, and a brightly-lighted restaurant was doing a rushing business. I pulled the Mercury off the highway and coasted to a stop, gunning the motor affectionately before I turned the key. It growled a response and died. In the restaurant I got a cup of coffee at the counter and carried it back to one of three phone booths in the rear. I placed the coffee on a small shelf, got out a handful of silver, lit a cigarette, and went to work.

Sandy's voice sounded faint and far away.

"This is Jim, honey."

"Where are you?"

"Somewhere on Route 20. How's everything?"

"Ralph's worse, Jim. I called the hospital, and they told me. His temperature is up, and he's not responding to treatment. They had already sent a car for Dad, and he's at the hospital now. Dr. Mazzini is still with him, but—"

"I'm sorry, Sandy."

"I—I know you are."

"What's Judy doing?"

"Still sleeping." It seemed to me that Sandy's voice held a bitter edge.

"If you want to go to the hospital, I'll come and stay with her."

"No, don't do that. I—I can't do anything for Ralph . . . Jim, how have you been?"

"I think I'm going nuts."

"What?"

"Never mind." I paused. "Listen, Sandy, I'd better come over there."

"I—I am a little scared. It's kind of spooky out here. But I'm all right. You do what you have to do."

"Chin up," I said.

"Sure, Jim."

I hung up, fed more money into the slot, and waited maybe three minutes before Eileen Fortune's breathless voice said, "Yes?"

"This is Jim Bennett, Eileen. Is—"

"He's gone!" she cried. "Ralph's dead! I knew it, I knew it...." Her sobbing filled the booth.

"Listen," I shouted. "Damn it."

"Tell me," she whimpered. "I—I'll be brave."

"He's not dead, but he's worse. His condition is critical, but there's still hope." I didn't know if there was any hope for Ralph, but there was no harm in telling her.

"Is *she* with him?"

"Who?"

"Judy."

"No."

"She killed him. She *meant* to kill him, because she's jealous. She's got Ralph's blood on her hands. She—she's a Jezebel, a—a—"

"Stop it," I snapped. "Shut up. Is your father home yet?"

"Papa? No."

"Where is he?"

"I told you—"

"He's not at Dan's Place. Have you seen Earl Seltzman?"

There was silence on the wire. Then she said primly, "Of course not. I am engaged to Ralph, and it would not be proper for me to be seeing Earl."

"You let him take you home last night."

"That—that was different."

"I see," I said. "Is Earl there now?"

"No. Really, Mr. Bennett—"

"Good-bye, Eileen."

"Thank you for calling. I—I'll pray for Ralph."

"Do that." I hung up.

Outside the booth a young grave-eyed man in the uniform of a state trooper stood waiting for me. I gazed at him, took a sip of coffee, and said, "Guilty, Sergeant."

"Is that your black Mercury outside?"

"Yep."

"Lucky you made that curve," he said shortly. Over his shoulder I saw that everyone in the restaurant was looking at us.

"Damn lucky," I agreed.

He held out a hand. "Driver's license, please."

I handed him my wallet, and he flipped through the cellophaned compartments. He gazed at my private cop's license issued by the Cleveland Police Department. He studied it carefully, frowning a little. Then he looked at me and his eyes were friendly. "So you're Bennett?"

I nodded, and drank more coffee. It was getting cold.

"Down here on a case?" he asked.

I nodded again.

"Care to tell me about it? I've heard of you since I was a kid."

"Sorry, Sergeant. Confidential."

"I understand," he said seriously. "I'm on patrol between here and Wheatville tonight. I picked you up just outside of Ridge Center.

Can I help?"

"Not right now. Maybe later. Where are you stationed?"

"At the barracks in Wheatville. Gilmore's my name. If you need me, they'll put it on the radio and I'll be on deck."

"That's damn nice of you. I appreciate it."

He grinned modestly, showing very white and even teeth. "I never thought I'd meet you. I've been thinking a little about going into the private investigation field...."

"Come and see me," I said. "We always need good men."

"I've got a day off next Thursday," he said eagerly. "Fine. I'll be in the office, as far as I know."

"Thank you," he said, and added wistfully. "Would you want an escort, to wherever you're going?"

"No, thanks."

He held out a hand, and I shook it, and everybody in the restaurant relaxed and went back to the coffee and doughnuts, their hamburger and french fries. The trooper saluted smartly, and went out, the state's finest, and a damn good thing.

I had another cup of coffee and smoked another cigarette, and I thought hard and concentrated and my brain went around in fuzzy circles. After a while I went out and got in the Mercury. The bullet holes in the windows leered at me, like two evil little eyes. I drove back toward Ridge Center.

At a sedate forty-five miles an hour.

CHAPTER FIFTEEN

Everything was in the past now. It was four o'clock on a Sunday morning and in a few hours it would be dawn and a new day would begin. Everything that had happened since Friday night would never happen again, not in exactly the same way, not for anybody. And oddly enough I wasn't tired anymore. I had gone beyond the barrier of fatigue and the need for sleep. I wasn't even hungry, and I didn't want a drink. I was in a happy limbo, suspended delicately between the world and space, and it seemed that my mind worked smoothly and calmly on oiled bearings.

I thought of all of it, taking each little scene as it happened, all the spoken words, the gestures, inflections and expressions of the people I'd met, the living and the dead. Once again I was walking across the brown fields, the shotgun in the crook of my arm, Sandy beside me. I saw Ralph climbing the ravine; the shotgun pellets rattled on my hat brim. I heard the second shot, and I saw Ralph fall, and the pheasant rising into the sun. I was kneeling beside Ralph, seeing his bright blood staining the leaves, and the torn horizontal furrows slanting across his leather jacket. I saw Judy Kirkland below me, climbing the steep side of the ravine, and I heard her dismayed voice....*I was standing down there in the thicket, and I saw a bird fly out of the ravine . . .*

It was all there, very clearly; old Rex Bishop grinning at me in the sunlight, the ancient rifle under his arm; the hot light in Dr. Anthony Mazzini's eyes as he slapped Judy Kirkland; the fluttering of Daisy Brown's eyelashes, the sharp needle feel of a puppy's teeth on my fingers; the softness of Judy Kirkland's lips and the smell of Scotch whisky; Sandy's kisses, too, and her stricken face in the windy night outside the hospital and her broken whisper, *Jim, what are we going to do?*

I stood on the crest of a ravine beside a beech tree; I laid on the bricks of an alley; I sat behind the wheel of my car, and the sound of the bullets carried the same whispering death. I sat at a bar beside a down-on-his-luck cattle buyer, and I heard the slow laconic voices of two beer-drinking farmers. Texas beef in Ohio, test tube calves, an all-night poker game, an old man on the village square cackling in the night, a swollen-eyed girl sobbing on my shoulder; a silver flask, a hammer hitting a gun barrel, the thin soft feel of Earl Seltzman's pale face as I slapped him; a famous writer in bed with a Jezebel, rats swarming in a barn, a sheriff working overtime, a drunken executive relaxing with a redhead on the pretext of hunting non-existent deer.

I laughed softly as I drove along.

The road unwound and the fields and the dark farmhouses drifted past and the moonlight was very bright. The rain had blown over, the wind had died, and the trees stood tall and straight along the road and across a line of hills on my left. It would be colder by dawn, much colder, and I was glad I'd had anti-freeze put in the Mercury the week before. The windshield began to frost a little, and I turned on the heater. The car grew warm, in spite of the holes in the windows. I relaxed and drove comfortably along, feeling oddly serene and at peace with the world. The rage was still with me, but I had it chained and was petting and soothing it, telling it to wait for just a little longer. I was like a lover, too. A lover returning to his sweetheart after a long absence, anticipating the remembered delights, but content to wait until they could be savored at leisure, because they would be so much sweeter after being so long denied.

I could afford to take my time. In the dash compartment I found a pint bottle, half full of bourbon. I decided that I wanted a drink after all, and I sipped at it as I drove along and I was happy. There was a sadness, too, because of Ralph Hollis and Rex Bishop. I couldn't help what had happened to them, but I could avenge them, and I was happy about that. And down beneath it all was my own personal rage, and I fed the fuel to it lovingly, because I wanted it to grow blazing hot.

And then I looked in the rearview mirror, and I saw it behind me on the road, its lights off, but with the moonlight glinting on glass and chrome, the pale ghost car. I patted the .38 in my pocket and said crooningly, "Come on, you bastard, come closer, just a teeny bit closer."

But it didn't, and presently I didn't see it anymore. I knew it was still there, somewhere behind me, as it had been for some hours on this cold November night, waiting for a chance to strike again, but I didn't worry about it now. I had been the hunted, and now I was the hunter. I pulled over to the side of the road and stopped, waiting expectantly. But no ghost car drifted up beside me; it refused to take the bait, and the road behind remained wide and empty.

I drank a little more whisky, lit a cigarette and hummed to myself:

> *I've been consulted by Franklin D.,*
> *Greta Garbo has had me to tea . . .*

Presently I eased the Mercury out on the road and continued toward Ridge Center. It was twenty minutes until five o'clock in the morning when I stopped on the curve of a hill beside a mailbox lettered with the name of J. E. Fortune. The dim light still burned in the front room of the small house. I turned off the car lights, slid over the seat, got out quickly on the right side, and crouched down in the car's shadow. In the moonlight I could see that the road behind was empty, at least to where it curved down and around a patch of dark woods. The early morning air was bitter on my cheeks, and in the stillness I could almost feel the cold creeping over the land. It would be twenty above zero or colder by daylight, I thought, and I shivered inside my overcoat. I waited maybe five minutes, but there was no movement on the road, no pale glitter of the ghost car. At last I stood up and faced the house. A shadow moved behind the drawn blind of the front window.

After one last glance down the road behind me, I walked on the grass beside the stone drive to where it curved around the back of the house. There, partially concealed by an unpainted sagging shed, was a shining pale car, a pastel color, maybe sky-blue, but I couldn't be sure in the moonlight. It was a new Cadillac. I crept up beside it. There was no one inside. On the door were gilt initials: *E.K.S.*

The burly man at Dan's Place had been correct. Earl Seltzman was indeed making hay with Eileen Fortune while Ralph Hollis lay near death in the hospital. I wondered how long he'd been here. If he had followed me from the intersection at Route 20, he must have circled around and arrived here ahead of me. Once more my fingers touched a car's exhaust pipe. The Cadillac's was warm, but not hot, and it didn't mean a thing to me.

But he was here. I began to tremble. For seventeen hours I'd been on a blind trail, a trail which was ending here at five o'clock in the morning. Three times in those seventeen hours somebody had tried to kill me, and I felt the rage grow hot. It could be traced back to the wilderness; kill or be killed, eat or be eaten. Elemental emotion, primitive. I tried to grin, to rationalize everything, but it was no good. I couldn't forget the sound of the bullets, the feel of them, and something seemed to coil and uncoil in my stomach.

I walked swiftly around the house to the small front porch. I didn't bother to look down the road again, and I banged loudly on the door. Without waiting for a response, I turned the knob. The door swung open and Eileen Fortune stood staring at me. Her face was still puffy, her eyes still red, but she had combed her blond hair, and put on a frilly pink robe over the faded nightgown. Her bare feet were now covered with pink satin slippers edged with fluffy white fur. Behind her Earl Seltzman got furtively up from the divan. His heavy red coat hung over a chair.

He started to speak, but Eileen's wailing voice drowned him out. "He's dead! You've come to tell me!"

I gazed at her with distaste. Apparently she thought that my sole purpose in life was to keep her informed about the condition of her betrothed. With one eye on Seltzman, I said, "He's probably dying— maybe dead by now."

She dug her fists into her eyes and began to sob wildly, a gasping unpleasant sound. Seltzman strode to her, grasped her by one arm. "Stop it!" he shouted, jerking her arm. "You said you didn't care if Ralph lived or died, that you'd marry me."

She kept on sobbing. He shook her arm some more, and she twisted her body, gasping, her mouth open, trying to free herself. He attempted to pull her to him, to embrace her, and he uttered some muttering sounds that made no sense to me. Apparently they had both forgotten my presence.

"Can't you wait?" Eileen sobbed. "Can't you be decent? You could let me alone until Ralph is buried." She struggled in his embrace, and he tried to force her to him, his glasses glinting wickedly.

"Let her go," I said.

He looked at me over her head. "She's hysterical," he panted. "She doesn't know what she's—"

I slapped him then, and I didn't worry about his glasses. The crack of my palm against his cheek was loud in the room. His head jerked sideways, and he lost his grip on Eileen, who stumbled to a chair and sat sobbing with her hands over her face. Seltzman turned slowly, his thin face contorted, like a kid about to cry. He assumed a ridiculous fighting pose with both fists raised, and he shrilled something and started for me. "Remember your glasses," I said.

He kept coming. I kicked him in the stomach, not too hard. It was hard enough. He doubled over, gasping. I raised my fist, intending to bat him behind the ear. But I paused. Suddenly it wasn't fun. I wasn't enjoying it, after all, and I was bitterly disappointed. I had been looking forward to this moment, and now it was nothing. But he was game. He came for me again, breathing hard. I held him off with a hand on his thin chest and caught his wild swings with a forearm. Then I crowded him, pushed him back to the divan, and shoved. He went down, struggled to get up.

"Stay," I said.

He stared up at me, his thin mouth working. "Damn . . . you . . ." He pushed upward.

I raised my fist. He sank back, his eyes glaring hate. "Brute strength," he panted. "I—I can't fight you."

"You tried, sonny. That's all anybody can do. Let's talk a little."

"Why should I talk to you?" he said bitterly. "You, you . . ." He took a deep shuddering breath. "I—I can't stand it anymore."

"Can't stand what?"

He moved his hands wildly. "This. You. All of it."

"You shot Ralph Hollis, didn't you? Because you hated him for taking your girl away from you, because with Ralph out of the way you could have her back. Isn't that right, Earl?"

"Is Ralph dead?" he asked in a dull voice.

"I don't know, but Rex Bishop is dead. It's murder, Earl—maybe two murders. Rex surprised you shooting at me, and you had to kill him, to keep him quiet. You tried to kill me, because you saw me snooping around the ravine, and you knew I was suspicious."

"No," he whispered, his chin trembling.

I clenched a fist, involuntarily, and the rage began to burn again. "Why did you run out on me at Dan's Place last night, and then wait in the alley, and—?"

"No, no," he said hoarsely. "Listen—"

"Shut up." I was almost shouting. "You shot at me again in front of your house, and you followed me in your car with the lights off, waiting for another chance, and you turned on the gas in Judy Kirkland's bedroom and typed a confession note for her, and you—"

"Stop!" he cried shrilly. "I—I—" His thin pale hands fluttered, and he seemed to be having trouble breathing.

"Talk," I said from between clenched teeth, and I raised my fist. "Damn you, talk."

Behind me I heard Eileen's voice. "Forgive him," she pleaded. "Don't blame Earl."

I turned. She was standing now, the frilly pink robe hanging open, her hands clasped before her. "Earl sinned for me," she said passionately. "It was wrong of him to do that to Ralph, but I am to blame. Earl sinned because of carnal desires, and I tempted him. I am guilty of false pride and vanity. I promised to be Earl's wife and then I broke my promise and became engaged to Ralph, not for love, but because it gave me pleasure to take Ralph away from Judy. I—I hated Judy, you see. I have always hated her. And poor Earl, he did not understand, and he—he killed, because of me. I am the guilty one."

I gazed at her a little uneasily.

There was a small sound behind me, and I turned. Earl Seltzman was staring at Eileen with a look of incredulous horror. He pointed a finger and stuttered, "S-s-she—"

"Never mind, Earl," I told him. "I'll call the sheriff, and you can tell him all about it."

"Tell him, Earl," Eileen pleaded. "Confess. I'll be by your side."

He stared at her blankly, his thin mouth working. There was saliva on his chin.

I said, "Earl, everything adds up. You knew that we all were going hunting yesterday morning, and so you took to the woods, too. You saw us head for the ravine and you waited on the hill across from the ravine, and on a level with the crest. You also saw Judy down in the thicket, or maybe you didn't see her. It doesn't matter. When Ralph reached the top of the ravine, you fired at him and then ducked. Judy fired, too, at a pheasant, but her shot did not hit Ralph. She was standing directly below him, and the shotgun charge which struck Ralph slanted horizontally across his chest. If Judy had hit him, the torn grooves in his jacket would have been vertical, because she fired from below—I saw her climbing up the side of the ravine immediately afterward. You counted on it being called a hunting accident, didn't you?"

"No," he said in a choked voice. "I—I didn't mean for Ralph to be killed—"

"You were scared afterward, weren't you, Earl?" I broke in. "You hung around, out of sight, to see what went on. At noon you saw me coming across the fields. You ran to your farm and got a rifle—or maybe you had it with you—and you saw me at the spot where you'd shot Ralph. You knew then, for certain, that I was on your trail. So you shot at me, and I dropped. You thought you had killed me. But old Rex Bishop, fixing a fence down in the bottom, had seen you. He approached you, accused you, and you had to kill him. That was the second shot I heard. Then you went away, started drinking, and came to the ravine later in the afternoon, to the scene of your killings. Rex was still where he'd fallen, but I was very much alive and digging your bullet from the tree. That shocked you, and you would have made certain that I was dead—if I hadn't taken your shotgun. You went away, and you brooded and worried. When I found you in the poker game, you became more worried. I was hounding you, and you had to get rid of me. You gave the men a story about my being an insurance salesman, and they stalled for you. You sneaked out, hid in the alley, and when I came out, you tried once more and missed. You hung around, followed me. When I stopped at your house, you tried again and missed again. But you stayed on my tail." I paused, watching him.

He gulped and said shrilly, "It's crazy. I didn't do any of that."

"Don't lie, Earl," I said gently. "You followed me to Route 20, to the truck stop, and back again. When you saw that I was headed for Eileen's house, you circled around, got here ahead of me, to make me think you'd been here all the time." I turned to Eileen. "How long has he been here?"

"Forgive him," she intoned. "Please."

I peered at her, saw the odd flat look in her eyes. She seemed to be in a kind of daze, and maybe I should have slapped her out of it, but I didn't. Instead, I said to Seltzman, "How did you manage to lock Judy's door from the inside, after you turned on the gas?"

His thin body twitched, and his tongue kept darting in and out of his mouth, over his prominent teeth. His face held a waxy pallor, and he stared at Eileen like a man transfixed. And suddenly he spoke in a rising voice, like a woman on the edge of hysteria. "She don't know what she's saying! Don't you listen to her!"

"Never mind," I said wearily. "You can tell the sheriff. She can tell him, too."

"Sheriff?" he mumbled.

"Yes," I said, feeling suddenly a deadly fatigue. "Murder is not permitted by law. I'm sorry as hell."

Eileen's voice rose in anguish. "Oh, Earl!"

I turned my head, and that moment, from the corner of my eye, I saw Seltzman make a stealthy movement toward the front door. I shouted to him to stand still. He kept moving, faster, scurrying along the wall. I started for him. Eileen flung herself against me. "Let him go!" she cried. "Take me! I'm the guilty one. I led Earl on, I tempted him...."

I pushed her away from me. She stumbled to the floor and crouched there, on her hands and knees, her yellow hair falling over her face. Seltzman was reaching for the door knob, and I said, "Hold it, Earl. Don't be a fool."

He swung toward me, his back against the door, and he cried in a wild shrill voice, "I'm not going with the sheriff! You can't make me!"

"But I can," I said softly.

He began to sob, his eyes squeezed shut, his mouth puckered, an ugly sight. I decided that he and Eileen made a good pair. Both were emotionally unstable, and probably immature. A small-town Sunday school teacher, who was having her brief moment of glory; a shy and sensitive and sullen man, who should have maybe been a poet or a painter, but had forsaken his yearnings, probably because of parental domination, for animal husbandry and agriculture. I shuddered a little and thought that it was very unfortunate that Ralph Hollis had happened to catch Judy Kirkland in bed with a casual writer friend. On the rebound he'd become engaged to Eileen Fortune, leaving Earl Seltzman out in the cold, and frustrated and bitter. If none of it had happened, Judy would have married Ralph, Eileen and Earl would have spoken the vows, and everybody would have been happy. Maybe.

"Earl," I said, "are you going to behave while I call the sheriff, or will I have to beat the hell out of you?"

"Don't you touch me again," he said in a low desperate voice. "Don't you dare. I—I'll kill you."

I took a grim step toward him. He avoided my gaze, a sly look on his face, and his hand moved. Suddenly I was looking at a small blue automatic. I was dumfounded. I hadn't figured him for the kind to carry a pocket gun, but I should have known better. He was of the unpredictable type, the dangerous ones. I stood still, feeling the rage again, and the fear, too, the same fear I'd felt when he had faced me drunkenly with the double-barreled shotgun. He wasn't drunk now, but he was on the borderline of something, maybe the borderline of reason, and it would only take a little thing to make him squeeze the trigger.

Eileen moaned, "Don't kill again, Earl, please, please...."

He stared at her, the horror again in his eyes and he said in a strangled voice, "Don't talk like that. It's crazy."

"I forgive you," she crooned. "Earl, my darling, it was always you. I never loved Ralph. You know I never loved him, that it was you. Please put down that nasty gun. We'll face it together, side by side."

But he was watching me. He couldn't hear her anymore. I took a step closer, so that I could reach him in one dive, if I had to, and I kept my gaze on the gun. It never wavered, and I didn't like that. Suddenly he sighed, a deep hopeless sigh, and his face took on a slack stupid look, and it seemed to me that his eyes behind the rimless glasses held no expression whatever. He had been fighting something, a dark, secret something, but it was over now, and he was at the end of his rope.

"All right, Earl," I said soothingly. "Use your head. Give me the gun." I held out a hand and took another step forward.

And I stopped.

The gun barrel moved a half inch, and it bore directly on the pit of my stomach. His thin lips pushed in and out over his teeth and he braced himself against the door.

"Earl!" Eileen screamed. "No, no!"

I wanted to jump for him, to reach for my own gun, to yell at him, to do anything, but I stood rooted. He began to tremble, and I saw his finger grow white on the trigger. There wasn't time for anything, not anymore.

There was a sudden slamming sound. I heard Eileen's crazy cracked scream, and I felt sick and I wondered when the pain would start. But there wasn't any pain, and I realized suddenly that the sound had been a car door slamming just outside the door. Earl Seltzman moved his eyes, for just an instant, and I jumped for him, got the gun, wrenched it from his fingers, and brought my fist up against his angular jaw. He hit the floor without a sound, and I dragged him away from the door.

Footsteps sounded on the porch, and the door opened. Behind me Eileen gasped, "Papa!"

When I looked up, she was in the embrace of Jake Fortune.

CHAPTER SIXTEEN

I stared at him stupidly. His heavy red face beneath the cream-colored hat held a sober and serious look as he gazed at Earl Seltzman on the floor. Then his gray yes, wide-spaced, like his daughter's, met mine over her shoulder, and silently asked a question.

"Papa, Papa," Eileen sobbed, and he held her close.

"I had to hit him," I said. "He pulled a gun on me, and he was jittery and ready to shoot. Thanks for slamming your car door. It gave me a chance to jump him." I stood up wearily.

Jake Fortune frowned. "Earl pulled a gun on you? Why?"

"Papa," Eileen sobbed. He patted her shoulder.

"You may as well know," I said. "He shot Ralph Hollis—on purpose— and he killed Rex Bishop, because the old man caught him shooting at me."

His frown deepened. "But I thought that Judy—"

"She's out of it," I said, and I looked around for the telephone. "I've got to get the sheriff out here."

Eileen left her father's arms and knelt beside Earl Seltzman. Her fingers caressed his thin slack face as she murmured, "It's all right, darling, don't you worry."

Jake Fortune gazed at me bleakly. "So Earl really tried to kill Ralph?"

"I'll tell you about it later. Where's the phone?"

"In the kitchen." He shook his head and swore softly.

"Watch him," I said.

He nodded.

The phone was on a shelf above the kitchen sink. I asked for Sheriff John Morrissy and got him almost immediately.

"This is Jim Bennett."

"Yes," he said quietly.

"Haven't you gone to bed yet?"

"I'm in bed now. The phone's right beside me."

"End of the hunt," I said. "It was Earl Seltzman. You can forget about going to Cleveland. Earl will have a rifle some place, and it'll match the bullet I dug out of the tree, and the bullet in Rex Bishop. I've got Earl out here at Jake Fortune's place."

The line was dead for a moment, and then I heard him sigh. "I see," he said in his grave, quiet voice. "I'll be right out."

"Thanks." I hung up and looked at the gun I'd taken from Earl Seltzman. It was a .25 caliber Colt. The clip was full, with a cartridge in the firing chamber. I put it in my overcoat pocket, along with my own .38, and went back to the living room.

Seltzman was sitting in a chair, leaning forward with his forehead in a palm. There was a bluish spot on the side of his jaw, and it appeared to be swelling. I rubbed my knuckles reflectively. Eileen was standing beside him, a hand on his shoulder, a maternal tender look on her face. Jake Fortune hadn't moved from his spot by the door. He said, "It's cold in here. I'd better go down and stir up the fire." As he moved across the room, he said to his daughter, "Eileen, make us some coffee." He went out through the kitchen, and I heard him going down some steps. Eileen left Seltzman's side and moved into the kitchen. She didn't look at me.

"Earl," I asked, "where's the rifle?"

He didn't answer.

"The rifle, Earl."

"I don't have a rifle," he muttered.

"You may as well tell me," I said. "We'll find it anyhow, and you'll save the sheriff a lot of trouble. Just tell him the whole thing, Earl. It'll be easier that way—for you, for everybody."

"You can't arrest me," he said sullenly.

"Yes, we can."

"I want a lawyer," he said.

"All right."

"I'll talk to him," he said, "and nobody else. Franklin Hoffman, in Cleveland."

"The sheriff will get him for you. I'm sorry I had to hit you again, but you shouldn't have pulled a gun on me."

He took a deep breath. "I—I didn't know what I was doing. Between the two of you, Eileen and you, I—I lost my head, I guess. I didn't intend to shoot you. I just wanted to scare you, to keep you away from me. I wanted time to think about what you said, and what Eileen said, and—oh, God...." He began to sob, a dry rasping sound.

Dimly below me I could hear Jake Fortune shaking the ashes out of the furnace. Eileen was making domestic sounds in the kitchen. Presently I smelled coffee brewing, and Eileen came into the room. She went past me, paused long enough to gently rest a hand on Seltzman's head, and then went up the stairway. Seltzman, quiet now, took off his glasses and began to wipe them with a handkerchief. His thin face looked naked and pinched, rodent-like, and he avoided my gaze. I heard Jake Fortune come up the basement steps, and his voice came from the kitchen, "Coffee's ready."

"In a minute," I said.

I heard a car stop outside, and I got up and opened the door for the sheriff. His grave eyes glanced at Earl, and then at me directly. "I'm taking your word for this."

"I'll be responsible," I said, handing him Seltzman's little automatic. "Assault with intent to kill. That's enough to book him. I'll be down later. He wants his lawyer—a man named Franklin Hoffman in Cleveland."

Morrissy nodded and spoke gently to Seltzman, "Come on, Earl."

"Can you handle him alone?" I asked.

"He won't cause any trouble. I've known Earl all my life."

From the kitchen Jake Fortune said quietly, "Hello, John."

The sheriff nodded, tight-lipped, said, "How are you, Jake?" and laid a hand gently on Seltzman's shoulder.

Earl got slowly to his feet, picked up his heavy red coat from the chair, and moved to the door, not looking at any of us. The sheriff said, "Better put on your coat, Earl. It's cold out."

Obediently Seltzman hunched into the coat. Morrissy opened the door. Eileen Fortune came down the stairs. She was wearing the bluish tweed suit with the frilly white blouse, and was carrying a coat over her arm. She had applied lipstick to her small thin-lipped mouth, her blond hair was smoothly combed, and she looked quite attractive, in spite of the red puffiness of her eyes. She said to Morrissy, "I want to go with him."

"All right, Eileen," he said gravely, "if you like."

Seltzman stood woodenly, his head down.

I said to the sheriff, "His car's around in back."

"I'll send somebody for it." The three of them went out, Eileen and Earl first, the sheriff following. I closed the door and went into the kitchen.

Jake Fortune sat at a table drinking coffee. He had taken off his camel's hair overcoat and unbuttoned the collar of his flannel shirt. I said, "Eileen went with him."

"I heard. Kids do crazy things. She and Earl figured on getting married, and then something happened. The first thing I knew, she was engaged to Ralph Hollis, and—"

"I know," I said.

He sipped at his coffee. "I didn't want to be in there when John Morrissy came. I've known Earl since he was a baby."

"Yes," I said dully.

"Take off your coat," Fortune said. "Sit down and tell me about it."

I poured some coffee. "It's a long story, and it's been a long night."

"For me, too," he said. "After I saw you at Dan's place, a farmer asked me to come out and look at a sick cow. I'm kind of a half-assed veterinary." He smiled faintly. "A midwife for cows, that's me. This cow was having trouble dropping a calf, but old Dr. Fortune pulled her through. Pretty little bull calf. Took me most of the night."

"You came home just in time," I said, sipping the hot black coffee. "I owe you a drink—or something."

"There's a bottle in the cupboard," he said.

I shook my head. "Not now."

"I hate it," he said, "about Earl. And Eileen. I didn't know that she cared about him anymore...." He drank more coffee. "But I can't interfere. She has to live her own life."

"Yes," I said, and I carried my coffee to the phone. "Excuse me," I said to Jake Fortune. I lit a cigarette, and asked for the Ridge Center hospital. To the female who answered, I said, "Is Miss Doyle busy?"

"Yes, she is—oh, just a minute." I heard her call, "Mary Lou," and then she said, "She was just passing the desk—here she is."

A soft cool voice said, "Yes."

"This is the friend of Ralph Hollis."

"Who?"

"The man who gave you twenty dollars."

"Oh, yes." There was a lilt in her voice, and she remembered me very well.

"How is he?" I gripped the receiver, prepared for the worst.

"Oh, much, much better!" Her voice seemed to sing. "We're all so happy about it. His temperature is going down at last, and he's breathing easier. Dr. Mazzini says he'll be all right now."

"Good. Is Dr. Mazzini there now?"

"No, he left a short time ago, as soon as he knew that Ralph was past the crisis. Dr. Mazzini has been wonderful."

"Thanks, Mary Lou," I said, and hung up. "Ralph's going to be all right," I told Jake Fortune.

"Well," he said dryly, "that's one good thing that's happened tonight. Ralph's a good steady boy, and he and my daughter—" He stopped abruptly, remembering, no doubt, that his daughter had gone with Earl Seltzman to the jail house.

I picked up the phone again and asked for the residence of Miss Judy Kirkland. I waited for ten rings before an old thin voice said, "Hello, hello."

I knew then that the operator had given me the Kirkland farm, the home of Judy's maiden aunts. "I'm sorry," I said, "I was calling Judy, and—"

The old thin voice said shrilly, "Judith is not here."

"I know. I'm sorry."

"I will have you know that it is six o'clock in the morning here in Ohio. I suppose you are calling from Miami or Los Angeles, and did not realize?"

"No, ma'am," I said. "I did not realize."

"In the future," the voice said coldly, "please call Judith at her place on River Road. She spends very little time here."

"Yes, ma'am."

"What is your name, sir?"

"Doakes," I said. "Joseph."

"You must be Judith's writer friend. I read your last book, sir, and found it most objectionable. I suppose it sold very well?"

"Five million copies," I said. "And Metro bought the movie rights."

"You writers would sell your souls for money, would you not?"

"Yes, ma'am. Body *and* soul. I'm sorry to have disturbed you. Good-bye." I hung up, quickly.

"Wrong number," Jake Fortune said.

I grinned at him, and lifted the phone once more. When the operator answered, I said, "Miss Judy Kirkland, on *River Road*, please."

She said stiffly, "The number, sir, is—"

"Never mind the number. Just ring her."

She rang her. No answer. I waited through innumerable rings before I hung up. I looked blankly at Jake Fortune. "That's funny."

"What?"

Once more I lifted the phone, asked for the Homer Hollis place. Sandy answered right away. "Jim, I knew it was you."

"Good news about Ralph," I said.

"You heard?"

"Yes. I called the hospital. It's wonderful news. Where's Judy?"

"Dr. Mazzini came and took her away."

"When?"

"Oh, maybe a half hour ago."

"Was she awake?"

"No. He wrapped her in a blanket and said he was taking her to the hospital, and carried her out to his car, and drove away. I locked up her house and came home."

"They're not at the hospital."

"Then where are they? Where did they go?"

"I don't know. Go to bed, Sandy. I'll be out there pretty soon."

"Jim, where are you? What have you been doing?"

"Never mind, for now."

"Jim, I—"

"Get some rest, Sandy." And once more I hung up.

CHAPTER SEVENTEEN

I stared at Jake Fortune.

"You look like you need that drink," he said.

"No."

Through the window I saw that the night was beginning to turn gray. The morning would soon be here, and there was nothing more that I could do. My anger was gone and I had a taste of ashes in my mouth, and I wasn't very proud of myself. I had stalked a mortal enemy, because I'd been afraid and wanted to live, and because there had been the rage, the desire to fight back. My motives had been purely selfish and personal, except at the very beginning, when I'd gone alone back to the ravine, to see what I could see at the spot where Ralph had been wounded. But even then my motive had been largely curiosity, and habit, resulting from years of investigation work. I was glad that Ralph was going to live, but nothing I had done had helped him. Dr. Mazzini and modern medicine could take the credit for Ralph's life. But old Rex Bishop was dead, and nothing could help him. Maybe he was happier now, and I hoped he was. But he might have lived a little longer, enjoyed the small things in life that pleased him. I didn't know what the old man liked; his pipe, maybe, a good dinner, a soft bed, a drink of whisky, memories of the women he'd known when he was young, his guns, the slow talk of cronies around a fire, yellow wheat waving in a field, the rustling of tall corn stalks, the morning sun....

But I knew with a kind of ashamed sadness that from the moment the bullet had hit the beech tree beside my head, my motives for doing what I had done had been selfish. It had been a silent hatred for an unknown enemy, and there had been fear, too, but the hatred and the selfish rage, had kept me from running back to Cleveland. And then I thought suddenly and bitterly that if I had gone back home and had let things alone, Rex Bishop would still be alive. If I hadn't gone back to the ravine, Earl Seltzman would never have shot at me; Rex Bishop would never have seen Earl shoot at me. He would not have accused Earl of shooting at me, and Rex would still be alive.

It was a hell of a thought, a terrible thought, and it was true. What had I gained? Ralph Hollis would have lived anyhow. I had merely tracked down and caught the man who had tried to kill him. Justice would be done, at the cost of Rex Bishop's life, but there were many murderers, and would-be murderers, running around loose in the world. Earl Seltzman would probably never try to kill again, but who can tell about that? And what difference did it make in the whole scheme of things? Because of me, Rex Bishop was dead.

The taste of ashes was very bitter, and I said to Jake Fortune, "I think I'll have that drink, after all."

"Right behind you," he said, and added, "I'll have one, too."

I opened the cupboard, took out a bottle of bourbon that was more than half full, and placed it on the table. Then I got two glasses and sat down.

Fortune said, "Ice? Water?"

I shook my head, poured whisky into the glasses. Both of us drank it straight, and between drinks I stared at the amber lights on my glass. I didn't talk, and neither did Jake Fortune, and we took turns filling the glasses. It was like a wake, and it would not have been difficult for me to believe that the corpse of Rex Bishop was in a flower-banked coffin in the next room.

At last Jake Fortune began to talk. In a slow quiet voice he told me about his years of farming, his marriage, the death of his wife, his experiences in World War I as a supply sergeant in Alabama, about cattle, crops, and the weather. I didn't mind, and I only half listened, realizing that somehow he knew what I felt. There were questions he wanted to ask me, I was sure of that, but he didn't ask them, and I was grateful.

His voice droned on, and I stared out of the window. Daylight now, with the hint of a red sun behind the distant woods. Whisky for breakfast, I thought, and will Eileen teach her Sunday school class this morning?

Jake Fortune said, "It's morning."

A thin shaft of cold pale sunlight hit the brown bottle between us and I saw that the bottle was empty, as empty and as drained as I felt in my mind and heart. He was just an old man, I told myself, and he would have died soon anyhow. Snap out of it, Bennett. Get on your feet and go to the Hollis farm and go to bed. Sleep a while and forget, and go back to Cleveland with Sandy, back where you belong. You've done enough damage here and *why did he have to wrap her in a blanket and take her away in the middle of the night?*

I looked at Jake Fortune. There was a gray stubble on his broad red face and his gray, wide-spaced eyes were bloodshot. He looked old and tired and worn out, the way I would look in another ten or fifteen years, maybe the way I looked now. "Go to bed, Jake," I said. "Don't mind me."

He gave me a tight smile, and he said, a little thickly, "I guess I'm a little drunk."

"Me, too." I pulled a hand down over my face, felt the stubble on my own cheeks, and I asked the bottle, "Why did he do that?"

"Who do what?" Jake Fortune said.

"Doc Mazzini. He took her away. Wrapped her in a blanket and whisked her away. To the hospital, he said. But they didn't go to the hospital."

"Who did he whisk?"

"Judy Kirkland."

"A hell of a note," Jake Fortune said. "I wish we had more whisky."

"I wish, too," I said, and I looked at the bottle. It seemed to dance up and down, and a small angry voice was screaming at me. It was as if the voice belonged to the bottle and it was trying to tell me something. I listened attentively. The bottle was brown, the color of new Springtime beer, and inside it two midget farmers were standing at a midget bar and one of them peered at me over his beer glass. He was saying something, but I couldn't hear him, and I mumbled, "Damn it, talk louder."

Jake Fortune said, "Wake up, Bennett."

I regarded him through half-closed eyes. I knew that I had dozed off, that I had been dreaming, and I tried to remember when I'd slept last. My eyes drooped, and the little farmers at the midget bar inside the bottle were still there, and a tiny little voice was coming to me across a vast windy plateau, and there was a lovely background of Bunny Berigan's music. I heard the voice then, clear and bell-like, above the muted brass, and it was saying, *Jake, I saw you over on Seltzman's place around supper time . . . around supper time . . . around supper time....* It was like a record trapped in a groove.

I opened my eyes wide. It was an effort, but I kept them open. Jake Fortune sat easily, a loose smile on his heavy mouth. I said, "Jake, how did you make out in Cleveland yesterday?"

He lifted his thick shoulders. "Not so good. A bank there is putting the squeeze on me."

"We all have troubles," I said. "Too bad you had to leave the hunting party yesterday morning. I'll bet you were pretty surprised when you got home last night and heard about Ralph Hollis and Rex Bishop."

He stopped smiling, and something seemed to shift and move behind his eyes. "Yes, I was," he said.

"Let's see," I said, "it was around eight-thirty last night when you came to the hospital, wasn't it?"

"Around there." He stirred in his chair.

"And you'd just got back from Cleveland?"

"That's right. But what—?"

"What's that farmer's name?" I broke in. "The one with the pregnant cow—where you spent most of the night?"

"Albert McCrory."

"Has he got a phone?"

"No, he hasn't. What're you getting at, Bennett?"

"Let's take a ride out to Albert McCrory's and have a little talk with him," I suggested.

"I don't get it," he said. There was sweat on his forehead. He took one of the yellow pencils from his shirt pocket, one of the pencils that had no doubt been in his pocket the first time I'd met him at Homer Hollis' house, and he began to tap it on the table top.

"I just want to ask Albert McCrory if you were really there," I said.

"Goddamn it, what's wrong with you? You *must* be drunk."

"Only a little, Jake," I said. "Not near drunk enough." I was looking at the pencil in his hand, and in my mind I was again in Judy's Kirkland's bedroom peering at a key, and at a tiny yellow fleck on the inside of the ring end of the key. All of the events from Friday evening until now, this cold bright Sunday morning, seemed to swirl wildly, like the snow in an old-time glass paperweight, and everything drifted down and settled and all of it was there for me to see.

It had been there all the time, but I had let my anger and my fear blind me, and I had gone on the prod for the obvious one, the one who in my mind had the most to gain. I had been all wrong, and I was sorry. This was my day for regrets. I didn't have it all, but I had most of it, and the knowledge made me a little sick.

I said, "Jake, it was you, and not Earl Seltzman, but you were willing to let him take the blame for it."

He gazed at me for a long moment, and then he smiled, the most humorless smile I'd ever seen.

CHAPTER EIGHTEEN

The sun had climbed higher and now a shaft of it fell across the table between us like a glittering white blade. Jake Fortune's gray eyes held a vacant faraway look, as if he were musing over the years gone by and all the mistakes that make up every man's life.

I said, "Tell me about it, Jake—or would you rather wait and tell the sheriff?"

He swung his slow gaze toward me. "What difference does it make?"

"Not much," I said. "Your alibis are no good; you were not in

Cleveland at all yesterday, and you were not being midwife to a cow last night. One of those farmers in the bar last night spiked your Cleveland story by saying he had seen you at Earl Seltzman's farm around supper time. And you left tracks. There'll be fingerprints, somewhere, and the rifle you used. It'll make it easier if you talk."

"It won't make it easier for me," he said.

"No," I admitted, "it won't. Murder is murder."

He sighed. "This—none of this would have happened, if Earl had loaned me the money I need. I'm in a jam with a stock syndicate in Cleveland. I sold a herd and I didn't pay off. I needed the money for—for other obligations. They gave me until tomorrow. Earl said he would give me the money, if I would talk Eileen into marrying him. I think she likes Earl well enough, but it was a hell of a thing for a father to do. I did it, or tried to. But women are damned funny. She refused to break off with Ralph Hollis, but she did say that if it weren't for Ralph, she'd marry Earl. I got the idea then, but I went the limit and told her about the money jam, and I'm damned if she didn't say if I had sinned, I would have to pay for my sins. Me, her father. And she said it as cool and prim as hell. Maybe she was right, but it rocked me." He paused, gazed out of the window, and then back at me. "So you see what I had to do then."

"Get rid of Ralph," I said.

He nodded slowly. "I thought about it all Friday night, and I couldn't see any other way out. I thought about it so much, I guess I went a little crazy. The Saturday morning hunting party seemed to be the answer to everything, but when I learned that you were a detective I got scared and almost gave it up. Then I got brave again, with the help of a bottle, and figured I could get away with it. So, after we went out yesterday morning, I suggested that we split up, figuring I could sneak away and get a shot at Ralph. With so many hunters around, it would be called an accident, especially if nobody could tell who fired the shot. With Ralph gone, Eileen would marry Earl, and I'd have the money. It would have worked, too, if it hadn't been for you." He gazed at me steadily, and something ugly began to build up in his eyes.

"Yes," I said. "So you faked a telephone call, sneaked back out, saw us heading for the ravine, planted yourself on the hill, and when Ralph showed, you let loose. Judy Kirkland happened to be down below, in the thicket, and that helped—"

"Don't hash it all over," he said wearily. "I heard what you told

Earl. I followed you around tonight, not Earl, and after you stopped here I parked down below the hill and came into the kitchen and I heard it all. Then I went back out to my car, drove up to the house, and came in."

"Poor Earl," I said sadly.

"To hell with him," he said bitterly.

"He's not such a bad guy," I said gently. "He tried to protect you, and your daughter, whom he madly loves. He had a problem, and he wasn't talking, not until he knew the score. When Eileen heard me accuse him of trying to kill Ralph, she believed me, thought he had really done it—for her. That almost drove Earl crazy, trying to figure it out. For all he knew, Eileen might have been mixed up in it, too. He—"

"Hell, no," Jake Fortune said harshly. "Earl knew the score. Right after I saw you carry Ralph away, I guessed that he was still alive, and I began to run. I met Earl, and I lost my head, and I told him what I'd had to do—because he wouldn't loan me the money. I told him that I'd swear I'd seen him shoot Ralph, out of jealousy, and because he wanted Eileen. The whole country knows that she jilted him for Ralph. I told him that you might come snooping around, and to watch the ravine—I didn't want to take a chance on being seen there. Then I left him, got a rifle, and waited behind a rail fence out back where I could watch the ravine. At noon you showed up, began your damned poking around, and I took a shot at you." With his left hand, he lifted the empty bottle. "All gone," he said.

I said, "And Rex Bishop, fixing a fence in the bottom, saw you shoot at me, and he came up to you and asked questions—and you shot him."

"I never saw the old bastard. I was watching you. He came walking fast up along the fence, and he was mad. He knew I'd shot at you, because he told me he'd been watching all along. He began to shout at me, and he pointed at the ravine, and—oh, Christ. I always liked old Rex, but I had to shoot him, to keep him quiet."

I shivered, thinking of all the things that made a person kill, and I said, "Jake, there's a woman, I suppose?"

His heavy mouth went loose, and he gave me a boastful grin, "Two women, by God, and I'm fifty-six years old." He leered at me lewdly. "A blonde in Cleveland, and a brunette in Toledo. They cost me a hell of a lot of money."

"I'll bet," I said. "When did you get the idea about Judy Kirkland?

When I told you in Dan's Place that she blamed herself, that she was drinking heavily, and did not want to face Ralph's folks?"

"That gave me the idea," he admitted, smiling at me. "There was no harm in trying. I went out to her place. The lights were on, and it was wide open. I found her upstairs on the bed, passed out. I locked the windows, rigged a pencil with a cord tied to it, and stuck it in the key. I read it some place, and it worked." He fingered his empty glass, smiling remotely, remembering his cleverness.

"It's an old trick," I said. "You ran the cord from the pencil under the door, turned the key until the bolt was almost ready to click shut, closed the door and pulled the cord. The pencil acted as a lever and flipped the key over, locking the door from the inside. The pencil fell to the floor, and you pulled it out under the door. I saw the yellow speck on the key last night, but I didn't tumble until now that it was paint from one of your damned pencils. You couldn't be certain of what Earl Seltzman would do, so you tried to frame Judy, too."

He tossed the pencil he'd been holding across the table. "Maybe that's the one I used," he said.

"There'll be dents in it, from the pressure on the key," I said.

"Why don't you look at it and see?" he invited.

I let the pencil lay and watched him. "And then you typed the suicide note on Judy's typewriter."

"With one finger."

I thought of old Rex Bishop, and of Judy, too. She would have died if I hadn't found her as I did. Maybe, for me, in the final scoring, the one life would cancel out the other. I hoped so, and I said, "You followed me to Dan's Place, knowing that I was looking for Earl Seltzman, because I'd been to his house. You went in ahead of me, warned Earl that I was hunting for him. He ducked out the back door, after telling his poker pals that I was a pesky insurance salesman, and to cover for him. He was already leery of me, because I'd slapped him around a little, and he didn't know what you were up to. You knew that I would guess that Earl had scooted out the back door, that I would come out that way, too, and you waited behind the can in the alley, and—" I stopped, remembering the sound of the bullets.

"I'm a rotten shot," he said. "Always have been." The blade of sunlight had moved to his face, highlighting the stubble on his cheeks. His gray, wide-spaced eyes held a blank, flat look, and his heavy mouth was slack. It seemed to me that we had been sitting there forever, and it suddenly occurred to me that he hadn't left his chair since I'd joined him, after the sheriff had left, and I realized that he had kept his right hand beneath the table.

"You missed me three times," I said.

"I won't miss now."

The fear returned, and I had a wild desire to jump up and run. But with the fear there was the rage, suddenly flaming, and at the same time another part of my brain cautioned me to be crafty, to induce him to delay the moment when he would decide to pull the trigger of the gun I knew he held beneath the table. "It won't work," I heard my voice saying. "They'll get you, Jake."

"Earl's car is out in back," he said. "The keys are in it and the tank is full. I checked, before I came in. The tires on my car are bad, but in Earl's car I can get a long way, maybe to Mexico. I've still got a couple of thousand in cash from the Cleveland cattle deal." He paused, and said in a whisper, "Buck up, Bennett." His teeth showed between his lips. "You can only die once."

I looked at him in the morning sunlight, in the peaceful quiet of the kitchen, and my soul began to whimper. There was still so much I wanted to do in this world, so many things, and I said, "Don't do it, Jake," but I knew that it was just a baby's cry in the wilderness. There was no time to get my gun, no time for anything, not even a prayer, and there was death in Jake Fortune's eyes, in the sudden brutal slant of his jaw; I heard it in his labored breathing.

Violently I pushed against the table, and my chair went backward. The bottle and glasses crashed to the floor, and the kitchen roared with the blast of his gun. It was as if a baseball had been thrown, quite hard, against my right side, above the belt. The impact made me gasp and I slammed on my back on the kitchen floor. My legs felt dead, but there was no pain.

Jake Fortune was on the floor, too, twisted sideways, the table on top of him. I clawed the .38 from my overcoat pocket, pushed myself to one elbow, tried to steady the gun. Fortune rolled clear of the table, and he fired as he rolled, the bullet splintering the wooden cabinet beside my head. I fired, my wrist wobbling, and I knew that I had missed. A flower pot on the window sill behind him flew to bits. He pushed himself upward, swaying on his knees. I had plenty of time to aim carefully. The kitchen seemed to jump with the muzzle blast and a little black hole appeared in Jake Fortune's shirt over his right shoulder. The impact rocked him, and his gun arm dangled limply.

"All right, Jake," I said. "You're done."

Grimacing, he grasped his right wrist with his left hand and he brought the gun up and around. I yelled, "No!" but he swung the gun toward me.

There was only a split second of time left, and I didn't have any choice. I shot him in the right eye.

The linoleum was slippery with our blood, Jake's and mine, and there was a giddy singing sound behind my eyes. I turned my head slowly, saw the telephone cord leading up from the bell box on the wall. I reached out a heavy hand and pulled on the cord. The phone tumbled off the shelf above to the floor beside me. I pulled the receiver toward me and I suppose I asked for Sheriff Morrissy.

Everything was white; the sunlight slanting through a window, the bed I was in, the gown I had on, the walls around me. Even my hands looked white against the sheet over me. I moved my fingers. I tried to move my legs, but I couldn't. It seemed as if the lower part of my body did not exist. There was no pain, no feeling of any kind. It was very strange.

Close beside me a soft voice said, "Hello, Jim."

I turned my head. Sandy sat there, the sunlight glinting on her bronze hair. There were tears on her face. She reached out and touched my hand. Her fingers felt cool and wonderful. Behind her stood the tall gaunt form of Homer Hollis. He smiled shyly.

"Hi, folks," my voice said.

An elderly gray-haired nurse came in. I closed my eyes. There were whispers, and Sandy's fingers left my hand. "You're fine, Jim," her voice said close to my ear. "Everything's fine. Sleep now." I felt her lips on my cheek. Presently I knew that she was gone.

I heard a faint clink of glass on metal. I opened my eyes. The nurse was at a steel table by the foot of the bed filling a hypo needle. I said, "What time is it?"

She smiled at me, glanced at a wrist watch. "Almost twelve o'clock noon."

"What day?"

"It's still Sunday."

I closed my eyes again, remembering that final and terrible scene in Jake Fortune's kitchen. I'd killed another man—how many now?

I tried not to think about it. "I want to see John Morrissy," I said.

"Later," the nurse said soothingly. "You've had a spinal, and a little ether, and you must rest now. Dr. Sweet will be here to see you before long."

"Where's Dr. Mazzini?"

"Nobody knows," she said. "He left a note last night for his landlady, Mrs. Brown, saying that he'd be gone for a day or two. It's rather odd for Dr. Mazzini to go away like that. Fortunately, Dr. Sweet—"

"Listen." I pushed myself up from the pillow.

"Now, now." She hovered over me. "We mustn't get excited." I felt the prick of the needle in my arm, and then the gentle pressure of her hands against my shoulders. I sank back and closed my eyes.

Sometime during the afternoon I awoke. The spinal anesthesia had worn off and my legs felt tingly and there was the beginning of pain in my side. Old Dr. Sweet came in, smelling strongly of whisky. He punched and probed, checked my bandages, looked at a chart, grunted, and barked at me, "Hurt yet?"

"A little."

"It will, it will. A forty-five slug. Just missed the lower duodenum. Goddamn lucky. Bowel wounds are hell, even with penicillin—don't let anybody tell you different."

"Where's Dr. Mazzini?" I asked, thinking vaguely that I'd asked it before.

"Skipped. Now I got the whole goddamn county to take care of."

"Thanks for taking care of me."

"You'll get a bill, don't worry." He went out.

The elderly nurse came in, gave me another hypo, and I slept some more. At dusk they brought me some soup and tea, and afterward I tried to sleep, but the pain was bad and I couldn't. Sheriff John Morrissy came. He talked to me, and I remembered his grave quiet voice saying something about Earl Seltzman, but it was all foggy. He went away. Sometime later on there was another hypo, and then blackness.

Sun again, the white walls. The pain was dull now. More tea and toast and a soft egg. Even a cigarette. And Sandy.

"I was here last night," she said, "but you were sleeping."

"Yes," I said. There was a happy shine in her brown eyes I'd never seen before.

"Do you feel better?"

"I feel fine."

"Dr. Mazzini's back with Judy. They went to Kentucky and got married. Isn't that wonderful?"

"Dandy."

"Judy called me. She was so happy she could hardly talk—because she's married to Dr. Mazzini, and because she hadn't shot Ralph. I guess the doctor just kind of kidnaped her. Cave man stuff." She laughed happily.

"He'll make her behave," I said. "What about Earl Seltzman and Eileen?"

She stopped laughing. "Eileen's taking her father's death pretty hard, and—" She paused, and gazed at me soberly.

"Don't be delicate," I said. "I killed him. I had to."

She touched my cheek. "I know, Jim. Nobody blames you. You're a hero in this town. After Earl talked with his lawyer from Cleveland, Earl told Mr. Morrissy all about it—about how Jake Fortune had told him what he tried to do to Ralph, and how he threatened Earl. Poor Earl went half crazy, I guess, trying to decide what to do about it. He loves Eileen, and Jake was her father, and when you accused Earl, Eileen helped it along because she really believed that Earl was guilty, that he had tried to kill Ralph because of her, and Earl didn't know what to do. Mr. Morrissy came out to the house and told us all about it. He found a rifle in the creek on Jake's place, and it matched the bullet you got from the tree, and the bullet that killed Rex Bishop, and Mr. Morrissy said there would be fingerprints, and he found an address book in Jake's pocket, and letters from two women—one in Toledo and one in Cleveland—asking him for money. And two men from Cleveland came to town looking for Jake, and Mr. Morrissy said that Jake had stolen money from these two men, and there was a lot of money in Jake's pockets—"

"I know," I said. "Tell me about Eileen."

"I talked to her. Her father's funeral will be on Tuesday. She and Earl are getting married soon afterward."

"How's Ralph? How does he feel about all this?"

"He's fine. They say we can bring him home the last of the week. I don't think he felt too badly about Eileen. He didn't say much about it, but I'm sure he never really loved her. It was just that Judy—" She smiled at me. "Ralph will be all right. He's got big plans for the farm, he and Dad."

I thought about Earl Seltzman and Eileen Fortune. Earl could help her with her Sunday school lessons, and they would probably have at least six children. I hoped that none of them would inherit Earl's prominent teeth. And Judy Kirkland and Dr. Mazzini would be fine together. They would love passionately, and quarrel passionately, and he would slap her around when she needed it.

I said, "You'd better call the boss in New York. Tell him I fell off a bar stool or something."

"I've already called him," Sandy said. "He swore horribly—because there isn't any fee."

"Didn't he express any concern about me?"

She laughed and her eyes danced. "He said you were a simple-minded fool for risking your neck when there was no money in it for the agency."

"Yes," I sighed.

"But he ordered me to report it as an agency job—so that your hospital and medical expense will be paid under the state occupational compensation laws," Sandy said.

"That's real kind of him."

Sandy laughed again and I looked at her. "There are stars in your eyes," I said. "Why is that?"

Her eyes avoided mine, but the stars were still there. "Because Ralph's going to get well," she said softly, "and—and you're all right." She touched my hand. "I guess I'm just happy, Jim. Aren't you?"

"Sure," I said, and I thought that everybody was happy, except Rex Bishop and Jake Fortune.

And maybe they were happy, too.

THE END

THE WIDOW AND THE WEB

Robert Martin

For Barbara

CHAPTER ONE

The river was not the Ohio, but it was almost as wide and much muddier. The yellow water, deepened by the April thaws from the hills, rolled thickly in the rain beneath the King William Street bridge, which linked Steel City's main business section and a grimy area which dwindled at last to the beginnings of the hills and the small blackened miners' shacks. The state highway wound through the hills and up to the plateau beyond and the country north. Route signs told me that the highway followed King William Street through the city, but Royal Street, as the hotel clerk had said, was two blocks from the bridge, a narrow brick-paved street choked with dingy bars and beer spots, their dirty front windows showing identical closed Venetian blinds.

There was also a succession of store fronts with a variety of merchandise on display behind murky panes; used television sets with ten inch screens, parakeets and gold fish, musical instruments and popular records at bargain prices, drugs and patent medicines, wine, beer and Choice Liquors, men's suits at One Half Off, groceries and meats, surgical appliances with Trusses Fitted by Our Experts, watches and diamond rings (You Name Your Terms), a glittering stack of auto accessories, from studded fender flaps to Cadillac fins and imitation Buick portholes.

Between the stores were occasional frame houses which had withstood the commercial invasion, and one of these houses, far down the street, bore the number 436. A small faded wooden sign imbedded crookedly in the damp clay of the narrow front yard read: *O. R. Vincetti, M.D., Physician and Surgeon.* I parked between a muddy pickup truck loaded with empty chicken crates and a 1937 Ford painted a wicked pink, and walked across the street. As I moved up the cracked cement walk leading to Dr. Vincetti's office, I saw that the other half of the structure was occupied by a man named Donald X. Weese. Peeled gilt lettering on the window proclaimed him to be an Electro-Health Therapist with Deep Massage by Appointment. A porch ran across the entire front of the building, with a dividing rail between the two professional establishments.

I climbed the slightly sagging steps to Dr. Vincetti's side of the porch, opened a door covered with cracked white paint and bearing a cardboard sign which read WALK IN. I stepped into a dusky room smelling strongly of iodine, alcohol, stale fried hamburger, stale tobacco smoke, heavy sweet perfume and burned gas fumes. A row of straight wooden chairs were arranged around the walls, and a heavy oaken table in the center bore an uneven stack of medical journals and tattered popular magazines. In a corner was an old-fashioned porcelain fireplace which had been converted to gas. Two pallid clay logs on stained brass andirons burned flickeringly with a blue hissing sound. Facing me was a door bearing a standard printed sign, no doubt the gift of some pharmaceutical house, which read: *The Doctor is In. Please Be Seated.*

The chairs were all empty so I had my choice. I picked one as far removed as possible from the fumes of the hissing gas logs, and took off my hat. From behind the door I heard a few muttered words, but the door didn't open. I lit a cigarette and looked around for an ashtray. The only one in the room was a small pink porcelain clamshell on the mantel above the fireplace. I dropped the match to the worn linoleum, which was of a dismal brownish hue. I flicked my ashes there, too. It didn't matter, not in the whole scheme of things. They'd have to sweep sometime, and my few ashes wouldn't make any difference. In fact, beneath the chairs were a scattering of ground-out cigarette butts and little swirled piles of gray ashes.

I reached out and took a magazine from the pile on the table. It was a *Time*, two years old. I tossed it back. Nothing is more dead than a back-dated news magazine—unless one is interested in history. I wasn't, and I sat and smoked. The voices came to me again, a woman's and a man's, low and intense, and once the man shouted something. I leaned forward, trying to catch the words. But I couldn't, and I sighed regretfully and settled back again. If Dr. Vincetti had a female patient in there, he certainly was not treating her with professional courtesy.

I coughed loudly and moved my chair with a thumping sound.

The voices stopped abruptly, and the only sound was the obscene hissing of the gas, like a trapped snake coiling restlessly in a pit. I smoked my cigarette until it burned my fingers, and then I dropped it and ground it out on the brown linoleum. I shifted my hat from one knee to the other. The door opened and a woman stepped out. She was wearing a white nurse's uniform, not quite clean, and it fitted her full figure too tightly. The white fabric over her hips and breasts was stretched to the ripping point, but her waist was surprisingly slender; it was belted snugly and the gleaming gold cap of a fountain pen peeked from a pocket over the ridge of her right pelvic structure. At first glance she appeared blowsy, too ripe, but as I watched her I saw that she had once been pretty, perhaps beautiful, and she still was, if you overlooked the soft puffiness beneath her chin, the faint sacks of flesh under her slightly bloodshot grayish eyes. Her hair, beneath a white cap, was dyed a brassy red. Full lips, coated with orange lipstick, held a sensual, sullen expression, and she seemed to regard me with a hot hatred.

"You wished to see the doctor?" she asked in a dead impersonal voice that rasped a little. Listening to the voice, I decided that it was not unpleasant, that it was a voice that might even excite some men, even with the rasp and the sullenness.

"Yes," I said, and I stood up.

Her slow gaze went over me. "Are you ill?"

"No, ma'am. I just want to see the doctor."

Her big body seemed to stiffen, and her eyes shifted for just an instant. She leaned against the closed door, rolling her hips a little, a provocative gesture, maybe from habit, and she spoke softly, but the faint rasp was still there, like a fingernail on a slate chalkboard, and I shivered slightly. "What about?" she asked.

"A business matter," I said. "My name is Bennett, and I'm with the Industrial Welfare Commission."

She said insolently, "The doctor is busy. Perhaps you could come back later."

"Perhaps," I said, "but I think not." I gazed at the empty room, the empty chairs, at the dismal emptiness of everything. "It will only take a minute or two."

"What will?" Her voice was almost a purr, below the rasp. I thought about it, that rasp in her voice. It could be from whisky, or a sore throat, or a sinus condition, or maybe at one time she had swallowed a jigger of sulphuric acid; that would cause a rasp in her throat, at the very least, even if she had been pumped out immediately, or had been given the antidote of huge quantities of milk.

"My business," I answered, aware that a small sound had come from behind the door, a sound like the tinkle of glass, maybe a bottle neck against a tumbler. I glanced at my wrist watch. One-thirty in the afternoon. A little early for a drink, unless one had not yet had lunch. Or unless one didn't care about lunch, and was getting a good start on one's pre-dinner drinking, a very good start.

She said, "What *is* your business?"

"I told you," I said wearily. "Insurance, just dreary old insurance. The State Welfare Commission."

She seemed to relax, and a little of the hate left her eyes. "I see," she said. "At first, I picked you for a drug salesman, or appliances, and we don't need any aspirin or forceps, or scalpels, or tongue depressors.... What case are you working on?"

"Shannon," I told her, "George Shannon. If I could just talk to the doctor for a minute...."

"Shannon," she said thoughtfully, pursing her full lips and puckering her finely plucked eyebrows. "I seem to remember...."

"Fractured skull," I said. "Dead. Ferris Abrasives."

"Yes. I remember. I handle all of the doctor's reports on industrial claims. I thought it was all settled?"

"Not quite. There are just a few details left. If I could see the doctor ...?"

She shook her head slowly. "I told you the doctor is busy. I can answer any questions about the Shannon case."

"What's the doctor doing?" I asked. "Playing solitaire?"

She looked at me, and the hate began to creep back into her eyes, and her mouth twisted a little, making it ugly. "Go away," she said. "Go the hell away. He's drunk."

"Why didn't you say so? What'll you do if a patient comes in?"

"We don't have many patients," she said bitterly. "But if we do, I'll take care of them—or tell them the doctor is out."

"You'd better take that sign down, then," I said.

She glanced at the sign on the door, and laughed shortly, an unpleasant sound. "He's always in—he sleeps in back."

A crashing sound came from beyond the door. It startled but the woman merely sighed. "He fell off the chair."

"Maybe we'd better look," I suggested.

Something like a groan came out to us, and a kind of thumping sound. The woman reached for the knob, and then hesitated, a tiny frown of worry on her forehead.

"Go ahead,"told her. "Don't mind me. Maybe he's hurt."

She gnawed at her plump lower lip with strong white teeth, and then abruptly she opened the door and entered. As I followed, she snapped at me over her shoulder, "Close that door."

I kicked the door shut and looked around. The room contained standard doctor's equipment, none of it new, a desk, several chairs, a glass-doored bookcase filled with medical volumes, an electric sterilizer, a glass instrument case containing a jumbled array of scalpels, forceps, hypodermic needles, gauze, bandages, tape. A row of shelves in one corner bore jars and bottles of drugs, varicolored capsules, liquids and tablets. A dusty window behind the desk looked out on a dirty court cluttered with garbage cans and metal drums full of trash. Beyond the court the tops of the stores along Royal Street were like uneven blocks stacked against the gray April sky.

I didn't see Dr. Vincetti immediately. On the green blotter of the desk was an empty bourbon bottle, an overturned glass. A big metal ashtray beside the bottle was heaped with cigarette butts, a few of them with an orange stain on their tips, which, I noted, matched the color of the woman's lips. She moved quickly around the desk and stooped down, so that all I could see of her was the white starched cap. She said something in a soothing, maternal voice, and when I moved around to the side of the desk I saw that she was tenderly stroking the high pale forehead of a man lying between the desk and the wall, with a chair overturned on his legs.

He was fully dressed in a neat dark gray suit, clean white shirt, sober blue tie and polished black shoes. He was not young, but not old, either, and he had a thin, high-cheekboned face and very dark brows. Except for graying hair over his ears, he was almost totally bald. His eyes were peacefully closed, and there was a happy smile on his thin, sensitive lips. The woman placed an arm beneath his head and looked up at me. "Open the door behind you."

I turned, opened a door between the instrument case and the drug shelves, saw that it led to a short hall, and turned back. The woman had lifted Dr. Vincetti to a sitting position, and his head lolled limply. I grasped his legs and together we lifted him and carried him through the doorway and down the hall. We passed a bathroom on the way, and at the end was a bedroom containing twin beds, both unmade, a dresser littered with mingled male and female toilet articles, a worn leather chair, a floor lamp and an open closet in which hung bright dresses and several men's suits. We laid him on the nearest bed. The woman unbuttoned his shirt collar, took off his shoes, and gently covered him with a blanket.

"There, baby," she said tenderly. "Sleep." She turned to me, sighed, and said, "Thanks. I can do it alone, but it's nice to have help."

"You're welcome," I said politely, and followed her down the hall to the office. She closed the door firmly, dropped the empty bourbon bottle into a wastebasket, moved to a tall steel filing case and said briskly, "What did you want to know about the Shannon case?"

"Just what happened—from the doctor's viewpoint."

She shrugged. "It's all on file." She pulled out a drawer, flipped through some manila folders, and took out a white card. "Shannon," she said, "George Allen. Age thirty-six, married, one child, named Jonquil—isn't that a hell of a name for a kid?—lathe operator, Ferris Abrasives, claim number WU-554368, state of—"

"I know," I broke in. "I've read the report, and the doctor's certificate of death. I just wanted to talk to him before I saw the widow, to ask him what he found when he first examined George Shannon, the circumstances."

"I was with him on the call," she said impatiently. "Dr. Vincetti is the company physician for Ferris Abrasives. He does all their physicals and treats most of their accident cases." She paused and her lips twisted a little. "It's about the only practice he has left. Oh, industrial work is fine for a young man just starting practice, but Dr. Vincetti...." She paused and glared at me defiantly. "He's a *good* doctor, a surgeon, one of the finest. Five years ago he had a clinic in Baltimore and was president of the Maryland medical association. He—oh, to hell with it. What else do you want to know?"

"And now he just—drinks?"

She nodded gloomily. "Mostly."

Outside in the waiting room we heard a door open and close. The woman crossed the office, opened the door, and I heard her say, "I'm sorry, dear—the doctor was called out on an emergency, I don't know when he'll be back."

A soft female voice said something low, entreating, desperate, and the woman said sharply, "I told you he isn't in. Perhaps you'd better see another doctor." She closed the door and said to me, "She's been here before, maybe sixteen years old. I know what she wants— abortion." She paused and added proudly, "That's one thing he hasn't done."

"But dope, maybe?" I asked gently.

"Damn you," she said viciously. "We've been hungry sometimes, but we've never peddled. Why don't you get the hell out of here?"

"I'm sorry," I said.

"I treat more patients than he does," she said. "All the minor stuff— colds, penicillin shots, knife cuts, infections, black eyes, bruises. We get a lot of that here, mostly people who can't pay." She sighed. "But we make out."

"Then you're really a nurse?"

"Registered. I was with him in Baltimore, and I stuck with him."

"Why?"

She looked at me insolently. "Now, that's a bright question. Why do you suppose?"

"I see," I said. "Why did he leave Baltimore?"

"Why, why, why," she mimicked. "I thought you just wanted to know about the Shannon case?"

"I do, but my mind is open. I suppose it was the old story; he operated while he was drunk and the patient died. He was sued for malpractice and the state lifted his license?"

"That's good," she said scornfully. "That's really good. You should write books . . . He didn't drink in Baltimore. That came after."

"After what?"

"Oh, God," she sighed. "Why am I talking to you? What do you care?" The hate was in her eyes again.

"I like people," I said. "Most people, anyhow."

"Rot," she said. "People are poison." She smiled a little. "Are you married?"

"No."

"Neither am I," she said carelessly. "Would you like a drink?"

"The bottle is empty."

"There's more, never fear. There's always more. We have whisky, even if we have no bread."

"As long as you have the necessities...." I murmured.

She moved to the drug shelf, her hips moving as if they were on oiled bearings. From behind a row of gallon jars filled with pink, red, blue and white capsules she took a full bottle—bonded bourbon, I noted from the label—and broke the seal with a fingernail. "We drink the best," she said. "Eight years old, one hundred proof. I like it straight. You want water, something?"

"No, thanks."

She placed a smudged glass on the desk and set upright the glass which was lying there. "They need washing," she said, "but don't worry about it—the whisky will make them antiseptic."

"I'm not worried," I said.

"Worry, worry," she said, pouring. "Everybody worries too much." She handed me a glass, half full, said, "Excuse me," and left the office. I heard her locking the outer door, the one to the street. I waited, holding the glass. She came back, dusting her hands briskly. "There! The shop is closed for the day. Let 'em pound." She picked up her glass. "Where were we?"

"In Baltimore," I said, sipping the whisky. It was smooth and hot, rich with the aged corn flavor.

She drank, a big swallow, and coughed slightly. When she spoke, the rasp was more pronounced. "Deah old Baltimore," she said mincingly. "We had *such* a charming practice there, all the lovely society ladies, pregnant, poor dears, more often than they liked. And then Deborah—she was the doctor's lovely wife—drank too many martinis one gay evening and became indiscreet and very careless. The doctor found her, when he came home from the hospital at three in the morning, in bed with a nice young boy, the life guard at the country club swimming pool where Deborah liked to relax in the sun on the afternoons when the doctor was busy in his office or at the hospital making money for her, and the children he wanted, but never had."

She drank again, and smiled at me, showing her strong white teeth. "We closed the office the next day, the doctor and me, and we left Baltimore, and we stayed in Florida for a time, and Mexico, and then we drifted around for a while and finally came here, God knows why."

"And the drinking started?"

"Not here—it just continued here. He started the drinking in Miami, and in Mexico he became very good at it—he loved the tequila. At first, I drank with him just to keep him company, but now I like it, too, and we drink together, and he talks about Deborah with a shine in his eyes, and I listen, and then he goes to sleep, happy, like you saw him. It's funny—when he's sober he hates her, and when he's drunk he loves her and forgets that he hates her, and he just remembers good things—their honeymoon at Lake Placid, the weekends in New York, the babies they both wanted and the one born dead, and no more to come, ever—I've heard it all a million times." She lifted her glass high and pirouetted before me, arching her back, thrusting the big breasts. "I could have babies, easy. I'm built for it, aren't I?"

"Yes," I said, drinking too quickly, and coughing.

"But I have a baby," she said softly. "He is like a baby."

"Yes," I said again, still coughing.

"Come on, loosen up." She snapped her fingers. "Tomorrow will never come, but if it does, let's pretend that it's Sunday, with funny papers." She drained her glass, poured more, and offered the bottle to me.

I shook my head, and stifled the coughing. "And now he can't stop the drinking?"

"Are you crazy?" she asked scornfully. "Of course he can, and so can I, but we like it. Anybody can stop drinking, if they really and truly want to. It's just a habit, like smoking, or chewing gum, or eating candy bars. More people die from overeating than overdrinking, really. But if it gives us pleasure, and we aren't harming anyone else, why shouldn't we drink? Life is short, and pleasures are few. Of course, the hangovers used to be ghastly, but the doctor invented a cure, a powder he mixed up. We take that in the mornings, and—bingo!—we feel fine."

"He should put it on the market," I said. "He'd make ten billion dollars."

"We don't care for money," she said. "He has his dreams, and I have him...." I thought I detected a glint of tears in her grayish eyes, but I wasn't certain. She drank again, and said soberly, "Tomorrow he'll go back to work, and make some money, and he will hate her and love her and it'll build up, and then he'll start drinking and only love her again."

I said, "He's a weak son of a bitch."

"Yes, he really is. Me, I'm just a bitch."

"No," I said. "You're all right. Tell me about the day you went with him to the Ferris Abrasives plant, when George Shannon fell from that ladder."

"A one-track mind," she said, "if I ever saw one."

"That's me."

"There isn't much to tell," she said. "The plant nurse called, and said there'd been an accident, and could the doctor come right away. I said yes, and we went. He was sober that day. They had carried Shannon to the dispensary. A quick examination showed there was brain hemorrhage. He died in the ambulance on the way to the hospital. I was beside him, checking his pulse. It just stopped. The autopsy showed multiple skull fractures in the occipital area—cracked like an egg shell."

"Did he say anything before he died?"

"Just one word—it sounded like a name, maybe 'John,' but I couldn't be certain."

I nodded, remembering the reports I'd read. "He probably started to say 'Jonquil,' the name of his small daughter."

"The devoted father, at death's door, thinking of his offspring," she said bitterly. "Very touching."

"Yes," I said, finishing the whisky. "You and I wouldn't know about that, not being parents."

"No," she said, "and to hell with it. How about another drink—what did you say your name is?"

"Bennett—James Bennett."

"Drink up, Jim. Be merry." She removed the white nurse's cap and ran a hand through her brilliant hair.

I shook my head. Even the smell of the whisky was beginning to nauseate me a little. Maybe it was the gas fumes filtering in from the waiting room. Suddenly I wanted to get out of there, away from this woman and the man who slept soddenly in a mutual room down the hall. I wanted to smell fresh air. I put the glass on the desk and moved to the door, noticing that she had turned the sign over. It now read, *The Doctor is OUT*.

The woman said, "What happened? Doesn't the state believe that Shannon is dead?" She laughed shortly, and drank again.

"We know he's dead, all right. This is just routine, before I approve the application."

She lowered the glass and stared at me over the rim. There were tiny brown flecks in her gray eyes, like a cat's. "He fell from a ladder twenty feet to a cement floor, and landed on his head. Is that right?"

"That's right."

"I suppose somebody pushed the ladder—on purpose?" she said jeeringly.

"Don't be melodramatic," I said. "This is just an industrial accident."

She shifted her eyes, gazed at the door leading to the hall and the bedroom at the end, and then she said in an odd strained voice. "Is—is he in trouble?"

"Why do you ask that?"

"I thought this case was all settled, and now you show up, asking questions. Who are you? The police?"

"I told you who I am, and he's not in trouble. I just wanted to talk to him. His medical report seems to be in order and agrees with the autopsy."

"Then, why . . . ?"

"I'll come back tomorrow. Will he be sober then?"

She shrugged carelessly. "Maybe. Maybe not." The neck of the bottle clinked against the glass as she poured more bourbon, and her hand shook a little.

Something stirred uneasily in my brain, and I asked carefully, "Has he been in trouble before?"

"No, he hasn't been in trouble before," she said in mocking, mincing tones that grated on my nerves.

"He had trouble in Baltimore," I said gently. "He still has the same trouble."

She flung the glass at me. I jerked my head, and it shattered against the wall. She came toward me, showing her fine strong teeth, and the hate in her eyes was like a blaze. "Damn you," she said in a low choked voice. "Damn all of you smug, normal people.... He's mine, and I won't let anything or anybody hurt him. Do you hear?"

"Yes, ma'am."

I backed away, through the waiting room, past the hissing fireplace, to the outer door. I unlocked this door, and as I stepped to the porch I turned and saw her watching me, the bottle in her hand. I smiled at her and closed the door. She must have jumped forward instantly, because I heard the key turn on the inside. I stood on the porch a moment, aware of her intense listening presence a few inches away behind the locked door, the door that led to wonderful dreams, and shame, and sick remembrance, and maybe love, of a sort, and a creeping horror.

CHAPTER TWO

The rain had stopped, and it was colder, the clear sharp coldness of early April, with pale sunshine on the street. A stubby shadow moved ahead of me as I crossed to the Mercury, and I looked at my watch. Three o'clock in the afternoon. I turned the car around in an alley and drove back down Royal Street to King William, and over the bridge. On the bridge I looked back, but I couldn't distinguish Dr. Vincetti's office from the rest of the buildings, and I thought of the woman back there, behind the locked door with her bottle, and of the man on the bed, dreaming of his beloved, in an alcoholic world where everything was clean and normal, a world in which a hardworking doctor did not come home at three in the morning to find his wife with a young and muscular beach boy.

The taste of Dr. Vincetti's whisky was bitter in my mouth, and I remembered the smudged and sticky glass with a faint shudder. I lit a cigarette and tried to stop thinking about the neat and antiseptic doctor trapped in a hole with a sensual, big-breasted woman in a soiled white uniform, a woman with the soul of a mother and the heart of a whore. Maybe she wasn't so bad, after all. Maybe it was me. Maybe I'd seen too much and done too much, mostly in the wrong places and with the wrong kind of people. Maybe I was the wrong kind of people. I should have been married long ago. It wasn't natural for a man not to be married, they said, the married ones. I should be busy reproducing my kind, God knew why, and paying off the mortgage and attending parent-teacher's meetings and frying hamburgers at the school lawn fetes. I should be going to service club luncheons and joining heartily in the group singing, and heading committees for the advancement of the community, maybe even serving on some town council helping to decide serious problems like sewage disposal and juvenile delinquency.

I left the bridge, thinking these dismal thoughts, and turned right at the corner where the Blue Ridge Hotel towered into the sky and drove across the city to the industrial section, to Carbon Street.

It was a smoke-blackened apartment building, and the address checked with the one in my note book—545. I parked at the curb, crossed the sidewalk, entered a small foyer and scanned a row of mailboxes until I saw one labeled Mr. and Mrs. George Shannon, Apt. 2-6. The Mr. and had been crossed out with a pencil. A stairway carpeted with a threadbare rug went upward into gloom. There was the faint smell of soap and antiseptic and long-ago cooking, and the place looked clean. I moved upward to a dim silent hall, 2-6 was three doors down, on my right.

A tiny blond girl answered my knock and gazed up at me with big solemn blue eyes. I'm not very good at guessing children's ages, but I decided that she couldn't have been older than four or five. I looked down at her, cracked my face into the smile reserved for kids and imbeciles, and said, "Is your mother at home, honey?"

She shook her small head and said seriously, "No. My mommy has gone away for a long time, and my daddy, too."

"That's too bad. Are you alone?"

"Oh, no! Elaine is here, and Uncle Vernon, too. He's nice. He calls me Blondie. Sometimes he takes Elaine and me for a ride, and he brings me toys and candy."

"Good for Uncle Vernon," I said, and peered into the apartment. What I could see of it looked neat, and was attractively furnished. From beyond my line of vision I heard voices, and a woman said, "Who is it, Jon?"

"A man," the little girl said.

I removed my hat and waited.

A woman appeared in the doorway and gazed at me questioningly. Her eyes were a deep blue and her short black hair curled crisply around her small face. Her skin was clear and milky, her nose short, the mouth a little large, but soft-looking and well-shaped. She was wearing a thin pale gray sweater, dark blue slacks, and soft white leather moccasins. The sweater fitted her very snugly, and I noted the slim gentle lines of her body.

"Mrs. Shannon?" I asked politely.

She nodded. "Yes." Her voice was soft and clear.

"My name is Bennett. I'm with the Industrial Welfare Commission, and I'd like to ask a few questions in connection with the death of your husband."

The blue eyes clouded, and for an instant her lips quivered. Then she said quietly, "Please come in."

I moved inside and closed the door. The little girl gazed up at me with curious eyes. "Is he a nice man, Elaine?" she asked.

The woman smiled faintly. "Of course, Jon." She motioned me to a chair.

I was about to sit down, when a tall young man entered the room through an open doorway leading, I saw, to a bedroom. He was maybe thirty, or a little younger, with a pleasant boyish face and dark brown hair trimmed short in a modified crew cut. He was wearing a gray flannel suit, and carried a gray tweed topcoat and a brown hat. He glanced at me, nodded briefly, and said to the woman, "I'll see you later."

"Perhaps you'd better stay," she said. "This gentleman is from the Commission—about George's death." She turned to me. "Mr. Bennett—is that right?—this is Mr. Dorr. He is the personnel manager for the Ferris Abrasive Company—where my husband worked."

As I shook hands with Dorr, I said, "I've seen your name on the company's accident reports."

He smiled ruefully. "I guess we have our share of injuries, the same as any other plant. But George Shannon was our first fatality in five years." He shook his head and sighed. "Too bad about George." He paused and peered at me curiously. "Aren't you new in this territory? What happened to Lew Kingston? He had this claim."

"Lew was transferred," I said. "I'm just picking up the loose ends on this, winding it up."

He nodded. "I see. Lew was a good man, very thorough, but always ready to give the working man a break. If I can be of any help...."

"It's just routine now," I told him. "There doesn't seem to be any doubt that Mr. Shannon was accidentally killed in the course of his employment."

"That's right," Dorr said. "Open and shut. I have certified the facts of the accident and requested that the claim he allowed. Dr. Vincetti signed the death certificate—skull fracture."

"Yes," I said. "I talked to Dr. Vincetti's nurse."

Dorr nodded at the woman, patted the little girl's head, and said to me, "Glad to have met you, Bennett."

"Thanks. You'll get a copy of my report from the Commission."

"Good." He went out.

The little girl said to the woman, "Uncle Vernon is nice, isn't he, Elaine?"

She flushed faintly. "Yes, dear. Why don't you go color a picture? Your crayons are on the floor beside your bed."

"I'll color an Easter bunny," the little girl said happily, and ran into the bedroom.

The woman said to me, "Mr. Dorr has been very kind since my husband was—was killed." She hesitated, and her gaze shifted away. "It—it's been rather difficult, for Jon and me."

"You have my sympathy, Mrs. Shannon," I said. "There seems no doubt that the ten-thousand-dollar death benefit will be paid you shortly. I am here to get your signature on a release form, but I must have proof that you were Mr. Shannon's legal wife—just a formality. May I see your marriage certificate?"

"Of course," she said quietly. She left the room and returned almost immediately with an embossed paper and handed it to me. I noted that Elaine Margaret Belsa and George Allen Shannon had been united in holy matrimony in a small town in Kentucky eight months previously. As I handed the paper back, I said, "The little girl—she is your husband's daughter by a former marriage?"

She nodded. "Yes. Jon is my stepdaughter. My husband's first wife died two years ago."

"Jon," I said, "without the 'h'?"

She smiled. "Her name is Jonquil, but George always called her Jon, and I do, too. It was his pet name for her."

"I know," I said. "Dr. Vincetti's nurse told me that your husband said her name before he died."

"He—he loved her very much."

I said, "I don't want to bother you, but I need a few details, for my report; on the day of your husband's death had he complained of feeling ill?"

"No. He went to work in good spirits. It—it was Jon's birthday, and he had promised to take us to dinner that evening. He—he never came home...." Her voice broke, and she turned away, her slim shoulders trembling a little.

I moved to her, touched her shoulder. "I'm sorry."

She turned slowly to face me. "We'd been married only a short time. It—it was quite a shock, when Mr. Dorr came and told me...."

"Of course," I said gently, thinking of the other widows I'd talked to in the weeks since the New York office had transferred me from the Cleveland territory to this state. All of them, the widows I'd seen, had one thing in common—their husbands had died in a factory, like George Allen Shannon. Death on the production line, an accident. Another widow, another statistic.

It was a new kind of work for me. The boss in New York was promoting something, and I was the guinea pig. His crafty old brain had conceived the idea that professional detectives, working with the safety technicians and special agents of the various state workmen's compensation boards, and applying standard methods of criminal investigation to the specialized field of industrial hazard, would be effective in preventing death on the job. He cunningly picked out a mid-Southern state with high rate of industrial fatalities and opened his campaign: Listen, gentlemen, we have trained investigators at your service, men schooled in the art of detection. There is a culprit for every crime, no matter if the crime is murder, or the crime of a drill press without a guard, or the crime of oil-soaked waste in a dusty corner. Stop Industrial Deaths in Your State. Cut Your Insurance Costs. Reduce Employer's Premiums. Our Service is Professional, Second Only to the FBI. The cost....

The workmen's compensation board of this state had taken the bait. They were faced with a new election, a new governor. Pressure was on from the labor unions, the press, and the public. They were snatching at straws, and they sent a requisition, in triplicate, to the New York office, for the services of one man, on a trial basis, for a period of three months. The boss called me, chuckling gleefully, and I could almost see him in his massive paneled office, with the box of black cigars on his desk beside the decanter of bourbon, his thin old lips beneath the clipped white mustache curling in the wolf's snarl he called a smile. "You've been working pretty hard, Jim, my boy. This is sort of a little vacation for you. I thought of you right off. You put it over, and the other states will fall in line. We'll need a hundred extra men to handle it, when it gets rolling, maybe more." I could see him licking his lips at the thought of the fees. "Just keep your eyes open, and act smart—"

"But I don't know a damn thing about a factory," I protested. "It's not like tailing a sticky-fingered bank clerk to the racetrack, or slapping a murder charge on the faithful family butler, or finding a restless wife shacked up with a television crooner. If a guy gets hurt in a shop, or killed, that's it. Nobody did it to him, except maybe a damned machine, and—"

"Now, now," the boss said soothingly. "I want to give it a try, and you're my top man, you know that. We're approaching this whole business of industrial safety and accident investigation from a new angle. Why, son, our methods, combined with the technical knowledge of the safety engineers, will revolutionize the whole structure of workmen's insurance. Think of the men who have died in the factories of America, of the poor grieving widows, the innocent, fatherless little children, the—"

"Oh, shut up," I told him. "All you're thinking about is how many men you'll have planted in the different state insurance setups making money for you."

"Now, Jim," he said in a hurt voice, "that ain't the right attitude."

"My God," I said, "private dicks snooping around a shop trying to find out why Joe Doakes stuck his finger into a buzz saw! You'll never sell the idea."

"Hah," he said.

"I won't do it. To hell with it."

I heard his hollow laugh as I hung up.

Two weeks later I walked down the marble corridor of a state capitol building and stopped before a frosted glass door with black lettering: *Industrial Welfare Commission—Office of Chief of*

Investigation. I was on a three months' leave of absence, with the Cleveland office in charge of Alec Hammond, my chief assistant, and Sandy Hollis, my secretary.

I met Austin O'Connor, the fussy, cold-eyed chief of claims investigation, and the other men in the division. For the most part they were friendly and capable, and they indulged in a minimum of kidding about whisky, blondes and .45 automatics in shoulder holsters. I spent a week in the main office learning routine and then they sent me out with an investigator named Al Purdy, a short thick-bodied man with keen little black eyes and a ready grin, who had started with the Commission as a clerk in the claims section and was now a specialist in checking on persons alleging permanent total disability. I learned a lot from Purdy, and even acquired a little of his enthusiasm for the work, and was with him in Steel City when they sent me the file on George Allen Shannon.

We went over the file together in my room at the Blue Ridge Hotel, and Purdy said, "A cinch, Jim. Lew Kingston checked it before he was transferred. All you gotta do is see the widow and get her to sign off, and maybe make a routine check with the doctor."

And that is why I visited the office of Dr. Vincetti, and met Elaine Shannon.

"Is that all?" she asked in her quiet voice.

"Just one thing more," I said, remembering the manual I'd studied. "You have the choice of drawing the ten thousand dollars death award in monthly installments, or in a lump sum."

"What does it matter, Mr. Bennett? It won't bring my husband back."

"Maybe it will help—you and the child."

"Money," she said bitterly.

I said, "It you have no preference, it is the policy of the Commission to pay the sum in monthly installments. In that way we feel that the worker's dependents will receive benefits over a period of time, and you will have a regular income for a number of years."

"No," she said suddenly, and there was a faint harshness in her voice. "I want it now—all of it. I don't want checks arriving every month, reminding me that George...." She turned away.

"Very well," I said. "I will recommend that it be paid in a lump sum." From my pocket I took a printed form, laid it on a table, and handed her a fountain pen. "Please sign this." She turned, signed quickly. I folded the form and moved to the door.

"Thank you, Mr. Bennett," she said in an oddly soft voice.

"All part of my job," I said smugly, like any bureaucrat. "You should receive the money within a week or ten days."

The little girl came out of the bedroom. "Good-bye, man."

The woman smiled at her.

"Good-bye," I said to both of them, and went out.

CHAPTER THREE

At the bottom of the stairs, opposite the row of mailboxes, was a door labeled *Superintendent*. I pressed a bell-button and waited. Behind the door a dog began to bark furiously. I pressed the bell again. The dog's barking became frenzied. The door opened and a small white fox terrier darted out between my legs and began to dance around, his shrill yapping quivering my ear drums. I muttered under my breath and kicked tentatively. He backed away, showing small white teeth, yip, yip, yip. I grinned at him, stooped over and offered a cautious hand. He sniffed my hand doubtfully, but his yips subsided. I patted his small head. He licked my fingers eagerly and wiggled his hind quarters.

Behind me a voice said, "Be careful, mister. Tippy doesn't like strangers."

I looked up at a stout gray-haired woman wearing a flower-printed apron and purple house slippers trimmed with white fur. Beneath the apron was a sober black dress. Her eyes were bright and very black, and her skin held a smooth quality in spite of the tiny wrinkles at the corners of her eyes and around her pleasant mouth.

"At first he wanted to chew me up," I said, smiling, "but now we're pals." I stood up straight and removed my hat. The little dog sat on his haunches and gazed up at me with soft brown eyes.

The woman smiled. "Tippy doesn't usually make friends that quickly."

"I get along with dogs," I said.

"And old ladies?"

"Usually," I said, still smiling. "Except my Aunt Edna—she disapproves of smoking."

"And drinking, too, I bet."

"Strong spirits are the ruination of mankind, Aunt Edna says."

"Bosh," the woman said. "It's all amatter of moderation. What are you selling?"

"Nothing.

"I don't have any vacancies."

"I'm not looking for an apartment, either. I'm with the Industrial Welfare Commission. I've just seen Mrs. Shannon, upstairs, about her husband's accidental death. Could I ask you a few questions?"

"Sure, sure. Come on in." She smiled as she stood aside. "You have an honest face, and you took off your hat—I can tell you've had the right kind of upbringing." She held out a hand. "I'm Mrs. Ryan."

Her clasp was firm. "My name's Bennett," I said. "I'll only take a minute of your time...."

"Bosh. An old woman has nothing but time." She motioned me to a chair. As I sat down, the little dog hopped to another chair, stretched out his small pointed nose between his forepaws, and watched me brightly. The place was too hot and had a faint dog smell, but it was clean. There were several deep old chairs, a worn red velvet sofa, an old-fashioned glass-doored bookcase stuffed with volumes. From where I sat I could see some of the titles; *A Girl of the Limberlost, When a Man's a Man, A Pictorial History of the Spanish-American War, Janice Meredith, When Knighthood Was in Flower*, and what looked like the complete works of Zane Grey. Before a big window facing Carbon Street stood an oaken table, which I remembered was of a type called a "library table," upon which were set numerous photographs in cardboard frames of children and adults, and a large gilt-framed one of a smiling fat man in an engineer's cap waving a gloved hand from the window of a locomotive. A framed motto on one wall read: *Home Is Where the Heart Is.*

Mrs. Ryan sat on the red velvet sofa, smoothed the apron over her broad thighs, and smiled at me. "I'm sure it's all right," she said, "but do you have any, well, identification?"

I opened my wallet and showed her the card Austin O'Connor had given me which stated that I was an authorized agent of the state. She nodded, and then saw my police license card in the opposite compartment. Her black eyes widened. "A private detective, too?"

"Yes, ma'am. I'm down here on special assignment for the state."

"Then—?"

I shook my head, smiling. "No murders, no blackmail, nothing like that. The agency I work for is experimenting with the possibility of selling its services to the various state workmen's compensation offices. You see, some private investigation agencies specialize in providing bonded guards and watchmen for industrial plants, banks, cash payroll agencies, even to some police departments. My agency has limited itself to private investigation on a national scale; now they are attempting to branch out into industrial accident investigation, on a fee basis. We feel that our specialized knowledge, methods and experience will be valuable to—"

"Never mind," she broke in. "I understand. They've handed you the job of checking on George Shannon's death?"

I nodded. "It's routine, but if the state likes the way I operate, the results I obtain, and if they feel they are getting their money's worth, then maybe they'll use men from my agency again."

"Doesn't it seem pretty tame—after what you've been doing?"

"It's different," I admitted.

"Maybe some time you'd tell me about some of the cases you've had. I read mysteries all the time, and listen to them on the radio. I'm thinking of buying a television set. Mrs. Lindstrom, across the hall, has one, and she asks me over. They're really quite exciting—the stories on TV, I mean. Is it really like that?"

"No, ma'am," I said sadly. "Not usually. Now, if you would just tell me how long the Shannons have lived here...."

"Of course," she said. "Don't mind an old woman's curiosity. They've been with me about six months."

"Good tenants, would you say?"

"Very good. Quiet, never any loud parties, always paid their rent on time. I feel sorry for Mrs. Shannon and the little girl."

"I understand she is her stepchild—Mr. Shannon's daughter by a former marriage."

Mrs. Ryan nodded. "That's right, Mr. Bennett. But her own mother couldn't have cared for that child better than Elaine Shannon has."

"You would say they were a happily married couple?"

"Yes. It's a shame he had to be taken, but it's something that comes to all of us, in one way or another. My Herman was killed on the railroad nine years ago this Easter." She nodded at the large photo on the table. "That's Herman, taken the year before the wreck. He was an engineer, Chicago to Cincinnati." She sighed heavily. "We had wonderful times. Never any kids, though—it's the one regret of my life." She sighed again. "But I shouldn't complain. The company pays me a small pension, and I used the insurance money for a down payment on this place—I'll get it paid for, too, if I live long enough. It's not a fancy neighborhood, but the people are good working folks, and I like it here. I've got eight apartments, and the tenants pay their rent on time—except when the shops are laying off or on short hours. Then I carry 'em, but I don't get stuck often.... Would you like a bottle of beer?"

"No, thanks, Mrs. Ryan. I appreciate what you have told me." I stood up and moved to the door. Tippy, from his place on the chair, cocked a lazy ear.

"I hope Elaine Shannon gets that insurance money," Mrs. Ryan said. "She can use it, with the little girl and all."

"I'm sure she'll get it," I said.

"Are you the one who decides?"

"No—I can only report and recommend. It's up to the Commission after that, but I don't think there'll be any question about it."

As I opened the door, I caught the glint of a pistol lying on a shelf beside a flower pot spouting a drooping ivy. Guns interest me, and I peered closely. It was a make and model I hadn't seen in a long time, a Stevens .22 caliber single shot, with an eight-inch barrel and black walnut stock. "Nice little gun," I said.

"It was Herman's," Mrs. Ryan said. "He was a crack shot, belonged to the railroad pistol team and several gun clubs. It was his hobby. Got a whole drawer full of trophies. He taught me to shoot but I don't get much chance anymore, except at the rats in the backyard. The police gave me permission to shoot them."

I grinned at her. "I've got a gun in my bag at the hotel—how about letting me help shoot the rats?"

"Any time," she said. "No matter how many I kill, there's always plenty around." She shivered a little. "I hate 'em. To me, a rat is worse than a snake. On Sundays, Herman and I used to go out along the river and shoot water moccasins. If you come back here, bring that gun. What is it? A Colt .45 automatic? Or a Luger?"

I gave her a look of mock pain. "Please Mrs. Ryan, not a Luger. I carry a Smith and Wesson .38."

She nodded in approval. "A good gun—not too heavy, but heavy enough."

I put on my hat. "Thanks, again."

Tippy wiggled a little as I went out.

After the heat of Mrs. Ryan's apartment, the cold April wind made me shiver and I turned up my coat collar as I walked to my car. All over the neighborhood whistles were blowing. I looked at my watch. Four o'clock in the afternoon. The street began to fill up with cars, and men and women swarmed the sidewalks, many of them carrying lunch boxes. I got into the Mercury, but I couldn't back out because of the steady stream of cars, so I took a printed form from my brief case and read it over:

Investigator's Report of Death in Course of Employment. George A. Shannon, deceased—The Ferris Abrasive Company—Claim No. WU-554368. Under a section headed Conclusions and Comments I wrote in ink: *Witnessed proof of marriage. Interviewed nurse of attending physician, and also landlady, who verified fact that deceased's widow, Mrs. Elaine Shannon, was living with him at the time of his death. Marital relations apparently good. Employer certifies death as arising from deceased's employment. Recommend that maximum death award be paid beneficiary, Mrs. Elaine Shannon, in a lump sum.*

I was learning the patter of the state Commission boys, and I smiled to myself. Maybe I'd missed my true calling. This work was similar to private investigation, and yet it was different. I had in the past worked mostly for individuals, some rich, some poor, but now I was working for a state, a great commonwealth. I was a representative of the state, and of the people whose taxes paid my salary. I was the defender of the workers, the men and women who performed the jobs in the factories so that all the people could drive cars and watch television, and do a Monday's wash in a porcelain cabinet and cool their beer in a deluxe refrigerator, and shave without lather or blades and wake in the morning to coffee already made and hot, and watch the toast pop up. I was beginning to feel a little like one of these people who, with dignity and skill, performed the jobs that made the goods that sold to the world and kept the wheels turning and the paychecks coming in. I was beginning to feel that the work I was doing had meaning and direction, and for the first time I hoped that the boss's scheme would be successful.

I sat for a while, my hands on the wheel, waiting for the after-work traffic to thin. I had other calls to make in this city; a man who had lost an eye when a casting chip had pierced it. He hadn't been wearing safety goggles, although the company provided them, and I shook my head in disapproval. I was beginning to be safety conscious, too. And there was a woman with an industrial dermatitis which patch tests had failed to isolate, and I thought about her and others. I would see them and get their stories, and I would report, stating the facts as I found them, and let the Commission take its course. I thought of George Allen Shannon, dead now and buried, another statistic, and I wondered what kind of a man he had been. I thought of Elaine Shannon, left behind with her husband's daughter, and I hoped that the Commission would pay the full benefit. It was the least the state could do for one of its workers who had died while doing his job.

And I also thought, Get off the soap box, Bennett. You abandoned the role of crusader when you left the law and stored your diploma to work for a sly and greedy old man. You're here in this city because the old man wants to make more money, God knows why, and your loyalty lies with him. Do your job here, but remember the long pull, and don't get too sentimental about George Allen Shannon, deceased, or his pretty widow. George isn't the first man to be killed on the job. It happens every day, all over the country, in all the states, to men working for a paycheck to feed a wife and kids. It's not your fault that a man refuses to wear safety goggles, or that a woman is allergic to dust, an oil, an acid, or that a man loses his grip on a ladder and falls twenty feet to a cement floor, as George Shannon had. Take a notch in your belt, Bennett, and look at these things objectively. You can't control what people do; all you can do is try and help them after they do it.

The clock on the dash of the Mercury told me that it was four-thirty in the afternoon. I opened my briefcase, which was still a strange object to me, and took out the file on George Shannon. I thumbed the typed pages and checked the two witnesses to the accident resulting in Shannon's death—Vernon H. Dorr and John R. Riggio. I realized suddenly that Dorr was the name of the man I'd met in Mrs. Shannon's apartment, the neat and sincere personnel man for Ferris Abrasives. I didn't reread their testimony, because I'd read it all before my visit to Dr. Vincetti's office, but I checked Riggio's address—1821 Maple Road. He should be home by now, I thought, if the Ferris plant worked the standard first shift of seven to four. But where was Maple Road?

I rolled down the window and called to a man passing by with a metal lunch box under his arm. He stopped, grinned, and by pointing, arm waving and wrist motions, directed me to Maple Road. I thanked him, a little confused, and drove away. I was surprised when I found Maple Road without any trouble.

It wasn't a road, but a narrow brick street, and there weren't any maples, or any trees at all. It was across the river, one block from Royal Street and Dr. Vincetti's office, and it was lined with stores and houses, perhaps a shade more genteel than Royal Street. 1821 was a big old frame house, gray with coal smoke, with gables and a wide front porch. A sign nailed to one of the porch pillars said *Rooms for Rent—By Day or Week*. I went up on the porch and pressed a bell-button beside the door.

A thin woman with a sallow face and dull eyes opened the door and gazed at me wearily.

"Does John Riggio live here?"

"Yes, but he ain't here now." She started to close the door.

"Just a minute, please. Do you know where I could find him?"

"At the bowling alley, I guess. This is his bowling night, and he went to his room just long enough to change his clothes, and I saw him go out carrying his bowling bag. He bowls on his shop team."

"I see," I said. "Is Mr. Riggio married?"

"All of my men are single. I don't rent rooms to couples, and no women. Women just cause trouble."

"Yes, ma'am. What bowling alley?"

"The Happy Time—over on Prince Richard Street."

"Thank you."

Her drooping mouth moved in what might have been a smile, and the door closed.

I knew where Prince Richard Street was, and I drove back across the river. The Happy Time was a long, low cement-block building with a gaudy neon sign over the sidewalk. On one side of it was a parking lot, but it was full and I drove around the block twice before I found a space two blocks away. I walked down to the Happy Time. Before I reached it, I could hear the rumble and crash of the balls and pins.

Inside it was bedlam. There were eight alleys, all full, and the bowlers milled around in the smoke and the shouting and the wooden roar, many of them with beer bottles in their hands. In the slots on the backs of the raised spectators' benches were rows of empties. I moved past a glass counter bearing a cash register and displays of bowling balls and equipment and back past a row of steel lockers to a small bar. A glance told me that the bar was dispensing beer and soft drinks only. I bought a bottle of beer and carried it to the alleys. A white-coated youth wheeling a cart filled with empty beer bottles hurried past me. I stopped him and said, "Busy night, huh?" I almost had to shout above the clashing sound.

He wiped a sleeve over his face. "Golly, yes. Industrial league semifinals. They started early, and they'll be bowling until midnight."

"Is there a team bowling for Ferris Abrasives?"

"Oh, sure." He pointed to a far alley. "They're in the first bunch, over there." He hurried away with his bottles.

I moved along the aisle between the spectators' seats and the benches for the bowlers. It wasn't difficult to find the Ferris Abrasives team; they wore yellow shirts with red lettering on the backs proclaiming the name of their company. I stood beside the scorekeeper and looked down at the black-crayoned names on the pad—*Fingerhuth, Stofer, Funderburg, Riggio, Ives.*

I drank the beer and watched the scorekeeper until he marked a strike in the line opposite *Riggio*. Then I looked up. A big man with a broad dark-skinned face and, short curly black hair turned away from the foul line, laughing, his teeth flashing white. Two yellow-shirted bowlers clapped him on the back. One of them handed him a beer bottle, and he tilted it high. I moved up to him and said, "Nice rolling."

He leaned toward me. "What?"

I made the motion of throwing a bowling ball and nodded in approval. He nodded and smiled, and I said loudly, "Your name is Riggio?"

"Yes." His lips formed the word, but I didn't hear it above the crashing of the balls and pins. He tilted the bottle again.

"Could I talk to you for a few minutes?" I shouted.

"What?" He leaned forward, showing his white teeth.

"I'd like to talk to you about George Shannon."

"Who?"

"George Shannon," I said loudly. "I'm with the Welfare Commission."

"Too bad about George." He shook his head sadly.

"I need your verification of the circumstances. If you just—"

"Come on, Riggio!" somebody yelled behind me. "You're up. Get another strike!"

Riggio looked at me, shrugged helplessly, took a swallow of beer, and moved up to the ball rack. One of his teammates took the bottle of beer from his hand. I yelled at Riggio, "I'll see you at the plant tomorrow."

He turned his head. "Okay."

I watched a moment. He threw his first ball into the gutter. A groan went up from the yellow-shirted ones. His second ball knocked down three pins, and another groan filled the air. Riggio turned away from the foul line, spreading his arms in apology. Close beside me a man yelled, "Don't worry, Riggio. You'll get 'em the next time!"

I walked away. Obviously it was not the time to get routine testimony from a witness to an industrial accident. I moved back along the alleys, finished my beer, placed the bottle in one of the slots on the back of a bench and went outside.

The April night was soft and quiet, and I was glad to be out of the Happy Time, the smoke and confusion, and the deafening crash of bowling balls against the pins. I lit a cigarette, walked to my car and drove across the city to the Blue Ridge Hotel. As I got my key, the clerk handed me a letter. It was a cheap white envelope, with the address penciled in sprawling letters: *Man in Charge of Geo. Shannon Case, Industrial Welfare Commission. Personal.* It had not been opened and had been forwarded to me in Steel City by some conscientious clerk at the state office building in the capitol. I carried it up to my room, sat on the bed and opened it.

Dear Sir: I can't keep quiet no longer. Geo. Shannon didn't have no accident. I saw what happened. I don't want no trouble and I can't tell no more, but I'm telling you true—Geo. Shannon was murdered.

One of Geo.'s Fellow Workers.

CHAPTER FOUR

I read it over maybe three times, slowly. Then I put it in my briefcase, along with the file on George Shannon, took off my coat and shoes and stretched out on the bed. The sky beyond the window changed from blue to a smoky gray and after a while, with the coming of dusk, the lights from the street below tinted the grayness. My thoughts fell into an old deadly pattern. Once more I was working for the agency, and suspicion and fear and death were riding the night. I had been away from it for a little while, in a world where a machine was the villain, or a dust, an acid, or maybe just human carelessness. In this other world no human was trying to hurt another human, but I was back again in the world where people deliberately hurt other people, in one way or another, and I hated it.

It was just a scribbled note, no doubt written by a crackpot, but it had put my thoughts back into that other world, the cruel one, and I couldn't escape it. I thought dismally that maybe the boss in New York, in his shrewd slyness, had sensed that all industrial deaths were not accidental, and that I would learn that this was true. No one knew what that wicked old man really thought, ever, and maybe he had sniffed profit in the possibility that death in a factory could be murder, probably was murder more often than anyone had ever dreamed.

The thought made me shiver a little, but at the same time I could imagine the boss chuckling and rubbing his hands at the publicity the agency would receive if one of its men uncovered a murder, in the guise of accidental death on the production line. That, alone, would justify his argument that men trained in criminal investigation should be on the payrolls of the state insurance offices. And why not? People in the factories were like people everywhere. They loved and hated, and could kill, if the desire was strong enough and the conditions right. I thought of all the accidents I'd investigated, the wicked machines I'd peered at, and I grew a little cold. If a man wanted to kill a man, in a factory, the possibilities were limitless; a loose nut on a safety guard, a cracked grinding wheel, one slip over a cauldron of molten steel, a cut safety belt, a wrong signal to a man on a high-tension wire, a laboratory explosion, gears, knives, presses, chopping machines....

Who could prove that it hadn't been accidental? A man was dead. A faulty machine, a ladder slipping, carelessness, maybe, and that was all. The state would pay the sum they had placed on a man's life, the widow would grieve, and somewhere in the shadows a murderer, never to be found out, chuckled gleefully and took what he wanted from the death of the man—a wife, a sweetheart, money, revenge.

Stop it, Bennett, I said to myself. You've developed a warped way of thinking. You're a guinea pig out here, far away from your home state, doing a job for your boss and this great commonwealth, and murder isn't on the program. Have a drink, Bennett, and forget that silly note from One of Geo.'s Fellow Workers. Just go about your business and get that ten thousand dollar check for Elaine Shannon....

Maybe I dozed a little, uneasily.

At six o'clock I got up, turned on the lights, washed my face and combed my hair, put on my shoes and coat and went down to the hotel bar. Al Purdy was sitting on a stool drinking beer. He gave me a sidelong grin. "Howdy, Jim. I figured you'd show up. Have a drink?"

"Sure," I said, sliding onto the stool beside him. "Is this on your expense account?"

"You know better, my friend," Purdy said. "Drinks never appear on an expense sheet to the Commission." He hunched his heavy shoulders and leaned toward me, grinning. "I'll tip you off—seeing as how you're new. You add your drinks to the cost of your hotel room or dinner or something."

"But that's cheating the state!" I said in horrified tones. "I'll have a dry martini—on your hotel bill."

Purdy laughed, motioned to the bartender, ordered a martini for me and another beer for himself, and said, "Hard day?"

"Not bad. How did you make out with Lame Back Flannagan?"

"Wait'll you hear," Purdy said. "The claims board will blow its top."

"What happened?"

"Well, as you know, Lame Back has been drawing his thirty-five a week regular for—let's see—twenty-two weeks. Total disability, he claims—said he couldn't even press a button on a punch press. Today I tailed him. He's working full time for a brewing company—and still drawing his disability compensation. I snapped a string of pictures of Lame Back heaving beer cases around." Purdy smiled in satisfaction. "That ought to convince the board that he's faking that back injury."

"It should," I said. "You were suspicious of Flannagan from the start, weren't you?"

"I sure was, but I couldn't prove that his back didn't hurt him, and neither could the doctors. Back claims are the worst—hard to pin down. A man says he hurt his back lifting something, and he can't work, and maybe he can't, most of the time, but not Flannagan. It's guys like him who make it tough for people on the level."

"What do you do now?" I was familiar with the case of Flannagan, a chronic applicant for disability compensation. Purdy had told me all about him, and had given him the title of "Lame Back."

"Shut off his compensation checks, and sue him for the money already paid him—not that we'll get it."

The bartender brought our drinks. Purdy sipped at his beer and said thoughtfully, "On the other hand, today I saw a man named Max Reardon, a real hardship case. He's in a bad way, flat on his back. Silicosis, advanced. His lungs are almost solid. Max's wife wants to work, but they can't get anybody to take care of the kids. I'm going to recommend that he be placed on permanent total disability, with compensation back to the day he had to quit work, plus all medical expenses. And I'll see that he gets the best doctors and all that. It's the least I can do." He sighed. "This is a thankless job we've got, but when you can help a man like Max Reardon, well, I guess it's worthwhile."

"And helps to make up for the fakes like Flannagan?" I asked.

Purdy nodded, his broad friendly face serious. "I've seen a lot of borderline malingerers, but Lame Back is an out-and-out fraud. I'll burn the hell out of him. How'd you make out with Mrs. Shannon? I met her right after her husband was killed, when Lew Kingston had the claim. Quite a looker, huh?"

"Very attractive," I admitted. "The little girl is cute, too." I was on the point of telling him about the note from One of Geo.'s Fellow Workers, but decided to wait a while. I finished my drink, refused Purdy's offer of another, bought him a beer and waited until he'd finished it.

"How about a movie, after we eat?" he asked.

I shook my head. "Me for bed."

We left the bar, and as we entered the lobby on the way to the dining room I saw Elaine Shannon turn away from the desk. She was wearing a loose tweed coat, no hat, and her short curling black hair glinted almost blue in the light. She hesitated, gazing uncertainly around, and then she saw me and came across the lobby with a swift, long-legged stride.

I said to Purdy, "Wait, Al."

Then she was standing before me, and I saw that her small oval face was pale. "I've been trying to find you," she said. "They told me you were not in your room, and . . ." She paused and gazed at Purdy.

"I believe you've met Mr. Purdy," I said. "He's with the Commission, too."

"Yes, ma'am," Purdy said, removing his hat. "I was with Mr. Kingston, right after . . ." He stopped, embarrassed.

"I remember," she said quietly, and her gaze returned to me. "I—I'd like to talk to you, if . . ."

"See you later, Jim," Purdy said. He nodded at Elaine Shannon and moved across the lobby toward the dining room.

She moistened her full lips with a pink tongue. "I'm sorry to bother you, but it's about my—my husband."

"No bother," I said. "We can go in the bar."

"I'd rather not. Perhaps someplace more private . . .?"

"My room?" I asked, feeling a sudden faint sense of excitement. I'd had it before, when I'd first met her, four hours earlier. There was something about her grave manner, a smoldering something I couldn't define, maybe a feeling of restraint, a veiled challenge, mockery, something. You have it, not too often, an immediate attraction for a woman when you see her for the first time. I suppose the feeling is different for every man, but you have it, and you can't explain it. It's not beauty or a pleasing figure, although Elaine Shannon had both. It's a manner, a tilt of a head, a scent, the tone of a voice, a way of moving, of clothes. Not necessarily more alluring than a million other women, but different—for you, anyhow.

She was still wearing the pale gray sweater beneath the topcoat, but had changed the slacks for a gray flannel skirt. I touched her arm, seeing the tiny movement of her small high breasts beneath the sweater, and I smiled.

"Your room will be fine," she said gravely, "if you don't mind."

"Not at all," I said, steering her toward the elevators.

As we stepped inside and turned, before the door closed, I saw Purdy standing in the dining room doorway gazing at me with raised eyebrows.

CHAPTER FIVE

She declined my offer to take her coat and she sat, rather stiffly, on a straight chair beside the writing desk. I offered her a cigarette, and she accepted. I lit it for her, placed an ashtray on the desk. Then I tossed my topcoat and hat across the only other chair in the room and sat on the edge of the bed. My room was on the fourth floor and the noise of the traffic came faintly up to us through the closed windows. The room was too hot, as most hotel rooms always are, and the steam bubbled gently from the radiator. Outside in the corridor the elevator doors opened and closed, and muffled voices drifted over the half-open transom.

From where I sat I could see the white tile of the bathroom, and I heard the soft dripping from the shower head, which I had vainly tried to turn completely off that morning. The thought occurred to me, and I admit it, as all men must, if they are honest, that I was alone, behind a spring lock door, with an extremely attractive widow; we were here together, at her request, in this quiet room. I thought about it, quite seriously, but at the time remembering my official duty and my responsibility to the state.

How did other men rationalize these things? I could make a tentative advance, if I were so inclined, and her response would tell me where we went from there. It would be a game, the oldest game in the world. The trouble was, I was not yet quite sure how I wanted the game to end or to begin, if I really wanted it to begin. I just felt the excitement, growing a little now, and I wished that I knew Elaine Shannon better, that I could have known her in some other way, in a normal man-meets-woman manner, in a bar, maybe, or at a friend's house, without the official facade between us. I sighed and made up my mind. She was the widow of a man killed in a factory accident, and I was the Industrial Welfare Commission, doing my duty.

She said, "Mr. Bennett, there is something I want to tell you." She gazed down at the un-lacquered nails of one hand and added in a lower voice, "I—I should have told you before."

"Yes?"

She took a deep breath and gazed at me directly, her eyes like blue mirrors. "It's about George. Yesterday I received a letter. It said that he had not died accidentally, that—that he had been murdered. I didn't know what to think. It worried me and—"

"Who wrote the letter?"

"It was signed 'One of George's Fellow Workers'—that was all."

"I see," I said.

"After I thought about it, I realized that if it were true, it might mean that I would not get the insurance money. I didn't tell you, because I wanted time to think. It seemed fantastic, and yet—you see, it's just little Jon and me now, and I need the money, very badly. Tonight I decided I'd better tell you—or the police. It seemed the honest thing to do. Nothing will bring George back to me, no matter how he died, and I want to do what is right...."

"Of course." I leaned forward and touched her hand.

She smiled, almost shyly, and I took my hand away. "Do you have the letter with you?" I asked.

She shook her head. "No. I locked it in a drawer at home."

"I'll pick it up in the morning. It's probably just the work of some crank, but I'd like to see it... How did you know where to find me?"

"I just called the hotels until I found the one where you were registered. There are only three main hotels in town." She looked down at her nails once more. "Do you forgive me for not telling about the letter?"

"Of course," I said. "It probably doesn't mean anything."

She stood up and took a deep breath. "I feel better now." She moved to the door.

I stood, too, and I said, "Have you had dinner yet?"

Her eyes were startled. "No. I—"

"Would you have it with me?"

She hesitated and a faint flush touched her cheeks.

"Strictly business," I said gently. "I can probably think of a few more questions to ask you."

Suddenly she smiled, showing small white teeth. "I'd love to. It's been a long time since I've—not since . . ." A hint of tears glistened in her eyes. "I'll have to call Mrs. Ryan. I left Jon with her."

I nodded at the phone on the desk. She turned away from me, spoke briefly in low tones, and faced me. "All fixed," she said brightly. "Mrs. Ryan is a wonderful person. I told her I'd be home in an hour."

We left the room and walked down the corridor to the elevators. As we entered the lobby, Al Purdy came out of the dining room. He gave Elaine Shannon a look of quick approval, winked at me, and moved away toward the desk, walking with his short-legged roll, like a sailor on the deck of a pitching schooner. In the few weeks I'd known Al Purdy I'd come to like him. He was friendly, like a collie dog, and capable and honest. His philosophy of life was simple; do his job, collect his pay, look forward to the weekends with his wife and two children (he had proudly shown me their pictures a number of times). All Al Purdy wanted was to live in peace with his fellow men, to have the things he wanted for himself and his family—food, clothing, a paid-up life insurance policy, a decent automobile, a television set, a drink when he wanted one. In another twelve years, he had told me, he would be eligible for the state pension, his kids would be through school, and he would devote his time to raising mink. He had just bought a pair of albinos for breeding, and had added them to the fifty other mink he kept in pens in his backyard.

I often wished that I could be like the Al Purdys of this world, satisfied with their lot, content with the world, ambitious for something they knew they could achieve, with moderate luck, and asking for nothing more. Happy men, the Al Purdys, and I envied them. I had no wife, no responsibilities, and yet I was restless. I worried about the present, the future and where I would be ten years from now. Nobody cared except myself, and that was the strange part.

Only a few tables were occupied in the dining room, and when I looked at my wristwatch I was surprised to see that it was twenty minutes until nine o'clock. When we were seated, I asked Elaine Shannon, "Drink?"

"No, thank you." Her gaze roved around the big room, and she seemed a little embarrassed, faintly ill at ease.

A waiter brought menus, and I ordered a martini for myself. Elaine Shannon studied the menu, and I noticed the white cleanness of her scalp where her black hair was parted. I recommended the ham with raisin sauce, and she said, "It sounds good—I'll have it."

My drink came and we ordered. I began to talk to her about ordinary things—the weather, of course, a movie I'd seen the evening before, a book I'd read on a recently lonely night in my hotel room, small things. Presently she smiled and touched my hand. "Please—don't mind me. I'll be all right. It's just that I haven't been with any man, like this, and I—" She lowered her eyes and turned her water glass slowly around on the tablecloth.

Our dinners arrived then, and as we ate she seemed to gradually relax and began to respond a little and to answer the few questions I inserted from time to time. I learned that she had been born in a small hill town in West Virginia. Her father had been killed in a coal mine cave-in, and she had quit high school to work as a waitress in order to support her invalid mother. There were no other children. Her mother died, eventually, of tuberculosis, and Elaine had sold the household effects to pay for the funeral. Then she took a bus to Steel City, where she found work on the inspection line in the plant of the Ferris Abrasives Company. There she had met George Shannon, the father of little Jonquil, whose wife had died two years previously. After her marriage to Shannon she quit her job and stayed in the apartment on Carbon Street to take care of Jonquil.

It was a commonplace story, reminiscent of the type found in the confession magazines, but she told it simply and I believed it. I guessed she had loved Shannon; whenever she spoke of him a little catch entered her voice.

I said, "What are your plans now?"

She lifted her round shoulders beneath the thin sweater. "Go to work. We had a little saved, but it's almost gone now, and I'll have to work. The insurance money, if I get it, will be held for Jon's education. Vernon—Mr. Dorr—has offered me my old job back at the plant. I'll have to find someone to take care of Jon."

"Mrs. Ryan?"

"Oh, no, I can't ask her. She's been very kind, but I'll need someone to stay with Jon all day, feed her and watch her. Mrs. Ryan is busy with the apartment house—she does most of the cleaning herself. Maybe I can put Jon in a day nursery. There's one here, and it's not too expensive."

As the waiter brought our coffee, she said abruptly, "I can't get that letter off my mind. What do you think about it?"

I shrugged, thinking of the letter I, too, had received. "I wouldn't be too concerned. There are some queer people in this world. Your husband's death has been certified as accidental. All the evidence points to it, and I don't mind telling you that I have already recommended that the state pay you the ten thousand dollars."

"Thank you," she said gravely. "But what will you do about it? The letter, I mean?"

"Maybe try and check on it, if we can. Those things are usually difficult to track down."

"Will you let me know, if you learn anything?"

"Certainly."

She stood up. "This has been very nice, Mr. Bennett, but I'd better get home." As I held her coat for her, she said softly, "Thank you very much."

"May I drive you home?"

She turned slowly to face me, a smile touching her lips, a slow smile, wise, the smile of a woman who knows that a man is attracted to her. We faced each other, aware of what lay between us, and she said, "Thank you, but I have a car outside."

"I see," I said bleakly.

"It was George's pride and joy, the car," she said. "Every Sunday he would wash and polish it."

"I see," I said again, like a fool, knowing that I had been properly rebuffed, and suddenly the world seemed a lonely place. Buck up, Bennett, I thought. She's just a woman, a widow, and there are a million others waiting around the corner to be met.

She moved out of the dining room to the lobby, and waited while I paid the check at the desk. When I joined her, she walked swiftly through the revolving door to the street, and in the cold April wind she turned to face me, buttoning her coat at the throat. The wind tossed her short black hair, her lips were very dark against the pale glow of her face and her eyes darker in the light which slanted across the sidewalk from the hotel.

"Where is your car?" I asked.

"Just down the street," she said carelessly. "I can make it."

"I'll pick up that letter in the morning."

"All right."

"Around ten?"

She nodded, her gaze remote, and she turned and walked swiftly away with her head high, her short hair blowing about her face. I watched her, and I shivered in the wind, because I'd left my coat and hat in my room. Then I moved along the side of the hotel until I came to the corner and saw her cross the street and get into a shiny five-year-old Plymouth sedan. I moved back into the shadows as she drove past, the directional lights of the Plymouth winking red at the intersection, signaling a left turn, toward the factory district and Carbon Street, and then she was gone. I walked swiftly back to the warmth of the hotel.

Al Purdy was at a booth in the bar, drinking beer and reading a newspaper spread on the table. He grinned at me as I sat down opposite him. "Nice babe," he said, folding the paper.

"Business," I said.

"Nice business. Have a beer?"

I shook my head. A waitress moved up. I said, "Bourbon and soda," and looked at Purdy. "Are you tied up in the morning? Anything special?"

"Well, Jim, I'll tell you; O'Connor called and told me to tail a blonde here who has been drawing temporary partial for weak eyes caused by spot welding. He wants me to check and make certain she's wearing dark glasses all the time, like the doctor ordered. Ain't that a hell of an assignment? But you know Old Maid O'Connor—the suspicious type."

"Yes, I know. Can you skip O'Connor's blonde? I might need some help in the morning."

Purdy took a long swallow of beer and then gazed at me steadily over the rim of the glass. "You look serious, Jim," he said quietly. "What's up?"

"I don't know. Probably nothing. But I've got to find out."

"Yeah?" Purdy said softly. "Tell me."

I told him quickly about the two anonymous letters from One of Geo.'s Fellow Workers, the one I'd received and the one Elaine Shannon had told me about. When I'd finished, Purdy drank the last of his beer and sighed. "I know," he said. "I've seen 'em before. I guess the Commission gets maybe a hundred screwball letters a day."

"Do you check them all?"

"Hell, no. We don't have time."

"Do you think we ought to check these?"

He gave me his crooked grin. "You're the big-time private dick—I'd like to see how you operate."

"Then we check?"

"Yep," Purdy said. "It won't do any harm. I'll be on deck in the morning."

CHAPTER SIX

When I entered my room it seemed that the subtle scent of Elaine Shannon was still there, and I saw the red-tipped stub of her cigarette in the ashtray. I undressed, put on pajamas, got the file on George Shannon from my briefcase, propped myself on the bed beneath the reading light and flipped through the various forms, letters and reports. I came to one headed STATEMENT OF EMPLOYER, which was stapled to a long pale green form bearing much fine print and many lines filled in with typewritten words. I read:

George A. Shannon, deceased, was a lathe operator in the main finishing department. At 10:05 A.M. on the day of the fatal accident he was engaged in his regular job of cutting unfinished abrasive grinding wheels down to exact tolerances with a steel cutting tool, when a maintenance repair man, John Riggio, hoisted a twenty-foot ladder to the skylight near Shannon's lathe for the purpose of replacing a broken pane. Riggio was carrying tools, and he asked Shannon if he would follow him up the ladder and hand him the skylight pane. Shannon agreed, and, carrying the pane of glass, he went up the ladder behind Riggio. While they were at the top, the ladder slipped and Shannon fell to the floor, striking his head and fracturing his skull (see medical report). Shannon was immediately carried to the plant dispensary and the company physician, Dr. Ordway R. Vincetti, was called. Riggio had saved himself from falling by clinging to a rafter beneath the skylight. The plant nurse, Mrs. Mary Koontz, administered first aid to Shannon. The doctor arrived promptly, about fifteen minutes after the accident, and after a quick examination an ambulance was called. Shannon died on the way to the hospital.

The statement was signed, *Vernon H. Dorr, Personnel Manager,*

The Ferris Abrasive Company.

I turned the pages, quickly scanned the brief preliminary report made by Lew Kingston, who had originated the investigation just before his transfer, and came to the testimony of the two witnesses, John Riggio and Vernon H. Dorr. I had been a little surprised that Dorr had been a witness, especially since I'd met him at Mrs. Shannon's, but I reread Riggio's signed statement first. It was similar to the employer's report, except for the ending: *I was standing on the ladder, two rungs above Shannon, removing broken pieces of glass from the skylight, when suddenly I felt the ladder slip out from under me. I grabbed a rafter just beneath the skylight and hung on. I heard the ladder fall to the floor, and when I looked down I saw Shannon lying on his back below me.*

Vernon Dorr's statement read: *I was walking through the finishing department and I saw Riggio and Shannon on the ladder. I stopped beside the ladder and gazed up at them. My attention was diverted and I looked off across the department. That was when the ladder slipped. I tried to steady it, but it fell to the floor. Shannon hit the floor violently right beside me. I immediately directed that he be carried to the plant dispensary....*

I lit a cigarette, placed an ashtray on a chair beside the bed, and turned on through the thick sheaf of papers. I came to the autopsy report. It was signed by Dr. Victor Van Horn, a pathologist employed by the Industrial Welfare Commission.

GENERAL DESCRIPTION OF BODY: The body is that of a well-developed, well-nourished white male measuring 74 inches in length and weighing about 160 pounds. The body had been embalmed and the abdominal and thoracic organs trochered. The scalp is covered with brown hair. The pupils are round, regular and equal. There is a small amount of pink fluid in the nostrils . . . No scars, no area of trauma.

ABDOMINAL CAVITY: The body is opened by a straight-line incision. Except for embalming fluid the peritoneal surfaces are smooth, shiny and dry.... HEAD: Incision in scalp reveals hemorrhage into the right temporal muscle.... After calvarium is removed it is noted that there is a large subdural hematoma. The blood in this area is coagulated. Hemorrhage has been recent, the clots still being very friable.... The brain weighs an estimated 1500 grams.... Surface vessels engorged.

FINDINGS: Death due to comminuted fracture in occipital area with subdural hematoma.

In spite of the medical language, it was a fairly familiar story to me, and I thought of all the post mortem examinations I'd witnessed, the reports I'd read. *Comminuted fracture in the occipital area with subdural hematoma.* That meant many fractures with bleeding. I remembered what Dr. Vincetti's nurse had said. Cracked like an egg shell. The subdural hematoma meant that Shannon could have been conscious, even lucid, for a brief time before he died.

I turned more pages, noted that the death certificate had been signed by Ordway R. Vincetti, M.D., and I came to a final printed question: *Do you certify that accident occurred on employer's premises and in the course of claimant's regular duties?*

Yes, Vernon Dorr had written.

I replaced the file in my briefcase and thoughtfully lit another cigarette.

The phone on the desk rang shrilly. I moved across the room, picked up the instrument, said, "Yes?"

"Mr. Bennett?" a breathless voice asked.

"Yes." I knew the voice, and I gripped the phone a little tighter.

"This is Elaine Shannon. Could—could I see you for a few minutes?"

"Now?"

"Yes, if it's not asking too much. You—"

"What's the matter?"

"I—I'd rather not tell you on the phone, and I can't leave Jon. Could you come out here?"

I glanced at my wristwatch, aware of the excitement again, remembering her presence in this room a few hours before. Twenty minutes after ten. I hesitated only an instant, and then I said, "All right. I'll be there in twenty minutes."

"Thank you," she said quietly. "I'm sorry to bother you...."

"No bother." I hung up.

It was a quarter of eleven when I stopped once more before the apartment building at 545 Carbon Street. There was a light showing from beneath Mrs. Ryan's door. I crossed the small foyer and went quietly up the stairs. The hall above was dimly lit. A brown teddy bear with an eye and an ear missing lay on the floor close to Elaine Shannon's door, and I smiled, thinking of little Jonquil. I knocked softly and waited.

From inside a low voice said, "Who is it?"

"Bennett," I said, a little annoyed at the rapid beating of my heart.

A key turned, the door opened and Elaine Shannon stood aside as I entered. She closed the door quietly and turned to face me. She was still wearing the thin gray sweater and the gray flannel skirt. Her face seemed pale, I thought, and her eyes were big and dark. I looked around for the little girl and saw that the bedroom door was closed.

She saw my glance. "Jon's asleep," she said, and turned away to crush out a cigarette in a glass ashtray on a table. The room was gently lighted by a shaded lamp in a corner and it seemed quiet and peaceful, away from the world.

I took off my hat and stood stiffly, aware of the scent of her, of the clean slender curve of her back above the small hips. "What's wrong?" I asked, realizing that I spoke in hushed tones, probably because of the quietness of the room and the little girl sleeping beyond the door.

She turned toward me. "Maybe I shouldn't have called you, but I thought perhaps you should know what—what happened. It may not mean anything, but . . ." She took a deep breath and avoided my gaze.

"Tell me," I said.

"Well, when I left you this evening, after I was halfway home, I suspected that a car was following me. At first, I thought it might be you—seeing that I got home safely." She gave me a faint brief smile.

"It wasn't."

"Please sit down. And don't look so—so grim. It probably didn't mean anything."

I remained standing. "What didn't mean anything?"

"This thing that happened. By the time I got here, I was sure the car was following me. After I stopped, it passed me and stopped, too. I was afraid to put the car away—the garage is in the alley at the rear of the building—and so I left it on the street. I got out and started for the building. A man got of the car and followed me. I started to run and he ran, too. I reached the entrance, and went into Mrs. Ryan's apartment. I told her about it, and she took a pistol and went outside to look, but the man was gone, and the car, too. Mrs. Ryan wanted me to stay with her, but I wanted to put Jon in bed— she was up much too late as it was—so Mrs. Ryan came up here with me and stayed awhile. She wanted to stay with me tonight, but I wouldn't let her. She likes to be in her own place, with Tippy—he's her dog . . ."

"I know," I said. "I've met Mrs. Ryan."

Her blue eyes widened. "You have?"

"This afternoon, after I left you. Routine check." I smiled at her. "You passed with flying colors."

A faint flush touched her cheeks. "I didn't realize that you would investigate so thoroughly."

"Ten thousand dollars is a lot of money, and the state just wants to be certain that the recipient is worthy, and all that."

"Am I worthy?"

"I think so," I told her.

She avoided my gaze, turned half away, and lit a fresh cigarette. "I wouldn't have called you," she said, "if something else hadn't happened. Mrs. Ryan left, and I locked the door and put Jon to bed. The telephone rang. It was a man and he said—" She frowned slightly, puckering her lips. "He said, 'Burn that letter, and stay away from Bennett, if you don't want any trouble.'"

"Is that all he said?"

"Yes. He just hung up."

"I see," I said, not seeing at all. "Did you know the man's voice?"

"No. It sounded sort of muffled."

"Did you get a look at him or his car?"

"Not too good a look. The car wasn't a dark color, like black, and it wasn't real light, either. Maybe a medium blue or green—and it was fairly new, I think. The man was tall, wearing a dark overcoat—I just had a glimpse of him."

"Would you recognize him if you saw him again?"

"No. I didn't see his face at all."

"I'm glad you called me," I said, knowing that I was telling the truth, because it had given me the opportunity to see her again, if for no other reason. I admitted it to myself, with no mental hedging. "Now that I'm here, would you give me that letter you received?"

"Yes," she said. "But why did that man follow me, and then call and say what he did?"

"I don't know."

She moved to the bedroom, softly opened the door and entered. I unbuttoned my topcoat, sat down and lit a cigarette. She came back into the living room and silently handed me an envelope. It bore the same penciled printing as the one I had received. I took out the single sheet of paper and read: *Dear Mrs. Shannon: This has been worrying me for two months and I've got to tell it. I didn't want to get mixed up in it and I can't tell no more, but I'm telling you true that your husband was killed on purpose. I also wrote the Welfare Commission and now maybe I can sleep better. One of Geo.'s Fellow Workers.*

I put the letter in my pocket. "Thanks. Either a crackpot is just trying to stir something up, or—" I paused and added, "Don't worry—and thanks for telling me."

She frowned faintly. "I don't want any trouble. I just want to make a home for Jon. It's the least I can do, and the insurance money would help."

"Yes," I said, and stood up.

"Must you go?" she asked quickly.

"No, but it's late...."

"Please stay a while." Her eyes shifted, and the faint flush touched her cheeks, and the small breasts lifted a little beneath the sweater.

"Scared?" I asked gently.

"A—a little."

"Don't be," I said, wondering gloomily if I ought to offer to camp in the hall outside her door for the rest of the night. She asked, "Would you like a drink?"

"Yes, if it's all right."

Her chin lifted a little. "Why wouldn't it be? George would want me to have friends."

"Am I your friend?"

"I hope so." She smiled, and there was a faint provocative light in her eyes. "You are, aren't you?"

"Yes—if you want me for a friend."

"I do," she said soberly. "Please take off your coat. I have some bourbon—it's been in the cupboard for ages—but no soda. Would water be all right?"

"Water's fine," I said, taking off my coat, moving right in, following her to the kitchen. "Can I help?"

She smiled at me over one round shoulder. "If you like."

I broke out the ice cubes while she got the whisky and glasses. She couldn't find a jigger, and so I poured the glasses about a third full and added water to the ice. Then we carried the drinks into the living room and sat side by side on a divan. We talked of a number of things, and she told me of the week she and her husband and the little girl had spent the previous summer in a cabin in the Michigan woods. "It was wonderful," she said softly, her eyes shining in remembrance. "The nicest time I ever had in my life. The days were warm and sunny, the nights cool, and we had a birch fire in the fireplace. George fished, and Jon and I walked along the beach, and once we had a fire on the beach and roasted hot dogs, and after Jon had gone to bed George and I would sit in front of the fire in the cabin and have a drink. The wind would blow the pines and the loons would cry—they scared me. In the mornings sand would be drifted under the kitchen door, and the sky was blue and the woods were green, and the coolness. I never had anything like that in Virginia—I never had anything there, but work and taking care of my mother, and my father coming home at night, black from the mine, too tired to do anything but sit and drink—when he had money for whisky. My mother begged him to get out of the mine, but he never would. He loved the mine and he hated it, and it killed him... ." She paused and gazed down at her glass, and I could see black lashes against one cheek.

"Go on," I said gently. "Talk about it."

"That was a bad time," she said in a low voice. "It was just my mother and me, then, and she died one night while I lay beside her. She just sort of sighed and turned on her side and she was dead. I was terrified and I ran to a neighbor's house up the mountainside and they came and covered my mother. I cried then, and the neighbors took me in, but I didn't like it there. The man began to touch me, whenever he had a chance, and one night he came to the room where I slept on the floor on mattresses with their children, and I hit him with my fists and scratched him and ran out of the house to the bus station and came here. I got a job at Ferris Abrasives, and met George, and—"

She gave me a twisted smile. "I'm sorry. This must seem very sordid to you, but I've never talked about it much, not even to George, and I wanted you to know what it meant to me to have a home of my own, and the love of a man like George." She lowered her eyes and added in a quiet voice, "My husband is gone now, but I'm going to try and keep the home he made for me. It's just a little apartment, sixty dollars a month, but I like it, and Jon likes it, and . . . well, I want to keep it, if I can."

"Of course," I said, and reached for her glass. "Can I make you another drink?"

"Yes—if you'll have one, too?"

I went into the kitchen, made two more drinks, and carried them back to the divan. She said suddenly, "Are you married?"

I shook my head. "Not yet"

"I knew it."

"How?"

She said seriously, "I don't think you would have stayed and had a drink with me—if you had been married."

I smiled. "Is that a compliment?"

"I meant it as one," she said, and added hastily, "Not that there is anything wrong in our having a drink together. It—it's been fun."

I placed my glass on the table beside the divan and put an arm around her shoulders. Her body stiffened slightly and she gazed down at the glass she held with both hands. I pulled her to me, and she began to tremble a little. She tilted her face then, her eyes closed, and I kissed her, gently at first, and then hard. Her lips were cool and soft, and they moved a little beneath mine.

"Wait," she murmured, and she leaned forward to place her glass on the table beside mine. Then she turned, blindly, and her arms went around me and her small slender body was against me. Her lips were cool no longer, but hot, and her fingers dug into my shoulders. My hands slid to the soft hollow above her hips, and her body moved, and I held her close.

Suddenly she strained away from me, and I let her go, not wanting to, and she said breathlessly, "No," and she reached a trembling hand for her glass.

I felt faint anger, and I said, "I'm sorry," knowing that I wasn't sorry, and hoping that she wasn't, either.

"Don't be," she whispered, not looking at me. "I wanted to kiss you." She sighed, a sibilant shuddering sound. "Let—let's leave it like that." Her short black hair was tousled, and a crisp curl lay across one cheek. She pulled the gray flannel skirt down over her knees and sat straight on the divan, not looking at me.

I offered her a cigarette, but she shook her head. I lit one and blew smoke at the ceiling. It was time to go, I thought, maybe past time. And if I knew what was good for me I'd go and I wouldn't come back. All you've got to remember, Bennett, is that she's the beneficiary of a death award from this great state and it's your job to find out whether or not her husband died in the course of his employment. Just remember that, and forget that she's a young and desirable woman, and keep your love life out of your professional life. She asked you here because she was scared, and you can't blame her for that. She told you a touching story of her childhood, and you had a drink and you made the pass you've been wanting to make since you met her. And you've had your answer—anyhow, half an answer—so let it lie, like she said. What the hell, Bennett? You know other women, even if they are four hundred miles away. What about that long-legged blonde in Police Records at the City Hall? And the grass widow with the yellow Cadillac in Lakewood? And what about Sandy Hollis, your ever-faithful secretary, holding down the office for you? If you were smart, you'd ask Sandy to marry you and settle down—if Sandy would have you—and forget Elaine Shannon and the blonde and the grass widow and all the others.

Across the room a telephone jangled. Elaine Shannon looked at me quickly, her eyes big and startled. I said, "Want me to answer it?"

She nodded silently, watching the phone, as if it were alive. I got up, moved to the phone on a small table against a wall. "Hello."

A man's guarded voice said, "Who is this?"

"Why?" I asked.

The voice said harshly, "I want to talk to Mrs. Shannon."

"You can talk to me."

"Is she there?" The words were clear, yet faintly muffled, as if the speaker were talking through a handkerchief.

"If you'll give me your name—"

There was a sharp click in my ear. I replaced the phone and looked at Elaine Shannon. "A man. He wanted to talk to you. He hung up."

She gazed at me silently, a flicker of something in her eyes, maybe fear. I moved over and stood looking down at her. "It was probably the same man again, the one who called you before."

"Yes." She shivered a little.

"If it rings again tonight, don't answer it. And keep your door locked."

She nodded.

I hesitated, and then I said, "Maybe I'd better tell the police. Do you want me to do that?"

"Whatever you think best. What does it mean? Who is that man?"

"I'll try and find out." I picked up my hat and coat and moved to the door. "Good-night."

She didn't move, but sat staring at me soberly. "I shouldn't have kissed you," she said. "I—I keep thinking of George...."

"I know," I said.

"George is dead. Maybe he wouldn't care. Do you think he would care?"

If I were a two-months-old corpse, I wondered, would I mind if my wife kissed another man? "Maybe he would," I said. "I'm sorry."

"Don't be, please.... Will I see you again?"

"Sure," I said, and I tried to smile. "I'll call you tomorrow."

"All right."

"Lock your door."

She nodded. "It's automatic, but I'll check it to make certain." She stood up, smoothing her skirt. I went out, closed the door and waited until I heard the catch click from the inside. Then I went down the stairs.

CHAPTER SEVEN

The light was still shining from beneath Mrs. Ryan's door. I knocked softly. Inside the little terrier began to bark, and Mrs. Ryan opened the door. When she saw me her broad pleasant face broke into a smile. The dog ran out, sniffed my shoes, and began to wag his stubby tail.

"Nice Tippy," I said.

Ryan said, "He knows you now, Mr. Bennett. Will you come in?"

"For a just a minute, if you don't mind." I took off my hat and stepped inside. As she closed the door, I said, "Mrs. Shannon called me about that man who followed her. She said she came in here with you, and that you went outside to look. You didn't see him?"

She shook her head. "Nope. He'd scooted, car and all. If I'd seen him, I'd have put a bullet in his gizzard. Anything I hate is a woman molester. Slimy." She made an expression of distaste. "Why, the poor girl was scared stiff."

"She still is, I'm afraid," I said. "Whoever the man was, he phoned her twice since—once while I was there. What do you think about notifying the police?"

"No harm, but I don't know what they can do—except maybe keep an eye on things around here. I'll tell 'em. The cops on the beat here are good friends of mine."

"Good," I said.

"Mrs. Shannon is a mighty pretty woman," Mrs. Ryan said. "Mighty pretty, and a widow, too. She'll have to get used to men noticing her, now that her husband is gone. It's natural but not that what happened tonight. If a man can't come courting, open and above board...." She sighed. "It takes all kinds, though. I'll keep an eye open tonight. There ain't much that goes on in this building, day or night, that I don't know about. For instance, I heard you go up the stairs to Mrs. Shannon's over an hour ago." She grinned at me.

"Yes," I said, feeling a faint irritation. "She asked me to come. I'm in charge of the investigation of her husband's death, and—"

"Don't get stuffy, son," she said, still grinning, "and you don't have to explain to a snoopy old woman. She's mighty pretty—"

"You said that," I told her.

"So I did. Ain't that liquor I smell on your breath?"

"We had a couple of drinks," I admitted, wondering why I felt obliged to explain. "She was frightened, naturally."

"Of course," Mrs. Ryan said. "Her husband has been gone for over two months now, and you can't blame her for getting lonesome. Every woman should have a man. Of course, I don't have a man anymore, either, but Herman and me had our life, and a good life too. When he was called, I didn't want another man—there's only one Herman. I picked up the pieces and made a new life. But Mrs. Shannon is young yet, and the little girl needs a daddy...." She brushed a hand over her eyes. "Oh, bosh. Let's have a beer, son."

"Thanks, Mrs. Ryan, but it's after midnight . . ." I opened the door.

"All right," she said cheerfully. "I'll have one, anyhow. Herman and me used to drink, three, four bottles apiece, every Saturday night, when he wasn't on a run. Of course, it ain't Saturday night now, but Tippy likes beer. I give him a saucer full, and you should see him lap it up! I talk to Tippy, late at night, and when I hear the train whistles I think of Herman, riding the cab...."

"Yes," I said. "Good-night, Mrs. Ryan."

"Good-night, son. Don't forget we got a date to shoot rats."

"I won't," I promised, and closed the door.

Carbon Street was dark and quiet, with only a few cars at the curb before several bars and tiny hamburger places. My car was parked beyond a dark alley entrance at the side of Mrs. Ryan's apartment house. I walked in the wind, thinking of Elaine Shannon, and started across the alley. Behind me I heard a soft scraping sound, like feet moving on cement, and I started to turn. An arm snaked out and hooked beneath my chin, jerked me backward into darkness. I went off balance, clawing at the arm, but it was like a steel band. I felt frantic fear and I struggled violently. Warm breath touched my cheek and a voice grunted in my ear. "Stay away from Elaine Shannon. Hear?"

I kicked and tried to twist free, and I gulped for air. Something exploded against my head and I soared away into an enormous starry silence.

A white light probed any eyeballs. I brought up a hand in protest, tried to shield my eyes. But the light bore steadily on me, and I squinted at it from between spread fingers. I knew that I was lying on the cement of the alley, and the memory of Elaine Shannon was like a ghost beckoning to me in the far depths of the night. My head throbbed wickedly. I moved my hand to a spot behind my right ear. There was a lump there, and my fingers grew sticky and warm. The white light blinded me and I said viciously, "Take that goddamn thing away."

Above me a voice said, "Drunk, huh?"

I muttered a word, something obscene, and pushed myself to one elbow. A hand grasped my arm and pulled. I stood up and leaned dizzily against a wall. There was a soft click and the light went off, and the sudden complete blackness was worse than the light. Then a dim glow filtered back and I saw the thick outline of a man, the glitter of a badge, and the metallic gleam of a flashlight. The man was standing in the alley entrance, between me and the light from the street, and I couldn't see his face. He leaned down, picked up my hat, and handed it to me.

"Thanks," I mumbled. "Somebody slugged me."

"Come out here." A hand tugged on my arm, pulled me to the sidewalk. The streetlight fell across the man's face, and I saw that he was a policeman, young, with pale eyes in a tanned face. He tucked the flashlight under one arm and hauled out a leather-covered book. "Robbery, huh?"

"No," I said. "Wait a minute." I felt for my wallet. It was gone. "Yes. Robbery."

"How much money?"

"Fifty or sixty dollars." It was difficult for me to stand steadily, and the pain behind my ear seemed to be spreading through my brain and made me squint my eyes. I leaned against the building and took a deep breath of the cold air.

The policeman peered at me. "I guess you're not drunk, mister.

What happened?"

I told him, and he wrote in his book. Name, address, occupation. When I had finished, he snapped the book shut. "I saw your feet sticking out from the alley. Get a look at him?"

"No. He grabbed me from behind. Damn near strangled me."

"State Commission, huh? Working on a casein town?"

"Yes. I was seeing the widow of a man killed at Ferris Abrasives."

"Would that be George Shannon's wife?"

"That's right."

"Know her well. I knew George, too. A nice couple. Got a cute little girl. Live at Mrs. Ryan's. I know pretty near everybody on this beat . . . You want to see a doctor?"

"I'll be all right." I nodded at my car parked just beyond the alley entrance. "That's my car. I'll just go back to the hotel."

"Turn around," the policeman ordered. "Let's look at it." Obediently I turned while he peered at the lump behind my ear. "Not too bad. Must have used a sap. Soak it in cold water and take a couple of aspirins."

"Yes, officer."

"What hotel? The Blue Ridge?"

I nodded.

"Can you make it all right?"

"Sure." I started to move away.

"I'll report it, but I don't suppose it'll do any good—since you didn't get a look at him. I'm sorry about your money."

"So am I." I paused and looked at him. "You might be on the lookout for a tall man in a dark overcoat."

"I thought you said you didn't see him."

"I didn't. Watch for him anyhow—especially around Ryan's apartments."

"What if I see a tall, guy in a dark overcoat, maybe acting suspicious?"

"Nab him, and call me at the hotel."

"I don't get it, mister. If you—"

"Never mind," I said wearily. "I don't get it, either. Thanks, for everything." I walked, fairly steadily, to my car and got in. As I drove away, I glanced in the rearview mirror. The young policeman was standing on the sidewalk gazing after me.

It was a quarter of one in the morning when I reached the Blue Ridge Hotel. There were plenty of parking places along the curb and

I left the car, after locking it and noting that the parking meter hours did not begin until nine in the morning. I should most certainly be up and about before then, I thought grimly. There were a number of things I wanted to do in the next twenty-four hours. Up until now I had been a man working on an insurance investigation, a routine job, except for the attraction Elaine Shannon had for me, but now it had turned into a personal thing. A man had slugged me and robbed me; that was personal, and he warned me to abandon my work on the Shannon case, to forget it. But I couldn't, not now, even if I wanted to, and wasn't working for the state. To hell with the state. If I had to serve it in order to learn who had struck me from behind and robbed me, then I would do it, but my motivation from here on out would be selfish. Tenderly I probed the lump behind my ear, and I felt the beginning of a slow rage.

In the lobby of the hotel, Al Purdy was sitting in a leather chair and staring moodily out of a wide window overlooking the street. As I walked toward him, he turned his head and his eyes widened in surprise. "My God, I thought you were in bed."

"Why aren't you?"

"I'm worrying about my mink. The weather has turned colder and I'm afraid my wife forgot to turn up the oil heater in their pen. A mink is a delicate animal."

"Why don't you call her?"

"At this time of night? Are you crazy? It would scare her silly." He peered at me closely. "Where you been? You look a little pale around the gills."

"I feel pale."

"You didn't answer my question."

"I had to go out."

"On business?"

"Certainly," I snapped. "Why the hell else?"

He grinned at me. "Don't be touchy. Was it Mrs. Shannon?"

I nodded.

"I envy you, pal. In all my years with the Commission, I never drew a dish like that to investigate." He sighed. "All I ever got was saggy old blisters with fourteen kids." He squinted his eyes at me. "What's the matter with you? You act jittery."

"Is the bar still open?"

"Sure. I just left it."

"Come on." We entered the bar and sat in a corner booth. Purdy had beer and I had a bourbon and soda. I told Purdy about what had happened in the alley entrance on Carbon Street.

Purdy whistled softly, and then grinned. "Maybe you'd better file a claim with the Commission for injuries suffered in the course of duty."

I touched the lump behind my ear. "The way I feel now, I think I'll ask for temporary total disability."

"She's real nice," Purdy said thoughtfully. "Mrs. Shannon, I mean."

"Yes."

"What goes on? How do you figure it?"

"I don't know," I said, thinking of the hot velvet of Elaine Shannon's lips. "I thought tomorrow morning we'd run out to Ferris Abrasives and snoop around a little."

"So that's what you had in mind?"

I nodded.

"Okay," Purdy said cheerfully. "I told you I'd be on deck. Will you feel up to it?"

"No, but we'll go anyway." I stood up. "Meet me at nine."

"Right," Purdy said.

We said good-night at my door, and he moved down the hall humming a little tune. At the corner he turned, grinned at me, and said, "Nice."

"Go to hell," I told him, and entered my room. If Purdy figured that I'd been slugged by one of Elaine Shannon's jealous boyfriends, maybe he was right. She was certainly attractive enough to have many male admirers, myself included, even if she was a recent widow, and in spite of what she had told me about being a recluse since husband's death.

I went dismally to bed. My head still ached, and I didn't go to sleep for a while. I was botching things up, and the boss would be sore. The professional detective, loaned out on a trial basis to a state workmen's insurance set-up, was acting like a rookie cop falling for one of the girls on his first bawdy house raid. It wasn't like that, of course, but it was similar, in principle if not in actuality. Remember this, Bennett: You're here in this state to make a good impression, to sell them on the idea of hiring men from the agency, and here you are, getting emotionally involved with a soft-voiced widow who only wants to collect the ten thousand bucks from the state, to which she is entitled, and bring up her stepdaughter in decency and dignity. She has no doubt been nice to you because she thinks you have the power to pay her the ten thousand, which she needs so badly. I twisted uneasily and turned over, to ease the pressure of the pillow from the sore spot behind my ear, and after a while I slept.

Sometime during the blackness a shrill ringing sound brought me groggily upright, and I sat stupidly, my nerves twanging at the sound. When I realized that it was the phone, and not the crack of doom, I left the bed and groped my way to the desk, to the phone. I found it, fumbled, dropped it to the floor, found it again, and on my hands and knees held it to my ear.

"Yes?"

A man's voice, faintly muffled, said, "Bennett?"

"Yes."

He laughed softly. "Hi, Bennett. Your wallet's outside your door. Thanks for the fifty-six bucks. And don't forget what I told you about Elaine Shannon. I won't be so gentle the next time." He laughed softly.

"Listen, you bastard, I—"

He hung up, the soft laugh still in my ears.

I pushed myself upright, replaced the phone, groped along the wall until I reached the door. I turned the lock, pushed open the door. My wallet was lying on the floor of the hall. I picked it up, flipped through it. My money was gone, of course, but my papers and identification cards were intact. Across the face of my agency license was a penciled word, *Hah!*

I closed the door, turned on the lights, and picked up the phone again. When I got the desk, I said, "Did you notice a man in the hotel a few minutes ago—maybe a tall man in a dark overcoat?"

"What, sir? What did you say, sir?"

"Never mind," I said wearily. "Just never the hell mind."

CHAPTER EIGHT

The plant of the Ferris Abrasives Company was in the center of Steel City's industrial section, close to the river, and Al Purdy and I drove the length of Carbon Street to reach it. On the way, I pointed out Mrs. Ryan's apartment house, the alley where I'd been slugged, and the windows of Elaine Shannon's apartment. Purdy merely nodded and we drove on until we came to an area of high steel fences, looming black smoke stacks, acres of parking areas filled with cars, a scattering of restaurants, stores and beer joints. There were maybe a dozen factories in a space of ten blocks, including one steel mill and an assembly plant of a famous popular automobile. A long black and white sign running across the top of a jagged roof proclaimed the site of Ferris Abrasives. The wide mouths of maybe a dozen kilns yawned against the bright April sky, with black smoke rolling away from three of them.

Purdy said, "They have two tunnel kilns, too. Gas fired, with oil conversion. I've been here before. On the Shannon case with Lew Kingston, and another time, when a fellow got his arm under a press. Amputation at the elbow. He got permanent partial, seventy percent disability, for life."

"No guards on the press?"

"Oh, sure," Purdy said. "But the guy wasn't using 'em, and the foreman didn't notice. The company got soaked extra for negligence." He sighed. "It's the same way with goggles. You wouldn't believe the eye cases we have—all because they won't wear goggles."

I turned the Mercury into a wide cement drive and rolled along between a sea of parked cars until we came to a steel gate with a small white-painted building at one side. A gray-uniformed man stepped out and peered in the car window.

"'Morning, gentlemen."

"Good morning," Purdy said. "We want to see Mr. Dorr."

"Yes, sir." The guard handed him a visitor's form and Purdy signed for both of us. The guard said, "Just a minute," and went inside the gate house. We could see him speaking into a phone. He came to the door and waved a hand. "You can park over there."

I drove into a vast black-top area surrounding the plant and nosed up against a brick wall beneath a sign which read, *Parking—Visitors*. We got out of the Mercury and followed a cement walk bordered with the brittle dried bones of last year's flowers until we came to an ornate entrance flanked by two cement columns. Glass doors bound with brass swung inward into the moist steam heat and closed with a hissing sound. We stood in a marble-floored reception room with straight chairs around the walls and a table in the center loaded with dull-looking industrial trade journals and house organs. At one side was a switchboard with a bored-looking blonde before it. Three glum-faced men with briefcases on their laps sat along one wall.

We moved to the switchboard and the blonde noticed us and said coolly, "Mr. Purdy and Mr. Bennett—to see Mr. Dorr?"

"Yes, ma'am," Purdy said.

"You can go right in." She nodded toward a short hall off the reception room.

We walked past the three men, who gave us dull envious looks, and Purdy said to me behind the back of his hand, "One thing about working for the Commission—they never give you the brush-off."

At the end of the hall was a frosted door labeled *Personnel*. Purdy opened it and we stepped into a small plain outer office containing four straight chairs, a stenographer's desk, a typewriter, six tall steel filing cabinets and an insurance company calendar depicting a hunting scene, complete with speckled bird dogs and hearty bronzed hunters carrying bright blue-barreled guns, all against a background of clear blue sky and trees heavy with brown and gold leaves. Behind the desk sat a girl with hair the color of the brown leaves in the picture. She wore it tight and shining, pulled to a knot on the top of her head, and she had a milky skin and a faint dusting of freckles. Her mouth was very red, and when she spoke I thought that her voice was as well modulated as any movie star's.

"Mr. Dorr will be right out. Please have chairs."

I smiled at her, thinking that Vernon Dorr had very good taste in secretaries, and Purdy and I sat in two of the four chairs. Purdy said, "Thanks, honey."

She smiled demurely, lowered her eyes, and turned back to her typewriter. Purdy winked at me and tilted his chair against the wall. In some ways he reminded me of my assistant, Alec Hammond, back in Cleveland. They had the same sardonic glint in their eyes, the same careless attitude toward life, and the same stubbornness and sense of loyalty. Alec Hammond was loyal to me, and to the agency. Al Purdy was loyal to the state, really and truly, in spite of his sometimes-cynical attitude. Some ignorant people would call him a bureaucrat, but I had learned in the few weeks I'd known him that the tax payers were getting much more than their money's worth. The modest salary the state paid him could never compensate for Al Purdy's genuine liking for the people he dealt with, and his feeling for justice. He could be tough, as he was going to be in the case of the malingering Lame Back Flannagan, who was swindling the state, but he was also fair and compassionate, as with the case of Jim Reardon. I suddenly decided that I liked Al Purdy very much, and I hoped that he would achieve his dream of a pension, and a home in the suburbs, and a little mink ranch of his own.

From a door in the far wall we could hear the muffled drone of voices, a man's and a woman's. The voices stopped, a chair scraped, the door opened and Vernon Dorr came out. His tall form was draped in a brown gabardine suit, and a dark green tie was neatly knotted in the slot of his soft white shirt. With his clear eyes and crew haircut he looked like the All-American college boy, somehow younger and more boyish than I remembered him from our meeting the afternoon before.

He smiled, shook hands with Purdy, said "Glad to see you again, Al," and nodded at me. "Mr.....?"

"Bennett," I said.

"Oh, yes. How are you today?"

"Fine."

"Well, gentlemen," Dorr said, "come in my office. There is someone I want you to meet." He stepped aside and Purdy and I went through the door.

A woman was sitting by a glass-topped desk. She gazed at Purdy and me with cool impersonal eyes behind glasses with thick brown frames, Purdy gave her a friendly smile. She nodded shortly, flicked her gaze over me, and turned to stare out a window at a bleak skyline of jagged factory roofs. She was young, in her late twenties, I guessed, and was dressed simply in a plain gray wool dress. She wore no hat, and her brown hair was short and combed and parted in a plain fashion. Her clear white skin bore no cosmetic and her lips were pale, as all women's are beneath the paint. Her long slim legs were crossed, the skirt pulled primly down over her knees, and she wore low-heeled black shoes. She sat stiffly, but the pleasing contours of her tall body were subtly suggested beneath the dress.

Vernon Dorr closed the door and said politely, "Miss Shannon, this is Mr. Purdy and Mr. Bennett, both of the Industrial Welfare Commission." He paused, coughed slightly, and added, "Mr. Bennett is investigating your brother's death."

She swung her head quickly, and I smiled at her, but she didn't smile back. Al Purdy sat on a chair and swung his hat between his knees.

Vernon Dorr said to me, a trifle nervously, "Miss Shannon is the sister of George Shannon." He moved to his desk and sat down behind it. "She has some questions to ask about the payment of the death award for her brother. It's—uh—fortunate that you and Mr. Purdy stopped in this morning." He lit a cigarette, and then held out the package to the woman. "I'm sorry—will you have a cigarette?"

She shook her head, her lips tight. "I don't smoke, Mr. Dorr."

"Sorry," he murmured, and looked at me hopefully.

I said, "What questions did you wish to ask, Miss Shannon?"

She looked at me, and her eyes were as cold as any I'd ever seen. "Am I correct in saying that my brother was killed in the performance of his work with this company?"

Before I could answer, Vernon Dorr said hastily, "Of course, Miss Shannon. That has been established, and I have certified the application."

"Is that correct, Mr. Bennett?" she asked crisply.

I looked at Al Purdy. He gave me a crooked grin and shrugged. I turned to Miss Shannon and said gently, "It was correct."

"Was?" Vernon Dorr said sharply. "What're you talking about? George Shannon fell from a ladder, in this plant, and he was killed. It was accidental, in the course of his employment, and the state is obligated to pay the claim."

Al Purdy said quietly, "Vernon, for a personnel man, it seems to me that you're damn anxious to increase your insurance costs. Every accident is charged against your claim experience, you know that. You're responsible for safety and plant protection and working conditions, aren't you?"

"Yes," Dorr snapped, "but I can't control what a man does on a ladder."

I said to him, "I'd like to speak to you privately for a minute."

"About George Shannon's death?"

I nodded.

"We can talk here, then. Miss Shannon is his sister, and anything you have to say to me, you can say in her presence."

I looked at Purdy. He was the veteran state man, and would know the procedure. He shrugged again. "You're handling it, Jim."

I told them, as briefly as possible, about the anonymous letters received by Elaine Shannon and myself, the phone calls, the man who had followed Elaine, about the blow on my head and the warning I'd received. When I had finished, I said carefully, "I was about to close this case and recommend that the full death benefit be paid to Mrs. Shannon, but now—"

"How did she want it paid?" Miss Shannon broke in.

"In a lump sum."

"I thought so," she said bitterly. "Thinking of herself. She'll squander it, and nothing will be left for my little niece, Jonquil. I came to see Mr. Dorr this morning to see if the money could not be paid to some responsible person. My brother's wife is not a responsible person."

I said, "She told me that she wanted the money for the little girl, not for herself. And she is the legal beneficiary."

"Of course she is," Vernon Dorr said impatiently. "There is no question about that. But all this nonsense about mysterious letters and warnings—what do they have to do with it?"

"Maybe nothing," I said, "and maybe a lot." I caught Al Purdy's eye, and he nodded firmly.

"Cloak and dagger stuff," Dorr sneered. "You fellows have been reading too many detective stories. I don't know about the letters, and the man you say attacked you, but I do know that the money—"

"I want the money paid to me," Miss Shannon snapped. "George was my brother, and I'm Jonquil's aunt, her only living relative. I want the Commission to appoint me the administrator of the insurance money."

I shook my head, "I'm afraid that's impossible, Miss Shannon. The state compensation laws provide that benefits be paid either to the claimant, or to his or her dependents."

"I'll get a lawyer," she said firmly. "I'll fight it. That woman is not going to get her hands on that money."

Al Purdy said in his quiet voice, "Miss Shannon, I'm afraid that no one will receive any money until the cause of Mr. Shannon's death is definitely established."

Vernon Dorr said stubbornly, "He was accidentally killed while working in this plant."

"That remains to be proven," Purdy said.

Dorr looked at me and said incredulously, "You don't mean you're serious about this?"

I sighed and said, "Perhaps you and Miss Shannon have not realized the implication here. Mrs. Shannon is aware of it, and she has given her full cooperation, even though it may mean that she will not receive the money. You may as well face it—George Shannon may have been murdered."

There was a shocked silence in the office for maybe two seconds. Then Vernon Dorr spoke, his voice oddly strained. "But that's ridiculous. George Shannon fell from a ladder to a cement floor and died of a fractured skull. The autopsy showed that. And this company, through me, has officially certified that he died as a result of an accident in the course of his employment. What more proof does the state want?"

Al Purdy said, "It is our duty, as agents of the Commission, to investigate every fatal accident in this territory, regardless of the circumstances, or the employer's statement. We believe that further investigation of this case is justified. The payment of the death claim depends upon what we find is the true cause of death."

I gazed at Purdy in admiration. He knew the workmen's compensation laws, and he sounded like a lawyer. Behind him were years of industrial accident investigation, and I realized that I had a long way to go before I could really qualify as a state agent. It takes all kinds, I thought, with each of us knowing our particular job, as I knew mine with the agency, and all of us were indifferent, even contemptuous, of the other fellow's job and of the knowledge and experience which had made him competent in his job.

Miss Shannon said coldly, "And if you persist in this silly investigation, and decide that my brother did not die accidentally—then what?"

"Then no death payment will be made to the widow," Purdy said. "In this state, murder is not considered an occupational hazard—not in an industrial plant."

"I am not concerned about the widow," Miss Shannon said in the same cold voice. "I am only concerned about my brother's daughter. It's not fair to her."

"I'm sorry, Miss," Purdy said. "I hope we are wrong, but it is our duty to determine the truth."

She turned impatiently away, and once more stared out the window. I could see her clean profile, and the sudden trembling of her lower lip.

Vernon Dorr said to Purdy, "Can you give me any particular reason for your attitude? I mean, aside from what you have told me? Who would want to murder George Shannon? And why?"

"I don't know," Purdy said. "We're going to try and find out."

Dorr made a scoffing sound. "If I took seriously every crackpot letter I get from screwballs with imagined grievances...."

"We know," Purdy said wearily. "We get 'em, too. But we've got to investigate every angle."

Dorr muttered something under his breath, probably a swear word, and said in a resigned voice, "All right. Let's get it over with. What do you want of me?"

I said, "We want permission to inspect the area where George Shannon worked, and to interview the employees who were near him at the time of the accident."

"But Lew Kingston did all that," Dorr said impatiently.

"We know," Purdy said.

"Maybe I'd better call your chief," Dorr said. "Maybe I'd better tell Austin O'Connor about this."

"Call him," Purdy said. "We'll wait." He folded his arms and settled back in his chair.

Dorr flushed, and avoided Purdy's amused gaze. Miss Shannon moved a toe nervously and continued to stare out the window. From the outer office we could hear the steady tapping of the brown-haired secretary's typewriter. Purdy looked at me and winked. We both knew that a call to the suspicious and old-maidish O'Connor would only result in a shrill order to push to the limit the investigation of George Shannon's death. If there was a chance to save the state money, Austin O'Connor would pounce on it. Dorr knew it, too, and he didn't reach for the phone. He merely said in a tired voice, "Do you want to go back in the plant now?"

"If we may," Purdy said, somewhat smugly.

Dorr got up and opened the office door. "Joyce, will you please have one of the guards come in here right away?" He turned to us, his eyes bleak. "I hope you two know what you're doing."

Purdy grinned. "So do we."

"Please make your investigation as quickly as possible," Dorr said, "and try not to disrupt the employees any more than necessary. A thing like this, two strangers snooping around, asking questions, gets the whole shop in an uproar. The boys in Production will be on my neck."

"We'll do our best," Purdy said.

The door to the outer office opened and a slight, middle-aged man in a gray uniform entered and stood quietly. Dorr said to Purdy and me, "I'd take you back myself, but I'm pretty well tied up this morning."

"That's all right," Purdy said. "We'll tell O'Connor that you cooperated."

"Thanks," Dorr said dryly, and turned to the guard. "Pete, this is Mr. Purdy and Mr. Bennett, from the state Commission. They want to talk to some of the men in the finishing department, and to inspect the area where George Shannon worked. Please take them back there, and stay with them until they are finished."

The guard nodded, and said, "This way, gentlemen."

I said to Dorr, "We'll see you before we leave."

He nodded, and I glanced at Miss Shannon, but she didn't turn her head. I followed Purdy and the guard out the door.

CHAPTER NINE

The guard led us down a long hall past rows of office doors with black words on the glass—Sales, Production, Purchasing, Engineering, Accounting. Al Purdy said to me in a low voice, "I kind of took over back there, because I didn't want Dorr to get you out on a limb, but this is your baby. You do the talking. I'll just stand around and watch."

"All right," I said. "I figure that somebody who worked near Shannon wrote those letters. He's the man I want to pick out. Keep your eye on all of them—for signs of nervousness, anything unusual."

"Right," Purdy said.

The guard slid back a steel door and we entered a huge long room filled with hydraulic presses. Men were working at the presses and the hiss of many pistons filled the air. None of the men looked at us directly, but I saw many of them gazing at us from the corners of their eyes. Purdy noticed it, too, and he said, "You'll get used to it when you enter a production area. They know when a stranger is around, and they can spot a white collar a block away."

We left the rows of presses and entered another area where three white tunnel kilns stretched away across the cement floor. Steel trucks loaded with grinding wheels of all shapes, sizes and colors stood on tracks waiting their turn to enter the inferno of the kilns. "They burn 'em here," Purdy said, "before they go to the finishing department." He pointed across the huge room, and at the far end I saw the dim circular bulks of enormous round kilns. "They burn the big wheels in those, coal fired. Tunnel kilns are faster for the smaller stuff."

"Maybe you ought to ask Dorr for a job," I said, grinning.

"You learn a lot, over the years," he said seriously, "but one of these days I'll be up for retirement with the Commission. Of course, those guys back there on the presses make more than I do." He gave me a rueful grin.

"You can't have everything," I said, watching blue gas flame hissing into the ports of the tunnel kiln on our right. Although we were twenty feet away, we could feel the heat on our far faces.

"Hot job," Purdy said, "but the round kilns are hotter to work near, almost asbad as blast furnaces. You see, grinding wheels are mixed up out of abrasives and clay to hold them together, pressed into shape, and then burned until they are like stone—twenty-three hundred degrees in those tunnel kilns—and then they've got to be smoothed and finished. Then the steel or lead bushings are put in the holes and they're tested at almost twice the speed they'll run on a job—so they won't break in operation. When a grinding wheel breaks, it's worse than bullets, honest. The pieces go right through a man. But they got it down to a science now, and with the safety guards there isn't any danger. But a man running a grinder without guards is flirting with murder."

"Tell me more," I said. "You're better than an encyclopedia."

"Murder," Purdy said. "That reminds me. Here's the finishing department."

We walked through a wide archway and a high metallic whine hit our ears. The guard waved an arm and said in a loud voice, "Here you are, gentlemen."

There were six rows of lathes, of various sizes and construction. At each stood a man, and on the spindles and in the steel chucks were grinding wheels of all colors; gray, black, blue, white, some of an orange tint, and in all sizes and shapes. On metal stands beside the lathes were stacks of rough grinding wheels waiting to be trued and finished to the required sizes. And here, too, I was aware of the many eyes upon us, although every man appeared to be attending strictly to his job.

A shirtsleeved man wearing an unbuttoned vest, the pockets of which were filled with notebooks and pencils, came up to us. The guard spoke to him. He nodded and said to Purdy and me, "I'm the foreman of this department." He spoke loudly, so that we could hear him over the sound of the cutters biting into the rough abrasive, and pointed to a big lathe, painted green and cream, in the middle of one line. "That's where George Shannon worked, on that big automatic. He was a hole borer, too, one of my best men. Nice fellow, too. Too bad he got killed."

I nodded and looked upward. A skylight was almost directly above the big machine. The guard said, "You fellows go ahead and look around. I'll take you back to the office when you're ready." He stepped back and leaned against a steel post. A few of the men at the machines waved at him and he waved back, grinning. The foreman nodded at us cheerfully and sauntered away.

Al Purdy said in my ear. "Go ahead. I'll stand by."

I went to a machine on the line which ran beneath the light. Its operator was a young fellow in blue jeans and a neat tan shirt. He grinned at me, shut off his machine and listened attentively, his head cocked to one side. I told him who I was, what I was doing, and asked the questions: *Did you know George Shannon? Were you here the day he fell? Did you see him fall?*

He said he hadn't been working at Ferris Abrasives at the time of the accident, and went back to work. The second man, a fat red-faced man with a Dutch accent, told me the same thing. The third man was sullen, but he admitted that he'd seen Shannon after he fell to the floor. "He didn't say nothing. He looked dead. I helped carry him to the first aid room." He muttered something else I didn't catch, and I said, "What?", but he ignored me, and I moved to the fourth man.

He was a burly blond kid with yellow fuzz on his fat cheeks. He was ready for me. It was as if some type of communication, a radar-like message, had gone through the line of men. "Sure, I saw it all," he said. "It was just after rest period. George had drunk a Coke and put the bottle on the floor beside his machine. Just then John Riggio came up dragging a ladder and sets it up beneath the skylight. It's a big ladder and George helps him. Then Riggio hands George a pane of glass, points at the skylight, and climbs the ladder. George follows him up with the glass. His machine's going all the time, you understand? It's an automatic, and all you gotta do is let it run until the cut is finished. See?"

"I see," I said.

The blond kid turned around, to see if the others were watching him. They were, but you had to look closely to catch the veiled eyes, the alert watchfulness made without the turn of a head. "Well, mister," the kid said, hitching at his belt, "the next thing I know the ladder hits the floor and George, he's sprawled out, limp-like. Riggio, he's hanging by his fingernails from the rafter. He almost got what George got. Well, all the guys rush over to George. Mr. Dorr, he's there, too, and he tells them to carry George to first aid. Riggio, he managed to hoist himself to the roof."

"Thanks," I said. "Was anyone else around at the time. I mean, anyone from the office beside Dorr?"

"Office?" He looked at me blankly, as if I'd uttered a word in a foreign language. Then he said, "No—just Mr. Dorr. They say he was there, before it happened, but I didn't see him. I heard he grabbed for the ladder, but he couldn't hold it. I saw him after George fell, dancing around and hollering orders." He grinned at me. "You know how they do."

"Yes," I said, trying not to smile. "What's your name?"

"Prokoff," he said. "Louis Prokoff."

"Thanks, Louie." I moved down to the next man. His story was the same as Prokoff's, even to the Coke George Shannon had drunk.

The sixth man was tall and cadaverous-looking, with sunken cheeks and a long nose. He needed a shave, and his eyes were bloodshot. Like the rest, he was ready for me, and he shut off his lathe while he talked. His account was the same as the others. It was almost as if they had rehearsed it. He said his name was Eddie Fleet. "I always liked George," he began. "We was sort of buddies. He turned out a fair day's production, and he minded his own business. I saw him go up the ladder, and when I looked again he was on the floor and the guys was running toward him. I'm telling you true, that's all I saw." His little red eyes regarded me suspiciously.

"Thanks, Mr. Fleet."

"Mister, hell," he grunted. "Eddie's my name."

"Thanks, Eddie."

He gave me a half smile then, showing yellow teeth, and turned back to his lathe. In addition to a shave, he needed a haircut, and his overalls were greasy and sweat-stained. He started the lathe, ignoring me, and I moved away.

All along the line the stories were the same; George Shannon had climbed the ladder behind Riggio, carrying a pane of glass. The ladder had fallen, Shannon had hit the floor. Just an accident, a mishap in a factory, another statistic for the industrial accident reports. George Shannon, grinding wheel lathe hand, killed on the job. Another claim for the state Commission to pay, another widow, another child without a father.

I didn't take any notes. Men in a factory are suspicious of a pad and pencil. Maybe it's the old speed-up, boys, a time study. Maybe the front office has got something on us. Maybe they're going to pull something at the next union contract negotiation meeting. Don't tell 'em nothing. Play it dumb. They can't hurt you with something you didn't say. But, still, I felt that I could recite the story of George Shannon's death in my sleep. I talked to every man in the department, even though I was aware that the guard leaning against the post was beginning to fidget, and that Al Purdy was walking around restlessly. When I had finished with the last man, I walked over to Purdy.

"Notice anything?" I asked him.

He shook his head. "Nothing special. They've all been keeping an eye on you."

"I know."

The guard came up, said eagerly, "All finished?"

I nodded, and Purdy and I followed him back through the factory to Vernon Dorr's office. The brown-haired secretary looked at us brightly, showing white teeth against red, red lips. Dorr stood beside her, a sheaf of papers in his hand. He gave me an amused smile. "Well, Mr. Bennett, did you find the murderer?"

"Let's talk privately," I suggested.

"Oh, come now," he said, grinning. "We can trust Miss Crandell. She's secret agent number X-77."

"Very funny," Al Purdy said.

"I want to talk to this ladder man, John Riggio," I said. "The one who asked Shannon to carry the pane of glass."

"All right," Dorr said. "But isn't this all a little melodramatic? After all, it's just a simple shop accident . . ."

"If you think death is simple," Purdy said, "try it sometime."

Dorr stopped grinning, and said to me, "I'll have Riggio come to my office. Do you want to talk to him in private?"

"Not necessarily."

Dorr turned and entered his office. Purdy and I followed him. Dorr picked up the phone on his desk. "Call Maintenance," he said. "I want John Riggio in my office right now." As he replaced the phone, he said to me, "This is the damnedest thing I ever heard of. Murder, for God's sake!" He glared at me with hot eyes. "If Elaine—Mrs. Shannon—doesn't get that money, it'll be a dirty shame. She needs it."

Purdy said curiously, "Vernon, why are you so steamed up? What do you care?"

Dorr swung toward him. "I'll tell you why," he snapped. "When a man gets killed in this shop, I feel responsible. We owe something to his family. We're paying our share of premium rates to protect our employees, and I can't understand why you're stirring this up. It doesn't matter to Mrs. Shannon how her husband died—he's still dead, and she's got a little girl to support. I think this FBI business is silly, and these dark hints about murder are silly, too. You're supposed to be one of the top agents in the state, Al. But still a man who gives a working man a break. Why are you fooling around with this? Don't you have enough work to do or what?"

"Now, now," Purdy said soothingly. "Calm down. What happened to Miss Shannon?"

"She just left," Dorr snapped. "And that's another thing. She—"

The door opened and the secretary peeked in. "Mr. Riggio is here."

"Send him in," Dorr said sullenly.

The secretary disappeared, and John Riggio stepped into the office. His white teeth flashed as he smiled at Vernon Dorr. "They told me to come to your office. That is bad. Am I fired?" His voice held a faint accent which I had not noticed the evening before.

"Hell, no," Dorr said. "We wouldn't fire a good man like you." He nodded at Purdy and me. "These men are from the Industrial Welfare Commission. They want to ask you some questions about George Shannon."

Purdy said to Riggio, "My name is Purdy, and this is Mr. Bennett." He held out a hand.

Riggio hesitated, rubbing his right hand over the front of his greasy coveralls. "My hands are pretty dirty, mister. I've been packing the fifteen-hundred-ton press."

"That's all right," Purdy said, smiling. They shook hands, Riggio looked at me. Then he smiled. "Ah, we meet again."

"Yes," I said. "What did you roll last night?" I shook his hand, too. It was indeed dirty, sticky with black grease. But I didn't mind. I was once an auto mechanic, and I liked the feel and the smell of grease and lubricating oil.

"Four-twenty," Riggio said. "Not so good." He shook his head sadly. "I missed too many spares."

"It's not bad," I said. "I'm lucky to roll a hundred a game."

Dorr said curiously, "You two have met?"

"At the bowling alley yesterday," I told him, "but we couldn't talk—too much racket."

Dorr said to Riggio, "You know what the Welfare Commission is?"

Riggio nodded vigorously. "Sure, sure. It is the state insurance for working people. They paid me two years ago when I mashed my foot in a foundry in Wheeling. They paid the doctor and the hospital thirty dollars a week for me while I was absent from work. The Commission is a good thing."

"That was in another state," Dorr said, "but much the same all over the country."

"A good thing," Riggio repeated, nodding.

I said to him, "Will you tell us what happened when George Shannon fell from that ladder?"

He spread his hands and looked bewildered, "But I have already told that other man and Mr. Dorr, and they wrote it all down."

"I know, but tell us again—just how it happened."

"Well, let's see." He raised liquid brown eyes to the ceiling, frowning as he concentrated. "It was like this: I see there is a broken pane in the skylight over the finishing room. I carry a ladder and the glass to the proper spot. George Shannon, he is working right there. I have tools to carry, too, and I ask him if he will bring up the glass. We think the ladder is secure. It has on its legs—what do you call them, Mr. Dorr?"

"Safety shoes," Dorr said, "to keep the ladder from slipping."

"Yes," Riggio said. "We go up the ladder. I take out the broken pane and I ask George to hand me the new glass. Then I feel the ladder move, and I start to fall. I grab the rafter and hang on. I hear the ladder hit the floor and I look down. George is on the floor. I am sweating. I am shaking. But I hang on, and I pull myself up. A close thing for me, but poor George—he died. I blame myself. If I had not asked him...." He paused and shook his head sadly. "A bad thing. I feel it is my fault."

"It was nobody's fault," Dorr said. "It was just an accident." He looked at Purdy and me with a mocking smile. "Well, does everything check?"

"So far," Purdy said. He looked at me. "Right, Jim?"

I nodded.

"Then I'll send John back to work," Dorr said, "if you don't mind. He gets two dollars and sixty cents an hour."

Purdy made an elaborate gesture of looking at his wristwatch, and said, "He's been away from work about ten minutes. Send a bill to the state for his time."

Dorr's young handsome face flushed. "If the state's got so damned much money," he blurted, "why can't they pay a measly death claim to a widow without quibbling about it and dreaming up blood and thunder nonsense about murder?"

Riggio's eyes grew wide. "Murder? What is this about murder?"

"Never mind, John," Dorr said. "Thanks for coming up here." He looked at me. "Are you all finished with him?"

I nodded, and said to Riggio, "Thanks."

He hesitated, and then said, "You're welcome," and his white teeth flashed in his dark face. It struck me that he was a handsome man. With a mustache, he'd make an acceptable movie hero, Latin type. He put on a greasy felt hat and left.

"Damn it," Dorr said angrily, "there'll be a hundred wild rumors about George Shannon all over the shop before the noon whistle."

I said, "You mentioned murder in front of him. I don't think that was very smart."

Dorr started to say something, and stopped. He sighed, and pulled a hand down over his face. "I know," he said wearily. "I shouldn't have said it. I—I didn't think. They've been pushing me pretty hard here, and union negotiations are coming up, and now this...."

Purdy patted his arm. "Relax, pal. When we make our final report, we'll send you a copy. After that, it'll be up to the Commission." He nodded at me and moved to the door. "Ready, Jim?"

I said to Dorr, "Can your secretary give us the address of one of the men in the finishing department?"

Dorr's eyes narrowed. "Which one?"

"Eddie Fleet."

"Why do you want his address?"

"It'll be in the report," I told him, aware that Al Purdy was looking at me with a question in his eyes.

Dorr said carelessly, "Ask her anything you want."

"Thanks." Purdy and I went out.

In the outer office, Purdy said in a low voice, "What's the matter with him? Is he frustrated in love, or something?"

"Maybe."

"And what about this Eddie Fleet? Is he—?"

I silenced him with a wave of a hand and moved over to the secretary's desk. She looked up, gave me her bright smile. I said, "Will you let me have the home address of Eddie Fleet, in the finishing department?"

"Certainly," She stood up, smoothed her skirt over rounded hips, and moved gracefully to a tall steel file, and pulled out a drawer. "He lives at 616 Clinton Street," she said.

"May I see his record?"

Silently she handed me a large manila envelope with typed information on both sides. I saw that Edward Aloysius Fleet was forty years old, was married, had four children, three boys and a girl, ranging in age from nine months to eight years. He was buying his home, had finished the second year of high school, liked pinochle and bowling, had a brother and an uncle who also working at Ferris Abrasives, and had been in the company's employ for over ten years. Before that he had been a railroad brakeman, a truck driver, a gas station attendant, and a tree trimmer. Inside the envelope I found various data pertaining to Edward Fleet and his job—his photo, withholding tax signature form, his absence record (he was a steady worker, I noted), his hospital, surgical and life insurance coverage in a company-sponsored program, and a number of other records.

I handed the envelope to the girl. "Yours records are very complete," I told her.

"Thank you."

"How many shifts do you have working now?"

"Just two. The first shift quits at four o'clock."

"And that is when Eddie Fleet quits?"

"That's right."

Purdy said to her, "What time do you quit work?"

"Five o'clock." She smiled at him. "My husband picks me up."

"Pardon me," Purdy said, grinning. "I'm married, too."

"How nice," she said demurely.

We left her then, and went out to the steam-heated reception room. The bored-looking blonde gave us a mechanical smile as we passed her desk. Outside we stood a moment, and then started for my car. A woman was standing by the gatehouse, and I saw that it was the prim and cool sister of the late George Shannon. She stood tall and straight, her hands thrust into the pockets of a loose black coat, the April wind blowing at her short brown hair. She had removed the dark-rimmed glasses and in the sunlight she looked young and fresh, even without powder or lipstick. She saw us and moved forward, walking with a clean long-legged stride, the black coat flirting with her legs. When she reached us, she stopped and said to me. "I've been waiting for you. I want to talk to you."

"All right," I said, "but if it's about your brother's death, you'd better talk to both of us."

"Mr. Dorr said you were in charge of the case."

"That's right, Miss," Purdy said. "I'm just helping out." He moved away, winked at me, and said over his shoulder. "I'll catch a bus downtown. See you at the hotel."

"Wait, Al," I said, but he kept going.

I turned to Miss Shannon. "Do you want to talk here. Or shall we go somewhere?"

CHAPTER TEN

She started to speak, but in that instant a whistle blew shrilly. It was followed by other whistles all around us, making a raucous din of sound over the city. Her lips moved, but I couldn't hear the words, and I held up a hand and smiled. Presently the whistles stopped and almost before the last harsh note had died, the parking area all around us was filled with moving cars, jockeying and pushing for a place in line on the drives leading away from the plant.

She gazed about in surprise. "My, but they get out quickly."

"They're hungry," I said. "They've been working since even this morning. What time did you have breakfast?"

She laughed, and it changed her features. The prim stiff look went away, and her white teeth flashed and crinkles appeared at the corners of her eyes. "Late," she said. "At least nine o'clock." Suddenly she stopped laughing, and once more her expression became withdrawn and severe, and she said crisply, "We can talk here. I just wanted to ask you—"

On a sudden impulse I said, "Listen, you're not teaching the third grade now. Of course we can't talk here." I looked at my wristwatch. Twenty-five minutes until twelve noon. "We can talk while we're having lunch."

She looked startled. "Does—does it show?"

"Does what show?"

"That I'm a school teacher."

"Just a little. What's wrong with that?"

Her rounded chin lifted a little. "Nothing is wrong with it. It's a fine profession."

"One of the finest," I agreed. "Where do you teach?"

"In a little town twenty miles from here, up in the hills. And I teach the sixth grade, not the third."

"You're not teaching today. Playing hooky, huh?"

She smiled again, and I decided that I liked to see her smile. "No school today, because of a teachers' meeting. I skipped the meeting and decided to see Mr. Dorr and get this business about my brother settled."

"Do you live here in the city?"

She shook her head. "No. I room in a farmhouse near the school."

"Isn't that rather lonesome for you?"

The prim look appeared again, and her lips tightened a little. "Mr. Bennett, this conversation began with my request to speak to you— on business. Shall we keep it that way?"

"I mentioned lunch," I said. "I'm hungry. I'll even throw in a couple of martinis."

"I don't drink. Really, Mr. Bennett...."

I took her arm and guided her gently to the Mercury. Except for Elaine Shannon, she was the only direct connection I had so far with the death of George Shannon, and asking her to lunch was probably not standard operating procedure for an agent of the Commission, but back in Cleveland I was not hampered by any set procedure, or a restricted expense account. One thing about the boss—he never complained about expenses as long as he got results, and fat fees. At the car, Miss Shannon hesitated only a second, and then she got in.

As I started the motor, I said, "At the Blue Ridge Hotel they have a room called The Poinsettia Room. Good food, I hear. Okay?"

"I was there once, years ago," she said. "It will be fine. But, really . . ." She looked at me, and I saw the uncertainty in her eyes.

I said gently, "It's all right. My name is really Bennett, I'm a genuine state employee, and I'm not married. I'm assuming that you're not, either—not that it makes any difference."

"No," she said slowly, "I'm not married. I—I guess that shows, too. You see, when Mr. Dorr told me that you were in charge of my brother's case, I was prepared to dislike you. And when you said you were holding up the insurance payment, I was certain that I disliked you. It was silly, I suppose—I realize now that you're just doing your job."

"That's right. Are we all squared away now?"

"Yes." She smiled at me.

"Good."

As I started to drive away, a new blue Dodge sedan with Vernon Dorr at the wheel came from behind a building and went through the gate to the street. For no reason at all, I noted that the license number was X-566.

The Poinsettia Room was on the top floor of the Blue Ridge Hotel and was the Rainbow Room of Steel City. The windows overlooked the smoky city and the brown wooded hills beyond. The place was all chrome and red leather, and a small stringed orchestra softly played Strauss waltzes. I skipped a drink and we both ordered the luncheon special, broiled swordfish with coleslaw and tartar sauce. While we waited, she told me that her first name was Gloria, that she had been engaged to marry an airline pilot who had been killed in a crash in Florida three years previously. After that, I gathered, she had more or less withdrawn from the world and had buried herself in teaching.

By the time our lunch arrived I decided that I'd done quite nicely in the way of securing background information without seeming to pry. It was one of the things I'd learned over the years, part of the technique the boss insisted upon. It was a technique some of the state Commission agents I'd met could well copy. When dealing with people, individual backgrounds are important, and the lack of background knowledge often meant failure in any type of investigation. A blunt question and answer approach usually resulted in antagonism on the part of the person interviewed, and in the failure of the investigation. Go to the head of the class, James.

While I was thinking these smug thoughts, Gloria Shannon said suddenly, "This is very pleasant, Mr. Bennett, but as the walrus said, the time has come—but that's trite, isn't it?"

"Yes," I said, "but sometimes I like the trite familiar things—like shoes and ships and sealing wax—"

"And cabbages and kings," she finished for me. "Now that we've both been trite, I may as well confess that I feel a little like Alice." She gazed about the big softly-lit room. "I really do. It's been so long since I've been anywhere. I've been more or less buried out there in the country...."

"Lonesome?"

She nodded. "Mr. and Mrs. Stockmaster—they're the old couple on the farm—are nice, but they go to bed at nine every night, and, well, it's really been rather grim, now that I think about it." She smiled at me. "I must confess that you've made me remember that there are things in life beside teaching kids, and grading papers, and going to a weekly movie with a couple of other lonely teachers. I get up at six in the morning, in school all day, with maybe an apple and a sandwich for lunch, home at four in the afternoon, then nothing but supper with Mr. and Mrs. Stockmaster, and talk of crops and sick cows and the new neighbor two miles down the road. In the summer, it's a little better, but not much. I usually go to a maiden aunt's home in South Bend, and that's dull, too." She sighed.

"You're just wasting your young life," I said, intending to be facetious. "You'll be an old, old woman before you know it."

"Yes," she said soberly. "That's true. But I can't forget Mike—burned to death in that plane. Nobody can ever...." She averted her eyes, and I saw the glint of tears. "Mike liked things gay, a party every night, when he wasn't flying. We weren't alone very much, because he wanted people around him, lots of people. I think Mike was maybe afraid of something, maybe airplanes, but he'd never admit it. He had a South American run, and before his last trip he asked me to marry him. He said he was going to quit flying and get an office job with the airline, and he tried to laugh about it. He said he was getting too old to be a flyboy. We planned a house that last night, in Miami, and he talked of kids.... But coming up from Rio he ran into a storm, a hurricane, really, but he brought the plane in to a crash landing at Miami. The passengers and the rest of the crew got out, but they found Mike in the pilot's seat, burned...." She brushed a hand over her eyes and tried to smile at me. "I sound like a candidate for a lonely hearts club, don't I? I almost forgot what I wanted to talk to you about."

"Must you remember?"

She took her glasses from a pigskin purse and put them on, and suddenly she was cool and brisk once more. "I meant what I said about that money," she said. "I've already talked to an attorney, and he told me that if I can prove that my brother's wife is not competent to handle the money, the court will appoint someone who is."

"Meaning you?"

"Preferably," she said coldly. "Who else? I can't sit by and let Elaine throw away that money. In her hands it will never do Jonquil any good, and she is the one to be considered. After all, she's my brother's daughter, and Elaine is merely her stepmother."

"Why don't you like Mrs. Shannon?"

She lifted her shoulders briefly. "Frankly, I don't really know. I've never liked her, since the day George first brought her to meet me. I think she is shallow, insincere, and I don't trust her. Call it intuition, if you like. I've got a feeling that once she gets that money she'll disappear, and I won't see Jonquil any more. I—I love her very much. George and I were pretty much alone in the world, and Jonquil is all I have left of my immediate family. After Helen died—she was my brother's first wife—he and Jonquil stayed with me for a while, at the Stockmasters', and I feel like—like a mother to her. I should have something to say about her care and her future."

"Of course," I said, "but Mrs. Shannon impressed me very favorably." As I spoke, I thought ruefully, *She sure as hell did, Bennett,* and I went on. "She seems devoted to the little girl, and concerned about her future. I'm sure she'll take good care of her."

Gloria Shannon's eyes narrowed behind the glasses. "I don't agree," she said shortly. "In the first place, my brother didn't have time to really know Elaine before he married her. She rushed him into it. He was—was infatuated with her. I'll admit that she's attractive, and she has a demure, pleasing personality—when it suits her purpose. God knows what her background is. George never told me, except that she came from someplace down south, and that she worked at Ferris Abrasives—that's where he met her. But I've seen the cold, calculating look in her eyes, and I know that she has no real love for Jonquil. After all, Jonquil is really nothing to her."

I thought of the implications, the mother complex, resulting from tragedy and frustration, and of the smooth patter with which the psychologists and the psychiatrists would classify the case of Gloria Shannon, spinster, and I said gently, "Could you be a little . . . jealous?"

"Jealous?" she flared. "Don't be ridiculous, Mr. Bennett. Why would I be jealous?"

I thought, *You could be jealous of a woman who had a husband, a normal life, the companionship of a child, even if it were not her own, and all the things you're missing,* but I said, "Never mind. I'm sorry. You say you want the custody of the child, but how can you care for her? I mean, with your teaching?"

"It's all arranged," she said crisply. "She'll stay on the farm with the Stockmasters, and I'll be with her every day after school and on weekends and during the summers. She'll be of school age soon, and I can take her with me to the school where I teach. It's a good school, with classes from the first grade to the first year of high school. It would be an ideal arrangement."

"Mrs. Shannon may think differently," I said. "Maybe she loves

Jonquil, too, and has plans for her."

Gloria Shannon gazed at me thoughtfully. "You'll see," she said, smiling a little. "I'll find a way. Elaine has no right to that money or to Jonquil."

I was a little irritated and maybe it showed in my voice, "Can you give me a reason for your attitude?"

"If you mean have I caught Elaine mistreating Jonquil, no. But I've got a kind of fear—now that George is gone. I can't explain it, but I hoped you would understand."

"Even if I did," I told her, "there is nothing I can do. Mrs. Shannon is the legal widow of George Shannon, and she is entitled to the death payment. There is no way to get around it."

She said quietly, "And now we come to this; you mentioned this morning that my brother may have been—murdered. That's fantastic, isn't it?"

"No. It happens every day."

"Are you really an agent for the state Commission?"

"Want to see my badge?"

"Of course not, but you don't seem the type."

"Why not?"

"I—I don't know. I have a feeling I've seen you before."

I thought of a story in the papers six months before concerning my part in nabbing the murderer of an old man on a farm in Ohio. The boss had never been modest when it came to publicity for the agency and the people who worked for him, and I wondered uneasily if Gloria Shannon had seen that story, or perhaps another. I said, "I've never seen you before but that's my misfortune."

She flushed faintly. "Please—you don't mean that, I'm sure. Who would want to murder my brother?"

"I don't know. I'm trying to learn if he was murdered. All the evidence says that he was not. I hope not."

"But you've got to make certain?"

"Yes."

She sighed. "I don't understand. What makes you think that—?"

"Never mind," I broke in. "I'm probably way off the beam."

"But if it were true?"

"Not a dime would be paid by the state. Murder, in this state, is not an industrial occupation hazard."

Light glinted on her glasses as she turned her head to gaze out of the window. "Shall we change the subject?" she asked in a low voice.

"A pleasure. What are you doing tomorrow night?"

She turned her head quickly. "That is a very quick change, Mr. Bennett."

"Call me Jim," I said. "I think we should talk some more." I thought of Elaine Shannon, and I stirred uneasily. It suddenly seemed to me that George Shannon's death and the results of his death, were connected, in one way or another with his wife, Elaine, and his sister, Gloria. There was something below the surface, maybe a dark something, and I had to dig for it through Elaine or Gloria or maybe both or maybe nobody. You start something, and you are stopped, but you go on, through the contacts you have, or even without any contacts. I had the feeling that Gloria Shannon could tell me more than she had told me, if she would, and I wanted to know what she knew, whatever it was.

"I'm busy tomorrow night," she said coolly. "I plan to attend a lecture at the high school auditorium on The Role of the Teacher in the Child's World. I'm going with another teacher—a lady teacher, I might add."

"We can have dinner at least," I said. "Meet me here, in the lobby, around six."

"Well," she said thoughtfully, "the lecture isn't until eight . . ."

"Skip the lecture. We'll go to my hotel room and look at my portable etchings."

"Don't be crude," she said crisply. "Do you really want to see me again?"

"Why?"

I shrugged, and smiled. "Business, maybe."

"I think not," she said shortly. She took off her glasses, placed them in her purse, and then clicked the purse shut sharply. "Thank you very much for the lunch." She stood up and I stood, too. "Am I to understand that I cannot count on your cooperation in the matter of the insurance?"

I shook my head. "I'm afraid not. I can tell you better after I talk to a man named Eddie Fleet."

"Who's he?"

"A worker at Ferris Abrasives."

"But—?"

"My job is to establish the facts. That's what I'm trying to do. Then it's up to the Claims Board.... No dinner tomorrow night?"

She shook her head firmly, her lips a tight line.

"Some other time? Soon?"

"I—I don't know."

"It'll be a very boring lecture."

"I suppose so," she sighed, "but I promised my friend . . ."

"Bring her along," I said generously.

She shook her head, smiling a little. "Miss Cameron is past sixty, a lovely person, but . . ."

"But what?"

She gazed around at the Poinsettia Room. "She wouldn't feel at home here. Now, if it were a chicken supper at the church . . ."

"Maybe we can find a church chicken supper."

"I'm afraid not," she said. "Perhaps we'd better keep our relationship on a business basis."

"Why?"

She looked away from me, out over the city, and her lips trembled a little.

"Mike?" I said gently.

She turned abruptly and walked away. I left some money on the table and followed her out to the elevator. Both of us were silent on the way down, and when we reached the lobby she moved swiftly to the street entrance and out to the sidewalk. We stood there, with people hurrying past. The sun was gone and high in the sky clouds were scudding before the wind. A spattering of rain hit our faces. Gloria Shannon shivered a little and turned up the collar of her coat.

I said, "Can I drive you somewhere?"

She shook her head, her eyes clouded and remote. "Thank you, but I have a car. I left it in a garage to be serviced, while I went out to the factory. It should be ready now."

"Call me at the hotel—if you change your mind about tomorrow night."

"I won't change my mind." She looked away from me. "Goodbye, Mr. Bennett."

I watched her walk away and turn at the corner, and I thought, *Mike was a lucky guy—until his luck ran out. It finally killed him, what he feared, but other people must live, honey, and you can't bring back the dead.... You're quite a guy, Bennett—hell with the women, all right. A black-haired widow, and an old maid school teacher. Well, really not an old maid, not yet. But she's headed that way. She'll wither in a dusty schoolroom, unless somebody does something about it. You were a Boy Scout, Bennett. Have you done your good deed for today? Have you ever done any good deeds, Bennett?*

I went back into the hotel. Al Purdy was not in the lobby, the dining room, or the bar. I called his room. No answer. As I left the phone, the clerk came up and handed me a folded piece of paper. "Mr. Purdy left this for you."

Purdy had written: *Jim: How'd you make out with Miss Four-Eyes? If I wasn't married, I'd like to work on that a little. You sure get the breaks—Mrs. Shannon AND Miss Shannon, all in the line of duty, yet. Going to check some more on Lame Back and really sew him up good. See you tonight. Al.*

I left the hotel, and for the third time in two days I drove to Carbon Street.

CHAPTER ELEVEN

A new blue Dodge sedan was parked at the curb before Mrs. Ryan's apartment building. The license number was X-566. I parked beside the Dodge and smoked two cigarettes before Vernon Dorr came out and headed for the car. I rolled down the window and called to him. He turned, and when he saw me his handsome young face took on a sullen, stubborn look.

"Come here," I said.

"I'm in a hurry."

I got out and walked up to him. There was a smudge of lipstick on his right cheek. "Is it my turn now?" I asked.

"Your turn for what?" Today he was wearing a tan tweed topcoat over the brown gabardine suit, and a dark brown snap brim. He looked like the president of the Steel City Civic Club, which he probably was.

"To see Mrs. Shannon," I said.

He flushed. "I don't like that, Bennett."

"Call me Jim. All my friends do."

"I wouldn't say that we were exactly friends," he said stiffly.

"My enemies call me Jim, too."

"Oh, stop it," he said impatiently. "What do you want?"

"Is she alone now?" I felt a small anger. Maybe it was the lipstick on his face. Elaine Shannon's lipstick.

"Yes, she's alone," he said quietly. "I had to see her, to explain the delay in the insurance payment. It was all settled, until you got on the case. I'm going to fight it, Bennett. As a representative of George Shannon's employer I have that right—to see that his widow receives the benefits to which she is entitled."

"It'll raise your premium rate," I said.

"I think Ferris Abrasives can afford it," he said shortly.

I sighed. "Then you were seeing Mrs. Shannon—on business?"

"Of course. What else?" He was suddenly watching me carefully.

"All right," I said, and I added, "Uncle Vernon." It wasn't very nice of me, but I felt mean and nasty.

A hot light flared in his eyes. He started to speak, and then checked himself, and he glared at me, breathing heavily.

"Relax," I said. "No offense meant. Why don't you admit that you're in love with her?"

Still he didn't speak.

"It's nothing to be ashamed of," I told him, "and it's obvious. You've been seeing her often, and you're 'Uncle Vernon' to the little girl. I don't blame you for wanting Mrs. Shannon to get the money."

"You're crazy," he blurted. "My interest in Mrs. Shannon is entirely impersonal. It is my job to handle these things, to see that an employee, or an employee's dependents, receive the benefits to which they are entitled, and which my company is paying for. It's just— well, it's just my job."

"You'd better wipe the lipstick off your face," I said.

Involuntarily he placed a hand on his cheek, and he turned away. Suddenly I felt a little sorry for him. He wasn't very old, maybe in his late twenties, and I didn't know if he was married or not. I didn't care, and I gave him credit. He had come a long way, was probably a graduate of some college in business administration and personnel work and industrial relations, and he had a good job. It probably paid more than the agency paid me, and I was maybe ten or fifteen years his senior. And I could understand his attraction for Elaine Shannon. I could understand it very well.

He turned, blindly opened the door of his car and as he started to get in, I said, "Take it easy," intending to show him that I meant no ill will, but he said, "Go to hell," in a muffled voice and drove furiously away. I stood on the curb and watched him turn a corner with a screech of tires.

I moved down the sidewalk to Mrs. Ryan's apartment house and went inside. The small foyer was deserted, and Mrs. Ryan's door was closed. The little fox terrier, Tippy, barked halfheartedly at my footsteps. I went up the stairs and knocked on Elaine Shannon's door, feeling a faint excitement.

No sound came from inside, and I was about to knock again when the door opened. Elaine Shannon's eyes widened a little, and then she smiled. "Oh, hello. Come on in."

Today she was wearing a white short-sleeved blouse and a flaring black skirt. Her hair was tied in a knot on top of her head, and I saw that her ears were small and close to her head. Except for lipstick, she wore no make-up, and she had a clean scrubbed look, as if she had just stepped from the shower. She smelled clean, too, like scented soap, and she had a pert, little-girl look. Her small breasts beneath the blouse were high and virginal, and for the first time I noticed a faint dusting of tiny freckles over her short nose. Through the window behind her I could see the smoke stacks and the factories which surrounded Carbon Street, and in the distance the sky held an April haze, murky with the rain. The apartment was clean, as usual, and very attractive in the afternoon light.

She said, half mockingly, "Well, aren't you coming in?"

I moved then and stepped inside, taking off my hat. "I can't stay." I gazed around the apartment, at the closed bedroom door. "Where's Jon?"

"She's spending the day with her aunt—my husband's sister. She picked her up a while ago."

"Gloria Shannon?"

Her eyes were startled. "You know her?"

"I met her this morning in Vernon Dorr's office. I had lunch with her, too."

A small frown marred her smooth forehead. "I see," she said quietly. "Vernon—Mr. Dorr—told me that she had talked to him. She's a very nice person."

"She seems nice," I said politely.

"She doesn't like me. I suppose she told you?"

"Yes, she told me. Why doesn't she like you?"

"I—I don't know. I've wanted to be friends with her ever since George and I were married, but she seemed to—to resent me. I don't know why, unless she's . . ."

"Jealous?" I finished for her.

"Perhaps. She and George were the only children, and after his first wife died, Gloria took care of Jon for a time. She's very fond of her."

"I know," I said.

"But I love Jon, too. Can't she understand?" She clenched her small fists and her breasts moved with her quick breathing. "Jon is my husband's child, all that I have left of him. No one can take her away from me."

"That's between you and Gloria," I said. "I met Vernon Dorr outside, just before I came up."

"Yes?" she said quietly, and waited.

I thought, to hell with it, and I said, "Of course, you know he's in love with you?"

"Yes," she said again, watching my face. She must have seen something there, something I didn't want her to see, and she smiled a sort of secret little smile.

"Are you in love with him?" I felt a fool, a high school freshman, but I had to ask it.

"No," she said softly. "He has been wonderful to Jon and me, since George died. I may as well tell you—he asked me to marry him, just a little while ago, before you came. I like Vernon but I don't love him. Perhaps he thinks that he loves me. I let him kiss me today, but he knows how I feel. I loved my husband. I still love him."

"Your husband is dead."

"Yes," she said, almost harshly. "What do you want? Why did you come here?"

"Never mind," I said, and took a step toward her. Her clean fresh fragrance was all around me.

"But I do mind," she whispered, the secret smile on her lips.

Suddenly, above everything else, I felt irritation. She knew how I felt about her, and she was trying to make me admit it. I didn't blame her, but I blamed myself for getting emotionally involved, even to a small degree, with a woman I had not yet known for twenty-four hours. I dropped my hat to the floor and placed my hands on her arms, above the elbows, feeling the soft warm flesh beneath my fingers. She stiffened a little, but she gazed at me steadily and soberly, her lips parted slightly. I pulled her to me, and the stiffness left her body and she sighed a little against my cheek. Her lips were hot and clinging, but still oddly reserved, as if a part of her was far away, out in the blackness, maybe with the dead. I didn't care. I had her with me, in the land of the living, and we swayed a little as we embraced.

Cars went past on the street outside, a distant sound.

She pushed away from me, gently at first, and then in a kind of desperation. I released her and she moved to the window.

"You—you'd better go," she said in a low voice.

"All right. I'll go."

"Please don't be—angry. It's just that I. . ."

"I know," I said stiffly. "I came here to tell you that I think I've found the man who wrote the letters."

She turned slowly to face me, a slim silhouette against the window. "What letters?"

"The ones we both received—about your husband being murdered. I'm going to see him, ask him why he wrote them. I thought you should know."

"Who is it?"

"A man at the plant, who worked near your husband. He saw what happened. It might mean that you won't receive the insurance money."

She lifted her slim shoulders. "Do what you have to do, but it still seems fantastic."

"Did your husband have any life insurance of his own?"

"Only what the company carried for him—a thousand dollars. I'll collect that, if the state doesn't pay. It's—" She paused, searching for a word.

"Non-occupational," I said. "That means that they won't pay for a death due to accidents on the job."

"It'll be better than nothing," she said with a trace of bitterness.

"Any more phone calls?"

"No, not since last night, when you were here. Who is the man— the one you think wrote the letters?"

"His name is Eddie Fleet."

She frowned. "George never spoke of him. I—I don't understand any of this. Why would anyone want to kill George?"

"I'm trying to find out, and I'm probably all wrong. I hope so." I decided not to tell her about the man who had struck me the night before.

"I hope you are wrong, too," she said gravely. "Not because of the money, but because it isn't nice to think that someone hated George so much that they...."

"What are your plans?"

"I told you. Find someone to care for Jon, and go back to work."

"At Ferris Abrasives?"

"I don't know. I can, if I want to."

"Vernon Dorr will give you a job?"

"Yes, if I want one. He has offered to help me, in any way he can."

"I'll bet," I said, and I picked up my hat and opened the door. This was no place for me, not if I knew what was good for me. It couldn't lead to anything really good, not with a husband's ghost, and his little daughter, and Gloria Shannon's jealousy and frustration, and Vernon Dorr. The thing for me to do was to wind the damn thing up, one way or the other, and get the hell back to Cleveland. But why did I have to wind it up? Why couldn't I just let it go, let it ride? George Shannon was dead, and he would never be any deader. It didn't matter how he had died, and all I had to do was turn in a report of accidental death on the job and Elaine Shannon would get her ten thousand dollars. She deserved it. Maybe Vernon Dorr was right, and it was silly, all this cloak-and-dagger routine. Maybe I'd lived in the big city jungle too long—but it was because I'd lived in the jungle that I knew the signs, the spoor of death, and I couldn't ignore them. I didn't know yet how George Shannon could have been murdered, or why, but I couldn't forget it, not anymore, no matter what it cost anybody, Elaine Shannon or little Jonquil, or myself. And once again I felt the blow on my head, and I heard the muttered voice in my ear, and I knew that I couldn't stop, not even if the boss ordered me back to my post in Cleveland, not even if the state fired me. I would stay in Steel City until I had the answers, and then I would start to live again.

"Good-bye," I said.

She didn't answer me, and I went out, quickly.

CHAPTER TWELVE

It was a quarter of four when I entered the lobby of the Blue Ridge Hotel. Al Purdy's short thick form was slouched in a chair by the front windows. He grinned at me as I came up and pushed his hat to the back of his head. "Hi, Jim, I got all the dope I need on Lame Back, and knocked off. Where in hell you been?"

"A few places. You'd be bored if I told you."

He sat up straight. "Bored? With a dish like that Shannon babe?"

"Which Shannon babe?" I asked coldly.

"Well, both of 'em, since you mention it. Mrs. Shannon, and Miss Shannon. Even with the glasses and no lipstick she's a knockout."

"Who?"

"Don't confuse me. They're both knockouts. Right now I'm talking about Miss Shannon, the sister-in-law of Mrs. Shannon."

I said, "She merely has a sort of family interest in her brother's death."

"And in the insurance payoff," Purdy said. "I gathered that in Dorr's office this morning." He pulled at his lower lip and said thoughtfully, "Miss Shannon, huh? Do you mean to tell me that a gal stocked like she is ain't married?"

"She's frustrated," I said, and sat in a chair beside him, realizing that my head still ached dully, and that I was tired. "Look, Al, I've still got things to do this afternoon—will you do me a favor?"

"Sure, Jim—anything but murder." He slapped his thigh and laughed loudly. "I'll bet this routine state stuff seems pretty tame to you."

"Tame as hell," I said. "Look, the first shift at Ferris Abrasives quits at four o'clock. This morning I talked to a man named Eddie Fleet, and I got his address from Dorr's secretary—616 Clinton Street. I want you to go out there and talk to him, see if you can learn anything more from him. Maybe, away from the plant, he'll open up. I think he's our man."

Purdy cocked an eyebrow at me. "You're real sharp, ain't you? There was maybe fifty guys working fairly close to George Shannon when he fell off that ladder. Why pick out this Fleet? Didn't he give you the same story as the rest?"

"Yes. It's just a hunch. The person who wrote the notes to Mrs. Shannon and myself used a certain expression in both of them, a rather unusual choice of words. He wrote, *I'm telling you true.* This morning, Eddie Fleet used the same expression when I talked to him. I think he wrote the notes. Anyhow, it's worth checking. Maybe, by talking to him, you can find out if he's just a screwball trying to stir something up, or if he really knows something. If you think he does, I'll take it from there. Got it?"

"Well, think of that," Purdy said admiringly. "None of us ignorant state boys would have figured that out."

"Routine," I said, grinning.

Purdy stood up and cocked his hat over one ear. "I'm on my way. This'll be a little more interesting than tailing Lame Back."

"Just see what Eddie has to ay—if he says anything. I'll meet you here later."

"Okay," Purdy said, buttoning his topcoat. "Just call me Private Eye Purdy." He started to move away, and then turned and added, "Hey, Jim, maybe I oughta get me a .38, a fifth of rye and a blonde. Then I'd be a real private eye."

"Get going. Guns and booze and women just get you into trouble."

He went out laughing.

The police station in Steel City was on a side street four blocks from the Blue Ridge Hotel. I left the Mercury where I'd parked it and walked over. It was a modern little layout, complete with a fingerprint lab, two-way radio, and a crew of bright-looking young cops in neat uniforms. Apparently four o'clock was the shift change, because the station was full of them coming and going, many of them carrying lunch boxes, which they stacked on a table in the squad room. The young officer on the desk was grave and very courteous. He called the chief while the radio behind him cracked and muttered, and he smiled and said, "Go right in, Mr. Bennett. Second door on your right." He pointed to a short corridor.

"Thanks, Sergeant." I moved to the corridor, spotted the door and walked in.

The chief got up from behind a desk and we shook hands. He was a tall, thin man with smoothly combed gray hair, a clipped white mustache, and keen intelligent eyes behind gold rimmed glasses. He was not in uniform, but was wearing a neat blue suit, a white shirt and a red-dotted bow-tie. He looked more like a banker, or the president of a chamber of commerce, than a cop, and his voice was low and pleasant. His name was Jason Conway. He motioned me to a chair and we faced each other across his desk.

"Bennett—of the Industrial Welfare Commission?" he said pleasantly.

"That's right, Chief."

"It's a familiar name. Have you been with the Commission long?"

"Not long." I told him about the deal the agency had with the state, and how the boss eventually hoped to sell his services to the other state insurance boards.

When I had finished, he smiled. "I was sure I knew you—your name, at least. Weren't you on that shooting up in Ohio last fall? The old man—what was his name?"

"Rex Bishop. He was a nice old man."

"You had to shoot the killer, didn't you?"

I nodded bleakly, remembering a cold November dawn in a farmhouse kitchen and a man facing me across the table with death in his eyes. Once more I heard the terrifying blast of his gun, hidden beneath the table, and I felt the hammer-blow of the bullet in my side. The scar was still red and I would never again twist a certain way without feeling pain. I closed my eyes for an instant, trying to blot out the memory of how he had looked when my bullet had hit him in the eye, and the memory of the linoleum slippery with the blood of both of us....

"I know," Conway said gently. "Sometimes you can't help it."

"Yes."

"I have the newspaper story on file. And there was another job, before that. In Cleveland, a man hanged to a flagpole—"

"Yes, Chief," I broke in. "I don't want to waste your time—"

"I've always wanted to meet you," he said, "but I haven't been in Cleveland for twenty years. I met your boss once, at a policeman's convention in New York. Quite a character." He laughed softly. "But a fine old man. He gave us a damn good talk about identification of decomposed bodies—something you don't find in the manuals."

"He's a shrewd old bastard," I said. "Chief, what can you tell me about Dr. Ordway Vincetti?"

He grinned. "Is this state business, or agency business?"

"The state, officially, but you might say it was both. After all, if I do a good job for the state, it'll be a feather in the agency's cap."

"I see. Two birds, and all that. Is Dr. Vincetti connected with the case you're investigating for the state?"

I told him about the death of George Shannon, about all of it. About his widow, his daughter, his sister, the notes, the warnings, the man who had struck me, my visit to Dr. Vincetti's office, about Eddie Fleet. I didn't skip anything, except my mixed feelings for Elaine Shannon, and when I had finished, Chief of Police Conway gazed at me gravely and toyed with a yellow pencil.

"So maybe it's murder?" he said quietly.

"Maybe. I've got to check it—before I make a report."

"Need any help?"

"Not right now, thanks. Maybe later...."

"This is my town. If it's murder, it's my business."

"If," I said.

"What do you want to know about Dr. Vincetti?"

"Anything you can tell me."

He took off his glasses and rubbed the bridge of his thin nose with slender fingers. "Well, when he located here, I did some routine checking—I like to know who's who in this town. He left Baltimore because of some sort of wife trouble, quite a scandal, I guess. Then he drifted around with a red-headed nurse. She's still with him, by the way—lives with him, I guess. They both booze a lot, but they've never been picked up. He's a good doctor, I hear, when he's sober." He sighed and shook his head. "What a woman can't do to a man."

"No record of any kind, then?"

He hooked the glasses over his neat flat ears and looked at me. "Yes, he has a record, in Kentucky. He practiced in Louisville a short time before coming here. An insurance investigator caught him falsifying accident reports and collecting benefits for himself in the name of a fictitious claimant."

I leaned forward in my chair. "State workmen's compensation?"

Conway shook his head. "No, private, part of a health and welfare program a big foundry sponsored for its employees. He was the company physician, and he had access to the application forms. The foundry didn't want any publicity on it, because the insurance program was part of their union contract, and negotiations were coming up. They paid the loss to the insurance company and hushed it up. They fired Vincetti, of course, and that's when he came here. I never told anyone out at Ferris Abrasives about it, and I won't, unless he pulls something again. I figure a man is entitled to one mistake in his life."

"He probably needed the money for whisky," I said. "It's expensive, if you make a career of it." I stood up. "Thanks, Chief."

"Let me know how you make out," he said. "And call me—if you need any help."

"I will," I promised, and I left.

As I passed the desk, the young sergeant said politely, "Goodbye, Mr. Bennett."

I waved at him. "So long, Sergeant." The clock on the wall behind him told me that it was almost five o'clock.

I didn't see Al Purdy in the lobby of the hotel, and I bought a paper and went up to my room. I took a shower, shaved, and stretched out on the bed in my undershirt and shorts and read the paper. The ball teams were finishing their training in Florida, a man in Boston had killed an old woman with an axe, congressional groups were wrangling, the president was fishing in Bermuda, a new committee was investigating disloyal government minions, warmer weather and rain were promised for the next day, my favorite comic strip character had gotten himself into so terrible a situation that I despaired for his life, a new play called *Life With Sister* was a smash hit in New York, a scientific tome about the sexual conduct of East African gorillas was a runaway best seller, an airliner with fifty-four passengers aboard had crashed in Wyoming, a nympho movie siren had selected her sixth husband, a three-year-old boy had been lost and found in the Michigan woods, the cherry trees in Washington were ready to bloom and all was well with the world.

At six o'clock Al Purdy entered my room. He sank into a chair and mopped his broad red face with a handkerchief. "My God," he groaned, "the beer I've swilled. That Eddie Fleet must have hollow legs."

I tossed the paper aside. "Then you won't want any whisky from the bottle I've got."

"The hell I won't," he said. "Maybe it'll cut the beer a little."

I got the bottle from my bag while he brought two glasses from the bathroom. "I'll order some ice," I said.

"Tap water is fine with me," he said, pouring into the glasses and carrying them into the bathroom. He came back, handed a glass to me, and sat down again. "I went to Fleet's house first, but he wasn't home from work yet. His wife said I'd probably find him in a beer joint down the street, a place called the Red Bird Tavern. He was there, all right, drinking beer at the bar. I remembered seeing you talk to him this morning—tall, skinny guy. He remembered seeing me, too, and he was cagey. We drank beer and we talked, but he wouldn't talk about anything but his kids, his bowling scores and the Cardinals' chances this year. When I tried to pin him down about George Shannon, he just said he didn't know nothing—except that he told 'that other guy,' meaning you."

Purdy paused and sipped his drink. "But there was something funny. Right after I mentioned Shannon, he began to act nervous, and he kept looking over his shoulder, like he was scared of something. Pretty soon he wouldn't talk to me at all. I saw I wasn't getting anyplace, maybe making him sore, and so I bought him another beer and left."

"All right, Al," I said. "Thanks for the try. Do you think it would do any good for me to see him?"

Purdy lifted his thick shoulders. "It might." He grinned up at me from beneath his heavy eyebrows. "Maybe you big-time detectives got methods of—what do you call it? Interrogation? —that us hicks don't know about."

"I doubt it," I said. "Are you going to put that beer you bought on your expense account?"

"You're damn right I am! It was official business, wasn't it? I didn't want that beer."

"Of course you didn't," I said, grinning, and started to get dressed. "Where you going?"

"To the Red Bird Tavern. Think he's still there?"

"He'll be there for a week—just coasting on my beer."

"If he's not, I'll try his house. He's the only lead we've got."

"You mean, like a clue? That kind of stuff? That maybe his—uh— testimony will lead us to the—uh—killer?"

"Something like that."

Purdy shook his head. "My, my. I never thought I'd get mixed up in a sinister plot like this."

"You're not mixed up in it."

"I sure am. You're my partner, ain't you?"

"That's right, Al."

"Then I gotta stick with you—but I'd sure like to get home tomorrow. Honest, Jim, why don't we just send the claim to the office and let them worry about it? Tomorrow's Friday, and my wife's probably sick of feeding them mink, and she don't feed 'em right, anyhow. She always gives 'em too much, and we run out of meat, and then I gotta line up a dead horse and cut it up—I keep telling her not to give 'em so much. Horse meat is expensive, but she says the poor mink are hungry, and she tries to make pets of 'em. Then, when pelting time comes, and I start to break their necks so I can skin 'em, she carries on and goes in the house and won't watch. I feel like a murderer, but what the hell? A mink is only good for one thing, and that's its fur, and we need the money." He gazed morosely into his glass. "Some ranchers use gas to kill 'em. Maybe I oughta try that. What do you think, Jim? Do you think it would be more—well, humane?"

"When you're dead you're dead," I said. "I figure it doesn't matter how it comes even to a mink. Just so it's short and sweet."

"That's what I say," he said thoughtfully. "That's what I tell Alice, and sometimes the gas don't work right away, and—"

"Go get your dinner," I told him, as I put on my topcoat. "I'll be back."

"I drank my dinner, Jim, old boy." He lifted his glass. "This is dessert."

It was dusk when I reached Clinton Street, which was the next block from Carbon Street and Mrs. Ryan's apartment house. I thought of Mrs. Ryan, and her dog, and target pistol, and of Elaine Shannon and little Jonquil. I thought of Vernon Dorr, and Gloria Shannon, and I wondered if she still had the child. I felt a faint chill of uneasiness. Gloria had wanted Jonquil, and now she had her, and I hoped there wouldn't be any trouble. But a family squabble was not my worry; my job was to find a killer, if there was a killer, and settle the case of the state and George Allen Shannon, deceased. Then I could make a report and go about my business. I was lonesome for home and my familiar office, and I admitted to myself that I missed Sandy Hollis. I would call her when I returned to the hotel. Maybe I'd even run up to Cleveland over the weekend. it was only four hundred miles, and I could make it easily, and have dinner with Sandy on Saturday night. I began to make eager plans. I might even leave tomorrow evening, Friday evening, and I could be in my apartment by midnight. On Saturday Sandy and I could make a day of it—lunch, and maybe the ice show matinee, cocktails at the Statler afterward, followed by a thick steak at my favorite restaurant just off Euclid Avenue. I'd ask Sandy tonight, when I called her....

Ahead of me I saw the red neon sign of the Red Bird Tavern. I couldn't miss it; it was the biggest sign on the short street, and was shaped like a bird. I pulled into the first parking space I found and walked back. At this hour there weren't many persons on the street, and when I stopped and peered through the glass door of the Red Bird Tavern the place looked deserted. But I couldn't see much beyond a small foyer; most of the interior was blocked off by a high counter, and the big front window was shuttered with a Venetian blind. A small neon sign over the door read *Stag Only*. Well, Bennett, you're a stag—go on in. I went in.

It was a long narrow room with a bar down one side and a row of booths on the other. In the middle huddled some tables and chairs. At the back shone an ornate jukebox, silent. There was the smell of stale smoke and stale burned grease and beer, the smell of all such places from Long Island to Long Beach. A couple of men in leather jackets were drinking beer and eating sandwiches at one of the booths near the entrance, and at a far table four men were playing cards. There was no one at the bar. Behind the bar a gray-faced youth in a white jacket was chewing on an enormous sandwich consisting of what looked like rye bread, layers of ham, liverwurst and cheese. He gazed at me resentfully, chewing steadily, his cheeks bulging. I sat on a stool and said, "Hi."

He mumbled something that might have been "Hello" and kept on chewing.

"Bourbon," I said. "Water on the side."

"Blup," he said, and still holding the sandwich, he placed a glass on the bar, reached for a bottle, poured, reached again, turned on a tap, and put a glass of water beside the whisky, all with one hand. "Gaw," he said, chewing.

"Thanks." I laid a dollar on the bar. I wanted some ice in the water, and I wanted to ask him a question, but I decided I'd better wait until he'd finished the sandwich. He did, presently, and drew himself a glass of beer. He took a long swallow, wiped his mouth with a sleeve of his jacket, and said in a complaining voice to no one in particular, "Even barkeeps gotta eat sometime."

"That's right," I said. "Looks like rain."

He said, "Yeah?", picked up the dollar, gave me sixty-five cents change, and began to slosh glasses around in a metal sink filled with soapy water.

"Has Eddie Fleet been around?"

He lifted his chin toward the rear of the place. "He just went to the can."

"How about some ice in this water?"

He looked at me as if I'd asked for rattlesnakes' hearts on buttered toast.

"Just one little cube," I said gently.

He dried his hands elaborately, went to a refrigerator at the end of the bar, came back with an ice cube in his fingers and dropped it into my glass. Water splashed over the bar.

"Thanks," I said. "Kind of quiet tonight, huh?"

"It's supper time. They'll be in later. I'm off at seven. Been working since ten this morning."

"Many fellows from Ferris Abrasives hang around here?"

"From all the shops," he said. "This is a shop section. You oughta be in here on payday nights."

I looked at my wristwatch. "What's Eddie doing back there? Taking a bath?"

"He's probably passed out. There was a guy in here a while ago buying him beers as fast as he could swallow 'em, and Eddie was never a guy to turn down a free drink. His old lady has already called twice for him to come home to supper. Eddie works at Ferris."

"I know," I said, finishing the bourbon. "Pour me another I'll be right back."

I slid off the stool and walked back to the rear. The men in the card game paid no attention to me. I stepped into a passageway lighted by a dim overhead bulb. The smells were stronger here, and of a more pungent nature. On the right side of the passage was a door labeled *Gents* and at the end was another door, which probably was a rear entrance, maybe from an alley or a court. I opened the first door and stepped inside.

A man lay on the cement floor beneath a stained and crusted wash bowl, his face turned to the wall. He wore greasy overalls, a worn brown leather jacket and heavy shoes. A crumpled gray felt hat lay near his feet. I thought, *Purdy and the beer—he overdid it*, and I knelt down, very carefully, because the floor was damp, with small viscous puddles in the low spots. I grasped the man's shoulder, shook it, and said loudly, "Hey, Eddie, wake up."

He didn't move, and I pushed on his shoulder and turned him until I could see his face. The eyes were half open, and the pupil of the left one was oddly off center. The mouth was open, too, and I saw the tongue and the stained teeth, and the forehead dripping with blood from beneath the sparse hair above. A drop of the blood spilled to the back of my hand. It was warm. Hastily I wiped it off on Eddie Fleet's jacket, and I stood up. I didn't need to feel for a heartbeat, because I knew there wouldn't be one, not anymore.

Eddie Fleet was dead, and his troubles were over, and in that instant of realization it was odd that I didn't think of Eddie; I thought of his wife and his four children, the three boys and the girl, and something in the pit of my stomach coiled and uncoiled slowly.

CHAPTER THIRTEEN

I stepped into the passageway, tried the door at the end. It was unlocked and opened into a dark court flanked by a murky alley. I closed the door and turned at the sound of footsteps. Two of the men from the card game were coming toward me, headed for the door marked *Gents*. I moved quickly forward, placed my fingers on their chests. "Hold it, boys. Don't go in there."

"What the hell—?" one of them began.

"Never mind," I said, pushing them gently backward. They moved, reluctantly. "The cops will be here. You don't want to get mixed up in it." We entered the outer room, and the bartender peered at us.

One of the two men said, "Oscar, this guy says we can't go in the john. He says the cops are coming. What happened?"

The bartender looked at me blankly, his gray face slack. I said to him, "Go back and stand by the door. Don't let anybody in, and don't you go in. Hear?"

The two other men at the card table stared at us silently, and up in front I saw the faces of the two in the booth peering back at us. The bartender stuttered, "W-who are you? W-what's going on?"

"Do what I told you," I snapped. "Now."

He moved slowly to the end of the bar, wiping his slack mouth with a palm. "Are you a cop?"

"Yes." It was the easiest way.

He looked down the passageway. "Eddie Fleet went in there, and he didn't come out. Then you went in, and now you—"

"He ain't no cop," one of the men said suddenly. "I know all the cops in this town, and he ain't one."

They were all looking at me. Slowly the two men at the table got up and edged forward, and from the corner of my eye I saw the other two move around behind me. The men in the front booth got up and started back. The bartender's eye shifted and he reached furtively under the bar. I sighed and I thought dismally of the gun in my bag at the hotel. They made a ring around me, not too close yet, but their faces were silent and unfriendly. One of them said, "You guys watch him. I'll go back and see about Eddie," and he started for the passage.

I saw a telephone on a ledge at the end of the bar. I moved swiftly and turned, my back against the bar, my right hand in my topcoat pocket. "Stop," I said to the man moving.

He turned, saw the bulge of my hand and rigid forefinger in the pocket, and said softly, "A holdup, by God."

I waggled my finger in the pocket menacingly, thinking that it was a tired old trick. But they couldn't be sure it wasn't a gun, and the trick worked, at least for as long as I needed it to work. The bartender laid down the short axe handle he'd picked up, and all of them watched me while I grabbed the phone and said loudly, "Police Department."

That did it. They relaxed a little, and began to talk excitedly, but they still watched me. A quiet voice said in my ear, "Police."

"Is Chief Conway there?"

"He's left the station, but he can be reached at his home."

"Reach him. Tell him there's been a murder at the Red Bird Tavern on Clinton Street, and send a couple of men over here. My name is Bennett. I'll stay until they get here."

"Yes, sir," he said crisply. "Right away," just as if a murder happened in Steel City every hour. I gave Conway credit. He had his force trained nicely—no questions, no red tape, no hedging. A citizen had reported a murder, and the department went into action.

I hung up and gazed at the seven men watching me. "Relax, boys," I said wearily. "I'm not a cop, and I haven't got a gun, and you may as well know that Eddie Fleet is dead. He's been murdered, and he's on the floor of the john. I'm from the Industrial Welfare Commission."

They stared at me dumbly. Then the bartender started to speak, but before any words came out, the front door opened and two uniformed policemen strode toward us. They were young, neat, fresh-looking, and one of them held a hand on the butt of a gun in a holster strapped over his tunic. I left the bar and went to meet them. "I'm the man who called in. There's a body in the can. Just keep an eye on things until the Chief gets here."

"We know what to do sir," one of them said gravely, and both of them went down the passageway. I saw the light as the door opened. One of them went inside. The second one stayed by the door. Presently the first one came out and I heard him, say, "Get back to the car, Sam. I'll hold it here."

Sam walked past us briskly, said, "All of you men stay here," and went out the door to the street.

The bartender drew himself a beer and said plaintively, "Now, ain't this one hell of a note?"

I looked down the bar. At the spot where I'd been sitting I saw the amber glint of the drink I'd ordered. I moved to it and drank it down in one swallow.

The bartender moved up, said nervously, "That'll be thirty-five cents, sir."

It was quiet in the office of Chief of Police Conway. Outside in the squad room the radio droned intermittently, and footsteps kept passing along the corridor beyond the closed door. Conway sat behind his desk smoking a cigarette in a long ivory holder. Light from a small desk lamp glinted on the gold rims of his glasses and made hollows in his thin cheeks. I sat in shadow in a corner, my chair tilted back against the wall. The bourbon inside me had died long ago, and although I hadn't eaten anything since my luncheon with Gloria Shannon, I wasn't hungry. I didn't feel anything, except the beginning of fatigue and a sick sadness at the memory of Eddie Fleet. There was a light knock on the door, and Conway said, "Come in."

A young policeman entered with two cardboard containers and placed them on Conway's desk. The good smell of hot black coffee filled the air. Conway looked at me and nodded at one of the containers. I got up and moved to the desk and sat down. Conway said, "Thanks, Albert," and the young policeman left.

I sipped at the coffee. It tasted very good. "I blame myself," I said. "I should have taken things more seriously. He had a wife and four kids."

"You couldn't help it," Conway said.

"I could have gone to see Fleet myself, instead of sending Purdy. Maybe Fleet would have talked to me, and we could have protected him. Maybe he'd still be alive."

"You can't tell," Conway said quietly. "Anyhow, it's murder. The coroner says repeated blows on the head with a blunt instrument. Murder weapon missing."

"The well-known blunt instrument," I said bitterly. "He got it just before I entered the Red Bird, maybe after I got there. When I found him, he hadn't been dead more than a couple of minutes. Eddie Fleet was working near George Shannon, and he saw—something. So we start with the murder of Shannon."

"So it's murder now, for sure?" Conway said softly.

"It has to be. If it had been a simple accident, Eddie Fleet would still be alive. The killer was checking on me, following me—we know that—and Purdy, too, because we were working together. He followed Purdy to Fleet's home, and then to the tavern, saw Purdy trying to pump Fleet. He figured Fleet knew something. He waited. Purdy leaves Fleet, and then I show up. The killer was convinced then. He killed Fleet before I could talk to him—to keep Fleet from talking. Does that make sense?"

Conway nodded. "It does. How many persons knew that you were interested in Eddie Fleet?"

I frowned and thought back. How many, indeed? "Well," I said, "Mrs. Shannon knew it, and Miss Shannon—she's the sister of George Shannon—and of course Purdy, yourself, and Vernon Dorr, and Dorr's secretary."

"Vernon Dorr?" Conway asked. "The personnel man at Ferris?"

I nodded.

"I know him. Seems like a nice young chap."

"What do you know about him?"

He shrugged his spare shoulders and ejected his cigarette from the ivory holder. "Not too much. Comes from a good family. His father has taught biology in one of the high schools here for many years. Lives with his parents, not married, graduated from State University." He gave me a thin smile. "He hasn't any police record, if that's what you mean. Anyhow, he wasn't booked."

"Wasn't booked for what?" I asked sharply.

"Don't get excited," Conway said. "The charge was gambling, but we dropped it. Last January a reform mayor took office. You know— every so often a town must have one, and he made a big crusade of it. They still gamble here, of course, but it gave him a lot of prestige with the church crowd. Anyhow, we raided a joint over on Royal Street, across the river, and nabbed Dorr in a crap game, along with a few other solid citizens. The mayor said to hush it up—one of the gamblers was his brother-in-law. He said he just wanted the joint closed, and we closed it." Conway sighed and inserted a fresh cigarette into the ivory holder. "It's open again now, and the mayor is on another crusade."

"What's that?"

"A new city playground—to be built on land that he owns."

"I see," I said. I drank more coffee. "Maybe I'd better tell you that Vernon Dorr is in love with George Shannon's widow. In fact, he asked her to marry him."

Conway raised his eyebrows. "Is that so?"

"And he seems awfully anxious for her to get the ten thousand dollars insurance payment from the state."

"Maybe we'd better get Dorr down here."

"We'd better," I said. "Anyhow, Eddie Fleet worked for his company and he should be notified. An employee's death is one of the things a personnel man has to worry about."

"Want him picked up?"

I shook my head. "I'll try and call him first. What's his father's name?"

"Phillip." He tossed me a phone book. "Burbank Road, I think."

I found the number, and used the phone on Conway's desk. A rather shrill female voice answered and told me that Vernon was not at home, that he hadn't been home since he'd left for the office that morning.

"When do you expect him?"

"I can't say, really. He phoned late this afternoon that he had to work late and that he wouldn't be home for dinner. If you will give me your name . . ."

"Thank you, Madam. I'll call him tomorrow."

I hung up and said to Conway, "He may be at the plant." I thumbed the book again and called the Ferris Abrasives number.

A man said, "Ferris Abrasives, main gate."

"Can you ring Mr. Dorr's office?"

"No, sir. The switchboard closed at five, but he has a direct line. Call Park 834."

"Do you know if he is in his office?"

"No, sir, I couldn't say. I came on duty at six. He hasn't come in since then—not through my gate."

I said, "Thanks," pressed the receiver bar, and called Park 834. Conway watched me through the smoke from his cigarette, his thin face grave. While I waited, I shook a cigarette from a crumpled pack. Conway held a match for me. Dorr's voice answered then, and I said, "This is Bennett. Can I see you right away?"

"What about?" he asked sharply

Conway heard his question, and he shook his head at me. I said, "I can't talk on the phone, but it's important."

"I'm busy now," he said impatiently. "Can't you see me in the morning?"

"No."

There was a moment's silence. Then he said in a tired voice, "Where are you?"

"At the police station, in Chief Conway's office."

Another silence, maybe two seconds of it, and when he spoke his voice sounded strained. "The police station? Why are you there?"

"I'll tell you when I see you. And listen—can you bring a sample of Eddie Fleet's handwriting?"

"Eddie Fleet's—? Yes, I can do that, but—"

"Bring it, and hurry, will you?"

He said something, I didn't know what, and the phone clicked in my ear. I looked at Conway, and he said softly, "Will he come?"

"He'll either come, or he'll run. He drives a new blue Dodge sedan, license X-566."

Conway's thin jaw tightened a little. He pressed a button and spoke into an intercom box on his desk. "Radio the patrol car nearest the Ferris Abrasive plant to watch for a man named Vernon Dorr leaving there in a new blue Dodge sedan, license X-566. Tail him here. If he heads anyplace else, stop him and bring him in."

"Yes, Chief." The intercom clicked off.

"Just to make sure he comes." Conway's teeth showed in a tight smile.

"You've got an efficient little force here," I said.

"Law enforcement is an important business," he said seriously. "We've got a good force because we pay better than most departments this size. Here a cop makes almost as much as a kid running a drill press at, say, Ferris Abrasives."

"You pay a man right," I said, "and he'll do you a job. The trouble over the country is that too many bright young men shy away from police work because of the low pay and lack of future prospects. To me, it's just as important a work as teaching, or law, or medicine."

"Unfortunately," Conway said, "very few people think that. But we're getting them educated at last about better pay for teachers. I hope the police are next.... Do you really think Dorr is mixed up in this?"

I shrugged. "We'll talk to him."

"You do the talking. I'll listen. How did you happen to know his license number?"

"Habit. You get so you notice things like that, over the years."

"I'm afraid I'm more of an administrator than a cop," he said. "I don't seem to have the knack for detective work."

"It takes all kinds," I said, and looked at my watch.

"He should be here pretty soon," Conway said. "Unless he tried to skip." He drank the last of his coffee and lit another cigarette.

The intercom buzzed. "Mr. Dorr is here, Chief."

"Send him in." Conway opened a drawer on the right side of his desk, and I saw the blue glint of a revolver lying there. He left the drawer partly open and turned his chair so that his right hand and arm rested close to the drawer and partly concealing it.

I smiled at him. "What do you mean—you don't have the knack?"

He grinned a little sheepishly. "Well, Dorr isn't under arrest, and we'll be in here alone with him." He stopped grinning and said, "We were talking about murder, weren't we?"

"Yes, and you never know what a person will do when it's the big job."

"Even a nice young chap like Dorr," Conway said. "I've seen some pretty respectable-looking murderers."

"Me, too," I said, and I meant it.

The door opened and Vernon Dorr stepped inside.

CHAPTER FOURTEEN

Conway smiled at him. "Sit down, Vernon. Thanks for coming here. Mr. Bennett and I wanted to talk to you."

Dorr glanced at me, and then at Conway. He looked tired, and his young face seemed pale against the faint growth of a black beard. He was still wearing the brown tweed topcoat and the brown hat he'd worn in the afternoon when I'd seen him outside Elaine Shannon's apartment. He remained standing, and he said to Conway, "I've been working all day—didn't even stop for dinner—and I was ready to go home when Mr. Bennett called me. What's this all about?"

Conway looked at me.

I said, "Did you bring the samples of Eddie Fleet's handwriting?"

He reached inside the topcoat and handed me an envelope bearing the name of Ferris Abrasives, and their trademark—a spinning grinding wheel with bright sparks flying from it. "Still playing cops and robbers?" He tried to make it a sneer, but it didn't quite come off, and I saw the misery in his eyes. Eating out his heart for Elaine, I thought. That's what's the matter with Vernon H. Dorr. Today she turned him down, and he can't take it.

"It's not play," I told him. "Tonight another Ferris employee was murdered. We thought you would want to know."

"What do you mean—another employee murdered? What're you talking about?"

"George Shannon was the first," I said. "Eddie Fleet was the second. Somebody damned near clubbed his brains out."

He stared at me and his face seemed to crumple. He swallowed and his lips moved as if he were repeating my words in a whisper. And then he blurted, "Where did it happen? And how?"

I told him, all of it; why I suspected Eddie Fleet of writing the notes, of Purdy's talk with Fleet, of my visit to the Red Bird Tavern and what happened there.

"But who would want to kill Eddie Fleet?" he asked in a bewildered voice. "And why?"

I said patiently, "Because Eddie Fleet knew why George Shannon died, and Eddie was killed because somebody was afraid he'd talk."

"I—I see," Dorr said. He moved to a chair against the wall, sat down, and leaned forward. "I can't believe it. Maybe it was just a tavern brawl. Eddie drank quite a bit, and—"

"It wasn't just a tavern brawl," I said. "Eddie's death ties in with George Shannon. I think so and so does Chief Conway."

Dorr smiled faintly. He was under control now, and he said, "Of course, you and Chief Conway know about such things, but . . ." He moved his hands in a deprecating gesture.

"You're damn right we know about them," I said. "It would have been easy for me to mark up Shannon's death as accidental and forget it, but I couldn't."

"If you had," Dorr said hotly, "Eddie Fleet would still be alive."

He was right, and I felt the sick sadness again. I looked at Conway for reassurance, for comfort, and he nodded at me, like a compassionate father, trying to tell me that I had done right, in spite of the consequences, and he pointed a long finger at Dorr and said in an even cold voice, "That wasn't a very smart remark, Vernon. I suppose you feel that Mr. Bennett should have ignored his suspicions, just so Mrs. Shannon would get the insurance money and Mr. Shannon's murderer could go his happy way—to kill again?"

Dorr flushed and said hastily, "I—I didn't mean that."

"I hope not, Vernon," Conway said dryly. "It wouldn't look well on the record."

"Record?" Dorr stood up. "What is this?"

"A preliminary investigation of murder," Conway said grimly. "Sit down."

Dorr sat again, slowly. There was a little sweat on his face. He didn't look at me, but kept his gaze on Conway. I said, "You have admitted being beside the ladder when Shannon was killed. Didn't you notice anything unusual at all? Think back."

He swung his head toward me, and he said a little wildly, "What *could* have happened? I was standing by the ladder, and it just slipped, that's all. I tried to grab it, but I was too late and I couldn't hold it. *I* couldn't help it, for God's sake!"

Suddenly I decided to get it over with. There was no point in sparring around. I looked at Conway. He knew what I had in mind, and he nodded, his mouth a tight line. I said to Dorr, "Now, listen; I'm going to point out a few facts. If you want a lawyer, get one."

"You have that right, Vernon," Conway said quietly.

"Lawyer?" Dorr said. "Why would I want a lawyer? What're you getting at?

"Go ahead," Conway said to me.

I took a deep breath and said to Dorr, "I'm convinced that Eddie Fleet wrote the notes to Mrs. Shannon and myself. The samples of handwriting you brought will no doubt verify it. You've been in love with Mrs. Shannon. You're still in love with her. But she was married, before. You let her know how you felt and maybe she encouraged you. You developed a big passion, and on top of that you were gambling, maybe losing more than you could afford. With George Shannon out of the way, you would be free to marry Elaine, if she would have you, and she would collect ten thousand dollars. As her husband, you would have access to the money. You saw your chance when George Shannon climbed that ladder. You pushed it over, and then made a big show of trying to hold it up. Shannon fell to his death on the floor. John Riggio, at the top, barely managed to save himself. Eddie Fleet, working nearby, saw what you had done. But you were an official of the company, and he was afraid to say anything. But it worried him, and he finally wrote to Mrs. Shannon, and to me. When I asked you for Fleet's address, you became suspicious, and you followed me, and Al Purdy. You saw Purdy talk to Fleet at the Red Bird Tavern, and you saw me go there, too. You decided that Fleet had talked to Purdy, and was going to talk to me—about what he had seen. You saw Fleet go into the men's room, and you entered by the back door and killed him before he could talk to me. What did you use on him? A crowbar?"

I paused and glanced at Conway. He was watching Vernon Dorr, his hand resting on the edge of the desk drawer. Dorr said to me in a low, desperate voice, "You don't really think that, do you? That I killed Eddie, and George Shannon? Is this some kind of a gag?"

"I'm sorry," I said. "It isn't the first time a man has killed for a woman, and for money."

"But I didn't," Dorr said, his voice close to the breaking point. "I—I don't understand any of this. I love Elaine, that's true, but I don't need money. And maybe I was anxious for Elaine to receive the insurance payment—you can't blame me for that. But I didn't push that ladder, and I haven't been near the Red Bird Tavern today."

"Can you prove it?" I asked. "If you were working at the plant all day, and this evening, as you said, that should be easy."

He looked at me with a kind of horror in his eyes. "I can't prove it. After I left Elaine this afternoon, I just drove around, all over, out in the hills. That's why I didn't have any dinner, and why I was working tonight. I had to get some reports ready for the general manager in the morning. I went to the office about five-thirty, and I worked, and then you called me . . ."

"Did anyone see you?"

He pressed fingers against his eyes. "No, no. They were all gone. Even the gate man was gone, making a round with his punch clock. The gate was locked, and I parked outside and walked in to the office." He looked up at Conway and me and said, "Honest, I'm not your man. I—I love Elaine Shannon. I admit that, and I wanted her to have the insurance money, but I didn't...."

"All right, Vernon," Conway said kindly. "I've known your father for a long time, a fine man. It appears that in this matter circumstances are against you, but I have no legal authority to hold you. I accept your word—for now. You can go."

"Chief," I said, "listen. He—"

"Never mind, Bennett," he said in a strangely sharp voice. "You have your methods, and I have mine. I'm chief of police here."

"Yes, sir," I said, thinking that he intended to have Dorr tailed.

Conway said, "The evidence is all circumstantial. His story is as good as ours. If we had the weapon, fingerprints, or a witness—a live one . . ." He spread his hands in a hopeless gesture.

"Or a confession," I said.

"That would be nice," Conway said mockingly. He looked at Dorr.

"Do you want to confess?"

"Not to something I didn't do," Dorr said quietly. He stood up, not looking at me, and started for the door.

The phone on Conway's desk tinkled softly. He picked it up, spoke briefly, listened a moment, said, "All right. Thanks." He hung up and said, "Wait, Vernon."

Dorr, at the door, stopped and turned.

"I'm sorry, Vernon," Conway said, his thin intelligent face grave, "but I'm afraid you'll have to stay here—for the present."

Dorr stared at him, a stricken look in his eyes.

"A woman just called the desk," Conway said. "She didn't give her name, but she said that she is the wife of one of the men who was at the Red Bird Tavern tonight when Fleet was killed. She said her husband works at Ferris, and that shortly after Eddie Fleet entered the men's room, he saw a man in the passage who had just come out of the room. The man was carrying a heavy wrench, and he sneaked out of the rear door, the one that opens on the court. He recognized the man, but he didn't tell the police—because he doesn't want any trouble."

"Like Eddie Fleet," I said.

"Yes," Conway said.

Dorr stood still, his gaze on Conway.

I had a hunch what was coming, and I stood up and sauntered to the door. Dorr ignored me.

Conway said, "The woman is trying to persuade her husband to come down and tell us. She says she'll bring him as soon as she can." He moved in his chair, and I saw his hand move to the edge of the drawer. "It's a positive identification, Vernon. She said her husband named you as the man."

Dorr seemed to sway slightly. I moved a little, so that I could see his face. His eyes were closed.

They didn't put Vernon Dorr in a cell, but let him sit in an unoccupied office down the corridor, with a policeman at the door. Conway and I sat in his office, drinking more coffee. It was twenty minutes after eight in the evening. Conway had told me that the woman had called from a pay booth on Carbon Street, in a drugstore. He looked at a wristwatch. "Twenty minutes," he said. "She should be here by now."

"Maybe she's having trouble convincing her husband that he should tell," I said. "After all, Dorr is an official at the place where he works."

"I know," Conway sighed. "They don't want any trouble, particularly if it's connected with their jobs. But we have the names of all the men in the Red Bird Tavern tonight, and it shouldn't be too difficult to smoke out the one we want. It'll take time, though." Once more he looked at his watch. "We'll wait fifteen more minutes."

We drank more coffee, and smoked, and waited. We talked a little, but not much. Presently Conway said, "Time's up. Do you want to stick around?"

I stood up and stretched. "No, thanks. You won't need me."

"I'll have all the men who were in the tavern picked up," he said, "including the bartender. I'll question them one at a time, and see what happens."

"You'll hold Dorr?"

"I've got to, now."

"Maybe you'd better tell his folks."

"I will, I will," he said irritably. "That's a pleasant job, too."

I placed a hand on his shoulder. "Take it easy, Chief. I'll see you in the morning."

"All right."

I left him.

As I entered the lobby of the hotel, a tall young man turned away from the desk and came to meet me. "Mr. Bennett?" he asked, and I nodded. He had a blunt serious face and grave brown eyes, and was dressed neatly in a brown suit and a tan raincoat. He wore no hat, and the light glinted on thick brown hair. "I'm Jack Schultz," he said, "the president of the union local at Ferris Abrasives." He flipped open a wallet and showed me a paid-up membership card.

We shook hands, and I said, "Pleased to meet you, Jack. What can I do for you?"

He gazed around the lobby. "Can I talk to you for a few minutes?"

"Sure. How about a drink?"

He grinned, and shook his head. "No, thanks. How about over there?" He nodded at two chairs in a far corner of the lobby.

"Fine," I said. We went to the chairs and sat down.

He leaned forward earnestly. "I'll make it short, Mr. Bennett; after you were at the plant this morning with that other man, some ugly rumors started about the accident that killed George Shannon. The whole plant got in an uproar—you know how those things are. Guys kept asking me what was going on—they all knew that Shannon's death had been investigated before—and my production went to hell. You can't press grinding wheels and keep answering crazy questions every couple of minutes. So, to stop the rumors, I decided to go in the office and see Dorr. He wasn't in. His secretary couldn't tell me when he'd be in, but she gave me your name and said that you were with the Industrial Welfare Commission. When I couldn't reach Dorr tonight, I decided to ask you about it. I figured you'd be staying at this hotel."

He paused, and said soberly, "They're saying there's something funny about that accident. And now tonight I hear that Eddie Fleet was killed over at the Red Bird. The guys saw you talking to all the men in the finishing room this morning, and they tell me that the other man, the one with you this morning, talked to Eddie at the Red Bird. And then you go there and find Eddie dead in the can."

"News travels fast," I said.

He grinned. "You'd be surprised how fast it travels in a shop—and it's usually all wrong." He stopped grinning and said seriously, "I don't want you to tell me anything you don't want to, or can't, but I wish you'd give me something to take back—to stop the rumors."

I thought fast, and tried to decide which side I was on, labor or management. I'd never thought much about it before. I decided that I was neutral, and I hoped that in some distant utopia there would not be two sides, but a combination of two groups working together for the common good, and suddenly I didn't see any harm in telling Jack Schultz the truth.

"Jack," I said, "it's a kind of delicate situation, and it will probably be all over town tomorrow. There was something irregular about the death of George Shannon." I told him the story, as briefly as possible, and when I'd finished, I told him, "Use your own judgment about repeating what I've told you. You have the truth, as of this minute. Maybe I shouldn't have told you, but as a representative of the people out there I figure you have a right to know."

"I appreciate that," he said gravely, "and you can trust me." He grinned ruefully. "The hell of it is, the truth is worse than the rumors."

"I was afraid of that," I sighed. "Why don't you just stall until tomorrow? It'll be in the newspapers then, at least part of it, and you'll be off the hook."

"Thanks, Mr. Bennett." He stood up. "If we can be of any help to you . . ."

"I'll remember that." I walked with him to the revolving glass doors. "By the way, what do you think about Vernon Dorr and Mrs. Shannon?"

"She worked at the plant, you know," he said, "before she married George Shannon. Of course, we all knew that Dorr was making a play for her—you can't hide a thing like that in a shop." He frowned slightly. "But Dorr wasn't the only one—other guys made passes at her, too. She's very pretty."

"Yes," I said, "but business and pleasure don't mix, do they?"

"I guess not," he said quietly, "but we're all human."

I decided that I liked Jack Schultz, and I said, "How are your relations with the company? I mean, as an organization?"

"Very good. The company is fair with us, and we try to be fair, too." He grinned at me. "Of course, we've got to keep our guard up."

I laughed. "Oh, sure. If you didn't, you wouldn't be a good union. What about the company's guard?"

"They keep theirs up, too," he said, still grinning. "It works both ways." He held out a hand. "Thanks, again, Mr. Bennett. I hope I see you again."

"I hope so, too," I said, thinking sadly that I was almost old enough to be his father. But I didn't have any sons, not even a wife. "Are you married?"

"Sure. Three kids. My oldest boy is in junior high school. Made shortstop on the ball team last year."

"That's fine," I said dismally. If I got married tonight and started propagation immediately I would be practically senile before any son of mine would be old enough to play on a junior high ball team. It wasn't a very pleasant thought, and I was glad that I didn't have such thoughts often. "Good-bye, Jack."

He nodded and went out. Through the doors I saw that it was raining again. Jack Schultz turned up the collar of his raincoat and strode up the street. I turned away, and walked slowly to the bar, feeling old and tired. I had a hot beef sandwich and a bottle of beer. The beer tasted very good after all the coffee I'd had with Chief of Police Conway. Afterward I smoked a cigarette and thought of Elaine Shannon, and of Elaine's trim sister-in-law, Gloria Shannon, the frustrated school teacher. I thought of little Jonquil, Jon for short, a hell of a name for a cute little girl, and of Mrs. Ryan, and of Eddie Fleet, dead on a cement floor beneath a crusted wash basin. What was his family doing tonight, the wife and the four children? Grieving, of course, and no doubt making a deal with an unctuous undertaker. Blah blah down and so much a month, and it'll be a real nice funeral, Mrs. Fleet. You furnish the body and we furnish the coffin and the canned hymns on easy payments. I thought of Sandy Hollis, far away in Cleveland, and I knew regretfully that I could not make a weekend date with her now. Chief Conway would want me here, and it was my job. I thought of George Allen Shannon, a man I'd never seen, rotting now in a box deep in the earth of some lonely graveyard, and of a falling ladder beneath a factory roof, with Vernon Dorr at the foot of the ladder and a man named Riggio hanging desperately from a rafter, and once more I was in the untidy office of Dr. Ordway Vincetti talking to a red-headed nurse about two soiled and hopeless lives, and in my mind I rode in an ambulance beside a man dying of a fractured skull.

How long had I been in Steel City? Just since yesterday afternoon? That's all, Bennett, and here you sit at ten o'clock on a Thursday evening.

I paid my check and went up to my room. The door was still unlocked, as it had been when I'd left Al Purdy, and I entered. The lights were still on, and the steam-heated air held the odor of whisky and cigarette smoke, and a sweet odor that I knew and didn't want to smell now. But I did, and it was sickish, and I knelt on the floor beside the still body of Purdy. I saw the blood in his hair and the wet blackness of it soaking the rug beneath his head.

CHAPTER FIFTEEN

He was breathing heavily and pinkish bubbles came from his nose and lips. I stood up, thinking wildly of another man with a bashed skull, of Eddie Fleet, and I knew that the killer would not stop now. I was scared, but with the fear was a blind feeling of outrage, and my hand trembled as I lifted the phone. Standing astride Purdy's body I said savagely to a faraway voice, "This is 412. Send a doctor right away, and an ambulance!"

"But, sir—"

"Emergency, goddamn it!" I shouted. "Hear?"

I slammed down the receiver and gazed down at Al Purdy, at his broad friendly face, composed now, except for the thick breathing and the bubbles. I wondered bleakly how many minutes, or seconds,

Eddie Fleet had lived after his skull had been crushed, and I knew that there was nothing I could do for Purdy. If anything could be done, it was a job for the doctors, the surgeons, and I didn't dare touch him, or move him.

I stepped over his body and gazed around the room. It looked the same. My whisky bottle was on the desk, still almost half full. The bed showed the depression where I had lain. The only different thing was Purdy's glass. It was on the floor beside him, unbroken. I tried to picture what had happened, and I could see Purdy sitting comfortably in the chair, his back to the door, drinking the whisky, his "dessert" after drinking a beer dinner with Eddie Fleet at the Red Bird Tavern, and I saw the door open slowly and soundlessly, and the crouched figure with murder in one hand, the raised arm and the swift vicious descent, and Purdy's body crumpling forward....

Except for the gentle hiss of steam, and Purdy's breathing, more labored now, the room was so quiet I wanted to scream. I picked up the phone once more, told a cool impersonal voice that I wanted the police department. While I waited I tried not to look at Purdy lying at my feet, and when the quiet voice of the desk sergeant answered, I said, "Chief Conway, please."

"Just a moment." I waited a moment, maybe two moments. How long is a moment?

Conway's tired voice said, "Yes?"

"This is Bennett. Are you still holding Dorr?"

He hesitated, and then said, "No. The woman who called in never showed up with her husband. We rounded up all the men who were at the tavern. Couldn't crack any of them. I had to release Dorr."

"When?"

"Oh, maybe twenty minutes ago, or a half hour. We can always pick him up, if we want him."

"Did you put a tail on him?"

"This isn't Cleveland," he said, a trifle testily, "or Chicago. I didn't think it was necessary."

"You'd better pick him up then," I told him, trying to keep my voice steady. "Somebody just tried to kill my partner, Al Purdy—the man who talked to Eddie Fleet at the Red Bird. I think he's dying. I'm with him in my room at the Blue Ridge. A doctor and an ambulance are on the way—I hope."

"We'll put it on the radio," Conway said quickly. "I'll be right over. Stay there."

I hung up, realizing that I was sweating. I went to my bag, open on a small stand against the wall, and felt for my Smith and Wesson .38 beneath a pile of clean socks. It wasn't there. I dumped the contents of the bag on the floor. No gun. My lovely, cold, blue steel friend was gone, and I felt naked and afraid.

There was a soft knock on the door. I moved to it, opened it cautiously. A short man in a blue pin-stripe suit and a checkered vest stood there. "I'm the manager. You called for a doctor and an ambulance?"

I nodded.

"They'll be here any moment," he said. "What's the trouble here?" He tried to peer past me into the room.

I stepped aside and let him look. "Good heavens!" He breathed. "How on earth did that happen?" He looked at me suspiciously, fearfully, and began to back away.

"Somebody sneaked in and slugged him," I said. "Where in hell is that doctor?"

"He—he'll be here." He backed across the corridor and wiped his face with a checkered handkerchief which matched his vest.

From down the corridor I heard the elevator door open, and the murmur of voices. Four persons moved toward us, three men and a woman. One of the men carried a folded canvas stretcher. Another man walked beside him. Both of them wore white jackets beneath their open topcoats. Behind them was Dr. Ordway Vincetti. The woman beside him was his red headed nurse.

The hotel manager said nervously, "I must call the police."

"I've called them," I snapped. "Why did you get Dr. Vincetti?"

"We've had him before. Sometimes it's difficult to locate the other doctors, and Dr. Vincetti is usually available."

The group approached us and stopped. Dr. Vincetti moved forward, carrying a black leather bag. He was still wearing the neat dark gray suit, and his thin face was the color of death. But he walked firmly, as if he were concentrating on the effort, and he held his head high and a little to one side. His black Homburg and dark blue overcoat gave him a distinguished appearance. Eight hours ago he had been passed-out drunk, and here he was, on his feet, answering the call of duty. Maybe it was the hangover cure the red-head had told me about. I wondered if maybe he'd sell me a small supply.

The manager pointed at the open door. "In there, Doctor." Down the corridor a few doors had opened and people were staring at us silently.

Dr. Vincetti inclined his head gravely and entered the room. He didn't look at me, but the nurse, who was right behind him, gave me a startled glance of recognition. Then her grayish cat's eyes shifted, and she entered the room behind the doctor and closed the door.

The manager walked briskly down the corridor and I heard him speaking to the curious people in officious tones. "It's all right, folks. One of our guests is—uh—ill. Please go back to your rooms." The curious people ignored him, and he began to walk in a slow circle, rubbing his chin, and darting quick glances at me. The two ambulance men leaned against the wall. The one holding the stretcher had a deep nasty cough, and they both seemed bored.

The room door opened, and the red-head said, "All right, boys. Come and get him. Fractured skull, multiple, cerebral bleeding. St. John's Hospital. Take it easy."

They went inside. I heard Dr. Vincetti speak to them in a low gentle voice. The manager teetered nervously. The people in the corridor moved closer, peering. The ambulance men came out bearing Al Purdy on the stretcher. They had wrapped him in a blanket and only his nose and mouth showed.

The manager plucked at the sleeve of one of the ambulance men. "Please! Take the service elevator. I can't have you carrying him through the lobby."

"Ambulance is in front," the coughing one said, and he coughed. "Sorry."

"Really," the manager protested shrilly. "I must insist."

They moved on, ignoring him. The nurse came out of the room with Dr. Vincetti, and I heard her say to him, "I'll go with them, baby." Her voice rasped pleasantly. She entered the elevator behind the ambulance men. The door closed and the little red lights began to flash downward. Slowly the onlookers returned to their rooms. The show was over, and they hadn't even seen any blood.

Dr. Vincetti, carrying his bag, moved past me. I touched his arm, and he turned. "Bad, Doc?" I asked.

He nodded gravely. "Very bad. He may have a chance, but I can't tell now." His voice was low and liquid, very precise. His black eyes gazed at me, and I saw the pain in them, maybe despair, and a remote look, as if he were far away, maybe in Baltimore, "Is he a friend of yours?" he asked politely.

"Yes. Can I drive you to the hospital?"

"Thank you, but I have my car. They should have him ready by the time I get there." He started to move away.

Once more I touched his arm. "Should I go with you?"

He paused and gazed at me with his sad eyes. "You may, if you wish, but there is nothing you can do. Nothing but wait."

"My name's Bennett. You can reach me here. I'll be responsible for him, for your fee...."

"We are not worrying about responsibility, or a fee," he said gently. "A man has been injured." He turned and moved down the corridor to the elevator waiting with the door open. I gazed after him, watched him disappear, and when I turned I saw Chief of Police Conway standing in the corridor.

He smiled thinly. "We came up the back elevator." Beside him was a stocky, middle-aged man in plainclothes. He was smoking a pipe, and an elk's tooth dangled from a gold chain across his vest. His brows were iron gray, his eyes a bright blue. Conway said, "This is Lieutenant Valdo."

We shook hands and were about to enter the room when the manager came hurrying up. "Please, gentlemen, will you make it as unobtrusive as possible? The other guests...." He gestured down the corridor, where doors were beginning to open again. Maybe they'd missed something. Maybe there would be a few more crumbs of excitement.

Conway said impatiently, "Yes, yes," and we entered the room. I closed the door in the manager's anxious face.

Conway said to me, "The lab men are on their way here. If your man dies, this room will have to be gone over anyway." He and Lieutenant Valdo stood gazing about. I pointed to the spot where I'd found Al Purdy, and they peered at the blood-stained rug. Valdo got out a notebook and I began to give them the story. From down in the street I heard the sad wail of an ambulance siren.

Conway said, "Bennett, on your say-so, I ordered Vernon Dorr picked up." The laboratory men had come and gone, and the room was quiet. Lieutenant Valdo leaned against the door, moodily puffing on his pipe.

"Do you have any better ideas?" I asked.

He shook his head, and said slowly, "No, I guess not.... So your gun is missing?"

I nodded. "I figure the person who slugged Purdy took it."

"Do you want a gun?"

"Do you think I'll need one?"

"You never know. It looks like the killer of Eddie Fleet was afraid that Eddie had given information to your man, Purdy, and he tried to silence Purdy the same way he did Fleet. And he must also know that Purdy had talked to you. So . . ." Conway lifted his thin shoulders.

Something like the point of an icicle seemed to trace my spine. "I see what you mean, Chief. Maybe I'm next?" I tried to smile, but it was a poor attempt.

He grinned, showing his teeth, a wolf's snarl. Lieutenant Valdo moved forward, took a big Police Positive from his overcoat pocket and held it out to me, butt first. "It's loaded," he said. "The safety is on."

I hefted the gun, feeling its deadly balanced weight, and I put it, muzzle down, in my inside coat pocket. "Thanks," I said, my gaze avoiding theirs. The gun felt good beneath my arm and against my ribs.

Valdo said, "A little equalizing never hurts. No sense in playing ball without a bat." His blue eyes twinkled.

Conway said to Valdo, "Got all you need?"

Valdo nodded, buttoned his overcoat, put the pipe between his teeth and moved to the door.

I said to Conway, "One thing more; the hotel called Dr. Vincetti on this. He's gone to the hospital. His nurse went with Purdy in the ambulance."

"Was Vincetti sober?"

"Yes."

He sighed. "It's up to you. It's a little late, but we can still try to get another doctor."

"It's *too* late," I said. "Purdy can't wait." I remembered Dr. Vincetti's words: *We are not worrying about responsibility, or a fee. A man has been injured.* "I think Dr. Vincetti will be fine."

Conway said to Valdo, "Send a man out to the hospital to stay with Purdy. Right now." He gave me his wolfish grin. "Routine."

Valdo picked up the phone and spoke in low tones. Conway moved to the door and said, "It looks like the same weapon was used—the one that killed Eddie Fleet."

"Yes?" I said, thinking of Al Purdy and his dream of a little mink ranch.

Valdo left the phone and joined Conway at the door. Conway said to me, "Do you want to stick with us on this, or what?"

"I'll see you later. Let me know when you pick Dorr up."

"He's still your boy, huh?"

"How the hell can you be sure?" I asked, feeling sudden anger. "It's *somebody*, and Dorr had the motive."

"And the opportunity," Conway said softly. He reached out and patted my shoulder. "Take it easy." He and Valdo went out.

I locked the door and picked up the bourbon bottle. It was almost empty now, because a couple of the lab men had sampled it after the photographers had taken their pictures of the room. I took a slow drink and was about to take another when the phone rang. It startled me, and I almost dropped the bottle. I lifted the receiver, "Hello."

A woman's voice said, "Mr. Bennett?"

"Yes." The voice was familiar. I frowned, trying to place it. "I called earlier, and some man in your room said you were out and that he would tell you to call me."

I knew who it was then, and I said, "I'm sorry. The man couldn't tell me." It wasn't Elaine Shannon, but Gloria Shannon, my other love.

"Couldn't tell you?"

"Never mind. How are you tonight?"

"Just fine, Mr. Bennett. It's—"

"I thought we agreed to call me Jim."

She laughed softly. "I'm fine, Jim. It's rather late, but I wanted to tell you that I can see you tomorrow night, after all—if you still want me to. Miss Cameron has a cold and begged off, and I don't want to go to the lecture alone. Would you go with me? I'm sure you would enjoy it."

"I'm sure I would, too," I said, trying to remember what the lecture was about. "Can't we have dinner first?"

"Of course, if you like." There was a happy lilt to her voice.

"I like," I said. "What happened to you?"

"And why do you ask that, sir?" The coyness was almost painful, but I remembered her fresh good looks, even without makeup, and her tall marvelous body.

"Well, you sound different."

"Oh, but I feel different. I've been with Jonquil, such a lovable, wonderful child. I picked her up at Elaine's right after I left you this afternoon and took her out to the farm. We had a wonderful time. I let her help me bake a cake—I really make marvelous cake, chocolate fudge—and she was so cute. Mr. and Mrs. Stockmaster just fell in love with her, really. And listen to this—when I took her home tonight, Elaine was very nice. I asked her again if I could have Jonquil, and do you know what she said?"

"I can't guess," I said, gazing down at Al Purdy's blood on the rug.

"I'm afraid I've misjudged Elaine," she said. "She's a nice person, really. I—I guess I was jealous, as you said. She agreed to let me keep Jonquil, at least for a while. You see, Elaine has the offer of a job in California—in Sacramento, I believe she said—and she's leaving in the morning. I'm to pick up Jonquil then, about seven o'clock, and I'll have her all to myself. Isn't that wonderful?"

"Yes," I said in a dull voice. "Wonderful."

"You don't sound very happy." I could almost see her pouting prettily.

"Oh, but I am," I said sincerely. "Where are you now?"

"In a drugstore on Carbon Street. I just left Elaine. Jonquil and I stayed at the farm until after nine o'clock, and then I brought her in. I tried to call you from Elaine's apartment, and that man in your room said he'd—"

"You told me that," I broke in. "And so now you'll be almost like a mother?"

"Yes! Isn't it wonderful? And Elaine was so nice about it, and I know she loves Jonquil, too. I just had to tell somebody about it. I don't care about the insurance money anymore—just so I have Jonquil. Do—do you suppose I could bring her along with me tomorrow night? Just for dinner? We could take her back to the farm before we go to the lecture. Would you mind?"

"Not at all," I said. "We can play that we are parents, and we'll buy Jonquil a double chocolate sundae."

"Won't it be wonderful?" she breathed.

"Yes. I'm very happy for you, Gloria. May I call you Gloria?"

"Oh, of course! I'd love it if you did. May I call you James?"

"Jim—remember?" I said, still seeing Al Purdy's blood, drying now.

"All right—Jim. You're the first man I've become, well, friendly with, since...."

"I know," I said, thinking, *Since Mike, honey, and that's been a long, long time*. "About six tomorrow? Where?"

"I can't ask you to drive way out here in the hills just for little old me. I'll meet you at the hotel. Will that be all right—Jim?"

"Sure. I'll look for you and Jonquil in the lobby."

"Jim, perhaps I'd better leave Jonquil at home—this first time. We can take her with us later. She was up late tonight, and she should be in bed early tomorrow night.... Do you mind if I don't bring her?"

"Not at all, Gloria. Why don't you just come up to my room? We'll have a drink before dinner."

She laughed uncertainly. "Well, maybe just a teensy one. It's been so long . . ."

"Too long," I muttered.

"What did you say, Jim?"

"It's too long to wait," I said fatuously. "Can't I see you tonight?"

She hesitated, thinking it over. Then she said, "I—I'm afraid not. It's very late. Please don't be—impatient. Until tomorrow at six, Jim."

"It's a long time," I murmured. "Good-night . . . Gloria."

"Good-night, Jim." She hung up softly.

CHAPTER SIXTEEN

I called St. John's Hospital. A woman told me that Mr. Purdy was still in surgery and that it might be some time before a statement as to his condition could be made. I thanked her, pressed the receiver bar and asked the hotel operator to get me Miss Sandra Hollis, in Cleveland, Ohio, and I gave her the number. Yes, I would hold on. I held on, for five minutes, and I shifted around in the chair so that I couldn't see Al Purdy's blood. Female voices, in varying degrees of pitch and regional accent, came over the wire from Louisville to Cincinnati, to Columbus and Toledo, and once a Detroit voice got in there, and then I had Cleveland.

Sandy answered right away. Just hearing her voice made me feel better. "Jim, it's you!"

"Hi, honey. How's everything?"

"Fine. I—I've missed you, though."

"I've missed you, too."

"How're you making out down there in the hills?"

"Terrible."

"I'm sorry, Jim. I just knew you wouldn't like that dull old insurance work. When are you coming home?"

"I don't know," I said miserably. "I thought I might make it this weekend, but it looks like I won't get away now."

"Oh, Jim." There was genuine regret in her voice, and I could picture her at the phone on the little ivory-painted desk in her apartment. She was probably in pajamas, with her crisp bronze hair combed to a shine, and maybe her faintly freckled face cold-creamed, her brown eyes sad, her sweet mouth close to the receiver, four hundred miles away.

"I'll get home as soon as I can," I told her. "I'm in the middle of something here, and I can't leave now. It may be the break the boss was hoping for—if I can wind it up. The agency will be sitting pretty then, and the other states will fall in line."

"Are—are you all right, Jim? Is it bad down there?"

"I'm all right, but it's bad."

"Can I help?"

"You've helped just talking to me."

"I won't make any dates for the weekend—just in case."

"Don't do that," I told her, wanting her to just the same. "I'm pretty sure I won't—"

"I'll be waiting for you."

"You mustn't do—"

"Be quiet. I hadn't planned anything anyhow."

"How's business?"

"Good, but routine. Missing teenagers, jealous wives, suspicious husbands, a loan company embezzlement, a little blackmail." She laughed. "The same old stuff. Alec is handling it nicely."

"Give him my regards." Alec Hammond was the Cleveland office's one full-time assistant, and had been with me for years.

"I will, Jim—and I'll look for you tomorrow night, or Saturday."

"Keep your fingers crossed."

"They're crossed now. See?"

"This isn't TV, honey. Good-bye."

"Good-bye, Jim. Be careful."

Slowly I cradled the phone.

The room seemed deathly quiet. Even the hiss of steam had stopped, and I decided that the hotel, for economy reasons, had turned down the boiler pressure for the night when guests should be keeping warm in bed. For the first time I realized that I was still wearing my hat and topcoat, that they hadn't been off since I'd talked to Al Purdy, here in this room, before my visit to the Red Bird Tavern. I took them off, and my suit coat, too, and loosened my collar. It was then that I remembered the envelope containing the samples of Eddie Fleet's handwriting Vernon Dorr had brought me. The envelope protruded from the coat pocket into which I'd put Lieutenant Valdo's gun. I opened the envelope and took out several sheets of yellow printed forms covered with a penciled record of a day's production turned out by Edward Fleet, and they were signed by him. From my briefcase I got the notes received by Elaine Shannon and myself and compared the writing. I'm not an expert, but the notes and the production records appeared to be written by the same person, even to the method of crossing the t's.

So what? Eddie Fleet had written the notes, and he was dead.

I slumped in the chair, held the bourbon bottle on my stomach, and gazed at the wispy cobwebs in the corners of the ceiling. I took a slow sip of the bourbon, not really wanting it, and I lit a cigarette, not wanting it, either, and I sipped and smoked and thought. My brain moved in a sluggish circle, around and around, slowly....

A man falling from a ladder, no doubt screaming thinly, a widow grieving, a little girl without a father. Another man, in love with the widow—and had the police picked him up yet? A school teacher, yearning for the dead man's child, so that an emptiness in her heart could be filled. A doctor remembering forever a cheating wife, and a red-headed nurse who loved the doctor truly. A dead man on a cement floor in a tavern, another man crumpled in his blood on the floor of this room. A sincere young president of a labor union, a chief of police who looked like a college professor, an amiable middle-aged lieutenant of detectives, a Police Positive in the pocket of my coat on the bed, a jittery hotel manager, a coughing ambulance man, the gritty whir of a grinding wheel as a finishing cutter bit into the rough abrasive, the hiss of hydraulic presses, the roar of gas flaming into the ports of a tunnel kiln, the warm sweet taste of a widow's lips. And the little girl again, a blue-eyed child named Jonquil, after a flower that blooms in the spring, and called Jon for short.

And a man dying in an ambulance with a name on his lips.

Slowly my circling thoughts came to a stop. I sat very still for a time, sipping the whisky. I wanted it now, although I knew it wouldn't help. Nothing could help now, and nobody could help. Nobody but me. And maybe I couldn't help, either, but I could try. Help who, Bennett? The law? Yes, maybe the law? But don't think about help, Bennett. It is too late for help, and you can only avenge. Vengeance for George Allen Shannon and Eddie Fleet and Al Purdy, who was probably dead by now. He was a nice guy. They were all nice guys, with hopes and dreams and warm blood flowing. No more, Bennett, never no more. But maybe you can avenge them, if you're careful and smart. And lucky.

Carefully I placed the bottle on the desk. There was an inch of bourbon left, but I didn't want it. Maybe I'd want it afterward, but I didn't know. I entered the bathroom, washed my face in cold water, buttoned my collar and adjusted the knot of my tie. I needed a shave again, but I didn't care, and my hair needed cutting, as it usually did, because to me the time spent waiting in a barber shop is wasted time, gone forever. And nobody has enough time, not even a murderer in death row, who should be anxious to get the whole damn business of living over and done with.

The least I could do was avenge them.

I put on my suit coat, feeling the lovely weight of the gun, and then my topcoat and hat, and I looked in the mirror over the dresser and I thought, You look like hell, Bennett. You're getting old; you've got bags beneath your eyes, and the lines around your mouth are very unattractive. The thin white scar on your chin doesn't help at all, and you really should shave, but what of it? You're not going to a cocktail party at the Plaza and no velvet-skinned females are going to rub their cheeks against your chin. You're going on an errand of vengeance, maybe an errand of glory and prestige and financial gain for the agency, and you're all alone. You can't ask Chief of Police Conway to help, or anybody because you don't really know if you'll want help on this, or need it.

And you may as well face it, Bennett; you're going out now because you're scared and you don't want it to happen to you, the thing that happened to George Shannon and Eddie Fleet and Al Purdy.

I turned off the lights, stepped into the corridor and locked the door.

There weren't many cars on the semi-darkened streets, and the few people on the sidewalks seemed to be hurrying home. Most of the storefronts were dark, but there were lights in the bars and restaurants. I drove slowly across the city and listened to the tail end of a midnight news broadcast:

....Mr. Fleet was the father of four children and had been employed by the Ferris Abrasives Company. Chief of Police Conway is conducting an investigation. Earlier this evening another man was brutally beaten on the head, suffering multiple skull fractures, as he sat in a room of a local hotel. He is Albert M. Purdy, an accident investigator

for the state's Industrial Welfare Commission. He is in St. John's Hospital and his condition is described as extremely critical. Chief Conway has expressed the opinion that the murder of Mr. Fleet and the attack on Mr. Purdy are connected, possibly committed by the same person, and he expects to make a statement tomorrow. He expressed concern over the increase of acts of violence in the city during the past few months, and at the next council meeting he will ask for additional patrolmen. The weather for Steel City and vicinity will continue mild....

I switched off the radio. It hadn't taken long for the news to get into the public domain, even though Conway was hedging. It would be in the papers in the morning, and Jack Schultz would not have to explain to the union membership. The wire services no doubt already had it. People in Boston and Seattle and Santa Fe would read about it, and in Cleveland, too; and Sandy Hollis would maybe know what I'd meant when I'd told her that things were "terrible" in Steel City. I thought uneasily that I should make a report to my superior, Austin O'Connor, since Al Purdy couldn't, and I was an official state agent. But there was time enough for that.

O'Connor would immediately send men up here, and maybe he'd even come himself, and he would disclaim any responsibility on the part of the state, quoting in his shrill voice statutes, articles and sections of the workmen's compensation laws in an effort to prove that George Shannon and Eddie Fleet had not died as a result of anything connected with their employment. Some states, I knew, would regard such a situation otherwise. In these states an employer was responsible under the law for a man's unnatural death while on the job or on the employer's premises. I was inclined to agree that it was a more just interpretation; if George Shannon had not been employed by Ferris Abrasives and had not fallen from the ladder, no matter what the reason, he would still be alive. And if Eddie Fleet had not become involved in a situation arising from his employment with Ferris, then he would still be alive.

There was a fine line someplace, and I gave it up. Even my training in law, many years before, did not qualify me to interpret the various workmen's compensation laws of the different states. It required special study and training, and was a matter for the claims board to decide or the courts.

I knew one thing—I did not want Austin O'Connor stirring things up in his fussy, old-maidish manner. Not now. I would have to tell him, and soon, about Al Purdy, and Purdy's family should be notified, too. But not now, not tonight.

I turned the Mercury into Carbon Street and presently I was driving slowly past Mrs. Ryan's apartment building. Most of the windows were dark, but there was a light behind the closed blinds of Elaine Shannon's apartment. I parked at the curb and watched. A shadow moved behind the blind, and I stirred uneasily. The uneasiness had been with me for some time now, a tiny devil prodding at the back of my brain.

At the end of the block I saw the lights of an all-night drugstore. I left the car and walked down. Beyond it was the Red Bird Tavern, on Clinton Street, which crossed Carbon. The place was brightly lighted and was no doubt jammed tonight with the curious. Perhaps there was still a little of Eddie Fleet's blood on the floor. If there wasn't any blood left, Oscar, the bartender, could point to some damp spots and declare proudly that there, in that spot, was where Eddie Fleet got it. I entered the drugstore.

There were three phone booths in the back. I called the police department and asked for Chief Conway. The desk sergeant said, "I'm sorry, sir. He's out with one of the patrol cars. If it's urgent, I can contact him."

"Never mind." I called the hospital.

"No, sir," a woman said, "there is no change in Mr. Purdy's condition. He is still unconscious and Dr. Vincetti has issued no statement, except that Mr. Purdy's condition is as good as can be expected."

"Thank you," I said bitterly. "Thank you very much." Hospital attendant double-talk had always irritated me. A man could be dead, and his condition could still be "as good as can be expected." But I suppose they had their reasons. Maybe if I was on the telephone in a hospital I wouldn't tell anybody a goddamn thing.

I left the booth and stood in the fluorescent light which made the drugstore as bright as an operating room. A tired-looking female with too much lipstick and a startling mammary camouflage beneath a blue sweater consented to sell me a package of cigarettes, and I went out to the street. It was raining a little but not much, more of a mist than rain, and the air was balmy. I stood for a time, smoking and thinking, but knowing all the while what I had to do. I had to do it alone and decided at last that I'd better get it over with. I could be wrong, and I hoped I was, but I had to know.

I walked swiftly to Mrs. Ryan's apartment house and entered.

CHAPTER SEVENTEEN

The small foyer was quiet and dimly lit, and no light showed from beneath Mrs. Ryan's door. I went up the stairs, quietly and down the hall to Elaine Shannon's door. Light leaked from beneath it in a fan-shaped pattern over the worn carpet. I took a deep breath and knocked softly.

She didn't come to the door right away, but I knew she had heard me, and I didn't knock again. Presently I heard a soft movement inside, and her low voice came out to me. "Who is it?"

"Bennett."

There was a silence, and then she said, "Just a moment."

I waited, and in maybe a minute the door opened and she stood aside for me to enter. I moved inside, closed the door and turned to look at her. She was wearing a raspberry tinted silk robe belted snugly at her slender waist. The wispy lace of a pale green nightgown showed at the bottom of the robe, and on her feet were silk slippers which matched the color of the robe. Her hair was tied in a knot on the top of her head, and her small oval face was devoid of make-up. She looked about sixteen years old.

"I—I wasn't dressed," she said. "It's rather late...."

I took off my hat, feeling faintly awkward and embarrassed. From the first, her grave level gaze had made me feel that way. Behind her on a chair was an open suitcase. The door to the bedroom was ajar, and a dim light showed beyond it. "I'm sorry to bother you," I said, "but I heard that you were going away in the morning and I wanted to say good-bye."

"How did you know?"

"You didn't tell me," I said, with a trace of bitterness. "Miss Shannon told me."

"I see," she said quietly. "Gloria."

"She also said you've consented to let her keep the little girl."

She nodded slowly, and her eyes clouded. "I—I can't do anything else. I can't take her with me, and it will only be until I can send for her. I wanted her with me tonight. I—I'm packing her things. Gloria is going to get her in the morning." She paused, and she said with a faint hardness, "Why does it concern you?"

"It doesn't," I said. "I was just surprised—after what you told me about not giving her up…. Have you had any more trouble?"

Her eyebrows lifted slightly. "Trouble?"

"Any more threatening phone calls? Men following you?"

"No."

"Good," I said. "I'm sorry you're going away."

"I'm sorry, too." Her eyes softened a little. "Maybe we'll meet again."

"Maybe. Sacramento? Is that it?"

She nodded. "I have friends there. They wired me this afternoon about a job I can have, but I'll have to go right away. I've wired back, accepting it. I've got to work."

"You can work here," I said. "Vernon Dorr will give you a job."

"I've changed my mind," she said flatly. "I don't want to stay here, thinking of George. I want to go far away, and try and forget …"

"What about the insurance money?"

"If I get it, you can send it to me."

"You won't get it."

"All right," she said carelessly.

"Don't you want to know why you won't get it?"

"You told me there was some legal difficulty—about how George died. I—I don't understand these things…."

"Your husband was murdered," I said. "I'm sorry."

She hugged her arms as if she were cold. "He's dead," she said dully. "Nothing can bring him back. I don't want to talk about it, not anymore…." She glanced at the door, an invitation for me to leave.

"You knew he was murdered, from the beginning."

"No, no …"

"Have you seen Vernon Dorr tonight?"

"Dorr?" Her voice was faintly shrill, maybe the thin edge of hysteria.

"Vernon Dorr," I said gently. "The police are looking for him. The charge is murder."

She stared at me. "You mean that he …?"

"Yes," I said. "He killed your husband, because he's in love with you, because he wanted to marry you—and to also share in the insurance money. He killed a man named Eddie Fleet tonight, and he tried to kill my partner—maybe he killed him. Tonight a woman called the police and said her husband could identify Dorr. Eddie Fleet saw Dorr kick the ladder from under your husband, and Dorr killed Fleet to keep him quiet. He tried to kill my partner because he was afraid that Fleet had talked to him. Dorr told you what he had done to your husband, for love of you, and you knew."

She made a small helpless gesture, and tears glinted in her eyes. "What could I do?" she asked desperately. "He swore that if I told, he'd implicate me, say we planned it together. People at the plant knew about us, that Vernon loved me. He threatened me, and I—"

"What about the phone calls, and the man you said followed you. Was that Dorr?"

"Yes," she said. "Yes, it was. I was afraid to tell you that it was Vernon."

"Why did you tell me anything, then?"

"I—I don't know. I was frightened . . ." Her small mouth began to quiver and she placed her hands against her cheeks. Her body trembled with suppressed sobs.

"Will you tell the police what you told me?"

"Yes, yes." She turned away, sobbing brokenly. "I—I'm glad it's over. It's been a—a nightmare . . ."

"I know," I said.

Except for her sobbing, the room seemed suddenly quiet. And then from the bedroom came a clear, small voice. "Why, hello, Uncle Vernon!" the voice cried happily.

Elaine Shannon turned to face me and I was aware that she had turned, but I was watching the bedroom door. The little blond girl trotted out, rubbing her eyes. She was wearing pink pajamas with feet in them. She pointed a stubby finger at the bedroom. "I waked up, Elaine, and I seed Uncle Vernon in there. He's wight behind the door. Is he playing a hide game, Elaine?"

Elaine Shannon whispered to me, "Yes, he's there. I was afraid to tell you, I didn't know what to do. I—I think he has a gun...."

I lifted the Police Positive from my coat pocket and said, "Come out, Dorr."

He stepped slowly into the living room. He looked like a man who had been on a two-day drunk; unshaven, disheveled, his dark eyes burning in his pale face. He stood slightly stooped, his arms hanging loosely, his gaze on Elaine Shannon.

"Stand still," I said to him.

He didn't move or look at me. It was as if I wasn't there, did not exist. He spoke in a voice so low that I barely heard him. "Elaine, I heard . . . in there . . . what you said. Elaine . . ." His fist opened and closed, and his chin quivered a little, as if he were about to cry.

"I'm sorry, Vernon." Her voice was brittle, and her eyes shifted to me, and I saw the fear in them. She moved backward slowly, until she stood by my side, and I could smell the clean scent of her.

"Elaine . . ." Dorr whispered.

The little girl said happily, "I had fun with Aunt Gloria."

"Yes, dear," Elaine Shannon said in a choked voice. "Go back to bed. Please."

"But I'm not *sleepy!*" She jumped up and down and clapped her hands. "I wanna play hide games with Uncle Vernon!"

"Jonquil," Elaine Shannon said desperately. "Please . . ."

The little girl looked up at me with big eyes. "Are you a cowboy, man? I got a gun, too." She cocked a thumb at Vernon Dorr. "Bang! Bang! You're dead, Uncle Vernon!"

Elaine Shannon said something hopeless and unintelligible, moved swiftly to the child, skirting Vernon Dorr, and led her into the bedroom. The door closed, but the child's plaintive voice came out to us. "But, I'm not *sleepy* . . .!"

Dorr turned slowly, like a robot, and gazed dully at the bedroom door. I moved to the telephone, lifted the receiver to my ear, my eyes on Dorr. Elaine Shannon's muffled voice came from the bedroom.

"Western Union," I said.

Vernon Dorr turned ponderously and said hoarsely, "Bennett...."

"Have you got a gun?" I asked him.

"Gun?" It was as if I'd asked if he had a cobra in his pocket. "No, no...." I didn't want to look at his eyes, but I couldn't help it.

A female voice spoke in my ear, and I said gruffly, "This is the police department. We need some information—right now. Did you have a telegram from Sacramento today for Mrs. George Shannon, 545 Carbon Street?"

"I'm sorry, sir," the voice said, "but we are not permitted to give out that information. If you will—"

"Damn it," I snapped, "it's important that we know immediately."

"I—I'm sorry . . ." The female voice faltered.

I held the phone away from my mouth and said loudly, "Sergeant, put Chief Conway on this wire."

The voice said hastily, "Oh, I am sorry! You are the police, aren't you? One moment, please."

I waited and watched Dorr. He seemed to be staring at me, but he wasn't seeing me.

The voice in my ear said crisply, "No messages for that party. I'll tell the supervisor that you—"

"Never mind."

"Officer, will you please give me your name so that I can mark our records?"

I hung up, feeling sadness and a smugness, too, but the sadness was the stronger, and I spoke gently to Vernon Dorr. "Sit down. I'm not going to shoot you."

"Bennett, listen—"

"Not now," I said, and looked at my watch. Half-past midnight, two minutes after.

Elaine Shannon came out of the bedroom, softly closed the door, and turned to face us. I said to her, "You didn't have a telegram from Sacramento today. Why did you lie to me?"

She stiffened, and her face took on a strange hard look. "I don't have to explain to you. I've told you that Vernon—"

"Yes," I said harshly, "you told me, and to hell with it. Where's John?"

"I—I don't understand. Jonquil is in bed...."

"I don't mean little Jonquil, Jon for short," I said. "I mean John, your lover, John Riggio. Shouldn't he be here by now, to take you away?"

"Please don't—joke."

"I'm not joking."

She shifted her gaze, turned slowly and moved to the window.

"Stay away from the window," I told her. "Don't try to warn him."

She stopped and swung toward Dorr. "Vernon, don't let him talk that way to me! I—I truly believed that you—that you killed George . . ."

I saw the loathing in Dorr's eyes and I was glad. He'd be all right, after a time. Maybe he was all right now. He had loved her, and he had heard her tell me that he was her husband's murderer. She had told it to save another man and maybe herself. Perhaps Dorr still loved her, but the hate was there, too, and I thought I knew a little of what he felt.

He turned slowly, so that his back was to Elaine Shannon, so that he couldn't see her, and he said in an even voice, "It's all right, Bennett. Don't tell me you're sorry. I know how it was now. We both wanted her, Riggio and me, but he had the inside track, even before George died. Some nights I used to watch her apartment—like a lovesick kid." He gave me a stiff smile. "I guess that's what I was, for sure. I saw Riggio come up here often, and I—I died a little each time. You know?"

"I know," I said.

He took a deep shuddering breath. "Tonight, after you and Chief Conway talked to me, I couldn't forget what you said, when you accused me. I began to wonder—about a number of things. I came here, to talk to her. She was packing. I asked her where she was going, but she wouldn't tell me. She tried to make me leave, and I knew something was very wrong. Then you came, and I hid in the bedroom, and I heard what she told you...." He gazed at the floor and he said something I couldn't hear, except that it had "fool" in it.

"It's been rough on you," I told him, "but I had to find out the truth, and that's why I made her believe that I thought you had killed Shannon and Eddie Fleet. She saw a way out, and she took the bait. She was willing to turn you in for murder, to save Riggio. She lied about the job in Sacramento. Things were getting too hot here, and they were skipping. She knew that I was suspicious about her husband's death, and she told Riggio. He tailed me and tried to scare me off by slugging me and warning me. She faked the stories about the threatening phone calls, the man following her, to throw me off the trail. She told me about the note she'd received, the one poor Eddie Fleet wrote, only because she knew I'd find it out anyhow. Eddie wrote her that he was also telling the Commission. You see—"

"Never mind," Dorr said wearily. "I want to go home. Mother will be worrying and wondering where I've been." He looked at me, and asked quietly, "Riggio kicked over the ladder?"

"Yes."

He sighed. "I never suspected, until tonight. I was just standing there, that day, and the ladder moved, and I tried to grab it. I thought it was an accident, that Riggio had barely escaped falling, too—one of those things. But after you talked to me, I began to wonder. Do you know that Riggio did it on purpose?"

"Yes. Shannon mentioned Riggio's name, just before he died, and it all adds up."

Elaine Shannon was watching us with bright eyes, listening. I said to Dorr, "Dr. Vincetti's nurse was with Shannon, in the ambulance. She told me that he said one word before he died. The word was 'John,' but we thought he had referred to his little daughter, Jonquil, whom he called 'Jon' . . . thinking of his only child before he died. But he was trying to say 'John,' that John Riggio had kicked the ladder." I paused and said bleakly, "I've known that since yesterday afternoon early, but I didn't know what it meant until a little while ago."

"You can't think of everything," Dorr said harshly. "May I go now?"

"Sure."

"I'll be at home, if you want me." He moved to the door without looking at Elaine Shannon. "Good-night."

"Good-night."

The door closed softly behind him.

I gazed at Elaine Shannon. She lifted her hands and pressed the palms against her forehead. "This is all so—so fantastic...."

"Shut up," I snarled. "Where's Riggio?"

"Riggio? Really, this is so—so—"

"Fantastic," I finished for her. "Life is a fantasy, Mrs. Shannon."

She moved up close to me. I realized that I was still holding the heavy gun and I dropped it into a pocket of my topcoat. The top of her head was on a level with my second shirt button, and her eyes were sober and veiled. "Call me Elaine," she whispered. "You liked me, didn't you?"

"Yes," I said.

"And you have proof—about John Riggio? You can prove what you said?"

"Certainly," I lied. "We have fingerprints, the weapon that killed Eddie Fleet, all of it."

She sighed. "Poor, poor John. I couldn't help it. I was caught in a—a . . ."

"Web?" I said.

She nodded. "There was nothing I could do."

"Except try and throw me off the track, and tell me sad stories of your girlhood in the mountains. Did you make that up?"

She smiled faintly. "No, of course not. I read it in a magazine called *Romance Confessions*. I was born in Chicago, near the stockyards."

"I see," I said. "Now what?"

"Can't you forget this—this—"

"Fantasy?"

"This fantasy. That's what it really it. I couldn't help it, any of it. John made me call the police this evening. He—he was like a crazy man. I had to do it. I knew John before I met George, in Chicago. He followed me here. But I married George, because I wanted a home, security—things that John would never give me. But I couldn't break away from John. I saw him a few times after I was married, and Vernon Dorr, too, but it didn't mean anything. George worked nights for a while, and I was lonesome. And then John began to talk to me—about a way he knew to get rid of George, and get some money, too. I didn't know what he meant. He wanted me to go away with him, back to Chicago, but I told him I couldn't—not as long as I was married to George. He said he would arrange it, and then, a few days later, George was dead...."

"And you were glad?" I asked, very much aware that her body was pressing against me.

"No, no." She clung to me. "I—I don't know how I felt. I was sorry about George. I—I loved him, a little, and yet it was exciting, to think that John—can you understand?"

"Yes," I said.

Her arms slid around me. "Hold me," she whispered. "I—I'm scared. I didn't do anything, not really, but what will they do to me? The police?"

"I don't know."

"You want me, don't you?"

"Yes," I said, and it was the truth.

"I want you," she whispered. "Take me—now."

"Where's Riggio?"

"I don't know, really. I haven't seen him all day. I think he's gone away." She moved restlessly against me. "Don't talk," she whispered.

"I've got to call the police," I said.

"All right. Call them. But stay with me . . . tonight. I need you."

I put my hands on her shoulders, and I felt the warm flesh beneath the silk, and she moved against me with practiced movements. There was another word for it—expert. Her hips moved expertly, and I held her for a moment, suspended in some queer limbo that was neither desire nor hate, and I thought of George Shannon, going to work every day, trusting and loving his wife, working for her and his daughter, and all the time she was seeing John Riggio and Vernon Dorr, and God knew how many others. Men, it seemed, were her hobby, and she was good at it, confident in her innocent and lovely appearance, but it had backfired at last, and now she was using her ultimate weapon to get what she wanted, to get out of the web.

I laughed inwardly, maybe a trifle hollowly, and she tilted her face, her eyes closed, her lips parted. I kissed her hard, and it was very nice. She came against me with a little cry, trembling deliciously, and expert was still the word. I pushed her away then, not gently, and I said harshly, "For old time's sake, honey," and started for the phone.

"Stop." It was as if she bit the word between her teeth.

I turned slowly and thought with a forlorn bleakness that I was smart, all right, as smart as all hell. I knew how to handle women. I could take 'em or leave 'em, you know me, boys. And here I stood in the middle of the night facing a woman with my own gun in her hand.

"Put that down," I said unsteadily, and began to move toward her.

She backed up, and she held the gun with both hands, the muzzle four feet from the middle of my stomach. Even allowing for wobble and recoil, she couldn't miss.

"Don't move," she whispered. "Stand still."

I stood still.

There was a soft knock on the door.

CHAPTER EIGHTEEN

Elaine Shannon's eyes shifted, but the gun didn't. The knock came again, and the knob rattled gently.

"Let him in," I said.

She began to tremble, and this time she wasn't faking. I saw it in her eyes, a terrible indecision. Should she warn her visitor away, or open the door? She made up her mind, and began to move sideways to the door, her gaze on me.

I took a chance and shouted. "It's the police, Riggio!"

She sprang to the door then, twisted at the knob of the spring lock. "John, John!" she screamed. "Don't leave me!" She jerked at the door, but it wouldn't open, because she needed both hands to do it, one to turn the lock, the other the knob. But she tried to do it with the gun in her hand, sobbing all the while, "Don't leave me, don't leave me...."

I jumped for her, and she swung around, her face a mask of terror, and she brought the gun up, pointed it point-blank. I dropped to my knees as the blast hammered over my head and death sighed in the room. I grabbed one of her ankles, and jerked her down, my free hand groping for her wrist. The gun exploded again. I felt a gentle tug at my coat sleeve, as light as a skeleton's plucking fingers, and there was the bitter smell of scorched cloth. From the hall there came a quick thudding of running feet.

I felt the gun beneath my fingers, and I jerked it free, viciously, aware of Elaine Shannon's slender, white naked body writhing beneath me, the robe and the nightgown twisted around her waist. I tried to roll her away from the door, and her fingers clawed my face. I got to my knees, reached for the door knob, but she was beating me, scratching me, as silent as a killer tigress, and I couldn't move her away from the door. I put the heel of a hand beneath her chin and shoved her head back. I could see her face, ugly now, with all beauty gone, and I didn't mind hitting her with my fist. She collapsed, abruptly, with a little sigh. I stood up, rolled her over with my foot, jerked open the door and stumbled out.

The hall was empty, but I heard the frantic thud of feet on the stairs, going down headlong, and I ran for the stairway, the gun ahead of me. But he had too much of a start. He was probably to the landing by now, and I'd never catch him. "Stop!" I yelled. "This is the police!" but it was just a child's wail, without hope.

I was almost to the stairway when I heard the shot from below, one clear sharp crack, which echoed through the building. There was silence then, maybe a second of it. Then a slow, thumping sound came to me, and a whimpering cry that didn't sound human. I reached the stairway and stopped abruptly, my hand on the railing.

Below me in the foyer a man lay on the floor, writhing slowly and making animal sounds. Mrs. Ryan stood by the open door of her apartment. Her gray hair was in metal curlers and she wore a voluminous blue flannel nightgown which almost reached the floor. Her feet were bare. I went down the stairs slowly, and when I reached the bottom I saw that Mrs. Ryan held the long-barreled Stevens single shot .22 cradled over her left forearm.

We gazed at each other, with the wounded man between us, and she said, calmly, "Hello, son."

"Hello," I panted. "Thanks."

"What's the matter with your face?"

"Scratched."

She nodded at the man on the floor. "I winged him in the knee."

"Thanks," I said again.

"I was sitting in the dark," she said, "having a beer, Tippy and me, and thinking of Herman, when I heard the commotion upstairs. I got the gun, opened the door, and I saw him coming down the stairs fast, and I heard somebody yell something about police. He kept coming, and I aimed careful, for his right knee. A moving target is hard to hit."

I looked at the man on the floor, saw the twisted leg and the blood, and I said, "A bull's-eye."

"I never shot a man before."

"You picked a good time to start." I knelt down, and turned him until I could see his face. Hot dark eyes burned up at me, and the mouth worked in pain. "Damn you," John Riggio gasped. "Get—get a doctor."

"Right away, John. Take it easy." I felt in his overcoat pocket. My gun was there, all right, my lovely .38. I dropped it into my topcoat pocketand stood up.

He said something muffled and obscene, and turned his cheek to the floor.

I said to Mrs. Ryan, "Will you call a doctor? And the police? Get Chief Conway, if you can. I've got to go back upstairs." I touched Riggio with my foot. "Don't worry about him. He's not going anyplace."

"Maybe you'll tell me about it," she said. "When you get time."

"Sure."

The little fox terrier, his small teeth bared, came out from behind her and sniffed at Riggio's shoes. "Tippy will watch him," Mrs. Ryan said, and she smiled. She went inside, and I heard her voice on the phone.

I went up the stairs slowly. People were standing in the hall, and a man spoke to me, but I ignored him. I entered the apartment and closed the door. Elaine Shannon lay as I had left her. Her lips smiled sweetly, as if she was having a happy dream, and there was the beginning of a blue bruise on the delicate line of her jaw. Gently I pulled the robe and nightgown down over her pale nakedness, lifted her in my arms and carried her to the divan. She sighed once, still smiling, and her eyes remained closed.

Behind me in the bedroom I heard the little girl crying. It suddenly seemed to me that she'd been crying for some time, a plaintive background against fear and violence. I opened the bedroom door. Little Jonquil, Jon for short, stood in the middle of the room, her small face contorted and red, tears on her cheeks, sobbing brokenly. In one hand she clutched a brown glassy-eyed teddy bear. There was a clean, sweet child's smell in the room, and everything was very neat. An open closet door disclosed a row of miniature dresses with bows and laces and bright ribbons, and I thought that whatever Elaine Shannon had been, she had taken loving care of her husband's daughter, and once more I knew that nobody was all bad, not even a John Riggio, maybe. People did the things they had to do, because of one desperate compulsion or another, and that was the way it went into the record. And then I remembered George Shannon and Eddie Fleet, and Al Purdy, and I tried to summon the rage again, but it was gone and all I felt was a vast weariness.

"I waked up," the little girl sobbed. "I—I was s-s-cared. I heard a boom, boom. I—I couldn't open the door."

I went to her and knelt down and held her small body close, and I tried to think of the words one said to a frightened child. But I couldn't think of any, because I'd never known many children, and maybe that was my misfortune. So I patted her and said, "There, there," in what I hoped was a motherly tone and let it go at that.

Gradually her sobbing stopped, and wiggled from my arms. "Where's Elaine, man?"

"In the other room."

"I want to see her."

"She's—busy now. You'd better go back to bed, honey."

"Are you a cowboy? Where's your gun?"

"I'll show it to you tomorrow." I picked her up, carried her to the crib and laid her down.

She held the teddy bear and smiled up at me. "I like Aunt Gloria."

"She likes you, too. Close your eyes now."

To my amazement, she closed her eyes. "See," she said. "I'm sleeping."

"That's a good girl." I covered her with a soft pink blanket, tip-toed out, and quietly closed the door.

I moved to the divan and gazed down at Elaine Shannon. She stirred and opened her eyes, and instantly there was the fear in them, and the ugly remembrance. She began to cry silently, her lips moving, the tears creeping down her cheeks.

From the hall I heard the sound of excited voices. I opened the door and Chief of Police Conway walked in.

We sat in Conway's office, a sober group. Morning sunlight filtered through the Venetian blinds and made dancing lights in Gloria Shannon's brown hair. Vernon Dorr sat beside her and they whispered together. Conway was behind his desk. I sat beside him. I hadn't had much sleep, but I was shaved and showered and wearing my other suit, the brown one I'd brought along. Friday morning in April, and I thought of all the Aprils behind me and the Aprils I still hoped to see.

On Conway's desk lay a brown manila folder containing the typed and signed transcript of John Riggio's confession. An hour before I'd talked to Al Purdy in the hospital, and I'd called his wife and told her that Al would be fine. I'd called Austin O'Connor, too, and he was on his way from the state capitol. He had babbled enthusiastically about the "marvelous" work I'd done, and about how he would personally recommend that the state Commission employ permanently the services of experienced men from my agency. The boss in New York would be pleased, and I could almost see him rubbing his dry old palms greedily at the thought of the extra income. His idea had worked, and the other states, maybe all forty-eight of them, would fall in line. I decided that as soon as I got back to the office I would call him and ask for a raise.

Conway said to Gloria Shannon, "I understand that you are prepared to legally adopt Jonquil Shannon."

"Yes," she said, her eyes shining.

Vernon Dorr reached out and patted her hand. He looked good this morning, very fresh and bright, the sharp young executive. Maybe he hadn't forgotten Elaine Shannon, but he would, in time. I hadn't forgotten her, either, but I would, too—in time. I looked at Dorr and Gloria Shannon, and I thought they made a very attractive couple.

Conway said, "Bennett, do you have anything to say?"

"No."

"No charges of any kind to make?" His keen eyes peered at me from behind the gold-rimmed glasses.

"No," I said, and I stirred uneasily.

"Not against Mrs. Shannon, who threatened you with a pistol, and attempted to hinder you from doing your duty?"

"No charges," I said.

Conway frowned. "We have no legal evidence against Mrs. Shannon. John Riggio's confession has cleared her of complicity in the murders of George Shannon and Edward Fleet, and in the attack on Albert Purdy. But we know that she had guilty knowledge, and that she attempted to shield her lover, a murderer, from apprehension. Bennett, you're the only witness to her actions. You do not wish to testify?"

"I do not wish to testify," I said, avoiding Conway's eyes. There's a weak streak in all of us, I guess.

Conway sighed and said heavily, "Is it the opinion of those present that Mrs. Elaine Shannon be released from custody?"

"Yes," I said.

"Yes." Gloria Shannon's voice was sober.

Vernon Dorr nodded slowly, an odd expression in his eyes. He was remembering, maybe, and for a moment I was with him in his mind and heart.

"All right," Conway said shortly. "This meeting is dismissed."

Out on the sidewalk in the bright April sunshine, Gloria Shannon said to me, "About our engagement this evening—I—I'm afraid I can't make it. You see, I have plans to make, and arrangements, about Jonquil. Mr. Dorr has kindly offered to help me, and...."

"I understand," I said. "I'm afraid I'll be tied up, too."

She held out a hand. "Thank you, Mr. Bennett. Good-bye."

I clasped her cool fingers. "Good-bye, Gloria."

Vernon Dorr shook hands with me, too, his expression faintly embarrassed, and they walked away together, his hand on her arm.

In a bar around the corner I bought a double martini, extra dry, carried it back to a phone booth and placed a call to Miss Sandra Hollis, in Cleveland, Ohio.

THE END

More hardboiled murder mysteries by

Robert Martin

"If you're a fan of private detective novels, you really should check it out."
—James Reasoner, *Rough Edges*

Little Sister $9.99
A detective is hired to keep a young heiress from marrying the wrong man, but discovers a corpse in her car instead—but who is the dead man? Black Gat #27

The Pale Door / Death of a Ladies' Man $19.95
"... a page-turner of a good read it is, with more plot twists than Dead Man's Curve."—*The Minderbinder Review of Books*

Dark Dream / Sleep, My Love $19.95
The first two Jim Bennett detective mysteries. "Definitely in the Hammett-Chandler school of writing... Bennett makes an interesting character to follow. —*Mystery*File*

"Bob Martin was a very popular writer in his day... Quality-wise, I would say he wrote as well as early Ross Macdonald and John D. MacDonald."
—Jim Felton, *Mystery*File*

"In an era when first-person private eyes were often little more than boozing, wenching, wise-cracking ciphers, Bennett comes off as a real and intelligent human being."—Bill Pronzini, *Mystery Scene*

In trade paperback from:

STARK HOUSE PRESS
1315 H Street, Eureka, CA 95501
griffinskye3@sbcglobal.net   StarkHousePress.com

Available from your local bookstore, or order direct with a check or via our website.